Paul Bassett Davies has written for the stage, ra
worked with some of the biggest names in Brit
several award-winning short stories, columns and articles. At various times he
has been a cab driver, a welder's mate and a DJ in a strip club.

For more information see his blog, The Writer Type
http://thewritertype.blogspot.com/

Paul Bassett Davies is represented by Julian Friedmann at Blake Friedmann
Literary, TV and Film Agency.
info@blakefriedmann.co.uk
+44 (0)20 7 284 0408

Cover painting by Lee Madgwick.
To see more of Lee's work visit www.leemadgwick.com

PUBLISHED BY
writertype press

ISBN: 978-0-9575099-0-0

Paul Bassett Davies

UTTER FOLLY

One.

"Hello?"

"Ivan? It's Oliver."

"Olly. Shit. What time is it?"

"About seven."

"In the morning?"

"Yes, the morning, you dozy twat."

"Why are you whispering?"

"I'm at that girl's place. She's asleep."

"The one from the wine bar?"

"You should have stayed. They were both up for it. Her and her little friend."

"Unbelievable. You bastard."

"Anyway, listen, we're on. It's arrived."

"Really?"

"All good. I've had the message from my guy."

"Brilliant."

"So this might be my last chance to contact you. I might not be able to use the phone for the rest of the weekend."

"Why not? Where will you be?"

"It's perfect. The perfect alibi."

"What is it? Come on, tell me. Olly?"

"You'll find out. But the main thing is, you might have to make the call to James."

"Who?"

"The guy I've invited down there."

"Down where?"

"Fuck's sake, Ivan, wake up, dude. To Ullage. To the family place. So we can get him to pick it up."

"Oh, right. Because you won't be there."

"That's the whole point! So I'm not in the frame. Or you, either. Just don't use your own phone. Buy a cheap one and throw it away afterwards."

"Yeah, yeah, I know. I know. But..."

"What? What is it, Ivan?"

"Why is this guy going to your family place if you're not going to be there?"

"He doesn't know I'm not going to be there, does he? Not yet, anyway."

"Oh, right. Okay. But does he know what it's all about?"

"Of course he doesn't! Jesus, Ivan! That's not going to work, is it?"

"No. Right. Okay. So. This guy."

1

"What?"

"This is the guy you work with, right?"

"I wouldn't call it that. We're in the same office. We hang out sometimes."

"Hold on."

"What are you doing? Ivan? Hello?"

"I just need a piss. It's okay, I'm taking the phone."

"Oh, right."

"So, this guy James. What's he like?"

"He's just, you know, normal. Ordinary. Nice middle class boy."

"But he's reliable, right?"

"He'll do it."

"But he's going to suspect something, isn't he? I mean, when I tell him to go and collect the package."

"So what? What's he going to do, Ivan?"

"I don't know. He might try to rip us off."

"No way. Absolutely not."

"Why not?"

"He's just not like that."

"Or go to the cops?"

"No. He'd never do that, either. Not to me."

"Are you sure?"

"Yes, I'm sure! Christ, Ivan, stop nagging me. I've got it sorted."

"Listen, Olly, I've got money in this. Remember? My own fucking money."

"Okay, okay, sorry. Don't worry. Believe me, it's okay. He's cool. For a start, he's totally tripping on the whole family thing. He thinks it's Brideshead Revisited down there or something. It's really funny. Listen, you won't believe this: ever since I invited him down, he's been texting me about what to wear."

"What do you mean?"

"He wants to know what clothes to bring. You know, for the country house weekend. Fuck knows what he thinks he's going to be doing. Deer stalking in the ballroom. You know what these people are like. Oh, God, I can hear you pissing!"

"You just woke me up. I wake up, I have to piss."

"Do it against the sides, then."

"Fuck off."

"Anyway, don't worry about James. He won't know what's hit him. Especially when he meets Jess."

"Oh, right. The famous little sister you've been keeping me away from."

"Fucking right. I don't want some sleazebag like you sniffing around her. I guarantee you, she'll have James on a leash in ten seconds. He doesn't stand a chance."

"And you're sure he'll do what you tell him, right?"

"Yes, but you'll probably be the one who tells him. Because if you don't hear from me by ten tomorrow morning, it means I can't call him, so you have to make the call."

"What if he doesn't have his phone with him? Or he turns it off?"

"No one turns their phone off."

"No. Okay. But there's a back-up plan, right?"

"No worries. Plan B."

"What's plan B?"

"You don't need to know. It's a bit complicated."

"Why?"

"It involves this other guy. This kid. This neighbour of ours down there. He's a bit weird, that's all. But he'll be fine. He thinks the sun shines out of my arse."

"But it's cool, yeah? It'll work?"

"Yes, it'll work! Fuck me, Ivan, you're like someone's mother."

"I just want to be sure we do it right. So, what was this guy's name again? The one I have to phone?"

"James Burridge. I'll text you his number. Hello? Ivan? What's the matter?"

"Sorry. Wait. Ah. Oh, God. Did you say porridge?"

"Burridge."

"Oh. I thought you said his name was James Porridge. I just laughed so hard a big bubble of snot came out of my nose."

"Thank you for sharing that, Ivan."

"Oh, shit!"

"Ivan? Hello? Hello? Ivan?"

"Oh, God. Fuck."

"What?"

"Can you hear me?"

"Yes. Why?"

"I dropped the phone in the toilet. I think it's okay, though. Hello? Olly?"

"I'm going to say goodbye now, Ivan."

"Wait, wait. You're absolutely sure about this guy. James."

"I'm sure. He's perfect."

Two.

James unfolded himself from the car's back seat, hauled his bag out behind him, slammed the rust-pocked door, and stood in the sudden heat of the little square.

"How much is that?"

The driver squinted up into the sun and scratched his ear.

"Let's see, pick-up at the station, late train, waiting time, had to cancel another job, luggage supplement, I have to put that on, compulsory like, it's the insurance, in case of people chucking suitcases about in the back with sharp corners and damaging the seats, then there's time'nnerarfferbankolidayweekend let's call it thirteen pound eighty-five."

That seemed a lot, as it couldn't have been more than a couple of miles from the station. James searched for a ten and a five. Only tens. He gave the driver two.

"Ah, thanks very much, chief, have a good weekend," the driver murmured as the electric window began to slice up between them with a grinding noise.

"Actually, if you take fifteen and give me-"

The car was already yards from him, fishtailing in an accelerating turn up the hill, leaving a column of oily grey smoke and a sick, high-pitched whine in the air, both of which sank abruptly, as though exhausted, into the thickening late afternoon silence.

The hottest June for twenty years, according to the news.

It wasn't actually silent at all, when you listened to it. A soft, continuous chattering formed a dome of sound at the edge of his perception. Crickets, that would be. Or grasshoppers, which were possibly the same thing. But it seemed to make the village square more silent, somehow. James thought he heard a sheep cough. Or perhaps it was a fox, barking. Didn't they bark? Or was that badgers? The badgers all had TB these days, apparently, which might give them a nasty cough and perhaps make them bark as well.

He would soon learn to identify these characteristic sounds. The important thing was that he was out of London, in the country, the real country. James realized that he was basically a Country Person. Not for the first time, he considered the idea of wearing a tweed hat. Four years ago, on holiday in Ireland, he had bought a tweed hat and worn it with jaunty confidence, only to discover, as soon as he was back at college, that it was ridiculous. And so was the pipe. Anyone who tries to wear a tweed hat at the age of nineteen is bound to look like an idiot, although a man of twenty-three might be able to carry it off. But no one had smoked a pipe for years. He blushed as he thought about

4

how preposterous he must have looked. He blamed the old movies his girlfriend at the time had made him watch.

James noticed that for the last minute or so he had been staring at a very fat woman who was standing in the doorway of what appeared to be the only shop in the village and which also hinted, in a faded red sign, that it was the Post Office. She was staring back with dark, beady eyes that glittered from the fleshy folds of her face. James wanted to ask for directions, so he began walking towards her, smiling broadly and raising his eyebrows to imply that he'd been staring at her for that very purpose. She held his gaze until he was within a few feet of her and then turned, stepped into the shop and closed the door behind her gently but firmly.

Country folk, thought James; they were deeply private people. Discretion, reserve, simplicity - these were the qualities to cultivate.

He unfolded the crumpled piece of paper on which Oliver had put directions. He had hoped he wouldn't have to rely on this map, which consisted of a highly detailed drawing of an old-fashioned steam train running along rails that ended near the centre of the sheet, and a picture of a car marked 'Taxi' with an arrow pointing to a shaky circle marked 'Ullage Village' from where another arrow pointed towards a crude drawing of a house, labelled: 'House'. James looked around. A narrow lane led off down the hill. It was blocked by a rusting gate with a notice in which only the word 'Private' was legible. Three other roads led off the square. On Oliver's drawing the arrow pointed left, but was James facing the right way? As he searched for more clues in the beer-stained cryptogram he tried to remember if Oliver had said anything helpful when he gave it to him.

They'd been in a club, in London, three nights ago. Communication had been difficult; the bass notes of the music seemed to operate in a region beyond audible volume, agitating James's kidneys rather than his eardrums. Banks of revolving strobe lights, sweeping over the twitching throng that churned around him on the dance floor, evoked a bungled jailbreak from the innermost circle of hell. At some point James realised that Oliver was talking, at great length, about James coming to stay for the weekend.

"Keeps me sane, you know," Oliver shouted.

"What?"

"The country. It's an antidote."

"Really? What's it about?"

"What's what about?"

"The anecdote."

"No, that's a story."

"I know, but what's it about?"

A girl with very long legs was swaying between them, looking fiercely at each of them in turn as though she was following a tennis match.

5

"Yeah, right, what's it all about, Alfie?" she shouted, and laughed hysterically.

James noticed the legs because she was wearing a very short skirt. He was sure she hadn't arrived with him and Oliver, and yet he couldn't remember being in the club without her. Oliver was treating her like an old friend, clasping her waist in an absentminded way, but James was certain that Oliver had never met her before.

"You know the way the city fucks you up," Oliver said, penetrating the noise with no apparent effort now. Had the music changed, or was Oliver employing some kind of specialized vocal technique? It was the kind of thing he seemed able to do.

"Does your head in," Oliver said. "I couldn't survive without, you know, touching base, in the ecological sense. Balance, that's the important thing."

"Right, balance!" screamed the girl.

"You'll love it. And you'll love the family, too."

James must have accepted the invitation already, before this conversation, because now Oliver was drawing the map. Oliver was one of those people who talked quite naturally about "the family", and where James would have said "my mother", Oliver simply said "Mother". He'd always been like that, ever since James had met him. How had he met him, now he came to think of it? It couldn't have been more than two years ago, but he thought of Oliver as a long-standing and prominent feature of his social landscape. True, he did disappear for months on end, but as soon as he returned James would find himself getting drunk in interesting places with lots of girls.

James looked at the piece of paper again, tilting it so that the sun didn't bleach out the details. He hadn't noticed that it had symmetrical creases in it, so you could fold it into a little paper hat. Or a sort of envelope. The sort of envelope, in fact, that usually contained drugs. But those packets were usually quite small, and this one wasn't. Hastily, James stuffed the paper back in his pocket. Even if the drawing was accurate, and north was at the top, he had no idea which way north was. If he was a countryman, of course, he could tell by the sun, or the swallows or something.

A man pulled up next to him on a mountain bike. He was chubby and was sweating heavily. His wispy fair hair was plastered to his forehead and his cheeks were bright pink, like those of a corpse that has been retouched after a particularly disfiguring accident. He was wearing dirty jeans and a sweatshirt with the picture of Einstein poking his tongue out on it. James thought he looked about twenty-five.

"Looking for the Longbourne house?" the young man said.

"Yes, actually."

"Road on the left. Only a minute, up a slight rise, road goes up to the right, and the house is on the left through an entrance in a big stone wall."

"Thanks," James said.

"Down for the weekend?"

"Yes, actually. For the weekend."

"Friend of Oliver's?"

"Yes. Oliver's friend."

"Aren't we all?"

"Oh, yes, absolutely."

"I'm the vicar."

James looked at him. He wasn't sure if this man was really a vicar or perhaps had made some kind of joke. He seemed terribly young. But people did seem to be younger these days. As Oliver once said, "It's one thing when you know you're getting old because the policemen look like kids, but you're in trouble when the winos in the gutter start looking younger than you!" Although, as James had pointed out, what with the increase in homelessness, it was quite apparent that some of the derelicts on the streets really were very young. Oliver had dismissed this observation angrily as spoiling a good aphorism. It wasn't strictly speaking an aphorism, of course, but James had let that pass.

"Reverend Simon Cottle, St Jude's," the young man said, extending his hand. "But don't call me reverend, or anything like that. Call me Simon."

"James Burridge," James said, shaking the sweaty hand, and then suppressing the impulse to wipe his own hand on his trousers.

"Coming to church?"

"What, now?"

"No, no, I meant on Sunday. Although do come now if you feel like it."

"No, I'm fine thanks. I mean, not now, thank you."

"Here," the vicar said, "you're not charismatic, are you?"

James considered this question carefully.

"You know the sort of thing," Simon continued, "reborn in the spirit, mad staring eyes, grinning all the time."

"Oh, no, not at all."

"Thank God for that. I thought not, but I got worried when you said you wanted to come to church now. Not that I mind. But that lot can get a bit pissy. They turn up and demand to be let in at all hours so they can play the guitar and speak in tongues. Awful fucking racket. Puts the willies up my dogs. I'm a breeder on the side and the vicarage is next door."

"That must be difficult."

"Not really. It's a question of attuning oneself to the canine sexual cycle. But don't get me wrong - I've got an open mind. Who's to say it's not just the thing the dear old C of E needs right now?"

"Yes, who indeed?" James said, troubled by visions of evangelical dogs, babbling and copulating among the pews.

"Exactly," the vicar said. "I've written articles about it. The trouble is, you see, this idea of being utterly swept away by some kind of uncontrollable rapture invokes the whole concept of possession. And then the question is: Divine or Diabolic?"

"I suppose there's a lot to be said on both sides."

"Oh, it's not a question of sides. The great strength of the Anglican communion has always been our inclusiveness. Of course, if I found out that any of my congregation were actually possessed by the devil, I'd be furious. But look at it this way - someone who worships Satan is, at least, worshipping. It's a profession of faith, in its own way. It gives us somewhere to start. We must seek the common ground. In fact, that's the subject of my sermon on Sunday. I'm so glad you're interested, by the way. I take it that you'll be coming along, then?"

James experienced a familiar evaporation of will.

"Yes, I look forward to it."

"Great, see you there. Bless you, and all that."

Scooting his bike forward, he executed a neat little hop and jump which plumped his ripe bottom onto the saddle, and pedalled off in the direction of the right-hand road.

James picked up his bag and walked towards the left-hand road, which was formed by the row of buildings containing the shop, and one edge of a patch of dusty grass: the village green. On the green were an old-fashioned red telephone box, a concrete bus shelter, a litter bin, and an isolated hedge concealing nothing but itself.

Why had he brought so much stuff with him? He'd packed a broad selection of what he considered to be his smarter clothes, which he never wore. Many of them were too small for him, having last been worn, under duress, when he was a teenager. His bag was bulging with garments, each one remarkably inappropriate by itself and spectacularly so in combination with any of the others. He considered dumping some of the clothes in the bin on the green but it was already overflowing with putrid refuse.

After about a hundred yards the road began to rise and curve to the right, bordered on its left-hand side by a high brick wall. Another twenty yards brought him to a gap in the wall flanked by gateposts, one of which was topped by a large stone pineapple. All that remained of the gates were the rusty stumps of hinge-posts set into the stonework.

James paused and put down his bag. From the gateway, a gravel path led between dark green bushes. Through the dense foliage James could glimpse a house, closer than he'd expected. His idea of what the place would look like had been vague and fluid, but had included manicured lawns and sweeping driveways. The absence of these features gave him a tweak of unease as he realized that everything else he'd imagined about the coming weekend was just as likely to be wrong. Still, Oliver would be there - he might even be there already. He'd promised to phone when he was leaving London, and although

James's phone had remained obstinately inert it was very possible that Oliver had simply forgotten to call. He'd been unable to say precisely when he'd be leaving town because of the uncertain timing of an important business meeting, and this was also why he couldn't drive James down himself. James's own inability to drive had been a useful factor in the courtship of various girls with cars, who unfailingly tried to teach him. He found that the more hopeless he was as a pupil the more he would ignite a deep maternal lust in his teacher, and had so far avoided passing his driving test.

James picked up his bag, passed between the gateposts, and scrunched along the gravel path. He emerged through the evergreens to find that the path led, on his right, to the back of a large house with French windows on either side of half-glazed double doors. On his left a broad, untidy garden sloped down to a tangle of trees and bushes. Ahead of him was a collection of ramshackle tin-roofed structures, one of which was open-fronted and contained the rusting form of a still beautiful antique sports car. A door in a grubby shed next to this structure opened and a figure shambled out.

The man was elderly and lean - a stringy type, thought James, perhaps influenced by the amount of actual string that featured in the man's wardrobe, giving him the appearance of a loosely-tied parcel of old tweed and corduroy. He peered at James for a moment, then wandered towards him erratically. When he was a yard away he stopped and gazed at him with eyes that swam in a thin, rheumy soup. His richly veined nose quivered and he chewed at the yellowing ends of a shaggy white moustache for a while before slowly opening his mouth, from which emerged a hoarse croak:

"See that shed?" He jerked one thumb over his shoulder and James noticed that in his other hand he gripped an old-fashioned oil-can with a long, probing spout. "That's my shed, all right?"

"Fine," James said.

This seemed to satisfy the old man and he resumed his efforts to eat his moustache. James felt that, conversationally, the ball was in his court.

"Did I come through the wrong bit," he asked, "or is this the front?"

"It is now. They moved the road, didn't they? Typical, of course. Filthy trick, but then what do you expect?"

James shook his head sadly to indicate his opinion of devious road-movers. The old man began to wheeze through his nose as he worked up to his next speech:

"Bloody council. Moved the road up round the corner there and let the property spivs put a lot of bloody horrible little cottages in front of the front. Council on the payroll, of course, backhanders and bungs all round. Only too happy to oblige, I expect. They've had it in for the family ever since the business with the goats during the war. Family didn't do a sodding thing about it. Except quack like a lot of cretins, as usual."

9

James wasn't shocked by this lack of deference in the gardener, or odd-job-man, or whoever he was. He was obviously the kind of treasured retainer whose fierce loyalty to the family excused any eccentricity. It was essential not to patronize this type, with his deep, almost feudal sentiments. James addressed him in tones of earnest formality:

"You know, that's a shocking state of affairs, absolutely shocking, and I think you're quite right to be indignant about it. Tell me, may I enter the house through these doors?"

"Go where you bloody well like, as long as you stay out of my shed."

"Of course, of course," James said. Perhaps he should offer him a tip. He worked his hand into the pocket of his trousers, which were a little tight, having been selected from the smart-but-obsolete end of the range of clothes he'd brought.

"Right," said the old man, waggling the oil-can under James's nose, "I'd better go and oil the old bitch."

"Hang on," James said, still rummaging awkwardly in his trousers, "I've got something in here for you."

The man narrowed his eyes and peered closely at James.

"Did Oliver invite you down?" he asked.

"That's right! For the long weekend."

"Silly bastard."

The old man swivelled almost completely around then corrected his bearings and tottered down the sloping garden towards the trees and bushes at the bottom. It was clear to James that he was slightly gaga, but the family probably kept him on out of kindness and *noblesse oblige*.

James approached the double doors. Although they were now the main, if not the only entrance to the house, it seemed that no attempt had been made to improve or repair them since the days when they simply provided access to the back garden. He stopped and looked behind him. The old man was just about to enter the thicket at the bottom of the garden, picking his way with high, prancing steps, the oil-can held up before him like a ceremonial artefact. James turned back and tapped on one of the glass panels. The sun, fairly low now, shone on to the glass, making it impossible to see beyond it. He tapped harder and the glass rattled in its frame. Turning one of the round brass door-knobs, James opened the door and stepped inside.

The sunlight from behind him illuminated a short stretch of tiled hallway and made the gloom beyond it all the more impenetrable. James could just about see the foot of a staircase a few yards ahead of him, and doors on either side of the hall.

"Hello?" James said.

"Who's that?" replied a startlingly close voice from the shadows to the left of the staircase. He heard the approaching click of high heels on the tiles and a figure emerged from the darkness.

10

"It's only me," James said, his voice sounding thin and reedy in his ears, "James. You know."

A large, stately looking woman sailed into the patch of sunlight. She had the air of someone who has emerged from an expensive hairdresser's within the last few moments. Her face was attractive in a confident, English way and although it was comfortably plump a certain sharpness about the nose and eyes reminded James of Oliver.

"James?" she said, "James?" and began to walk, not towards him but to one side of him in a slow, circling movement which James found disturbing. As soon as he realized that she could see him only in silhouette and was attempting to look at his face, he co-operated by shuffling around so that they were both in the light. She considered him thoughtfully.

"James who?"

"James Burridge. Oliver's friend."

"Of course, how silly!" she cried in a husky drawl, "I do apologise, you must think me frightfully rude. The fact is, I completely forgot you were coming. Do forgive me. How marvellous that you could make it. I'm Daphne Longbourne, Oliver's mother."

She produced a dazzling smile that contrived to express both delight at his arrival and amusement at her own stupidity. James was so relieved that he began to chatter uncontrollably.

"I hope you don't mind me just barging in like that but I tapped on the glass and there was nobody there so I just came in, because I met this old man who was outside, your gardener I think he is, anyway, he said to just go on in because this was the front now. He's a bit of a cranky old specimen, isn't he? I thought he was rather funny, actually."

"Ah, yes," Daphne Longbourne said, "my husband."

James unhitched his bag from his shoulder and held it in front of him by the strap, inspecting it with furious concentration.

"Hah. Yes. Right. Right."

Finally he raised his eyes. Oliver's mother had resumed her thoughtful look. James lifted the bag, as if displaying a prize marlin.

"Heavy old thing. I'll put it down."

He dropped the bag onto the floor. There was a sickening shriek, followed by a ghastly scrabbling, then something erupted from beneath the bag and streaked away into the darkness. Daphne Longbourne raised one eyebrow by a millimetre.

"Mind the cat."

From somewhere above his head, James heard a creamy young voice:

"Mummy? What was that?"

Someone came running down the stairs and switched on a light. A girl of about eighteen was standing on the bottom step of the staircase. She was tall, about five feet nine, and was wearing jeans and a long, loose shirt. She had shoulder-length chestnut hair, a long straight nose, a wide mouth, large, clear brown eyes and James was in love.

"It was nothing, darling," said Oliver's mother, "just the cat. This is James, Oliver's friend."

"Hello," the girl said. "I'm Jessica, Oliver's sister."

James walked to the foot of the stairs.

"How do you do," he said.

He'd been practicing a new handshake recently, inspired by a television programme about body language. He straightened his arm smartly and swept it forwards and upwards in a low-slung arc, expressing ambition and dominance. At the same time Jessica descended the last step, so that James's hand sliced neatly up between her legs and came to rest snugly in her crotch. She didn't move, or even blink. Gazing earnestly into his eyes she asked:

"Do you fancy a bath?"

For an instant, James believed a miracle had taken place and this girl, responding to his unintentionally direct approach, was inviting him to have a bath with her.

"Because if you do," she continued, gently removing his hand from between her legs, "I'll go and put the immersion heater on for you. It takes a while to warm up. I always like to have a bath before dinner if I've been travelling, don't you?"

James took a pace backwards. He couldn't bring himself to meet her eyes and didn't dare look at her mother and so he addressed a space between them. He needed to be somewhere else. In a bath would do.

"Yes, fine. Lovely. If it's no trouble."

"None whatsoever," Jessica said, turning to go back upstairs. James finally looked at Oliver's mother, covering the moment with a blurted question:

"By the way, Mrs Longbourne, what's, I mean where -"

"Oh, please, call me Daphne."

"Yes. Okay. Um, I was just wondering where Oliver was."

"Oh, didn't you know?"

James was aware of a hollowness in the pit of his stomach. "Know what?"

"He won't be down today. We're not sure when he'll turn up. If at all."

James refused to let her words penetrate too far into his consciousness, where he knew they would cause havoc once he allowed himself to understand them.

"But why? I mean, where is he?"

"Well, when he phoned he said he was in a police station. He told Jessica he'd been arrested."

"Oh, God. Did they find anything?"

"Find anything? What do you mean?"

"No, no, nothing, I just meant why was he arrested. What for?"

Mrs Longbourne raised her head and called up the stairs:

"Darling, what was it that Oliver was arrested for?"

Jessica leaned over the banisters and her hair fell forward, concealing her face from James as she replied:

"Throwing cheeseburgers at a traffic warden."

"Oh, dear," Mrs Longbourne said, "has he done this sort of thing before, Jess, do you know?"

"Not with cheeseburgers. He did once hit a man from the Salvation Army with a pizza but that was an accident. Something to do with Frisbee technique. Anyway, I'll put the water heater on."

James turned back to Mrs Longbourne.

"What shall I do?" he asked, realising as he spoke that the question must sound inane. "I mean, perhaps I'd better go."

"Good Lord, don't dream of it!" cried Daphne Longbourne. "You know what Oliver's like. He may show up at any moment. You just make yourself at home and we'll have a lovely weekend with or without the silly boy. I won't hear of you not staying."

The doors to the garden were flung open and a man walked briskly in, slammed the doors behind him, strode up to Mrs Longbourne, clasped her about the waist and nuzzled his face into her neck.

"Hello, sexy!" he roared into her hair, "How about a little nap before dinner?"

"We have company, John," Mrs Longbourne said.

"Oh, really?" the man said, half-disengaging himself from the embrace and turning to face James.

James simply couldn't understand what he saw. It was the old man from the garden, whom he now knew to be Daphne Longbourne's husband, and so his amorous assault on her was explicable. What was beyond rational explanation, however, was the way the man had changed. The features were the same, but seemed fresher and fuller. The hair was thicker, the eyes clearer, the neck less scrawny. The body appeared more robust. The clothes, although composed of the same mixture of tweed and corduroy, were now neat and lacked the webs of string. The transformation was so eerie as to be supernatural. Just as James felt that he might give way to the need to run from the house, Daphne Longbourne spoke:

"John, this is James, a friend of Oliver's. James, this is John Longbourne, my brother-in-law."

An hour later James was lying in an old-fashioned bathtub that was long enough for him to stretch out completely, and nearly overflowing with pleasantly warm water. He was feeling better, but only slightly. Ever since he'd arrived at the house - arrived in Ullage itself, in fact - he'd had a growing sense of things slipping beyond his control. Everything that had taken place in the last two hours had an opaque, impenetrable quality. Everything he'd said and done was chronically embarrassing. Talking to Mrs Longbourne about her husband like that. The cat. Jessica and the legs. She was incredibly beautiful. He was sure there had been nothing under that shirt. He began to see, then feel the freedom of her breasts, moving beneath it. God, he was getting an erection. Something about the primal simplicity of this response was immensely comforting, and James closed his eyes, moving his hips so that the water lapped around his groin. There was a small pattering noise. He was probably splashing water over the side of the tub. He squeezed his eyes more tightly closed, savouring a final, delicious image, then opened them to check if the bath was overflowing.

Jessica Longbourne was perched on the end of the bathtub, dabbling her fingers in the water between his feet.

"Hot enough for you?" she asked.

James sat up abruptly and hunched forward, plunging his arms between his legs at the same time.

"I hope you don't mind me popping in," Jessica said. "You're not one of those people who gets stressed about bodies and clothes, are you?"

"God, no, absolutely not," James said with a scornful chuckle which came out, he found, like an attempt to clear his sinuses.

"In fact that's one of the things I came to tell you. We don't dress for dinner. Just wear any old thing."

"That's handy," James said, "because any old thing is precisely what I've brought with me."

Jessica laughed, throwing back her head and exposing her throat. Her laughter had a hint of her mother's huskiness in it, and suggested something wild and untamed simmering beneath a surface of poised sophistication. It was incredibly sexy.

"In fact," James continued, "my luggage contains a very impressive selection of any-old-things. I've cornered the market in that particular item of fashion and now you can't get hold of any-old-thing in London for love or money."

Jessica laughed again, but with more restraint. James wished he hadn't diluted the success of his original quip by extending it beyond its natural life-span. He always got carried away when he was nervous. One of his more sadistic tutors at college had been able to reduce him to imbecility simply by asking him a question and then staring at him without saying anything as James dug himself into an ever-deepening verbal hole.

"Anyway," Jessica said, "that was one thing I wanted to mention." She got up from the edge of the bath and wiped the condensation off the mirror over the sink. She began to pout at her reflection and toss her hair, striking different poses with a bewitching lack of self-consciousness as she continued:

14

"But I also thought this might be the only chance I got to explain things about Mummy and uncle John and Daddy before you got even more confused."

"Oh, God," James said, "I suppose your mother told you I made a complete fool of myself." He felt beads of sweat collecting on his face.

"Oh, don't worry, everyone gets mixed up until they know. I thought Olly might have told you about it, but he often forgets. You see, my father, Bill, that's who you met in the garden, he's seventy-five and Mummy's only fifty-six. And he's always been interested in machines and old cars and things, and years ago he joined this local club that restores those old traction engines; you know, like fancy steam-rollers with funnels and belts and everything? He's got one of them down at the bottom of the garden, actually."

"Ah, that explains what he meant by oiling the bitch."

"Oh, good. Anyway, he got friendly with this man who always brought his wife along, and he ended up having this sort of affair with her, because Mummy was never remotely interested in the steam engine things, and she used to hate the way he was always covered in oil and grease and made the house filthy. So I think the affair was mostly to do with them sharing an interest, really, not some sort of great sexual passion or anything. In fact I don't think Daddy had ever been too keen on that side of things. I think he was a bit baffled by it all, quite honestly. But still, Mummy was dreadfully upset of course, and she sort of turned to uncle John for comfort. He's Daddy's younger brother and he was staying with us a lot at that time because he'd just lost everything, including his house, when his business went bust. That used to happen quite a lot. He'd always be turning up with creditors breathing down his neck, sometimes even the police. He's not a crook or anything, it's just he's always had these business schemes that sometimes don't quite work out. Some of them are pretty impressive, actually. He once got five million quid from some Arabs, but then they got annoyed and tried to have him killed.

"Anyway, Mummy and uncle John had an affair of their own. I think it was partly because of the sex, because Daddy was so hopeless about that. Which was probably why his affair with this woman faded out after a while. And then he decided that he was much happier doing without the whole sex business, and women in general, really. By which time uncle John had become a kind of fixture, which Daddy didn't seem to mind at all. In fact he seemed quite relieved. So he fixed up the shed, and moved in there. He's even got plumbing in there. So now he spends all his time pottering about with his traction engine, and Mummy and uncle John live here in the house, and everyone's happy. I suppose we all take it for granted now, but I expect it all seems a bit weird to you."

She turned from the mirror and gave him a rueful smile.

"No, not at all," James said. "It all seems very civilized. I mean, people come to all sorts of arrangements, don't they? My great-aunt Jasmine was happily married to a bigamist for over forty years. She said it stopped him from cluttering the place up. She didn't like him coming into the kitchen, apparently. All four wives knew about each other and only one of them ever caused trouble, and after she died it turned out she had a string of lovers all over the West Midlands."

"What fun," murmured Jessica, turning to the mirror again and smoothing her eyebrows. "By the way, you know we're having people for dinner, don't you?"

"No," James said, with a pang of jealousy, "who is it?"

"Oh, they're great fun. Dave and Sylvia Silver. They're neighbours of ours. They bought the old manor house in the village a few years ago. He made a ton of money out of something to do with computers. You know how clever these people are."

"God, yes, I often think they must be a completely separate species. Because all that stuff is a total mystery to me. I think it's a particular gene or something."

"Exactly," Jessica said with satisfaction. "Anyway, Dave Silver's such a funny little man. He can't seem to think of what to do with all his money. He's bought a boat, and a house in France, and all that stuff. And can you believe it, they've got a butler! A real butler! Well, not a real one, actually, because it's not as though he comes from some family that's been in service for ages, or anything. They got him from some college, I think, where they train ordinary people to be butlers. But Dave's ever so proud of him, and he makes him answer the door, even if Dave's standing right next to it. It's terribly sweet. Anyway, they've just come back from Thailand, shooting elephants or something."

"I don't think you're actually allowed to shoot elephants these days."

"Or saving elephants, then. Yes, the shooting part was to do with filming them for this documentary about them being endangered. Dave Silver's put up the money for it and they let him say he's the producer. They're very into all that kind of thing, you know, the ecology and all that. They've put solar panels in the roof and they've got this mad windmill in their back garden."

"You mean like one of those wind-farm things with propellers?"

"No, a real windmill. It's in the grounds behind the house, and it used to be part of the village, where they all came to make bread and so on. And the Silvers have restored it. I think they want everyone in the village to start using it again, but nobody's remotely interested. Not with a Tesco only a few minutes' drive away."

James was getting cold and he needed to get out of the bath. He couldn't reach the towel-rail without exposing himself in a horribly ungainly way. It was bad enough already, without stretching and dangling all over the place.

"Could you pass me the towel? The pink one, your mother said to use."

Jessica flicked the towel from the rail and passed it to him. Instead of turning back to the mirror, she watched him with frank interest as he tried to stand up and wrap the towel around himself at the same time. Attempting nonchalance but hampered by modesty he clambered out of the tub, banging his ankle smartly against the cold tap.

"Ooh," said Jessica, with sympathetic wince, "that must have hurt."

"No, not really," James said, tears pricking his eyes.

"What you need is a drink. You can get one as soon as you come down because we all sort of congregate for drinks in the drawing room about half an hour before dinner, so that's nearly now. Or sooner, if the Silvers have arrived. They like a drink, I can tell you. Except for Richard."

"Who's Richard?" James didn't like the sound of him.

"Oh, he's a bit of a drag, I'm afraid. He's the son, he's about eighteen, and he mopes about the place being miserable. He thinks he's in love with me, apparently."

James laughed indulgently to cover his outrage. It was inevitable, of course. Any sane, heterosexual male was bound to be in love with Jessica. There were probably dozens of them lurking around. He began patting himself brutally through the towel.

"That's not the only reason he's miserable," continued Jessica. "He's doing the whole teenage rebel thing, you know, rejecting everything his parents stand for, and saying he hates all the money they've got, and he wants to return to his roots, with the clothes and the hair, and everything. I think he's terribly mixed up, actually."

"A Rebel Without a Clue," James said.

Jessica laughed as if she hadn't heard the line before.

"Oh, one more thing," she said, "then I'll let you get dressed. You'll meet Auntie Pru downstairs as well. She lives with us. She's John and Daddy's aunt and she's pretty ancient but she's terribly sweet. So she's my great aunt, really, but we all call her Auntie Pru. And her friend Joan lives here too. They were at school together years and years ago, and Auntie Pru sort of looked after her, because Joan was a bit younger, and she was terribly grateful, and they've been friends ever since. Olly and I used to call her Auntie Joan, but now we call her Spracky like everyone else because her name's Joan Sprackling. She sort of does things around the place."

"Right, I see," James said. He thought for a moment. "What sort of things?"

"Oh, sort of... jobs. Cooking meals and tidying up and things. She bustles about generally being helpful. Anyway, you'll meet everyone properly, and if you feel awkward you can always get drunk."

"Oh, God, I feel awkward enough already," James said, "so I'll probably have to get completely trashed."

Jessica laughed again.

17

"Do, by all means. Everyone else probably will. I'm afraid we're all terrible hounds for the booze. In fact, I'm going to go and start now, whether the Silvers have arrived or not. I'll be seeing you!"

She flung open the door and walked out without closing it.

Three.

James stood in darkness at the top of the stairs. He'd found some clean clothes in his bag that weren't too creased and which made him look fairly normal. He was feeling more optimistic about the weekend ahead of him. He couldn't believe that someone would stroll into a bathroom where they knew a person was naked without wanting to encourage the naked person to think that they at least didn't find him repulsive. If he could now make Jessica fall in love with him, and have sex with her, nothing else he could imagine about his future held any interest for him.

From somewhere below him came the sound of several people holding loud conversations. Good. It would be easier to face Mrs Longbourne again in a large group. He refused to think about the gracious way she'd tried to conceal her impression that he was clearly an idiot. He began to walk cautiously down the stairs, groping for a light switch. All he could see were two dim grey oblongs that glowed faintly in the distance and seemed to float about when he tried to focus on them. Half way down the stairs he realized they were the glass panels in the doors at the far end of the hall. It was getting dark outside.

A door was flung open on James's right and he froze as the hall was flooded with light and noise. A squat, bulky figure was silhouetted in the doorway for an instant before the door swung closed and someone clumped along the passage at the side of the stairs, opened another door, and was swallowed by the gloom. But the door into the room with all the people in it was still open a few inches and enough light spilled out for James to see his way down the rest of the stairs.

He hesitated. The person he'd glimpsed had been wearing a large hat, which he found disturbing. And there was a lot of noise coming out of the room. It sounded as if at least fifty people were in there, shouting and laughing at each other. The more people there were in the room, the easier it would be to avoid Daphne Longbourne. But on the other hand a larger gathering might include more potential suitors for Jessica.

James walked quickly and quietly down the rest of the stairs, tiptoed to the open door, and peered through the gap. By swaying from side to side he was able to take in most of the room and see that the noise was being produced by only a small number of people, all talking at once very loudly. Suddenly his view was blocked by someone who came and stood in front of the gap with their back to him, inches from his face. By craning his neck James was able to see that it was a young man, who'd positioned himself in the doorway and was gazing around the room while nibbling morosely on an egg sandwich. The boy looked about seventeen and had a faint, wispy beard. He was wearing a wide brimmed black hat and a long black coat like a character in a cowboy film. Over his shoulder James caught sight of a middle-aged woman impersonating a 1950s starlet. A tight, shimmering gold dress cradled her immense bosom, and her silver hair looked like sculpted candyfloss. Although she was ugly and was nearly as short as a dwarf, she tackled the part with panache, twirling her cocktail glass and throwing back her head as she honked with laughter at something that someone just beyond James's field of vision was saying to her.

It appeared to be some kind of fancy dress party. Blood rushed to James's brain, distributing ice as it went. Why hadn't Jessica said anything? He stood on tiptoe, trying to look over the head of the young cowboy to check if everyone in the room was wearing a costume. But the boy was too tall, and James gave up. He was about to turn and creep back upstairs when he heard himself being talked about.

"Is your friend still in the bath, Jess?" Daphne Longbourne said. Her voice was very close. She must have been standing just inside the room, to one side of the door. "I must say he's taking his time up there."

He heard Jessica's voice: "He's not my friend, Mummy, he's Oliver's."

"Rather extraordinary, to march in and demand a bath like that. And then to just trot straight upstairs and switch the immersion heater on in the middle of the day, never mind the cost. I know that people's idea of good manners has changed since I was a girl, but one does find it hard to get used to."

"Oh, Mummy, do chill."

Why didn't Jessica remind her that the bath had been her idea? And when she'd said he was Oliver's friend, not hers, she'd made it sound as if he meant nothing to her. But perhaps she was being deliberately casual about him in order not to arouse suspicion. In her mother's eyes she was, absurdly, still a teenage girl. She probably wanted to avoid embarrassing accusations of being infatuated with her older brother's friend.

"It looks as though the light's not on out there, Jess," Mrs Longbourne said. "The next thing you know, we'll have young whatsisname--"

"James," Jessica said. At least she remembered his name.

"James, yes, we'll have young James falling down stairs and breaking his neck, and then we'll have to get hold of poor old Doctor Bulmer. Someone had better go and switch it on. Richard?" She raised her voice. "Richard, will you be a poppet...?"

The boy who was standing in the doorway froze in the act of raising his sandwich to his mouth. A nerve in his cheek twitched. He examined the sandwich carefully, took a small, savage bite, and began to chew it slowly, gazing into the distance.

"Mummy!" hissed Jessica, in a voice that the boy could easily hear, "he won't answer if you call him that!"

"Oh, for God's sake, ridiculous boy," muttered Mrs Longbourne in a stage whisper. She cleared her throat and adopted the purring, sing-song tone of someone trying to persuade a child to go to bed: "Reuben, would you be an angel and switch on the light in the hall?"

The young cowboy didn't look at her. "I'm sorry, Mrs Longbourne," he replied, "but I'm afraid the sun has gone down."

"Yes, dear, exactly, that's why we need the light on."

"No, I mean I can't--"

"It's the Sabbath, Daphne!" yelled the short woman in the gold dress, from the centre of the room. "Once the sun's set on Friday he can't operate devices or any of that!" She spun on her stiletto heels to face the boy in the doorway. "Can you, darling?"

The boy looked down. James saw the back of his neck flush through his thin, untidy hair. Logic grappled with ignorance in James's mind. The Sabbath on Friday night: that was a Jewish thing. The boy was dressed as a rabbi, not a cowboy. But he was taking it a bit literally by observing the rules about switching lights on and off. Unless he was a real rabbi. No, he was too young, surely. But didn't they do things very young, the Jews? A school friend had told James that his *bar mitzvah* was his entry into manhood, and he'd only been twelve. But if the boy was a real rabbi, and he wasn't in fancy dress, what could explain the appearance of the woman who was obviously his mother, and the person with the hat he'd seen earlier?

"Oh, my goodness," cried Mrs Longbourne, merrily, "we certainly mustn't break the rules! I shall do it myself!"

The boy shuffled aside and James realised that Daphne Longbourne was about to emerge from the room. He hopped backwards rapidly.

"Look out, clumsy boots!" barked a hoarse voice behind him as something hard cracked into the base of his spine. He spun around and was prodded in the stomach with a tea tray wielded by a small, squat man wearing women's clothes. The costume included the large hat James had seen earlier. "Chop, chop!" snapped the transvestite. He drove James back towards the door by repeatedly poking the tea tray into his midriff, grunting playfully on each thrust. James staggered back and collided with someone. Even before he turned and grabbed hold of her to prevent them both from falling over, he knew it was Mrs Longbourne. He found himself standing just inside the brightly lit room, grasping her fleshy biceps. Her face was so close that he could see tiny, individual clumps of mascara stuck in her eyelashes. Her breath was slightly rotten beneath a warm veil of mint and whisky. She gazed at him expressionlessly.

"Drink?" she said.

Five minutes later James was finishing his second large glass of red wine. Jessica had detached him from her mother, grabbed a bottle, and steered him into a corner. James had told her about mistaking the gathering for a fancy dress party. She'd laughed so much that she'd had to put her hand on his shoulder to support herself, and she left it there while she explained who everyone was.

The squat little man in drag was Spracky: Joan Sprackling, Jessica's great aunt Prudence's friend. She didn't look quite so masculine in proper light, although she did have a faint moustache. Her blunt-featured face was broad, like the rest of her, and when she spoke it sounded like a dog trying to cough something up. She bustled about with little bowls of nuts and crisps, and tried to make people drink more. James liked her. Apart from her hat, her clothes were sturdy and practical. Her bust was constrained by a tightly buttoned little tweed jacket with lots of pockets, and below her long grey skirt two thick pillars of flesh overflowed the sides of heavy walking shoes. The hat, Jessica explained, was because of alopecia.

"My God," James said, "do you mean she's bald?"

"No, not completely. She's still got a bit of hair but it's thin and you can see a few little scabs on her scalp. It doesn't look too bad, really. But Auntie Pru says it makes her feel sick so Spracky always wears a hat. I think she rather enjoys it, actually. It gives her a chance to express her artistic side."

"Does she have sides? It looks to me as if she's only got a front that goes all the way round."

Jessica laughed.

"Come to think of it, though," James continued, "she's a bit of a work of art in her own right, isn't she? As if she'd escaped from some kind of exhibition."

"What do you mean?" Jessica said sharply.

James paused. "I just mean she looks, you know, quite striking."

"Actually, she's very creative. She does things with pine cones. And she's painted lots of water colours of the house and the grounds."

"Are they any good?"

"How can you tell?"

James laughed. Jessica was very witty in a delightfully dry, deadpan way. He looked around at the pictures in the room but they were all small sporting prints except for one large, faded oil painting in a gilt frame hanging over the fireplace. It showed a young woman in a purple dress sitting on a very ornate chair and looking cross.

"Oh, you won't see any of Spracky's stuff on the walls," Jessica said. "Auntie Pru doesn't like it."

James looked over at Jessica's great aunt, who was sitting in the far corner of the room. She was very well preserved for her age, which James took to be about ninety. She sat up very straight and her bright blue eyes were clear and piercing. There was an air of serene entitlement about her, an attitude which said that if you thought there was any problem about being a very old lady like her, the problem was yours, not hers. James could see that she must have been beautiful once. She still was, in a way.

22

She was talking to a tubby middle-aged man with crinkly grey hair and a sunburned face, who listened to her attentively, nodding and chuckling. Every so often he made a remark of his own, laughed at it, then bent over her and listened again.

"That's Dave Silver," Jessica said.

"Oh, right, with the windmill and the elephants, who bought the manor house. Reuben's father."

"Richard. Reuben. Whatever." She turned to face him and, with her back to the rest of the room, she made a dismal face and intoned in a deep, dreary monotone:

"Oh, God, I despise everything my parents stand for and they don't even notice when I get all religious and call myself Reuben, because they're so cool and liberal and they gave up being Jewish ages ago, I'm so depressed, I hate myself, I hate everyone except you Jessica, oh, God, I think I love you, shall I kill myself, oh boo hoo, poor me."

James tried to suppress his snorts of laughter as he noticed, over Jessica's shoulder, that Daphne Longbourne was looking at him. But Jessica was very funny; she'd even captured the way that Reuben's hoarse voice cracked and squeaked sometimes.

"And, of course," she said, in her normal voice, "what drives him absolutely crazy is the way his parents are so understanding and say it's just a 'difficult phase' he's going through, and try to be tremendously helpful. They even say they'll pay for him to go to some mad, fundamentalist religious college if he's really serious. It's so funny."

"Look out," James said, "here comes his mother."

"Introduce me to your handsome friend," the dwarfish woman said, laying a mottled hand with blood-red nails and several large rings on Jessica's shoulder. She exposed a set of dazzling white teeth at James. When she stopped smiling a web of white creases faded slowly back into her suntanned face. She wasn't really ugly, James decided, just matronly.

"We're doing well for handsome young men tonight, aren't we, Jess?" she continued, sweeping an arm that jangled with bracelets around the room.

James checked in case someone had just come in. As far as he could tell he was still one of only three men in the room under fifty. The other two were Richard, or Reuben, or whatever he was called, and Simon Cottle, the vicar. James had been surprised to see him here, and even more surprised to find he had a wife with him: a tall, heavy-hipped woman who stayed close to his side with the wary vigilance of someone who has been swindled into buying an unpredictable horse.

James was offended. He didn't think of himself as vain, but he knew he was quite good looking, and it was absurd to put him in the same category as the chubby, sweating vicar and this woman's ridiculous son.

"Sylvia," Jessica said, "this is James Burridge. James, this is Sylvia Silver."

The woman held out her arm and allowed her hand to droop as if inviting him to admire her collection of oversized rings. When James tried to shake the hand she fluttered it in his face and he realized he was meant to kiss it. She chuckled as he brushed his lips against her fingertips, grazing his nose on a large jewel. He let her hand drop as abruptly as he could. She was looking at him expectantly, as if waiting for a cue.

"That's right," she said eventually, "Sylvia Silver. What a name! I think it's the only reason Dave married me, you know. Made up his mind the first time he met me. Of course, I had to give him the idea."

"Oh, we love this story," Jessica said, implying politely that she'd rather not hear it again. James could see that her tact was lost on Sylvia Silver, who barely paused as she glanced at Jessica, then turned her full attention on James.

"Yes, the first time I met him, he started going on about the environment and recycling and all that - he was ahead of his time, you know, even twenty years ago he was a right little eco-warrior. I thought he was terribly serious. I mean, I fancied him like crazy, and I was trying to get him to ask me out, and all he could talk about was these poor old seagulls covered in oil and how he was giving all his money to Greenpeace! I thought he was a bit of a crackpot, to be honest. Can you imagine! There I am, trying to get all romantic, and he's talking about cleaning seagulls in his bath!" She spoke over little hiccups of her own laughter which now became a continuous, yelping convulsion: "I said to him, 'save some of that money,' I said, 'you never know when you might need to spend it on me!' He was gobsmacked!" The yelps of laughter took over and a wave of hilarity engulfed her.

The trouble with people who laugh at their own stories, thought James, was that they made it very difficult for you to laugh at them too. Sylvia took a deep breath, refuelling for more yelps.

"Well," she said, "he thought it was funny once he got over the shock, and when I saw he had a sense of humour I thought maybe he wasn't such a nutcase after all. That's what I always say. If you can have a laugh, you can't be all bad. Although he still kept going on about the state of the rain forest and saving natural resources. I found out later he'd only just got into it, so he had the zeal of a recent convert. So then I said, 'listen, if we got married, we'd be doing the alphabet a favour, wouldn't we? Instead of using up all those letters on my name, Sylvia Rabbinowitz, I'd be Sylvia Silver, and we could use all the letters left over on names for our kids. How's that for saving resources?' I don't know what got into me, I swear, because I was never brazen like that, never, but something just made me say it. And even though it was really just a joke, part of me was dead serious. And the funny thing was, he was, too. I could tell. He just looked at me, and he said, 'that's a very good idea.' Absolutely serious. And three weeks later we were married."

24

"It's a very sweet story, Sylvia," Jessica said, linking her arm through James's. "Would you like another drink?"

Sylvia ignored her. "Of course, now I'm just as keen as Dave. On the ecological side. In fact, it was my idea to restore a completely authentic windmill that we have in the extensive grounds of our residence. It used to be the manor house, you know, and it really is a most gracious dwelling."

James felt Jessica quiver as she clutched his arm. Her voice nearly broke as she said, "Yes, I told James all about the windmill. And the gracious dwelling."

"Did you dear?" Sylvia Silver said haughtily. Her manner had changed as she spoke about her house, as though she'd suddenly remembered to be someone else. James preferred the cheerful version who told stories about fancying her husband.

"Well, that's only a small part of our commitment to the environment," she continued. "As it happens, we've just returned from the far east where my husband is producing a documentary feature TV film about the plight of endangered elephants."

"And I can see you got a nice tan over there," James said.

"Oh, thank you, dear," said Sylvia, beaming at him. "Yes, you don't pick this up under a sun bed, let me tell you!" She held out her arms and rotated them with a clatter of bracelets as she admired them. "Of course, now they all say that we've got to stay indoors and be as white as bloody maggots, but that's where I part company with the global warming people and say, sod it, there's nothing like a nice rich tan, especially on a woman of a certain age, as the expression goes."

"I quite agree," James said, "although you haven't reached it yet."

"Oh, you sweetheart, how charming." She stroked his cheek.

James had only said it as a natural reflex to make himself agreeable. He was always doing this; being nice to people he didn't particularly like. He'd once been told by a girlfriend that he was too anxious to please people. Although he noticed that she didn't complain when she was the one he was trying to please. Sylvia gave his cheek a little pinch as she removed her hand. "Anyway, about these elephants..."

"I've already told him all about those, too," Jessica said.

"Have you, dear?"

"Yes, I've brought him up to speed on all your exploits to save the planet."

"I bet you haven't, love. Because what you don't know is that we've just bought a high bred car."

"A high bred car?"

"Yes, it runs on a mixture of petrol and spare electricity from the wheels. Dave can explain it to you. It's a Japanese make."

"Oh," cried Jessica with a little trill of laughter, "you mean a hybrid."

"They probably call them that as well. But the name doesn't matter. What's important is that it's another way of saving resources and reducing our carbon footsteps."

James saw his chance to spread some frost between himself and Sylvia Silver.

"Actually," he said, "I was reading something the other day about hybrid cars. You see, if you're going to buy a new car, then, yes, they are better for the environment. But by far the most ecologically sound strategy is to buy an old, used car. Because the vast majority of damage to the eco-system is caused in the process of manufacture."

"I'm not quite with you, dear."

"I'm saying it's better to buy something that's already been made and re-use it. That's the principle of re-cycling, after all. You could argue that it's very damaging to the ecology to encourage people to buy any kind of new car, hybrid or not."

Sylvia looked puzzled. "Are you saying we've done the wrong thing?"

Nearly there, thought James. "Yes, I'm afraid so. Not only is it a bad move ecologically, it's also a cynical marketing strategy to make more money for the automobile industry. They don't care about the planet, they're just riding a bandwagon because they know the days of the old gas-guzzlers are numbered. They're manipulating you. You're actually being even more of a dumb consumer than ever."

Sylvia gazed at him blankly. Maybe he'd gone too far by calling her dumb. Finally she turned and gave Jessica a girlish little slap on her shoulder.

"This young man and I have obviously got a lot to talk about! Promise me you'll sit him next to me at dinner."

After half an hour at the table John Longbourne distracted Sylvia Silver with a question about the village fete. At last James was able to give his attention to the food on his plate. He found it was stone cold. Earlier, he hadn't touched the soup whose aroma had tantalized him as it sat under his nose for ten minutes before Spracky removed the bowl. All he'd managed to do was gulp some wine each time Sylvia thought of a new question to ask him about himself. He was reluctant to tell her anything interesting as he wanted to save his best anecdotes for Jessica, and even though she was at the other end of the table he couldn't risk her overhearing something he might want to deploy later as spontaneous, freshly-minted conversation.

But the less he tried to say to Sylvia the more she seemed convinced he was an enigmatic source of wisdom which would be divulged only under relentless interrogation. At first she just made him repeat, in more detail, what he'd told her about hybrid cars, occasionally shouting across the table to inform her husband of something James had said, at which Dave Silver simply raised his eyebrows and nodded affably. Each time she did this she laid a hand on

James's arm, putting him on hold conversationally but also preventing him from lifting his soup spoon.

After a while her questions had become more personal, with a particular emphasis on James's childhood, and the inquisition began to take an ominously Freudian thrust. When she asked him how long he thought children should be breast-fed, it took a huge effort of will to keep his eyes firmly on her face and prevent them from straying down into the deep crevasse of her bosom. John Longbourne's intervention had come in the nick of time. James gave up on the cold food and leaned back in his chair, exhausted.

A strange noise made him glance to his left. He'd forgotten he was sandwiched between Sylvia and her son. The boy hadn't said a word so far. Now he was hawking something up out of his throat and trying to deposit it on his plate as discreetly as possible, even though no one but James was paying him any attention and the chair opposite him was empty. It was meant to be Spracky's but she hadn't sat in it yet. She appeared to be acting as a general servant, bringing in the food and clearing away the dishes, as well as attending personally to Auntie Pru, who sat opposite James. Every time Spracky served her, the old lady patted her hand in an absent-minded way without looking at her. Instead, her bright blue eyes seemed to be fixed permanently on James, and whenever he glanced at her he found himself under their piercing scrutiny. The first time it happened he'd smiled at her, but she hadn't returned the slightest acknowledgement. On each subsequent occasion that he met her inscrutable gaze he simply took a large swig of wine to cover his discomfort.

James waited until the boy had finished regurgitating his food, not wishing to embarrass him during the salvage operation itself, then turned to speak to him. He was scowling down at his plate, from which, like James, he'd hardly eaten anything.

"Not hungry, Reuben?"

Reuben gave a little jump and turned a pale, startled face to James. He stared at him with his mouth hanging open, saying nothing.

James tried again: "You haven't eaten anything."

Reuben looked down at his plate and muttered something James couldn't hear.

"I beg your pardon?"

Reuben hissed from the side of his mouth, like someone passing on dangerous information in a prison canteen: "I don't know if it's kosher."

"Why don't you ask?"

Reuben shook his head fiercely.

"I'll ask, if you like."

"No!" cried Reuben, at normal volume, then looked around furtively. "Sorry," he resumed in a whisper, "I mean, thank you but please don't. It doesn't matter."

"There must be something you can eat. What's the harm in asking?"

Reuben snorted derisively. "I never ask them anything," he said.

"Why not?"

"Because then they pretend to take me seriously and patronize the shit out of me."

"Who does?"

"Everyone."

James felt sorry for him. "I hope you don't think I'm trying to patronize you, because I'm not. I'm a bit lost here myself."

Reuben turned to face him again. A faint, sad smile was visible through the wispy hair around his lips. He wouldn't be bad looking if he tidied himself up a bit. "You'll get the hang of it," he said. He drained the glass in front of him. "Pass that wine, will you?"

James handed him the bottle of red that Spracky had just placed next to him. Reuben poured himself a full glass and topped up James's glass to the brim.

"Cheers." Reuben drank half the glass in one gulp. "And thanks."

"What for?"

"Calling me Reuben."

James shrugged. "Well, if that's what you want to be called, why not?"

"It's not as easy as that." Reuben finished his glass of wine and poured himself another one. James could see that he was fairly drunk. He was quite drunk himself.

He looked around the table. Everyone was drinking steadily; even Auntie Pru was making good progress. The only exception was the vicar's wife, whose name was Jane. She sat opposite Sylvia, on the other side of John Longbourne, who was at the head of the table. Dave Silver was next to her, manfully trying to keep a conversation going. But her attention was on the other end of the table, where Daphne presided, flanked by Simon Cottle and Jessica. Every time Jane Cottle heard her husband's raised voice or Jessica's laughter, she stiffened like a pointer and her eyes flickered towards the couple. It was evident, James noted with disgust, that Simon was trying to flirt with Jessica. But while it was clear to him that Jessica was merely being civil by paying attention to Simon and humouring his crude attempts to entertain her, he could understand why the vicar's wife might see things differently. Any woman would find Jessica a threat, especially a big, plain lump like Jane Cottle, with a frisky husband who was now spluttering into his wine over some inane remark he'd just made. At that moment Jessica glanced at James, rolled her eyes, and flashed him a smile of such intimate complicity that it sent a rush of warm blood pounding around his system. God, she was gorgeous. He had to sleep with her.

He was distracted by Spracky putting a dessert in front of him. James thought that it would probably answer to the name of trifle, but it represented a noble branch of that family, its heraldry displayed in layers of fresh fruit, sponge, custard, biscuit, fresh cream, ice cream, and a rich, dark sauce.

As he picked up his spoon, he felt a tug on his sleeve.

He turned to find that Sylvia Silver had stopped talking to John Longbourne, who knew what was good for him and was attacking his dessert without delay.

"Where were we?" she said.

"Oh, I don't think we were talking about anything in particular."

"Yes, we were discussing children's upbringing." She leaned towards him confidentially and dropped her voice by a couple of decibels. "You see, Richard is our only one, and we're terribly concerned about him."

Her son, on the other side of James, gave no sign that he could hear her as he drained another glass of wine.

"We were always very free and open about everything when he was growing up," Sylvia continued, "because that was what all the latest advice said, back then. And he wasn't a difficult adolescent. But now he's going through this very painful religious phase, poor lamb, and I can't help wondering if we got it all wrong. That's why I've been reading what Freud has to say about it. Now, tell me, quite honestly, where you stand on masturbation."

James put down his spoon.

Just before Spracky drove everyone from the dining room James managed to snatch a single mouthful of the pudding. His taste buds, soured by wine for the last two hours, exploded in a tiny orgy of sweetness that left him craving much, much more.

*

The rest of the evening is a collection of fragments that collide in James's memory. The only thread of continuity is alcohol.

Jane Cottle tries to stay close to Simon, but he always slips away. Jane stalks him, but he is smoke. James laughs. Look, he says to Jessica, it's like some weird kind of dance. Then Jessica's talking to someone else.

James finds the remains of some nuts and crisps in a couple of bowls on a little table. As he scoops them up, he feels a sharp slap on his hand.

"Naughty!" cries Spracky as she whisks the bowls away. "You can't get away with that. You young people won't eat proper meals, then you think you can make up for it with snacks."

James is talking to Simon Cottle and Dave Silver about religion. They discuss the pagan roots of the Judeo-Christian tradition. The ascendancy of monotheism in the west. Fundamentalism. Tolerance. Islam. Zionism. James contributes intelligent, judicious remarks. Dave Silver laughs a lot. Simon says that he and Dave are always having this debate. It's his ambition to convert Dave, he says. Dave professes no belief. He was never that observant a Jew anyway. James says he thinks he believes in some kind of higher power. When called upon, he can't quite define it. He never can.

"Do you ever talk to Oliver about these things?" Simon asks.

"Oliver? No, not really."

"But you're quite close friends, aren't you?"

"Yes, I suppose so. Quite close."

"Does he never talk about his deep spiritual feelings?"

"Who, Oliver?"

"You seem surprised."

"He's never really mentioned that sort of thing. Not to me, anyway."

"He speaks to me quite frequently. He's been asking my advice about various matters. He's thinking of renewing his confirmation in the Church of England."

James stares at the vicar. He realizes that Simon is older than he thought. His plumpness conceals the wrinkles in his face unless you look at him closely.

"Yes," Simon continues, "Oliver is a young man of profound yearnings."

Dave Silver catches James's eye. The look he gives him makes it clear that he knows the direction that Oliver's yearnings take, quite as well as James does.

Jane Cottle drifts into their orbit. With practised ease Simon moves away, uncoiling some kind of stored momentum that enables him to give the impression of having been on his way somewhere else even before his wife approached.

"So, I'd better check with Sylvia," he says as he leaves them, "about those details for the fete tomorrow."

Dave Silver chuckles and pats James on the back.

"Excuse me," he says, "I just need to water the garden."

James finds himself alone with Jane Cottle.

"So," she says eventually, her eyes following her husband across the room, "how did you meet Oliver?"

James is standing beside Auntie Pru's chair. Jessica was with him but she's gone. He'd sought her out, and she'd said would he be an angel and come and talk to Auntie Pru, otherwise she just gets stuck in a corner, and she'd led him to the chair and begun a conversation between the three of them, then left him there. James finds himself once more pinned down by the clear, blue gaze. He takes a drink from the glass in his hand. It appears that he's now drinking whiskey.

"Do you always drink a lot?" says Auntie Pru.

"No, not really. I mean, do I? I haven't, actually. Not that much."

"Nonsense. Every time I see you, you're knocking it back."

"It was very good wine," James says, lamely. "Hard to resist. Although, of course, they say that the better a wine is, the less you need to drink."

"Don't blather."

"Sorry."

"It's perfectly all right to drink. I happen to believe that men should be drunk much of the time. For the most part, it makes them more agreeable and easier to manage. The ones that become unpleasant or violent can usually find someone as vicious and tiresome as themselves to go off and have a fight with."

James notices that the old lady's teeth are grey and lustrous, worn down by age to tiny, delicate stumps. They remind him of the pearls on a Victorian necklace of his mother's.

"They're all my own," she says.

"I beg your pardon?"

"You were looking at my teeth."

"I'm very sorry."

"I don't care. I'm very proud of them."

"And so you should be. They're lovely."

"Watch your step. I know you're just trying to be charming, but I'm sure you don't really want to get my knickers off, do you?"

James can't think of a correct answer to this question.

"Don't worry," Auntie Pru says. "When you get to my age you can say more or less whatever you like. One of the few advantages."

"I suppose you can have a bit of fun with people, then," James says.

The old lady gives him a shrewd glance.

"You're not quite as stupid as you look," she says. "However, I doubt if you're clever enough for Jess. I assume you're in love with her, like everyone else."

"Who else is in love with her?"

"Oh, all the men," says Auntie Pru, vaguely. "I was the same at her age. They were all in love with me."

James admires the way she didn't add, "believe it or not," or something similar, as most women of her age would have done.

"Sometimes," she adds, gazing into the distance, "I wonder if it would have been less trouble if I'd been an ugly old boot like Spracky." She pauses. "Less trouble, but less fun, too." She looks up at him.

"All right," she says, "you can go now."

"How is Oliver getting on at work?" John Longbourne asks.

"He does pretty well, I think," James says.

"How do you actually measure success in game like PR?"

"I've been trying to find that out ever since I've been doing the job."

John Longbourne bares his teeth and expels a bark of laughter. The laugh, and the veins in John's nose, remind James of the old man he met in the garden. Bill. John Longbourne's brother. Oliver's father. He's out there somewhere now, probably in his special shed.

"I'm trying to encourage Oliver to branch out," John says. "But I find it quite hard to talk to him about these things."

"Where?" says James.

"Where what?"

"Branch out where?"

"On his own. He should start his own business."

"Really? What sort of business?"

"Oh, I've got a few ideas. I've had a fair amount of experience. Unfortunately I was rather badly let down on a couple of occasions. I trusted people I shouldn't have done. That's always been my trouble: I assume people are honest."

"Yes," James says, "me too."

"But Oliver's pretty shrewd. Wouldn't you say? I mean, you work with him; he's pretty sharp, isn't he, when it comes to business?"

James wonders if any of Oliver's activities could be described as business. He does as little work as possible for his employers, treating them as a source of patronage and subsidy for pursuits of his own. And while it's true that he's always making arrangements, and talking on the phone, and having meetings, either he loses interest in the plans he concocts, or he becomes obsessed with schemes that never amount to anything. However, James is aware there's a lot he doesn't know about Oliver.

"He always seems to be pretty busy, I'll give him that," James says.

"Exactly. He's got energy and business acumen; I've got the experience and contacts. We could do a lot worse."

"Are you saying you want him to start a business with you?"

"No, no, I'd only be involved in a consultancy capacity. My field is mainly commercial management. Of course, if you want to make a serious impact with a new company, you need a bit of capital." John Longbourne strokes his moustache. Suddenly he is struck by a completely unexpected thought. "You don't happen to know how Oliver's fixed in that respect, do you? Savings, investments and so on?"

"No, sorry. I've no idea."

"As I say, it's rather difficult for me to talk to him about these things. Not that there's any animosity. God, no; we're great pals. But certain things. Given the family situation. Not being his father. As you know. Do you? The set-up here with myself and Bill and Daphne. Did he fill you in?"

"Yes, actually, no, it was Jessica who told me, but, yes."

"Nice girl, Jess. Don't you think?"

"Definitely, yes."

"Anyway, it's all a bit delicate. I have to be discreet with Oliver. I don't want him to think that big bad uncle John is just trying to get his hands on the son and heir's money." He bares his nicotine-stained teeth again and emits one of his nasal, barking laughs. "I don't want to start looking like the wicked stepfather!"

James thinks that, at that moment, that's exactly what he looks like.

The sky is crowded with stars. More stars than sky. Amazing. Almost too bright and clear to be real. And they look so close. James can't remember ever seeing the night sky like this. He's only taken a few paces into the garden from the French windows but it's as though he's stepped into outer space, among the stars themselves.

Someone stumbles against him from behind.

"Sorry," Reuben says, steadying himself with a hand on James's shoulder.

"Are you all right?" asks James.

"Dunno."

They both breathe in the warm night air.

Reuben gazes up at the stars. "Makes you feel..."

"That's right," James says.

Reuben lets his head flop back to stare up at the sky directly above him. James grabs his arm to stop him from toppling over backwards.

"Oops," Reuben says. "Thanks." He lowers his gaze and turns to look at James, making an effort to focus on him. "You're all right."

"Thank you."

"No, really. You're all right."

James releases his arm gently, allowing him to find his balance.

"D'you know what?" Reuben says.

"What?"

"I love Jessica."

"Really?"

"Yes. But don't tell anyone. No one knows."

"Not even Jessica?"

"She might have found out," Reuben says. "I might have told her. When I was drunk. I think she likes me, though."

"I'm sure she does."

"Has she said anything to you about me?"

"No," James lies.

"I think she likes me. But as a friend. She probably thinks I'm too young. She doesn't take me seriously. I'm learning Hebrew, you know."

"That must be interesting. Is it difficult?"

"Fucking difficult. But I want her to see I'm serious about my roots. She's got roots. They've all got roots, these country families. But I've got roots, too. You see?"

"Is it working?"

"Not really. But it doesn't matter. Because I'm going to do something to prove I'm a serious player. Know what I mean? A player. That's what Olly says."

James wonders where Olly is and why he hasn't phoned him. He checks his mobile phone. When he was getting dressed, and thinking about etiquette, he concluded it would be acceptable to keep it on him, switched to silent mode. No messages.

Reuben grabs his arm. "And Olly should know, shouldn't he? He's a player."

"But what's Olly got to do with it?"

"Actually, it was Olly's idea, originally."

James doesn't like the sound of this. "What's he got you involved in?"

"It's a partnership. It means that soon I'll have a lot of money."

"How soon?"

"Very soon. You'll see. Olly's got this plan. In fact, you're sort of involved."

James becomes seriously alarmed. Olly's plans tend to disrupt the life of anyone who comes into contact with them, even accidentally. But to find out that you've been specially selected for inclusion in one of them is like seeing your oncologist approach along the hospital corridor with a set of X-rays and a grief counsellor. Bad news. James wants to shake it off and run away, like a dog escaping from a bath.

He grips Reuben gently by the shoulder. "Can you tell me about it?"

"Not just at this moment, no."

"Why not?"

"Because I'm going to be sick."

Reuben turns away and vomits into a flower bed.

All the guests have gone. Daphne Longbourne has said goodnight, and helped John Longbourne up to bed. Auntie Pru retired some time ago. James stands at the foot of the stairs. He wishes he'd managed to talk to Jessica alone but the opportunity never seemed to arise. He wonders if she's gone to bed without saying goodnight to him. Someone is making a noise with pots and pans, but that's bound to be Spracky. Then the door at the far end of the staircase swings open, the volume of noise increases for a moment before being muffled again, and Jessica is walking towards him.

"I was just helping Spracky," Jessica says, "but she's nearly finished now. She's sent me off to bed. Are you coming?"

"To bed?" says James.

"Upstairs. Do you know where your room is?"

"Yes, I can remember."

"And there's a loo right opposite you. Next door to my room. I'm just across the corridor from you. Just let me know if there's anything you need."

"When?"

"When what?

"I mean, you won't be asleep?"

"Oh, eventually. But I'm usually awake for quite a long time."

"What do you do?" James says. He can't believe he just asked her that.

Jessica gives a low, throaty chuckle. "Now, there's a question. Actually, I just lie there. Sort of waiting."

"What for?"

She shrugs. "Whatever's going to happen next in my life. I just lie there thinking about things, usually. I fantasize."

"What sort of things?"

"Oh, gosh," Jessica says, widening her eyes and adopting a brittle voice from an old British film, "wondering if I'll get a pony for my birthday, and when I'll see all my super chums from school, and how beastly it will be if nanny's too old to come to my wedding, because she's so jolly decent, and what kind of wedding dress I shall have, and all that kind of rot, don't you know?"

They both laugh. Then they stop and regard each other in silence for a moment. Jessica moves towards the foot of the stairs. She's very close to him. She leans towards him and drops her voice:

"I'm a healthy seventeen-year old," she says, "what do you think I think about?"

She kisses him on the cheek.

"Good night," she says. "I'll be seeing you."

She turns and runs up the stairs.

James sits on his bed. He's tried lying down but the room spins too much. Anyway, he doesn't want to go to sleep. He wants to answer the question that's tormenting him. Was Jessica inviting him to come to her room?

He alternates between being convinced that she's waiting impatiently at this very moment for him to knock softly on her door, and the certainty that if he does he'll make a complete fool of himself.

He replays their conversation at the foot of the stairs, examining every word for its meaning, turning it this way and that, like a jeweller scrutinizing a gem. In one light, everything she said to him is a blatant erotic signal which he's being incredibly dense not to recognize and act upon; in another, his alcohol-impaired judgment is allowing him to corrupt her entirely innocent remarks with his own lecherous optimism.

I'll be seeing you. That's what she said. Not 'see you in the morning'. It's obvious she meant that she'll be seeing him when he comes to her room. Or is it? It's just an expression, after all. But why use it at bed-time? Maybe it's a family thing. Sleep tight, don't let the bugs bite. That kind of thing. No, that's ridiculous.

But what about all the other things she said? She made very sure that he knows where her room is. Let me know if there's anything you need, she said, then told him that she'd be awake, waiting! What's wrong with him? Of course

35

she was inviting him to go to her! Any normal man would be there already. And when she kissed him good night, the way she pressed herself against him, it was unmistakeable.

Or was it? It was only a peck on the cheek, after all. She was just being friendly. And helpful, with that stuff about making sure he knows where her room is. What is he thinking of? Almost all he's done since he arrived is commit a series of excruciating social blunders. And now he wants to go barging into the room of a girl he only met this afternoon, who hasn't given him the slightest indication that she's interested in him. Although she did come and talk to him when he was in the bath.

It's driving him mad.

He needs a piss.

That decides it: he's definitely going to leave his own room.

He can make the next decision in a minute.

James stands in the corridor, appalled at the noise he's just made by operating the flush. The antiquated system gurgles and groans as it refills the cistern with agonizing slowness. He's acutely aware that Jessica is only a matter of feet away. He sees a strip of light beneath the door next to the toilet. She's in there, awake. Waiting for him. Is she?

Don't think, just do it.

He grasps the door knob, turns it very gently, opens the door, and walks in.

She's sitting on the bed, looking at him.

Not Jessica. Spracky.

Who is naked.

He looks away, horrified, only to meet the unblinking gaze of Auntie Pru.

Something is going on in this room that he doesn't understand, and doesn't want to. Things he can't allow himself to see. He tries not to look anywhere, and begins to back slowly towards the door, but certain images are seared indelibly into his mind.

Spracky's naked flesh. Except she's not completely naked, she's wearing some kind of massive and complex flesh-coloured corset. But it's hard to tell where the corset ends, and where her flesh begins. It spills down her body in an undulating cascade, like dough.

Auntie Pru, by contrast, is composed entirely of wrinkles.

She, too, is wearing some kind of corset-like undergarment. It appears to be made of leather and is like a straitjacket whose untied straps radiate out from the torso and connect with a network of other straps to form a mesh-like contraption that appears to be suspended from the ceiling. The whole thing is a kind of web, with Pru suspended at its centre, like an immensely ancient spider, completely still, silent, and alert.

He keeps edging towards the door but he can't tear his eyes away. Pru continues to gaze at him utterly impassively, but Spracky suddenly smiles at him, which makes him shudder. He notices that she's wearing riding boots and that there's a saddle beside her on the bed. Also a bridle, stirrups and spurs.

James inches backwards, trying to create as little disturbance as possible in the atmosphere of the room, hoping somehow to erase himself from both the space and the time in which this scene takes place, and to unmake its existence.

But as reaches the door, and his fingers close around its cold brass handle, he is frozen to the spot by a sight that threatens to pluck his mind entirely from its moorings, crush it like a paper cup, and toss it into a rubbish bin of madness. Auntie Pru begins to rise slowly into the air. She is levitating. Or perhaps undergoing the Rapture, spoken of so eagerly by evangelical Christians, and being received into heaven. James wonders briefly how she's going to get through the ceiling. As her rigid, upright body continues to rise, her arms spread out slowly as if she's being crucified. Delicate filaments of fine grey hair, like wispy clouds of spun silk, peep from the waxy folds and flaps of wrinkled flesh dripping from her armpits. James begins to tremble.

Suddenly, Pru descends several inches and then stops with a jerk. The web in which she's enmeshed gives a slight shudder. A corresponding movement from Spracky catches James's eye. He sees that she's holding one end of a rope attached to a series of pulleys from which the contraption is suspended. She has slowly been letting the rope slip through her fingers, and this has the effect, through a system of counterweights, of raising Pru up into the air. Now Spracky pulls on the rope gently, which lowers Pru back down so she's standing on the floor once more. Spracky turns to James again and her smile widens to a ghastly leer. Her eyes seem glazed. She releases the rope again, and Pru is propelled upwards, then she pulls down on it, and Pru descends again. Spracky repeats the process several times, so that Pru is dangled up and down, up and down, like a helpless marionette. All the while, Spracky grins at him, inviting him to admire this unspeakable human puppet show. Pru remains absolutely expressionless.

Finally James manages to get out of the room. The last thing he sees, as he closes the door softly, is a large structure like an oversized dog kennel, in the corner of the room. He recognizes some of auntie Pru's outer clothing strewn across its entrance.

James lies in his bed, the idea of sleep a quaint relic from an earlier age of innocence. Why didn't he notice that there was a door on either side of the toilet? He tries to forget what he saw but he can't. He will never forget.

Four.

Someone was scraping toast.

The sound was faint and distant but it was so familiar that James's brain, making a leisurely ascent to consciousness, identified it well before he was properly awake. Somewhere nearby a bath was being run, and in the background a hard-working hot water system provided a comforting cocoon of soft white noise. Birds were singing in the bright sunlight beyond the curtains.

James wallowed in a delicious combination of drowsiness and excitement.

It was the holidays and a long summer day of limitless possibility stretched out ahead of him. Perhaps he and Simmy Robshaw would ride their bikes all the way to the tunnel this time. He would promise his mother that he wouldn't go further than the far side of the common, and it wouldn't really be a lie, because the tunnel more or less joined up to the edge of the common if you didn't count the two roads you had to cross, and one of them never had any traffic anyway. Or maybe he should go and be nice to Justin Webb, in case he was getting the new Power Rangers video game today. But Justin didn't like Simmy at the moment, ever since the dog poo incident, which had actually been very funny, although James could see Justin's point, so James would need to find out about the video game before he made any arrangement to meet Simmy, because...

Holy shit.

James was awake. Dreadful images engulfed him. He had a pounding headache. He struggled to push his memories of the night before out of his mind, which made his head hurt even more.

He sat up in bed, slowly. The assault on the toast was taking place directly below him, and the noise was sneaking up through the floorboards: a thin, penetrating rasp that seemed to scrape the inside of his skull, as well as the toast, with every rhythmic stroke.

He thought about his father, who always made breakfast at the weekend and always burned the toast. One of his earliest memories was of lying in bed and listening to his father trying to salvage something edible from the charred slices of white Wonderloaf (later replaced by a more health-conscious wholemeal), a ritual that continued all through his childhood. It was the realization that the scraping was becoming hesitant and less vigorous - and finally, feeble and erratic - that brought home to him the reality of what was happening to his father, far more effectively than the brave, evasive little talks in which his mother tried to explain it to him. Poor Dad.

James cursed himself. He'd made the lethal error of giving way to melancholy while suffering from a hangover, aiding and abetting its power to demolish him.

He tried to assess the hangover's severity. It was certainly formidable, and far more sophisticated than a straightforward mugging administered by a night on the beer, from which he could usually recover by being sick and going back to sleep. This hangover was symphonic in its complexity. Beneath the usual clashing dissonance in its upper register, produced by hypersensitivity to light, sound and sudden movement, and the unpretentious but robust varieties of blunt pain throbbing through its middle range, James detected a quiet but ominous bass note of existential dread that rumbled through the foundations of his mental integrity, threatening to undermine it. He couldn't think of anything worse than being in this house and getting the horrors.

It was unlikely that a hangover of this type would allow him to go back to sleep, but he lay down anyway and closed his eyes. Miraculously, after a few minutes, he felt himself drifting towards a state which, while he knew it wouldn't be actual sleep, might at least provide a mildly refreshing doze. All he had to do was relax. Empty his mind. Refuse to think. Sail into a bank of dense, welcoming fog...

There was a sharp knock at the door.

James sat up quickly, and regretted it immediately.

The door opened and Jessica walked in. Her hair was wet and she was wrapped in a small towel that provided an absolute minimum of what James's mother would have called decency.

"I've left the water in my bath," she said, "It's still pretty clean. Or if you want, there's a much more modern bathroom upstairs that we put in when we converted the top floor, and it's got a fantastic shower, but the whole hot water system is a bit cranky, especially at weekends when everyone wants to use it, and you might have to wait."

When James tried to reply he found that his mouth was too dry to produce any sound. He swallowed painfully.

"Bath," he croaked. "Thanks."

"How's your hangover?"

"Brutal."

"Mine too," Jessica said cheerfully. "Do you fancy a cooked breakfast?"

At that moment James smelled bacon and coffee. He was famished. He nodded.

"What do you feel like?" Jessica said. "Bacon, egg, sausage, beans, tomatoes, mushrooms, hash browns, black pudding, anything. I expect there's even kedgeree."

The effort of selection was beyond him. "All of the above," he said.

"How would you like your eggs?"

"Scrambled. Like my brains."

39

"I'll go and tell Spracky."

"Wait."

Even with his mind severely impaired by the hangover some of James's basic mental faculties were beginning to function, kicked into action by powerful waves of sexual craving. Jessica was here in his room, hardly dressed. He was naked in bed. There had to be a chance she'd join him. He just needed to stop her leaving.

"What?" Jessica said.

"I wanted to ask you something."

She sat on his bed.

Just as he'd hoped. Now all he had to do was think of something to ask her. He sat up more, allowing the sheets to slip down and expose his whole torso. He'd been told he had an attractive body. He was lean and his muscles were well-defined but not exaggerated. He knew most women liked that look more than bulging, overdeveloped muscles. He was in good shape, and he always felt fit and healthy. He bent his legs slightly and leaned forward with his elbows on his knees, contracting his stomach in a way that made his abs look good.

"What?" Jessica repeated.

"Um... I just wanted to ask... have you heard from Olly?"

"No. Have you?" She leaned against his leg and draped one arm over his knee. Her hand was very close to his groin.

James picked up his mobile phone from the bedside table, which gave him a chance to shuffle forward a bit. Jessica's fingers were now almost brushing his crotch. He examined the phone and shook his head.

"Oh, well," Jessica said.

"Do you think he'll call?"

"No idea. But don't hold your breath."

James frowned and narrowed his eyes. "I wonder what's happened to him."

He didn't really care what he was talking to Jessica about, just as long as he could gaze earnestly into her eyes and speak in a low, sincere voice about something that sounded important. But having alighted on the subject of Oliver as a useful topic for the purpose, he realized that he was, in fact, still genuinely worried about his absence. He'd been very insistent about James visiting on this particular weekend. Why hadn't he shown up? The story of the arrest seemed vaguely farcical. Admittedly, that was pretty typical of Olly. But there was something suspiciously contrived about the whole thing. And then there was the mysterious plan Olly had cooked up with Reuben, who'd said that something was going to happen very soon, which could mean it would happen this weekend. And James was involved in some way. It was all very ominous.

He was still gazing into Jessica eye's. She was gazing back. All that separated her naked body from his was a few inches of space and a thin cotton towel. He placed his hand gently on her arm.

"I'm worried about him. Aren't you?"

"Not really. You know what he's like." She raised her eyebrows. "But what's the problem? Can't you have a good time without him being here?"

"Oh, God, no, it's not that," James said, "I just wondered, that's all. No, it's fine. If he comes, he comes, right? If not, no worries."

James tossed the phone back onto the bedside table.

Jessica stretched, and the skimpy towel parted at the side, exposing her whole flank and the curve of her breast.

He paused. Just a touch away. All he had to do was reach out. He leaned forward and moved his arm to encircle her. At the same moment she sighed, pushed against his leg, and sprang up from the bed. "You must be ravenous," she said. "I'll get Spracky to start your breakfast."

Timing, thought James. And he'd mismanaged the whole encounter by going on about Olly like that. It had made him look weak and anxious, dependent on Olly in some way. He decided that he wouldn't carry his phone around with him any more, to show Jessica he didn't care. He decided to leave it here in the bedroom and check for messages periodically.

As Jessica turned away and moved towards the door she unwound the towel and began to dry her hair with it, so that James caught a glimpse of her whole naked body from the back just before she stepped through the doorway.

"I'll be seeing you," she called over her shoulder.

The kitchen was bigger than some of the flats James had lived in. A dozen battered chairs fitted easily around the long, deeply scarred oak table in the middle of it. Spracky was standing at a double sink the size of a cattle-trough, wearing a shapeless mob cap like a Victorian parlour maid's. She had her back to him and any sound he might have made coming into the room was drowned by the clattering of the plates and pans she was washing up in a way that suggested they had personally offended her.

No one else was in the kitchen. James paused just inside the doorway. What if she made some reference to the abominations he'd witnessed the night before? He was wondering whether to leave quietly and come back later, when something struck the back of his leg with a soft blow. He jumped and uttered a hoarse squeak of surprise. He looked down to see the cat curling itself around his legs and purring loudly as it swished its tail against his calves.

"Don't encourage him," he heard Spracky say, "he's got fleas."

James looked up to see her scowling at him.

"Sorry," he said, and tried to back away from the cat, which wound itself around his legs even more tenaciously.

"Give the bugger a kick!"

James did as he was told, but harder than he'd intended. The cat skittered along the tiled floor, scrabbled to a stop, and padded from the room trying to look dignified.

41

"That's the style," growled Spracky. "Sit down, young man, sit down."

James sat in a chair half way along the table.

Spracky dried her hands on a filthy towel hanging beside the sink, then turned to face him. She looked him up and down slowly, narrowing her eyes and nodding judiciously, as if assessing his value as livestock.

"Yes," she said eventually, "you're as thin as a stick. I'm not surprised she said you want the lot."

"Sorry, who said what?"

"Jess. You've just missed her. That was the little madam's washing-up I was doing when you came in."

"Oh, I see. Where's she gone, do you know?"

"No idea. But she said you'd ordered a full cooked breakfast."

"Well, not ordered it. I mean, she asked if I'd like one, so I said yes, but I don't want to put you to any trouble. I'll have whatever's going, really."

"You'll have what you asked for."

"Right. Thanks. Is there anything I can do to help?"

Spracky laughed scornfully. "Don't be stupid. It's all ready for you over here."

She stumped over to an Aga cooking range that had been installed in the recess of a vast fireplace in which a medium sized car could have been parked without difficulty.

"Is that an Inglenook that's been opened up?" James said.

Spracky turned and beamed at him. For an instant he glimpsed a hint of something maternal in her smile. Until that moment he hadn't really considered that she belonged to the same species as someone like his mother, let alone the same gender.

"Well spotted!" she said. "That's exactly what it is. Can you believe it, some odious philistine had the whole thing bricked up in the nineteen twenties and put a gas fire in? It was Bill and John's father, Rollo, who opened it up again. Did it all himself, too. Stood there swinging a sledgehammer, stripped off, covered in dust. He was a fine figure of a man. Terrifically exciting."

"Yes," James said, "I can imagine." He saw her looking at him suspiciously. "I mean to see an old fireplace like that being opened up," he continued. "And I expect there were smaller brickwork pediments inside, dividing off the nooks themselves, which he must have taken down, too."

"Exactly right!" cried Spracky. She regarded him with something approaching approval. "All right," she said, "how old do you think this place is?"

"Well, that's a bit of trick question, isn't it? This kitchen is probably one of the oldest parts of the house. I'd say fifteenth century. Late fifteenth. The dining room is part of a much later addition, maybe early Georgian. It looks like a whole wing was added. And the living room's mostly Elizabethan, with a series of increasingly bigger windows added over the years. That's my guess, anyway."

"And a bloody good one, too. You know your stuff. I didn't know we had an expert among us."

"Not an expert, not at all. An enthusiastic amateur."

"You know a damn sight more than young Oliver, I'll tell you that, and he's lived in the bloody place all his life. Doesn't care a fig about it."

"It all depends on what you're interested in. It just happens to be a bit of hobby with me. In fact I used to think about becoming an architect at one time."

"Why didn't you?"

James thought about the abrupt move to the local state school after his father died, and the gradual fading of the prospect of a good university. He still could have done it, if he'd really wanted to, but something changed over the years. He wasn't quite sure what.

"It's a long story," he said. "But I've always loved old buildings and churches and things. Houses like this."

"Well, let's get you fed," said Spracky, opening one of the lower oven doors in the Aga, "and I'll tell you a bit more about the place."

She extracted a very large plate from the oven and deposited it on a place-mat on the table in front of him. It contained a huge, perfectly cooked breakfast, with all the ingredients that Jessica had mentioned, steaming gently.

"Tea or coffee with that?" Spracky said.

"Coffee, please."

"Careful, that's very hot."

She was right. The rim of the plate scalded his fingers when he tried to shift it towards him. He noticed that Spracky hadn't used an oven glove to carry it, though.

*

The fabric of the deckchair was sticking to his back again. He leaned forward to unpeel himself from it.

It was going to be another hot day. It was already a hot day, and it was still only just after ten. When Spracky had installed him in the deckchair at the top of the lawn she'd chosen the perfect spot. He was in the sun but his face was shaded by the tree beside him, and any extra glare was dealt with by the brim of the Panama hat she'd found him, which he'd pulled down over his brow, and his sunglasses. Spracky had also produced a pair of old sandals that fitted him. She'd even offered to find him some shorts after telling him how stupid he was not to have brought any of his own. But James had declined the offer and rolled up the legs of his trousers instead.

"Oh, well," Spracky had said, "trousers are neither here nor there."

James gazed out over the garden, stupefied by the heat and the remains of his hangover, which had diminished into a pleasant lethargy. The bath and the breakfast had helped, and once Spracky had discovered he was interested in the house she'd been very friendly, which made her seem almost normal. And she was behaving as if what he saw in her room last night had never happened, which suited him very well. James recalled her unearthly grin and her glazed eyes. Perhaps she just kept it all completely separate. She was a strange person, after all. But he wondered how much of her gruff eccentricity was an act. Maybe it had all started because she was shy, then the act took over. People did that. And everyone was weird in some way or another.

But James found it disturbingly easy to allow her to take care of him, as if he was completely helpless. It was some quality that she herself projected, he thought, which demanded a response of infantile dependence from other people. On the few occasions when he had come into contact with genuine servants he'd always been uncomfortable, which made him vulnerable to outrageous exploitation by them. But Spracky wasn't like a servant. She was more like a very bossy slave, or a character in a fable who insists on devoting herself to the service of the stranger who accidentally saves her life, whether the stranger likes it or not.

He realized he was nearly asleep. He heard footsteps approaching along the gravel path behind his deckchair and looked up to see John Longbourne standing beside him. Some newspapers were tucked under his arm and he was carrying a tall glass full of red fluid. He raised the glass.

"Cheers. Tomato juice. I find it always does the trick after a bit of a session. Especially if you forget to leave out the vodka." He winked at James. "I'm off to read the papers in the summer house. Have you been to the summer house?"

"No, not yet," James said.

"Charming spot. It's behind the sheds over there. Did you know there's a whole other garden back there?"

"No, I didn't"

"Want to come?"

"Not just now, thanks."

"Would you like some of the papers? I've got the Times, the Telegraph, and a couple of the chip wrappers."

"No thanks, I'm fine."

"Bloody hot, isn't it?

"Sweltering."

"Right, I'll be seeing you, then."

James watched him walk away along the path until he disappeared behind the sheds that James had seen when he first entered the garden. It was only once he was out of sight that James began to devote some consideration to the fact that John Longbourne was stark naked.

After a while he decided not to worry about it. If a man wanted to wander about with no clothes on in his own garden, that was his business. Although, strictly speaking, it was probably still Bill's garden. James wondered idly whether, if Bill were to appear unclothed as well, he'd be able to tell the two brothers apart. Bill's moustache was shaggier and more stained and there were more veins visible in his nose, although John was catching up quickly in that respect, obviously helped by a diet rich in alcohol. But it would mostly be a matter of posture, wrinkles and general skin condition.

He decided he wanted to stop visualizing naked, elderly men. But he found it difficult to erase the image of John Longbourne's long, spindly cock dangling inches from his face. He closed his eyes and the memory began to fade as he drifted back towards a state of semi-consciousness.

He heard a clattering noise beside him. He looked around and saw Jessica setting up a deckchair. She was wearing sunglasses and a long, loose shirt that came down to the middle of her bare thighs.

"Mind if I join you?" she said.

James began to struggle upright. "Do you need any help?"

"Relax," she said, and expertly flipped the deckchair into place without the usual wrestling match that James always underwent in the process.

Jessica nudged the deckchair closer to James's with her foot and extracted a thin, hand-rolled cigarette and a lighter from the breast pocket of her shirt. She lit the roll-up, inhaled deeply, and held it out to James.

"No thanks, I don't smoke."

"It's all right, there's no tobacco in it."

She held it closer to him and James caught a familiar, pungent aroma. He was taken aback. He didn't want to smoke pot right now. Sometimes he enjoyed it, especially when it made everyone laugh uncontrollably, and occasionally he liked the way it gave him a fresh perspective on things: what he could honestly describe as insights, when he could remember them. But he found its effects far more unpredictable than those of the other drugs he'd taken. He'd done coke a few times, mostly with Oliver, and usually in combination with a lot of alcohol, and even when he got wasted he always felt confident and gregarious in a way that overrode any sense of impairment. The same was true of ecstasy, which he liked, although it took him a long time to recover from it and he hadn't taken any for a while. But smoking weed, in certain moods and circumstances, made him nervous and unsure of himself, sometimes even paranoid. He was always troubled by a vague impression that he didn't quite know what was going on. As this was the predominant feeling he'd had, without the assistance of drugs, ever since he'd arrived in Ullage, he didn't want to risk making it worse.

"It's a bit early for me, thanks," he said.

"Oh, come on," Jessica said, "I hate getting stoned by myself. It'll be fun. Don't be such a wuss." She took another quick hit on the joint and waved it under his nose.

James took it from her. He tried to make it look as if he was taking a deep drag by including as much air as possible from the side of his mouth along with the smoke, then passed it back, exhaling as soon as he reasonably could. Jessica took another hit, held her breath, and passed it back to him.

"Go on, take it right in, or you won't get the benefit," she croaked, as she exhaled in short, controlled bursts.

James tried not to let the smoke get too far down into his lungs. He waited a moment, let his breath out, and passed the joint back to Jessica. She finished it in a couple of short, fierce drags, flicked the roach into the bushes, and stretched luxuriously.

"Ah, lovely," she said. "And there's plenty more where that came from. I've got a few dozen plants in the greenhouse. Not bad for home-grown, is it? Pretty strong."

James had to agree. Already a familiar cloud of befuddled anxiety was beginning to envelop him.

Jessica turned and looked at him, her hands on her hips.

"Right," she said, "get 'em off."

"Get what off?"

"Those trousers."

She took off her shirt. There was nothing underneath it.

The sight of her naked body affected James like a physical blow. He felt as if he'd been hit very hard by something that didn't hurt. She was perfect. Her breasts were small but full, with hard little nipples, and her legs were long and athletic. The tops of her thighs framed a neat, tightly-curled pubic bush. She put her hands on her hips again, as if pointing to it, and grinned at him.

"Come on," she said, "otherwise it's not fair."

James interrogated his brain for alternatives to what was about to happen but couldn't find any. He couldn't find much in there at all, in fact. He undid his trousers and took them off. Thank God he was wearing reasonably presentable underpants. He stepped out of them and placed them neatly on top of his trousers beside the deckchair.

"Doesn't that feel better?" Jessica said.

James thought about it. Did it feel better? It felt unusual. His body was strangely cool, even though he was standing in the bright sunlight, and he was very aware of his skin, as though he was trying it on for the first time, like a new suit.

Jessica flopped down in her deckchair, raised her arms, and clasped her hands behind her head, which had a truly fascinating effect on her breasts.

"Are you all right?" she said.

"Yes, fine." James stood uncertainly beside his deckchair. He had a vague feeling that if he sat down he would be committing himself to something.

"What's the matter?" Jessica said, "are you worried about sunburn? Because you're quite fair-skinned, aren't you? Do you want me to go and get some sun cream and rub it on for you?"

"No, that's fine, thanks," James said, and sat down.

Silence descended. James felt that it showed no sign of ascending again without his help. He groped around for a topic of conversation. He was sure there was something he'd been meaning to say for some time. He searched in his mind for it, but wherever he looked, it always seemed to have just left, like a train he'd narrowly missed, leaving a sad, palpable absence in the atmosphere. Or like someone you think you recognize from the back, who constantly turns a corner just ahead of you before you can tell who it is. No, it wasn't like that; it was more like... wait. What was he doing? Instead of remembering what he'd been meaning to say, he was thinking about the process of remembering. Thinking about thinking. He often did this when he was stoned. And now he was thinking about thinking about thinking. He was going around in circles. Like a vortex. A whirlpool. Or a spin dryer. Hold on. What had he just been thinking about? Spin dryer. Washing. Clean clothes? At least he wouldn't run out of clean clothes if he was going to spend most of the weekend in the nude. Nude. That was a funny word. Nude. It sounded like 'rude' and, also, it was rude. It's rude to be nude. Brilliant: a little poem. Or like something his mother would say. A rude nude. Nude. What did that word mean? Nude. Nuuuude.

"What did you say?" asked Jessica.

"Nothing. Did I?"

"You were muttering something about being nude."

"Oh. Sorry."

"Is it freaking you out a bit?"

"What?"

"The nudity thing. I assumed you were cool about it. We sort of take it for granted. We're not overlooked here, so when it's nice weather we often wander about with no clothes on. I suppose people would say we were naturists, except we'd never do it in one of those ghastly clubs where people play volleyball and smoke pipes and grin all the time, or go to some beach where all sorts of perverts hang out. But this is our garden, and we can do what we like, so why not? We all do it."

At that moment James caught sight of Daphne Longbourne at the far end of the garden, where it sloped down into the tangle of bushes and trees. She was carrying a gardening trug with some kind of vegetation dangling over its sides, and a trowel. She wore a sun hat and a length of fabric wrapped low around her hips, like a sarong, but nothing above it, leaving her impressive bosom exposed as she crossed his field of vision and took a path leading down through the bushes. Somehow she managed to look even more stately and dignified than she did with all her clothes on.

James thought about what Jessica had just said. They all did it. Suddenly a hideous image sprang up in his mind. "When you say you all do it--"

Jessica laughed. "Don't worry, you won't be seeing Auntie Pru out here. No, she hates the sun. And as long as she's inside, Spracky will stay in there too, looking after her. So you'll be spared that sight, at least."

"Sorry, I didn't mean to be--"

"Forget it. I agree; there are limits."

Silence crept up on them again. James felt time stretching out uncomfortably and once again he thought he ought to say something. But even though he'd only taken a few hits of the spliff, its effects seemed to be getting more powerful all the time and now his mental processes were in complete disorder. Finally he began to speak:

"That dope is..."

"What?"

"It's really..." James couldn't remember what he was going to say. "Sorry. I seem to have forgotten how to..."

"Speak."

"I'm trying to."

"No, I meant is that what you've forgotten how to do?"

No, not speak, exactly. It's as if I can't remember how to... to..."

"Think."

"I'm trying to. I just can't think of it."

Jessica giggled.

"No, that doesn't make sense, does it?" James said. "Although that's it, in fact. I've forgotten how to think. That's what I was going to say. I think." He was having some kind of trouble with his tongue, which seemed too big for his mouth, and the word 'think' was beginning to puzzle to him, locking itself up and hiding its meaning somewhere inside itself. "Sorry," he said, "I suppose I'm just really stoned."

"Good. Then you can just chill out and enjoy it, can't you?"

"Yes. Great," James said miserably.

Time crawled along.

"You know what?" Jessica said.

"What?"

"I've got the munchies." She stood up. "I'm going to go and make a peanut butter sandwich. Peanut butter and jam. Or cheese on toast. With Marmite. No, peanut butter and marmalade. Would you like something?"

"I don't think so. Not just now, thanks."

"Sure?"

"No, I don't think so. I mean, yes, I'm sure, thanks."

James's mind was churning. Something she'd just said had reminded him of what it was he'd been wanting to say all this time. What was it? Something to do with food. Marmite? Toast! That was it.

"I just wanted to ask you something," he said.

"Sure, go ahead."

"When I woke up I could hear this scraping noise. And it was Spracky, she'd burnt the toast. It went on for ages, she must have burnt a dozen pieces. It went on for so long that I went into a kind of dream about being a kid, because my father always used to burn the toast, before he died, when I was quite young. Well, obviously, before he died. He wouldn't have been doing it afterwards, unless it was a poltergeist type of thing."

"I'm sorry. What a shame."

"Oh, it didn't taste too bad. Just a bit charred."

"No, I mean I'm sorry about your father. Dying when you were young."

"Oh, right. Thanks. I got over it, I suppose. Although I once went out with a girl who said I'd never gone through a proper grieving process. But she was a geography student."

"Ignorant bitch."

"She was quite intelligent, actually. But that doesn't matter. She ended up being treated for depression, as it happens. I don't mean that that doesn't matter, by the way, because, obviously, it does. She married a man who designed bridges in the end. Or was it dams?" James realized he was getting off the point. "But what I mean about Spracky and the scraping is that I couldn't understand it. Because she's such a good cook, and so efficient about everything else, and yet she burnt all the toast. Do you see what I mean?"

"Oh, she always does it. She insists it's the only way to make proper toast. You've got to burn it slightly, then scrape it a bit. One of her odd little ways. Now, where's my fucking shirt?"

It was as simple as that. James couldn't believe that the question had seemed so important. It had been nagging at him ever since he'd woken up. But it was utterly trivial. And now that he had the answer, his mind felt empty.

"Of course," Jessica said as she looked around for her shirt, "you've got to remember that Spracky's on quite heavy medication."

Jessica located the shirt where she'd flung it down on the grass, just in front of her deckchair. She took a step forward and bent down to pick it up.

The effect on James was instant and dramatic. Up until now, and to his surprise, Jessica's nakedness hadn't seemed particularly erotic. She just looked healthy and wholesome, like an advertisement for something. But now, as she turned her back and bent down, keeping her legs straight and parting them very slightly, her buttocks were presented to him invitingly and he glimpsed the plump fruit of her labia peeping between the tops of her thighs. He had the fastest erection he'd ever experienced. He whipped the hat off his head and slammed it down over his groin.

Jessica turned around, slipping her shirt back on. She glanced at the hat.

"Are you getting sunburned down there?" she asked.

"No, I'm fine. Just thought I'd move the hat. Let my hair breathe. I mean my head, you know, it's getting a bit sweaty. Sticky hair."

"So, there's nothing you want from indoors?"

"No, I don't need any cream or anything."

"I don't know if we've got any cream anyway. I hadn't thought of that. Peanut butter and cream. Not a bad idea."

"No, I meant sun cream. When you asked before, and said did I want you to rub it in. So I'm okay. I don't need any rubbing." This was coming out all wrong. "I mean with sun cream. I don't need any sun cream. To rub in. Anywhere. Thanks."

Jessica raised her eyebrows and smiled at him. "You've got a one-track mind, that's your trouble."

James gave a feeble croak of laughter and held the hat down firmly.

Right," Jessica said, "I'll be seeing you."

She spun on her heels and walked away across the grass in long, springy strides.

James tried to think in a straight line. If only he could follow one train of thought, he might be able to make sense of things. Like Jessica. He still couldn't work out if she was encouraging him or not. She must have known what she was doing when she bent over in front of him like that. He felt a stirring beneath the hat. The human body was amazing. Even without the image in front of him, his eyes still visualized it so clearly that his brain instantly sent a message to his genitals. Like an electrical current. In fact, it was an electrical current, he seemed to remember learning. But then why didn't it give you an electric shock? There was blood involved as well. The member became engorged. Where did that phrase come from? School. He saw the lugubrious, mottled face of his biology teacher. The male member becomes engorged. He'd been no good at science. Okay at maths. He liked English, hated geography, mainly because of the teachers, who always seemed to be foul-tempered, quite liked history, wasn't too good at games but didn't mind them. At least games got you out of the classroom. He'd turned out to be quite a strong swimmer, and for a couple of terms he swam on the school team. But he lost interest quite quickly, which had happened with a lot of things. Perhaps it was true that he'd never mourned for his father properly. Why was he suddenly thinking about that again? There must be some chain of association. What was the last thing he'd been thinking about? Swimming. And before that, how games got you out of the classroom. And before that, about what classes he liked and didn't like. Geography: that was it. The girlfriend who was a geography student and had accused him of not grieving for his father. That's how he'd got there. It was all logical. Everything was logical. You could follow everything through a chain of connections.

He lifted his back from the deckchair again for a moment, to allow the sweat to drain away. The deckchair was logical. It was made of wood and fabric. Wood that came from trees like the ones he could see growing a hundred yards away. And the fabric - that came from plants, originally. Even if the material was plastic instead of fabric, that was made from oil, which was found in the ground, somewhere far beneath his feet. Like the iron in the rivets and bolts that held the chair together. He was actually sitting on a piece of furniture that grew organically out of the ground beneath it; grew out of this very garden, in a sense.

He looked around the garden. Where was everyone? Jessica had been gone for ages. Everything was very quiet. James began to feel a bit spooked. How long had he been out here, anyway? It was at least a couple of hours since he'd had breakfast, he was sure of that.

In the distance he heard a faint whirring and clanking, then a bell struck. That would be the church in the square, just next to the Post Office shop. The bell only struck once. One 'o clock already? That meant he'd been out here nearly three hours. A bit longer than he'd thought, but he might have dozed off at some point. Then the bell struck again. Two 'o clock? Surely not. Another stroke of the bell. Three? No, that was ridiculous. Then James realized it was probably going to strike twelve. So he'd only been out here a couple of hours after all. Yes, perhaps that made more sense.

The bell stopped after eleven strokes. That couldn't be right. Eleven? No, it was far later than eleven. That would mean he'd only been out here for less than an hour. That was inconceivable. His mind had taken long, complicated voyages that seemed to have spanned aeons and continents. And Jessica had been gone for half an hour at the very least. She'd said she was only going in to make a sandwich.

Food. James was seized by a sudden craving. Plain chocolate digestive biscuits. He must have some, immediately. But would they have any in the house? It had to be those particular biscuits: McVities plain chocolate digestives, nothing else would hit the spot. And if he went in and tried to find some, or asked Jessica or Spracky for them, and they offered him some other type of biscuit, and he refused, it would seem very rude. But it had to be plain chocolate digestives or nothing. He could taste the bittersweet chocolate on his tongue, and the crisp biscuit crumbling in his mouth. The shop. They might have some there. It was bound to be open at eleven on a Saturday morning. He put his hat back on his head. He was full of optimism and determination. Money. He'd need some money. He reached down to his trousers and felt in the pocket. Lucky he'd thought of that. He was pleased with himself: yes, his mind was still working logically.

Detective Sergeant Jarvis sat in his car drinking coffee and watching the Post Office. The coffee was cold and he was hot. He was forty-four, his bladder hurt, and he should have been an Inspector by now, at the very least.

The coffee was cold because his thermos flask was old and the seal leaked; he was hot because his car was even older and the air conditioning didn't work properly; his bladder ached because he couldn't risk breaking off surveillance to empty it, and he was still only a DS because sixteen years ago a man had ruined his life.

But this weekend it was payback time.

The bladder situation wasn't usually a problem. Years ago, when Jarvis first began to undertake prolonged surveillance operations, he'd invested in a contraption called The Trucker's Friend, which allowed him to piss through a tube into a plastic flask strapped to his ankle beneath his trousers. All he had to do was periodically unscrew the bottom of the tube and, if he was in his car, empty the flask discreetly out of the window. But today the top end of the device - a moulded plastic cup that fitted inside his underpants, with an internal rubber spigot like a loose condom - had become dislodged. It was the heat. Jarvis was a man who perspired freely at the best of times, and in today's sweltering conditions the plastic down there had become very slippery. About an hour ago he'd undone his trousers and was groping around trying to re-adjust the thing when something thumped against his window, right next to his head. Jarvis recoiled, spilling a residue of urine from the groin-cup onto his trousers. He looked up to see a boy of about ten, holding a football and peering in through the window. Jarvis hastily rammed himself back into the cup and zipped up his fly. The boy bounced the football against the window again and gave him a sly smile. Jarvis wound down the window.

"I'm going to tell my dad," the boy said.

"No, no, don't do that, son. I wasn't doing anything. I've got a medical condition."

"You're a paedo."

"No, I'm not, son."

"I'm going to get my brother, too. He does Thai kick-boxing. South Cotswolds championship bronze medal for the last three years. He's a psycho." He turned and began to amble away very slowly.

"Wait, son!"

The boy stopped.

"I'm a policeman," Jarvis said. "A copper."

Jarvis showed him his badge.

"I don't care," the boy said. "I'm going to go and tell my dad that I was playing here and a nasty man in a car was watching me and took out his willy."

"Listen, I'm on a special operation. Undercover. Like the secret service. You know, James Bond type of thing. Do you like James Bond?"

"No, he's a cunt. And if you're really a copper you'll get in even more trouble. They hate coppers in the nick even more than they hate nonces. They'll fucking castrate you in there. You're in deep shit, mate."

Jarvis sighed. He fished out his wallet and took out a ten pound note.

"Right. Take this, fuck off and keep quiet. Come back here at lunch time and I'll give you another one. But if you fuck things up for me you'll get nothing."

"What if you just drive off?"

"Then you'll still have a tenner, won't you?"

The boy thought about it. He took the note and strolled away, bouncing the football on the ground.

Jarvis hadn't been able to get the Trucker's Friend back into place properly when the boy had interrupted him, and now he couldn't risk any more groping around down there, even though he needed to piss, just in case the little bastard was still watching him. Keeping him under surveillance. Which was ironic, given that if he was, he was doing it with more success than Jarvis was achieving with his own efforts at clandestine observation. There wasn't really anywhere to park where he could see the Post Office and remain concealed. He'd done the best he could, by parking on the far side of the village green, as near the hedge as possible, but the longer he sat there, the more his presence was going to arouse suspicion.

Fuck it. He didn't care if it took all weekend and he had to pay off every rat-faced, chiselling little urchin in the village. He was finally going to nail his man.

Raymond Norfolk.

There wasn't a day in the last twenty years when he hadn't thought about that name. Raymond Norfolk, ex-rock-star, currently living in a mansion nine miles away, just outside Nether Gurney, the next village. Five years ago Norfolk had walked out of his band, The Hangmen, and bought the mansion, part of which he'd converted into a recording studio. Now he played the country squire, poncing about in a tweed cap and Wellingtons. He'd even started a small business, selling his own organic vegetables. But although he might not be a rock star any more - not in the way he used to be, filling stadiums, and causing riots and flying in private jets, and smashing up hotels - he still made records, and played gigs, and gave interviews, and got photographed leaving clubs with gorgeous women. He had a thriving solo career, as they say.

Just like me, thought Jarvis. A solo career. Because no fucker will work with me.

Obsessed. Vendetta. A loose cannon.

He'd heard it all, behind his back, and to his face.

"You've got the makings of a good copper, Jarvis," the superintendent had said to him, when he was twenty-five. "You could do well. Just keep your nose clean and your wits about you. And don't make it too personal. That's a mistake, son. Sure, you need a bit of fire in your belly sometimes, and you need to despise the scumbags you nick, but don't let them get to you. Understand what I'm saying?"

"Yes, sir."

"For example," said the superintendent, glancing at a file, "you seem to be devoting a lot of time to this Norfolk character. This rock star. My daughter's keen on his lot, as it happens. What's the problem there, Jarvis?"

"I'm sure he's into drugs, sir."

"They're all into drugs, son. Comes with the territory."

"I know, sir. But Norfolk is taking the piss."

"What, dealing, is he?"

"Yes, sir."

"Really? What sort of scale?"

"Can't really tell, sir. But I'm sure he's distributing cocaine to the other members of the band, at the very least."

"Hang on, son. Are you saying he's a dealer, or are you saying he's just scoring an ounce or so and flogging some to his mates to cover a few grams for himself?"

"I'm not exactly sure, sir, but--"

"Forget it, Jarvis. We're after the dealers, remember. The big boys. If this guy fucks up and hands himself to you on a plate, then by all means bust him. But you've raided him twice and got nowhere. Leave it. That's my advice, Jarvis. Just leave it."

But Jarvis wouldn't leave it. He didn't tell the superintendent that he and Raymond Norfolk had been at school together. They hadn't been in the same class; not even in the same year. Norfolk was two years older than him. Even though he now looked five years younger. How did they do it, these celebrity types?

Norfolk probably didn't even remember what had happened. Even back then, at seventeen, in his last year at school, he'd been a bit of a star. He already had a band that did proper gigs and got paid for them. Jarvis pestered him for weeks, bringing his guitar into school every day, begging Norfolk to listen to him play the songs he'd written, and every day Norfolk said he didn't have the time. And then, on the night of the school dance, when Norfolk's band set up to play...

The humiliation. Christ. In front of everyone. The bastard. The sadistic bastard.

Jarvis became a copper because he couldn't think of anything else to do, but he probably wouldn't have joined the Drug Squad if it hadn't been for Norfolk. When he saw how famous Norfolk was getting, and the kind of life he was leading, he knew there was only one person in the world he really wanted to see locked up. And drugs were the key, he was sure.

He kept his eye on Norfolk all the time. He fought off complaints of harassment. He had to be very careful after the two raids the superintendent referred to. He knew he wouldn't get many more chances. He went to every Hangmen's gig that he could. What he saw and heard, and what he read in the press, convinced him that Norfolk was using drugs, and every instinct told him that he was dealing as well. When colleagues challenged him as to why a successful rock star would need to deal drugs, Jarvis gave a variety of answers, the most frequent being another, rhetorical question of his own: Why does a dog lick its balls? Because it can, that's why.

Norfolk's style on stage was surly and combative, the rock and roll bad-boy rebel. He treated the audience like shit and they loved him for it. They went crazy. He encouraged and manipulated the frequent fights that broke out; sometimes he even leaped from the stage and joined in. Somehow, he always emerged unscathed, ready to pick up his guitar and come in right on cue with a windmilling, slashing chord at the end of the keyboard solo. Norfolk was a big, fit, handsome bastard and he could look after himself. But after watching it happen several times, Jarvis began to see how much of it was rehearsed and staged. The whole thing sickened him: the adulation, the groupies, the obscene amount of money Norfolk made by pretending to behave like a hooligan - not even a real hooligan, for fuck's sake, it was all bogus! - the total arrogance of the man. Worst of all, he was a terrific singer and wrote some great songs. Three of the band's singles got to number one in the charts and several more were top ten hits. Two albums went triple platinum. Jarvis loved some of those songs. It was intolerable.

Finally, Jarvis couldn't take it any more. He set up a raid after a gig at the Alexandra Palace in London. He led a team into the dressing room and they tore the place apart. They manhandled the groupies, trashed the instruments, and walloped any of the hangers-on who got in their way. Norfolk didn't even recognize him.

But it worked. They found drugs everywhere. Almost everyone in the dressing room was holding something. All small amounts - except for Norfolk. They found several grams of coke on him, and, as a bonus, a gram or so of morphine. The amount was just enough to charge him with Intent to Supply.

When the case came to court, five weeks later, they had to drop Intent to Supply because when you took into account the amount by which the drugs had been cut, it was borderline. But the judge was a ferocious old fart who didn't like arrogant young rock stars who earned more in a week than he did in a year. And it was a time when the government and the media were going through one of their periodic fits of hysteria about Britain's Youth Drug Shame. The judge decided to make an example of Norfolk with a custodial sentence on the possession charge. Six months in Pentonville.

The next two weeks were the happiest of Jarvis's life. People told him how well he was looking. He met a very pretty stenographer. He started going to a gym.

Then it all fell apart.

Norfolk had 'people' - his manager, his record company, his publishers, his publicists - and they were powerful people. They could afford the best legal help that money could buy, and some help that wasn't particularly legal, too. They found the weak spot. A young detective constable had been one of the Drug Squad team - it was his first bust - and they got to him. He was informed that one of the groupies was bringing a charge of assault against him that could put a serious dent in his career prospects. Then they made sure that his wife, who'd only been married to him a year, began to hear unpleasant details about the alleged assault, and then rumours that it wasn't the first time her husband had behaved like that. Then the young cop found out that people were saying it was a moody bust, there was something bent about it, and he was the one who bent it. Finally he cracked and told them that Jarvis had planted the drugs on Raymond Norfolk.

Which he had.

Jarvis was lucky to stay out of prison. Conspiracy to pervert the course of justice: definite bird - up to ten years. But the police and the defence managed to muddy the case just enough, and to cast just enough doubt on the evidence, and the young constable's motives and testimony, to get the charge dropped.

Jarvis's luck held. The superintendent liked him, even though he thought he was a nutter; at least he had balls, and he reminded the Super of himself when he was younger, and he got behind him. We all make mistakes, son. So Jarvis stayed on the force, by the skin of his teeth. He was demoted back to constable and transferred to traffic duties.

Norfolk was free, of course. But Jarvis was still a copper.

Jarvis worked his way back up the ladder. It was a long, slow climb. And it was a solo ascent. He'd never been particularly popular, and now he found that he didn't have any friends on the force at all. There was a bit of grudging support, but after the superintendent retired, he was pretty much on his own.

He found he preferred it that way. People didn't understand him. He couldn't find anyone to share his determination to keep after Raymond Norfolk. They thought he was weird, quite frankly - the way he talked about Norfolk all the time, even when he was off duty. Jarvis was aware that he was becoming an oddity, even a bit of a joke.

Why don't you just leave it, Jarvis?

But Jarvis wouldn't leave it.

He may not have had any friends but he forged some useful alliances on his way back up the ladder. Even if some of the allies weren't too crazy about it. As it happened, one of them was sitting in a car about two hundred yards away right now. He was parked just up the hill on the road between Ullage and Nether Gurney, watching the entrance to a muddy lane that ran behind the Post Office.

Phil Beamish was a Detective Investigator with Customs and Excise. Jarvis had met him eight years ago, just after he finally made it back onto the Drug Squad as a detective constable. Jarvis was put on a team that was ordered to investigate possible corruption at the Gravesend unit, where Phil Beamish was based. That was the way it worked: if a customs unit was under suspicion, then the police would conduct the inquiry, and if a police force was to be investigated - individuals were dealt with by the Internal branch - the inquiry would be conducted by a force from a different county, or by Customs if it involved drugs, immigration or smuggling.

Seven kilos of heroin had gone missing from the Evidence Room in the Gravesend unit. The Drug Squad investigation got nowhere. Someone had covered their tracks very carefully. But not carefully enough for Jarvis. He worked late, in his own time, probing, digging, persisting. He discovered that two months before the smack had disappeared Phil Beamish had been about to have his house repossessed. He was being pursued by the Child Support Agency. He drove a twelve year old Toyota. Two months after the disappearance, Beamish had quietly paid off his mortgage and straightened out the child support people. He still drove the twelve year old Toyota. He wasn't stupid. Jarvis liked that. He confronted Beamish quite amicably. He admitted he didn't have enough hard evidence to ensure a conviction but they both knew the score. The deal was that Beamish would become Jarvis's inside man in Customs and Excise, with special responsibility for any possible leads to Raymond Norfolk.

Because Jarvis knew - he just *knew* - that Norfolk was mixed up in dealing, probably smuggling as well. They were all wrong and he was right. He had to be. Otherwise he was nothing more than what they said: vindictive, obsessed, deluded. And that couldn't be right. Beamish kept his opinion to himself. He didn't have any choice about becoming Jarvis's ally, so he did what he was asked. And it didn't do Jarvis any harm to have a man inside Customs and Excise, regardless of the Norfolk thing. It helped him with a number of other cases, and he clawed his way back up to Detective Sergeant.

When Norfolk bought the mansion and started the residential recording studio, it all fitted into place. It was obvious to Jarvis: a certain type of band booked in for a few weeks and, in addition to the usual facilities, Norfolk supplied them with all the drugs they needed. Which could amount to a lot, when you took into account the inevitable entourage and all the visiting hangers-on, who included smaller scale dealers to sell to.

For five years Jarvis nursed his certainty but he could never persuade his superiors to sanction a raid or even a discreet investigation. They knew all about Jarvis and the bee in his bonnet. So Jarvis watched and waited.

Meanwhile, he and Beamish became friends of a sort, or so he liked to think. They were both single men who tended to have short-term relationships with women they met in their line of work. They drank together sometimes. Went out for a curry and ended up in a lap-dancing club. Screwed the same tarts. Jarvis knew he could trust him.

And then, two weeks ago, the big break had come. Beamish found out that Customs had intercepted a suspicious parcel, posted in Bermuda. It was opened and found to contain one-and-a-half kilos of cocaine. Not a huge amount, but it was high quality stuff, very pure. When Beamish told Jarvis the address on the parcel, he flipped: Ullage Post Office. Not ten miles from Norfolk's studio. Jarvis called in every favour he'd built up over the years and pulled every string in the web of grudging obligations he'd patiently woven, and persuaded his bosses to let him mount a special, short term operation. Customs didn't object too much: it was a piddling amount of coke by their usual standards, and if Jarvis was prepared to do all the work, and managed to roll up a network they could bust, then why not do what he asked? Which was to allow the parcel to go through and let Jarvis track it, keep whoever picked it up under surveillance, and set up a bust when he was sure he'd nailed the whole operation at this end.

Even though there was still a cloud over Jarvis, Phil Beamish had a clean record because Jarvis hadn't fingered him in the Gravesend investigation, and they were both equipped with digital cameras, to film the whole pick-up and delivery process, so Jarvis was covering himself against any potential allegations that the operation was bent.

It was obvious how Norfolk was running it. Relatively small parcels, posted from places like Bermuda - staging posts for coke that originated in South America - and sent to a selection of quiet rural Post Offices within an easy reach of the studio. Keep it small, keep it out of London. Smart. The names of the people to whom the parcels were addressed were clearly fictitious. Norfolk, or someone working for him, would turn up with some phoney ID - something made on a kid's printing kit would be enough to fool the yokels in these little country places - and pick up the parcel, and that was that. Next time it would a different Post Office and a different name. In this case, the parcel was addressed to a James Burridge, c/o Ullage Post Office. Jarvis had the name checked out: nothing on the Police National Computer, or any of the other more discreet data bases that the public didn't know about. Maybe James Burridge didn't exist, or was some old codger, or Norfolk had got the name from an old death certificate. You could still do that; bloody Frederick Forsyth had a lot to answer for. Either way, someone was going to turn up at Ullage Post Office today and pretend to be this Burridge character and collect the parcel. At a pinch, they might try to get in the back way. The only other possibility - that the woman who ran the shop was in on it - was a non-starter. Jarvis had checked her out thoroughly. Besides, it couldn't work that way: Norfolk would have to corrupt every sub-postmistress in the county. Although Jarvis wouldn't put that past him.

It was time to phone Phil on his mobile for the regular half-hourly contact they'd arranged. Jarvis had only just managed to persuade him to give up the time for this operation, and Phil had said he'd only stay until five. Jarvis was pretty confident that Norfolk would make his move today, because the Post Office would be closed tomorrow, and Monday was a Bank Holiday. But there was always the possibility that Norfolk would pull a stunt Jarvis hadn't anticipated. Jarvis took out his mobile and began to dial.

Then he saw a naked man.

The man was on the far side of the village green and he was heading for the Post Office. He looked quite young, and he wasn't completely nude because he was wearing a panama hat, sunglasses and sandals, but his tall, pale, lanky body still made a very striking impression.

Suddenly the young man stopped in his tracks. He looked around wildly, then down at his own body. Then he covered his genitals with his hands, turned, and ran away at top speed.

Jarvis's mind raced. Should he follow the naked man? No! Of course - that was exactly what Norfolk wanted him to do. It was a decoy. Jarvis was meant to chase after the nudist, at which point Norfolk, or another henchman, would slip into the Post Office, which they were obviously watching from some nearby vantage point, probably having sussed Jarvis, pick up the package, and disappear. It would only take a moment. Jarvis would probably find that the naked man was some village idiot who'd been paid to do it by someone he'd never seen before. Clever. Very clever, but Jarvis wasn't falling for it. Of course, he needed to check out the naked joker, but he could get Phil to intercept him. The guy had disappeared up the hill, towards where Phil was parked.

He dialled Phil's mobile number. Busy signal. Shit! The idiot was probably trying to phone him at that very moment. Come on, Phil, follow protocol - it was Jarvis's turn to call and, no matter what happened, you always followed protocol. That was the golden rule. He tried again. Still busy. Get off the fucking line!

*

59

James leaned back in his deckchair, breathing heavily. He didn't think anyone had seen him. It was only because of the wasp he'd encountered that he'd realized he was naked. Thank God he hadn't got as far as the shop. As soon as he'd got back he'd put his trousers back on. Enough was enough.

Jessica appeared beside him, licking crumbs from her fingers.

"Yummy," she said. She sat down on the grass in front of him and leaned back against his leg. "Been having fun?"

James decided not to tell her what had happened. Definitely not. He knew he could make her laugh with the story, but he was beginning to suspect that trying to make her laugh all the time with stories about his own ineptitude wasn't always working to his advantage. He'd been aiming to strike a tone of rueful self-deprecation and delightfully ironic self-awareness, but there was a chance she just thought he was a jerk.

"Have you been running?" Jessica said.

"Running? No. Just breathing. You know, exercises. Deep breathing. To relax." He demonstrated by filling his lungs and spreading his arms.

"Aren't you relaxed, then?" she asked.

"Yes, but you can never be too relaxed, can you?"

"A good point, well made. Shall we have another spliff?"

"No thanks, not for me."

"Perhaps you're right. It'll only make me want more food. In the end I had peanut butter and Marmite with very thinly sliced raw onion. And a little bit of cream cheese. Listen, I meant to say: just go and help yourself when you get hungry. I might go and get something else in a minute, actually. I forgot to make any tea with that sandwich. I really fancy some tea and biscuits. How about you?"

"I wouldn't mind a biscuit. I'm quite hungry."

"I'm afraid we've only got a limited selection. In fact, all we've got are McVities plain chocolate digestives. I adore them, especially when I'm stoned, so I always make sure we've got some in the kitchen. Are they all right for you?"

"McVities plain chocolate digestives?"

"Yes."

"In the kitchen?"

"Yes. Will they be okay?"

"They'll be fine."

"We won't be having proper lunch or anything today because of the fete," Jessica said. "There'll be tons of food there, so we can just graze all afternoon."

"Is this the fete at the Silver's place?"

"Yes, don't you know about it? Oh, God, you've just reminded me, I think I forgot to tell you: you're doing the bingo."

"What do you mean?"

"The bingo stall. You're running it. You know, clickety-click, two fat ladies, all that stuff. It's always the most popular thing because Dave and Sylvia lay on some really big prizes. People get quite worked up about it."

James felt a sudden chill. He thought the sun must have gone in but when he looked up there wasn't a cloud in the sky. "You don't mean you want me to be the announcer or the compere, or whatever it's called? The MC?"

"The caller. You'll be great at it! Sulky Richard was going to do it, but they phoned this morning to say he's sick as a dog, which is really good, actually, because you'll be much better. I'm going to dress you up."

"You've only just got my clothes off."

Jessica laughed.

That was good, James thought. If he kept it light and jokey maybe he could talk her out of the whole terrifying idea without letting her see how scared he was.

"No, really," she said, "I'm going to make you look like a bit of a spiv, you know, a sort of chav type wide-boy, with a little moustache and everything. Don't you think that'll be really funny? And you can do a Cockney accent. So it'll be just like the real bingo they all go to. Except for the accent. Maybe you should do a sort of yokel voice."

"I can't do voices."

"Well, that just makes it funnier, doesn't it? It'll be great. Everyone from the village turns up and loads of people from all the nearby villages, too. Because of the prizes. But you get some quite rough types, you know, some of the local farm workers, and some of the Polish lot who've been around for the last year or so, doing a lot of the seasonal picking. There's sometimes a bit of trouble, actually."

James thought he saw a possible escape route. "But if they take it all so seriously don't you think it might come over as a bit patronizing if I'm completely ignorant about the whole thing and I start taking the piss? I don't want to upset these local guys."

"No, they'll love it! Anyway, they aren't the worst. The ones who get really violent are all the more well-to-do types. Especially the women. If you want to see rampant greed there's nothing to match an upper-middle class woman. Last year I caught Jane Cottle pinching some poor senile old woman who was sitting next to her, really hard, trying to make her lose concentration because Jane could see she had a winning card. The vicar's wife! So, you have to keep them in line a bit, but it's all really good fun."

"To be honest," James said, trying to suppress a slight tremor in his voice caused by mortal terror, "I don't think I'll be very good at it."

"Don't be silly! Of course you will!"

"No, really. I'm a bit awkward about doing that kind of thing."

The truth was that any kind of public performance at all was a hideous, excruciating torment for him.

His earliest memory of real, crippling embarrassment was a school nativity play. The teacher organizing it had cast him as the narrator because she said he had a nice speaking voice. His role was to stand at the side of the stage and recite the well-known gospel story, while the other children, clad in the usual array of dishcloths, dressing gowns, cardboard wings and wobbly haloes paraded on and off as shepherds, wise men and angels, acting out the events he described. The narration was meant to be delivered at a measured, steady pace and the performance was timed to last about ten minutes. On the day, James waited for his cue, took a deep breath, blurted out the words, "And lo, it came to pass that certain poor shepherds...." and didn't stop. He gabbled through the story so fast that the children had to run on and off the stage to keep up with him, hissing at him to slow down as they collided with each other in a series of multiple pile-ups, tripping over the manger and dislodging the baby Jesus, who rolled off the front of the stage and into the lap of a veiled Muslim mother whose son was appearing as Joseph in the interests of enhancing inter-faith diversity, while the teacher, purple-faced with frustration, performed increasingly frantic semaphore from the wings. James was told later that he'd got through the whole thing in just over a minute.

Over the years the same thing happened whenever they gave him a part in a play. Before he even stepped onto the stage his costume was drenched in sweat. Then, quaking with dread, he either swallowed his lines in a stuttering whisper or rattled them out in a deafening, staccato monotone. But they wouldn't give up on him. The pedagogic theories of the time insisted that self-expression was vital for healthy juvenile development, and that even the most reticent child was a precious miracle of untapped potential; potential which must be nurtured, forcibly if need be, no matter how deeply it seemed to be hidden.

James remembered one particularly tenacious teacher who fancied himself as an astute educational psychologist, and who thought James's shyness could be cured by forcing him to join the debating society. He was a ferocious little Welshman with high ideals and good intentions but less common sense than a box of hammers. The more James pleaded with him to be spared the more he insisted on James participating. A year of recurring weekly agony brought James as close as he would probably ever come to committing a serious criminal assault. Then the man left the school to go and teach at a progressive establishment in the country where pupils were encouraged to set their own curriculum, treat the staff as equals or preferably inferiors, and smoke whenever and wherever they felt like it. James heard later that the place had burned down.

In his final years at school James developed a number of excuses to reduce the risk of public humiliation. Illness, pressure of exam work, and discreet hints about family problems too painful to broach had all been deployed. Since leaving school he'd managed to avoid any kind of public performance altogether.

But now Jessica was asking him to appear without a script in front of a large crowd of aggressive strangers in a highly charged scenario that would undoubtedly expose him to ridicule, hostility and possible violence.

"I'm really sorry," he said, "but I just can't do it. I'd be absolutely no good, really."

Jessica swivelled around and knelt between his legs. She rested an elbow on each of his knees, lowered her head, and looked up at him with big, puppyish eyes.

"But I want you to do it!"

"I know, and it's very flattering, but I can't. Sorry. I really can't."

Jessica sighed and laid her cheek on his thigh. She pouted, and squeezed his other thigh. Thank God he was wearing his trousers again. But the sudden bulge in his groin was unmistakeable and he saw Jessica's eyes flicker towards it. She rubbed her cheek softly against his leg and began to walk her fingers playfully up and down his other leg, bringing them closer to the bulge with each expedition.

"Please," she said. "Please, please, please?"

"No, sorry. Absolutely not."

"Just for me. You'd be such a star. Please say you will, James. Please?"

James shook his head. It was out of the question.

She gazed up at him. Very slowly she licked a crumb from the corner of her mouth, then ran the tip of her tongue around her moist, slightly parted lips.

"I'd be so grateful," she whispered huskily. "I really would."

"All right," James said.

Five

"There was something else," Jessica said, "but I can't remember what it is." She paused as they approached a corner in the narrow lane, and absently tore a leaf from the hedge. "No, I've completely forgotten. I expect it'll come to me later. Come on."

James reviewed the list of things Jessica had warned him to avoid at the fete. It included pretty much any kind of contest, especially tests of strength like the tug-of-war or 'hitting the thing that rings the bell with the wooden hammer thing.' According to Jessica, any demonstration of physical prowess at all might inflame the unruly element who would be present. She told him about a fight that had taken place two years ago, between some of the local farm labourers and the Polish fruit pickers. Although she referred to it cheerfully as 'an amazing punch-up', and made it sound like a boisterous saloon brawl in a film, where people hit each other with chairs and bottles that shatter harmlessly, she mentioned as an afterthought that three people had been taken to hospital, one of whom remained in a coma for a week. It was obvious to James that it was essentially a series of brutal beatings administered by vicious rustic psychopaths.

She'd also told him on no account to agree to judge any kind of competitive event, particularly if it involved the relative size and merit of plants or vegetables, or to give even a casual opinion on any edible produce that he might be offered. It would certainly be a trap. The cake contest, she said, was especially notorious; it was meant to be decided by secret ballot, but the competitors had mysterious ways of identifying the voters, and were capable of ugly reprisals. And he was to steer clear of anything whatsoever to do with children. She claimed she was doing him a favour by making him run the bingo stall, as it would prevent him from being roped in for any more potentially dangerous job.

James felt oddly detached from the ordeal ahead of him. He knew that some people, facing execution, arrived at a state of serene acceptance, and confronted their extinction with tranquillity. Others, of course, had to be dragged to the scaffold bellowing with terror. James had always felt that he probably belonged in the latter category, but perhaps something had changed. Perhaps it was a sign of maturity.

Or perhaps he was still a bit stoned.

Ahead of them people were turning off the lane and disappearing through a gap in the hedge. Jessica had protested that usually, to get to the Sliver's place, she'd simply walk along the main road from her house, and go up their driveway, but today they had to take the long route and go in the back way along with all the ordinary people. James had rather enjoyed the walk along the leafy, winding lane they'd joined at the bottom of the Longbourne's garden, although he was now sweating lightly.

They reached the gap in the hedge and James saw that Jane Cottle was sitting at a trestle table on the other side of it, selling tickets. Jessica strode past her.

"Hoy!" Jane shouted, "pay up!"

Jessica stopped and turned around very slowly.

"Who, us?" she said.

"Everyone pays," Jane said, rattling a large cake tin full of coins and notes, and flapping a book of thin paper tickets.

"But I've been helping to organize everything," Jessica said, "and James is doing the bingo."

"Everyone's been helping. Come on, it's only two pounds. It's all for a good cause."

"I haven't got any change."

Jane sighed and rummaged in the cake tin. "I expect we can find something."

James was aware of people coughing and muttering behind him. "I've probably got the right money," he said, groping in his pockets.

"No," Jessica said, "it's a matter of principle. I really don't see why we should pay, what with all the work we're doing."

"Everyone's paying," Jane said. "Even Simon, and he's done tons of work."

"That's his business."

"Look," James said, "let me pay, okay?"

"Good man," Jane said. "And how about some raffle tickets? You can buy them from me as well. They're only a pound each."

"We don't want any raffle tickets," Jessica said. "We should get free ones, anyway, because Mummy donated one of the prizes. She helped choose it, anyway."

"Oh, don't be ridiculous," Jane said. "It's too hot for this nonsense."

"In that case, Jane," Jessica said sweetly, "why don't you chill out?"

James felt a gentle pressure behind him and a hot breath on the back of his neck.

"Come on, pal," a low voice muttered.

James turned to find a beefy young man standing very close to him. He had a round, red face and thick black eyebrows that joined in the middle. He winked at James. "Get that bitch sorted," he said quietly.

James recoiled from a blast of beer fumes lightly scented with fried onion. There was another man standing close behind the first one. He looked like a larger replica of the same model and was probably his brother. He smiled at James unpleasantly.

The two young men created a powerful impression of raw meat. James didn't particularly like the way Jessica had been called a bitch, but perhaps it was the normal way they referred to women around here. He gave the two men a sardonic smile, hinting at friendly but not craven male solidarity, then turned back to Jane Cottle and fished some coins from his pocket.

"James, don't," Jessica said, "she can't make us."

"No, really, I want to pay," James said. He found that he only had three pounds in coins, so he took a ten pound note from his wallet. "I'll have six raffle tickets as well."

"Splendid," Jane Cottle said, giving him a collection of flimsy bits of paper.

He stuffed them in his pocket and took Jessica's arm, gently but firmly turning her to face the direction of traffic. "Come on," he said, "let's get in there."

"Gosh, now you're getting all masterful," Jessica said. But she didn't resist him, and James could tell she was glad he'd acted decisively to end the standoff.

There were a lot of people around. James and Jessica found themselves in a sizeable crowd that was shuffling off the rutted track that led from the gap in the hedge, and through a narrow gateway in a dry stone wall.

"I see you were making friends with the Pringle brothers," Jessica said.

"Who, those two guys back there?"

"The twin gorillas. Terry and Jason. There's a third brother, too, much younger. He's a real little vermin. He keeps trying to climb up on the wall when we're sunbathing. It's a good idea to keep on the right side of them. They tend to be the ringleaders if things kick off. Terry, the bigger one, is into martial arts. Kick boxing. Although you wouldn't think he could do much kicking or boxing, hauling that massive gut around."

"Sometimes these big people can be surprisingly nimble," James said. "Did you ever see that pop video of that fat bloke doing all kinds of back-flips and things? He wasn't really fat, just large. He seemed quite firm, in fact. Portly but firm. I think he was actually a ballet dancer."

"Well, I wouldn't ask Terry Pringle about ballet, if I were you. He was the one who put the Polish guy into a coma. You're not keen on that type of thing, are you?"

"What, putting people into a coma?"

"No, ballet. I always think it's such a weird mixture. Sexy and boring at the same time. They've all got amazing bodies, though. Haunches everywhere. Like animals. Great, strong haunches. And they're fantastically supple. They must be great in bed. But the actual dancing is all a bit dull, just sort of prancing around with a bit of leaping and twirling. Actually, I went to ballet classes when I was a little girl. It was only a phase, though, like ponies, and being a lesbian."

"When were you a lesbian?"

"I wasn't, really. It was just about having a crush on older girls, or teachers. Everyone went through it. Although I seem to remember we did a bit of snogging. And feeling each other up. That was after the ballet thing, when we were older. Nothing happened at ballet, it was all very tedious. The same little girl would always end up crying. You didn't even have to pull her hair or anything, all you had to do was call her names. There's always one like that, isn't there?"

James didn't answer. He'd seen the house.

Georgian; probably late Palladian. Not particularly big, but you got a better sense of the classic proportions from a smaller one like this, especially seeing it in its own grounds, which made you appreciate the way it filled the space it occupied so precisely. Clean lines, no decoration, just very simple architraves around the first floor windows. A conservatory had been added to the back of the house, which faced them, and James guessed it had probably started life as an orangery.

The house stood at the top of a wide lawn that sloped gently down to where they were standing, flanked by shrubbery and stands of trees. Even though people were swarming all over the whole area, which was covered with various stalls, rides, exhibits and marquees, James could detect the carefully landscaped contours underneath it all. There was a small ornamental lake on his left, and although it made no secret of its artificiality it still looked perfectly natural. It was all beautifully done.

The only problem was the windmill.

It was too near the house, for one thing, and it looked as though it dated from a much earlier period. Even if the house had been constructed on the site of an older building, James thought, you'd still expect the windmill to be further away. And it was strange that they would go to all the trouble of creating a superbly landscaped vista around a beautifully proportioned Georgian house without demolishing - or at least moving - something so incongruous.

"What do you think of the windmill?" Jessica said. "Isn't it fun? They've got it all working, you know."

"I'd be interested to know the history."

"Let's go up there. I expect old Max Fennel will be there. He'll be only too happy to blather to you about it for hours on end."

"Who's he?"

"He's been helping the Silvers restore it. He's fantastically knowledgeable about all that stuff. He knows all about the local history, although he's not from around here originally. He's a dean, or a don, or a professor, or something."

"Have we got time?"

"Yes, it's only two. You won't need to start the bingo until about three. It'll be much more crowded than this by then. Come on."

They wove their way up towards the windmill, through what James was beginning to realize was a very large event. When he'd first heard about the fete he'd pictured something small and quaint, with beaming ladies from the Women's Institute selling homemade jam, and a crusty old major putting the local pony club through its paces. But this was more like a big, noisy country fair. The atmosphere was convivial, but there was an edge of rowdiness to it. In some ways it reminded James of a rock festival.

"Where have all these people come from?" he said.

"Oh, miles away, some of them. There's a big car park in one of the fields over on the other side of the house. People come from all over the place."

"What's that?" James pointed to a long, thick log, like a telegraph pole, that was suspended horizontally between two trestles about ten feet above what looked like a giant paddling pool. There were stepladders at either end of the pole.

"The greasy pole! It's fantastic. Don't you know about the greasy pole?"

"I thought the greasy pole was something you climbed up, to be a success."

"No, it's a contest. Two guys sit on it and wallop the shit out of each other with sacks of flour until one of them falls off into the water."

"Christ. It sounds a bit dangerous."

"Well, the water's quite shallow, so people don't actually drown, even if they get knocked unconscious, which sometimes happens. It's all traditional, apparently. You see, when the Silvers revived the fete they did all this research into what it would have been like in the olden days. You know, like a medieval fair kind of thing. So they've got the tug-of-war, and the greasy pole, and the stocks, and things like that."

"The stocks?"

"Yes, people go in the stocks and have things thrown at them."

"What kind of things?"

"Oh, you know," Jessica said, "rotten eggs, soggy vegetables, shoes, old china."

"China? Are you sure?"

"Yes, the local guys do it to prove how tough they are. They like to get a few cuts and bruises, like a sort of badge of honour. It's all voluntary. Although I have heard that sometimes they make people go in there who don't want to. But it's all in fun."

"I don't think they would have thrown china at people in medieval times."

"Well, maybe not. I don't know. But it's the spirit of the thing that counts, isn't it? I love all that historical stuff. Like the windmill."

They both stopped and looked up at the windmill again. Now they were closer James could see that it was made entirely of wood. That didn't seem

68

right, somehow. And there was something odd about the sails. He groped for a dim memory of some knowledge on the subject, but couldn't locate it.

"I can just see it, can't you?" Jessica said, gazing at the mill with narrowed eyes and a dreamy expression. "All those serfs and varlets, and villeins, or whatever, all trudging up here with sacks on their backs, and those funny tights they all wore, with the pointy pixie shoes and floppy hats. I can just imagine it. It gives me the shivers. Like going back in time, to a hundred years ago."

"It would have been a bit more than a hundred years ago, if you're talking about serfs and villeins. That was in the middle ages."

"Well, two hundred, then. I was never very good with those details at school."

"When did you leave school, anyway?"

"The minute I was sixteen. It wasn't doing me the slightest bit of good. I think they should let you leave at fourteen, if it's obvious you're not the academic type. Let you get on with something useful."

"Like what? What are you planning to do with yourself?"

"I'm going into catering. You know, hotels and things. The leisure industry."

"Not a bad idea. It's a growth sector, and there are some very good catering colleges these days."

"Oh, I shan't bother with that. There's no substitute for starting at the coalface. You know, get stuck in and get your hands dirty. Learning on the job. Much better."

"So, are you going to look for work in a hotel?"

"Not exactly. Mummy's going to buy me one. Only a small one. The family's broke, but I think she's got some money of her own tucked away for it. Anyway, it'll probably do me good to start with something small. She says it'll be a good discipline."

She gave him a rueful smile.

"Oh, look," she said, catching sight of something over his shoulder, "there's Mandy, setting up the bingo."

James turned to see a large, open-sided marquee a few yards away. It was full of chairs - well over a hundred of them, he estimated. There was a table on a platform at the far end of the enclosure, where a skinny woman with streaked blonde hair was setting up a contraption like a hand-cranked tumble dryer. That would be the thing that jumbled all the balls around, James thought. The woman looked up and waved to them.

"Mandy will look after you," Jessica said.

James's stomach suddenly felt watery. It was the sight of all those chairs. The reality of what he'd agreed to do sprang into painfully sharp focus. A familiar paralysis began to grip his mind. Part of him had suspected all along that the calm detachment he'd been feeling was too good to be true. That part, it turned out, was right.

He gave a nervous cough. "What shall I do?" he said. He noticed that the pitch of his voice had gone up. "Shall I go and help her?"

"No, she's fine. She does it every year. All you need to do is turn up and make a bit of an act out of reading out the numbers."

"Right. That's all, is it?"

"Yes. Have a bit of fun with it."

Just then they heard cheering and clapping from further down the slope. James turned to see what was happening.

A huge machine like an old-fashioned steamroller was trundling sedately through the crowd, puffing clouds of smoke from its funnel. Instead of cylindrical rollers, it had four ribbed metal wheels that were at least six feet tall. Its body was painted bright green and red, with smart black piping. The network of brass tubes that encased the vast, cylindrical boiler gleamed in the sun. A system of gears, cranks, belts and pulleys whirred and slapped along its sides. James saw a jet of steam erupt from a shiny vertical pipe attached to one side of the driver's cab, and then a high-pitched whistle split the air. The crowd cheered.

"There's Daddy!" exclaimed Jessica, pointing at Bill Longbourne, who was waving at the crowd from the traction engine's cab.

When Jessica had told James about her father's hobby he'd never imagined anything so impressive. It was magnificent.

"He sets it up to do all kinds of things," Jessica said, "like sawing wood, or running this little merry-go-round thing with the drive belt. It's fantastically powerful. He says it's one of the most efficient forms of power you can get. The children absolutely love it, even the older ones. I think it's great that even though they've all got their snotty little noses stuck in computer games these days, they can still get into something like that. Daddy's really dedicated to the whole thing. You should see him, he's really patient with everyone, explaining how it all works and letting people have a go at running it."

James was surprised to hear the pride and affection in Jessica's voice. But why wouldn't she love her father? As he gazed at the traction engine he began to revise his opinion of Bill, who was clearly not quite the shambling geriatric he'd first taken him for. "I'd love to have a look at it," he said.

"I'll take you later on. He'll be here until late; he's often the last one to leave."

She turned and squinted up the field, shading her eyes. "Oh, good, Max is by the windmill. Let's get up there and catch him, so he can bore you to tears about it."

Max Fennel was sitting at a little table just outside the door of the windmill. He was a small, round man with a frizz of reddish hair framing a balding head, and he wore a polka-dot bowtie and a three-piece tweed suit, in which he seemed perfectly comfortable despite the heat. There were pamphlets, maps, prints and postcards spread out on the table, along with packaged cardboard model kits that you could cut out and assemble to create a replica of the mill. There were also dishcloths, oven-gloves, place-mats and mugs decorated with pictures of windmills, and small silver spoons with windmills on the ends of the handles. Several copies of a book called 'My Secret Past - Journeys through Hidden History' by Professor Max Fennel, PhD. FRHS., were displayed prominently. Everything was for sale, at prices James found surprisingly steep.

"Hello, young lady," said Professor Fennel, beaming at Jessica, "how's my favourite little ignoramus. Or should that be ignorama?"

"Don't be so rude," Jessica said.

"It's a compliment, my dear. I wish there were more delightful young barbarians like you. There is an unmanageable profusion of information in the world these days." He gestured to the copies of his book on the table. "And what good has all this scholarly toil ever done me, for instance? Here am I, grubbing around for a crust, while you lovely young people traipse about without a care in the world."

He sat back with a smirk, and poked his half-moon glasses back up his nose with a chubby forefinger.

"Max, this is James, a friend of Oliver's," Jessica said.

"Oho," cried Max, "if you're a pal of that young rogue, I'll count the spoons before you leave! No, I jest. Enchanted to meet you, dear boy. What do you think of our windmill?"

"It's very interesting."

"Ah, you find it 'interesting', do you? And what is the nature of your interest? Is it combative, like that of the melancholy Iberian?" He winked at James, then turned to smile at Jessica, raising his eyebrows. He turned back to James. "She has no idea what we're talking about, the lovely creature."

"Yes, I do," said Jessica. "It's Don Quixote."

"I am astonished! Although my admiration is somewhat tempered by your mispronunciation. The 'x' is silent in the Castilian fashion, and the Knight of the Sad Countenance is customarily referred to as 'Kee-ho-tay' although, interestingly enough, a contemporary medieval English pronunciation would have used a 'sh' sound for the 'x', something like 'Quee-shote.'"

"Oh, shut up," Jessica said, "you told me all that last time."

While they'd been talking James had discovered another thing that was wrong with the windmill. It was too small. And then his eye fell upon the packaged cardboard model kits on the table, and it all fell into place. The thing was basically a toy.

"It's a folly, isn't it?" he blurted out.

"I beg your pardon?" said Max Fennel.

"The windmill. It's a folly."

For a moment Max's face narrowed and hardened, then he coughed and spoke to James cajolingly. "No, no, we can't have that. The restoration of a wonderful old mill like this isn't a folly, it's a labour of love. Principally on the part of Mr and Mrs Silver, of course, who have devoted so many resources to it. And I assure you that many people, not least myself, consider it an extremely worthwhile undertaking."

"I don't mean that," James said, "I mean it's an eighteenth century folly, isn't it? Built after the house, probably. As a kind of amusement."

"I hardly think so, young man. This was a working windmill in medieval times, many years before the present house was constructed. No one would build a fully functional windmill like this for the sake of amusement, I can assure you."

"But didn't they do that kind of thing a lot in the eighteenth century? Pastoral romanticism? You know, like Marie Antoinette playing milkmaids in the artificial village at Versailles. It could be a folly from that period, surely? That would explain why it's so small, and so near the house, and why there's all that wood, with no stone or brickwork base, which you might expect in a mill of this shape."

Max Fennel stood up abruptly. "Why don't you come and look at the inside, and see all the working apparatus? You'll find it fascinating." He darted around the table and gripped James firmly by the elbow.

"Go ahead," Jessica said, "I've got a few things to do, and you two are obviously keen to have a chat. You can find your own way down to the bingo, can't you James? See you later. Bye, Max!"

Jessica twirled around on her toes and bounced away. James found himself being propelled towards the black rectangle of the windmill's open doorway.

Inside the mill it wasn't as dark as James had expected. Shafts of light fell from somewhere above him, illuminating the interior in dappled patches. There was a strong smell of fresh wood everywhere, like a timber yard.

"So," said Max Fennel, turning to James as soon as they were inside, "you consider that you know a bit about these things, do you?"

"No, not at all. It simply struck me that this place might have been built on some kind of whim. It all looks a bit artificial, that's all."

"Really? What do you think that is?" Max gestured to the grindstones and gears mounted in the middle of the floor, around a thick vertical shaft that disappeared into the gloom above them. "It all works. Of course, it's all been restored, and that may account for the patina of inauthenticity you claim to detect. But I assure you that you could bring a sack of grain in here this very minute and we could simply release the gears, and, if necessary, use the cranks to rotate the cap so the sails caught the wind, and the grain could be milled. It's fully functional, and always has been."

"Sorry, I'm not suggesting it hasn't always worked. I just thought it might have been built as a kind of... hobby." James was careful not to refer to it as a folly again. "Like a working model, out of interest. But if you say it's medieval, and functioned as the local mill for the villagers, I'm sure you're right. You're the expert, after all."

"Yes, I am, aren't I?"

They looked at each other in silence. Max had dropped the act. James knew the type. Minor public school, university, a mediocre degree, perhaps a research fellowship, then teaching - in all probability back at his own old school - having reinvented himself as a merry little pedant who would torment generations of schoolboys with sadistic relish.

James scuffed his feet in the clean, fresh straw that covered the floor.

"Look here," Max said, finally, resuming a more genial tone, "you're obviously a very intelligent young man. I'm sure I don't have to tell you that there's always a degree of ambiguity involved in a project of this nature, no matter how thorough the research. In fact, I call it an adventure. An adventure in history. The evidence in this case is, I grant you, equivocal. But it's impossible to prove that this windmill *wasn't* originally of medieval construction. So it's highly irresponsible to blithely tell all and sundry that it's an eighteenth century folly. That kind of talk is... is sheer folly!" He chuckled at his joke and beamed at James, willing him to join in.

James managed a smile. "Yes, well, I expect you're right."

"And to be quite frank with you, the research has been problematic. There are long gaps in the record for this whole estate. Much of the Longbourne material has gone missing. They've been very careless with things."

"What have the Longbournes got to do with it?"

"Didn't you know? This whole estate used to belong to the Longbourne family. An ancestor of theirs built the Georgian house here, on the site of an Elizabethan manor. The Longbourne ownership probably goes back to the conquest, although a peerage wasn't granted until the Stuarts, as far as I can tell. But in the eighteen-nineties there was some kind of scandal which resulted in the peerage being lost, and the family had to sell up. Various people owned the place after that, until the Silvers bought it four years ago. Fascinating history, but, as I say, frustratingly patchy for the scholar."

"Oh. I didn't know any of that," James said. He wondered why Jessica hadn't told him. Maybe it was considered to be in poor taste to mention these matters in families like hers. But it was also quite possible, given her shaky grasp of the general subject, that she had simply flung the information into the murky recess of her mind labelled 'history', where it was mixed up with pictures of Robin Hood signing *Magna Carta*, and Oliver Cromwell chopping off King Alfred's head for burning the Armada.

James looked at his watch. "Well, thanks for showing me around. Absolutely fascinating. And good luck with it all. Anyway, I'd better be getting off to the bingo."

Max planted himself between James and the doorway. "Look, with regard to Mr and Mrs Silver. I feel that there's no need to confuse them with the kind of ambiguity we've been talking about. Or anyone else, for that matter. Of course, you and I know that historical restoration will always involve a degree of individual interpretation. But others don't have quite such a sophisticated perspective. The Silvers are very committed to the idea that this was the mill the Ullage villagers made use of for hundreds of years. That is what has inspired them to have it restored, and to continue what they see as a local tradition. And since the facts are so difficult to ascertain with any exactitude, it's quite possible that they're right. So there's absolutely no reason to disappoint them. I'm sure you agree, don't you?"

James suspected that Max would be the one who was disappointed if the Silvers were told that the mill wasn't authentic. He was obviously enjoying his authority here, and was probably getting generous funding from them as well.

"Yes, of course," James said. "I wouldn't want to do that."

Max stepped aside.

James walked out into the glare of the afternoon. He set off down the hill towards the bingo tent, weaving through a crowd that was getting bigger and noisier all the time.

The seats were already beginning to fill up even though there was nearly half an hour before the first bingo game. Most of the early arrivals were old ladies.

"Hello, lover," Mandy said, "dressed for the part, I see. Very nice."

James had resisted Jessica's more outlandish attempts to outfit him but he'd agreed to wear a Hawaiian shirt of Oliver's that was decorated with surfing motifs and a vibrant sunset. He had to admit it looked pretty good on him, especially with the little straw trilby perched on the back of his head. He was glad Mandy thought so, too. She was wearing very tight jeans and a skimpy sleeveless top and although she was thin she had quite big breasts. Not bad for her age, James thought. The top was just a vest, really.

"They're genuine, darling," Mandy said. "Both of them." She gave a husky smoker's chuckle.

James realised he'd been staring. "Sorry."

"Don't apologize, lover. They thrive on the attention." She thrust her chest at him and winked.

James laughed unconvincingly. He knew he was blushing.

"Right, give us a hand to get the rest of these seats out, sweetheart," Mandy said, indicating some stacks of folding chairs. "I was going to keep these in reserve, like, but I think we'll be fucking rammed from the get-go today."

"They'll have a nice view right up your nose," Mandy said when they'd finished putting out two extra rows, bringing the seating right up to the front edge of the platform with the table on it. "Here, now I'll show you how to do the balls."

She led James up onto the stage, and he inspected the device that was set up on the table. It was a transparent plastic cylinder full of coloured ping-pong balls with numbers on them, mounted on a bracket so that it could be rotated by turning a handle.

"It's a piece of piss," Mandy said. "Just make sure you close this flap on the top here properly before you give the handle a couple of turns, otherwise all the balls come flying out. Then you pick one out, read out the number, and put it in that tub on the other side. Then, at the end of each game, you just tip the ones in the tub back into the tumbler. Go on, have a go, just to make sure you've got the hang of it."

James checked that the lid was firmly closed, then cranked the handle. The coloured balls exploded inside the cylinder, rattling angrily against its sides. A couple of very old ladies sitting together in the middle of the rows of seats jerked into life.

"Has it started?" croaked one of them.

"Full House!" screamed the other, with a cackle of laughter that quickly turned into a heaving, phlegmy cough. Her friend thumped her on the back until she wheezed into silence.

James stopped turning the handle, opened the lid, and plunged his hand into the mass of balls. It was an odd feeling, but not unpleasant. He plucked one out.

"Number thirty."

"Dirty Gertie!" yelled Mandy, and laughed.

"Do I have to do rhymes for all of them?" James asked.

"Nah, babes, just throw a few in now and then for a bit of a laugh. They're not all rhymes, anyway, the traditional ones."

"Oh, yes, that's right. There's Legs Eleven, isn't there? And Two Fat Ladies, for eighty-eight. Those come from the shape of the numbers, obviously."

"Yeah, same with Two Little Ducks for twenty-two, and Kelly's eye for number one. There's other ones that are obvious, too, like Key of the Door for twenty-one. But there's a few I've never worked out at all. Number nine: Doctor's Orders. And fifty-six: Was She Worth It. I mean, what the fuck is all that about?"

"Search me."

"You can make them up if you feel like it. But some of the callers don't bother with them at all these days. The punters don't really care, they just want the numbers. Whoa, steady there, lover, what are you doing? Used balls in the tub, darling, not back in the tumbler. Remember?"

"Oh, yes. Sorry." He'd been about to put the ball back in the cylinder.

"Right, now you've remembered, you can pop that one back in. Lesson over."

James fanned himself with his hat.

"I know," Mandy said, "it's a bugger, innit? Don't worry, the lads'll be here in a minute with something nice and cold. Ah, talk of the devils."

Two young boys walked up to them. They were both wiry, and had hard, watchful faces. The smaller one, who was about ten, heaved a large, clear plastic canister on to the table. Inside it, pieces of fruit sloshed around in a golden fluid, and beads of cold condensation ran down the outside. James swallowed. His throat felt like leather.

"Thanks, our kid," Mandy said to the younger boy. She unscrewed the container, filled two paper cups, and handed one to James. "Try that, babes. That'll wet you nicely."

It was like nectar. James drank the whole cupful and held it out for another. "That's fantastic. What is it?"

"Lovely, innit? Very refreshing. Fruit Cup. My sister makes it. These are her boys. Marcus and Darren. Everyone says they look like mine, but I think I'd know if they were. I've got two little buggers of my own, haven't I?" She laughed raucously at the boys, who nodded unsmilingly. The older one, Marcus, was clutching a large tin cashbox close to his chest. "Give us that, then," Mandy said.

The boy handed her the box as if it might explode. Mandy wriggled a small key out of the pocket of her jeans and opened the box with it. She extracted a thick wad of large, square bingo cards. "We look after these a bit careful, like. You'd be amazed what some people get up to, trying to get hold of these."

The two boys glanced around, as if expecting an armed assault at any moment.

Mandy checked her watch. "I think we better kick off. Right, you two, get these out there." She split the cards between the boys and handed each of them a leather satchel. "There's a good cash float in those, but try and get the right money off them." She also gave Marcus a large plastic carrier bag full of felt-tipped markers. "A pound deposit on the markers if they haven't got their own; four quid a card, no excuses, no exceptions, not for anyone."

"Yeah, yeah," muttered the boys, and walked towards the seats.

The noise in the marquee had now risen to a roaring babble. James looked around to see that the place was full. More old ladies had arrived, but there was also a wide variety of other people, from the type of middle-aged, middle class woman that Jessica had mentioned, in Laura Ashley frocks and sun-hats, to a contingent of rough looking young men at the back, including the Pringle brothers. Terry Pringle caught James's eye and grinned at him, revealing several gaps in his teeth, and gave him a thumbs-up sign. For some reason, his friends all thought this was extremely funny. James's throat felt dry again, and he lifted his hat and wiped his brow. Mandy gently took the paper cup from his hand and poured him another drink.

"Don't worry, lover," she said, "you'll be fine." She examined the drink container, which was now half empty. "I'll send the lads over to my sister for some more of this in a minute. Keep it coming nice and cold, eh? And as soon as they've got the cards out, we'll start. Now, the prizes are all on this list here. Just announce the prize for each game as you go along, but you can give a bit of a build-up for the ones coming later if you want. Tease them with a few hints. Although most of the buggers already know. They always find out somehow, no matter what we do. Here you go."

James scanned the list she gave him. There were eight games in all. The prizes were surprisingly valuable, with vouchers worth seventy and a hundred pound at stores in Bristol, a Fortnum and Mason food and drink hamper, and a table at a gourmet country restaurant which James recognized as the flagship of an obnoxious TV chef who threw saucepans at people. The prizes got progressively more impressive until the sixth game, for which there was a 'star prize' of a 'Home entertainment centre including DVD projector, £800 approx', then they diminished in value for the last two games.

"Why do you have the star prize in the sixth game?" he asked Mandy. "I'd have thought you'd save it until last."

"It's all about timing, lover. Some of the youngsters have a few bevvies. And the old dears can start getting cranky when they get tired. Sometimes it can kick off a bit. Nothing to worry about, though. Just keep the games going. And don't fuck up." She threw back her head and laughed hoarsely, then squeezed his arm. "No, you'll be a star, babes. No problem, just enjoy yourself."

The list was getting damp. James wiped his hands on his trousers.

When he first spoke into the microphone it didn't seem to be working, then it squawked with feedback when he raised his voice. He took it off its stand and examined it without knowing what he was looking for. When he tried to replace it, its bracket slid down the stand and he couldn't get it to stay at the right height. There was some derisive laughter from the crowd. James couldn't blame them. He felt that he might as well give up. He looked around helplessly then raised his hat, put his fingers to his head like a gun, and mimed shooting himself. There was more laughter, but suddenly it was warmer, with some scattered clapping. James finally got the microphone to stay in place. He glared at it, then cautiously put his lips very close to it.

"Stay there, you bastard," he muttered. His voice reverberated through the marquee in a low, husky growl. There was more laughter and a round of applause.

James looked up and saw rows of expectant, smiling faces.

Why did they suddenly like him? Somehow, he'd done something right. But what?

Then he got it. It was simple. Stop trying. Don't take it so seriously. Be an idiot. Who cares? No one.

He squared his shoulders, adjusted his hat, and waggled his eyebrows, in a show of getting down to business.

"We will now commence," he said. He looked at the list with the prizes on it. "The prize for the first game is..." He paused dramatically and widened his eyes. Some people laughed. He did a double-take, then peered at the list and whistled. The crowd responded with enthusiastic cheering. He pretended to faint. Some people in the crowd stamped their feet.

James was enjoying himself.

Towards the end of the fifth game, James found himself thinking that perhaps he'd discovered his true vocation. Maybe he should consider developing a stand-up act and taking it around the comedy clubs. He could end up with his own TV show. Why not? He had the crowd in the palm of his hand. He kept the patter to a witty but effective minimum, with the occasional mime, and he didn't attempt to find a rhyme or reference for every number, but when he did, the crowd seemed to appreciate the mild eccentricity of his choices.

"Number twenty-two," he called out, "the didgeridoo!"

That produced an ironic cheer, and a few good-natured shouts of "silly bugger," from the old ladies, and "wanker," from the lads at the back. They loved him.

The prize for this game was a washing machine worth £350. Excitement was mounting. James cranked the handle of the tumbler vigorously with one hand, and yanked on an imaginary bell rope with the other, imitating the sound of a steam-train whistle through the microphone. Some people in the crowd hooted along with him and laughed. Not quite as many as the first time he'd done it, but that was inevitable, James reasoned, when you lost the element of surprise. He extracted a ball from the tumbler.

"Number twenty-eight, Brandenburg Gate!"

"What's he say?" asked an old lady.

"Battenberg cake," said her neighbour."

James selected another ball. "Potassium: number nineteen!"

The crowd fell silent.

"Nineteen is the atomic weight of potassium," James said, "in the periodic table."

"How about Piss-offium?" someone at the back shouted.

"Bingo!" trilled a fruity voice. There were squeals from a gaggle of the Laura Ashley types in the middle of the crowd. One of them jumped to her feet. "I mean, Full House!" she cried, waving her card. "I've got it, I've got it!"

Her friends applauded and cheered, but there was also some booing, along with cat-calls and groans, mainly from the ranks of the old ladies.

"Now then, ladies," James said, "I'm sure we can all find it in our hearts to congratulate the lucky winner!"

"Fuck 'er," growled an elderly voice, "she don't need a washer. I do the cleaning up at her place and she's got a sodding great Hotpoint twin tub, brand new."

The winner whirled around, red in the face, scanning the crowd angrily. "As a matter of fact," she said, her voice becoming shrill, "I shall give it to my niece, who is about to be married and will be very grateful for it."

"She'd be grateful for anything!" shouted one of the young men at the back.

"The randy little mare!" called another, amid harsh laughter.

Two of the woman's friends stood up and began to shout at the boys to be quiet. James clapped his hands and leaned into the microphone. "Plenty more chances to win, ladies and gentlemen!" he boomed, "it isn't over until the fat lady sings!" He realized, too late, that the woman with the winning ticket was distinctly overweight. She turned to glare at him. James felt a tug at his sleeve. Mandy was beside him.

"Interval!" she mouthed.

"Oh, yes," James said, "we will now take a short break before the next game, which, I need hardly remind you, is the star prize game! Please take this opportunity to get some refreshments, and we'll begin again in fifteen minutes." He started to say that the game would begin promptly, but he was drowned out by the noise of people getting up and leaving. James wiped his brow and raised his paper cup, but it was empty. He was parched.

"Are you all right, babes?" Mandy said, looking at him anxiously.

"Fine, just thirsty."

She poured him a drink from the plastic container then hoisted it up to the light and squinted at it. "Nearly gone again. I'll send Marcus over to my sister's stall to get a refill." As she went off to find the boy she crossed paths with Jessica, who was grinning as she walked up to James.

"You certainly seem to be enjoying yourself," she said.

"How long have you been here?"

"I was just watching for some of the last game. You're putting on quite a show."

"I think I'm getting into the swing of it," said James, modestly. "You've got to get the right balance, you see. You've got to be confident without being over the top. And you've got to be able to judge the mood of the punters. That's always the key."

"That's always the key, is it?" she said.

James thought he detected a note of mockery in her voice. "Just remember," he said, "I didn't want to do this. It's actually very difficult for me. Every moment is a struggle. I've had to confront my inner demons to stand on that stage. And the only reason I'm doing it is for you. I hope you realize that. Because you said you'd be grateful." He gave her a roguish smile and winked. "Are you grateful?"

He found she was peering at him closely.

"Are you all right?" she said.

"Yes, I'm fine." Why did everyone keep asking him that?

"You seem a bit flushed."

"It's bloody hot work."

"Are you going off to get something to drink? Or to eat? I've only got a minute because I'm going back to help Daddy. He's fantastically busy. But I can go and get you something if you want."

"I'm okay, thanks. I'm not hungry, and I'll probably stick with this fruit drink that Mandy's getting."

"Well, if you do decide to go out for something, I've remembered the other thing I wanted to tell you. Jackie Leppard's cider punch. Some of them call it Scrumpy Cup. She's selling it at a stall just down the hill. She keeps topping it up with vodka, and the more she tops it up the more trashed she gets, and the more trashed she gets the more she tops it up, so it just keeps getting stronger. It's lethal. You can't miss her. She's a huge fat woman with a gigantic behind. And she always wears really tight, stretchy clothes so you can see all her bulges and folds and flaps and everything. It's disgusting."

"I think I'll stay here, actually. But if I do go out I'll flee at the first sight of a gigantic behind."

"Okay, I'll leave you to it." Jessica looked at him closely again. "Are you sure you're going to be all right?"

"Yes! God, stop worrying. I'm on a roll here. You can feel it, if you've got an instinct for these things. You sense the vibe."

Jessica nodded slowly. "I'll take your word for it. Have fun. See you later."

She blew him a kiss. James watched the sway of her hips as she wove her way through the disarrayed chairs, which had lost all semblance of the neat rows and aisles they'd been arranged into earlier.

"Here we are, lover," Mandy said, handing him a paper cup. "Go easy, though."

"Why?" said James.

"You're getting through a fair bit of that. Thank fuck Jackie lets me have it for free, 'cos she charges three pound a cup for it on the stall."

A tiny bell rang in James's mind. "Jackie?"

"My sister. Jackie Leppard. She makes this stuff every year."

"But she's fat!"

Mandy gave him a strange look. "Oh, you know her, do you? Not that I'll disagree with you; she could lose a couple of stone."

"Sorry. It's just that you're so thin."

"I suppose I'd better take that as a compliment."

"Sorry, no, what I mean is... if she's your sister, then..."

"What?"

"This isn't her scrumpy punch I'm drinking, is it? You said this was just fruit cup."

80

"Fruit cup, cider punch, scrumpy cup, it's all the same thing. Everyone knows what it is, whatever you call it."

"So it's got alcohol in it."

"Not half, lover!"

"But you didn't say."

"I thought you knew. Anyway, I reckoned you could do with a bit of Dutch courage. Getting a bit pissed up, are you? I'm not surprised, the way you've been knocking it back."

"Not really," James said. "That's the strange thing. I feel perfectly normal."

"You might feel that way, babes, but you're off your face, believe me." She laughed, put her arm around his shoulder and kissed his cheek. "That's the thing about this stuff. It tastes just like lemonade, and you think it's not doing anything. But it is, take my word for it. It creeps up on you. Never mind, you'll be fine. Just go easy on it, all right? We'd better start in a minute. I'll go and give out the cards out for this next game."

The place was filling up again. There was a loud clattering of chairs and a buzz of raised voices as people argued over where they were meant to be sitting.

James stepped up on to the platform. But the platform wasn't there. He trod down heavily on thin air, lurched forwards, tried to correct himself, overcompensated and toppled backwards. He found himself sitting on the grass, staring at the edge of the platform in front of him. How had that happened? Luckily he was behind the table, which hid him from the view of the crowd. He got to his feet and nearly lost his balance again. He must have stood up too quickly. He just needed a moment to clear his head. Not that he felt at all unclear. He was fine. Just a bit dizzy.

"Number sixteen - ruptured spleen!" James tossed the ball up into the air and attempted to catch it in his mouth, but it bounced off his teeth and flew into the crowd. Someone threw it back at him and, miraculously, he caught it in one hand. He bowed, and some people clapped. A few other people shouted things he couldn't hear. The air inside the marquee seemed to have been replaced by a thicker, more viscous substance. Sound throbbed against his eardrums in sluggish waves, and the mass of faces in front of him swelled and rippled as if they were made of glistening, brightly-coloured rubber. He cranked the handle of the tumbler again, deciding not to try the steam-whistle routine this time. You could have too much of a good thing. It was all about timing. He opened the top of the tumbler and plunged his hand into the balls as they came to rest. They felt cool and light, caressing his hand with a strange, shy intimacy. He dabbled his fingers around, enjoying the sensation. The coloured balls reminded him of model molecules in a demonstration he once saw on a visit to the Science Museum. His father had taken him.

Things seemed to have gone quiet. He looked up and saw that everyone was staring at him. It must be nearly the end of the game. He grinned and withdrew a ball with a flourish, like a magician, then covered it with his other hand and peeked at it slyly.

"Get on with it," someone shouted.

James peered at the ball. The number was blurred. Perhaps the ink had run in the heat. He narrowed his eyes until he could make it out.

"Number thirty-four... Repeal of the Poor Law!"

There was a swell of noise from the crowd. James realized it wasn't fair to assume that everyone could see how appropriate the reference was. Some of them might not have done nineteenth century constitutional history at school.

"It's not just a rhyme, you see," he said, delighted to be able to share some fascinating information with them, "because the Poor Law was actually amended in 1834! So it all fits with number thirty-four, do you see?"

"Fuck right off!" someone yelled above the hubbub.

James wondered if he was losing some of the audience. It was probably better to follow the general momentum at this stage, rather than try to build up any more dramatic tension. He spun the cylinder again quickly and selected another ball.

"Twenty-one!" he cried. "Legs of the door! No, wait--"

"We've fucking had that one!"

James ignored the objection. Best to press on. He spun the tumbler again. But he'd forgotten to secure the lid, and the remaining balls exploded from it in a demented centrifugal spray. James managed to catch one as it flew past him. He peered at it.

"Seventy-seven!" he shouted.

"Full House!" screamed one of the old ladies. Her friends cheered and coughed.

"Wait a fucking minute!" cried the voice that had called out earlier. It was one of the lads at the back. "We had that other one before! He's done twenty-one twice!"

There was an angry groundswell of support for his complaint.

"Makes no difference," shouted one of the old lady's friends, "she's still won!"

"Bollocks! If he hadn't done that one twice, my last number might have come up! I only had one to go!"

"Me and all!" cried someone else.

James realized what had happened: he'd put the last few balls back into the tumbler, instead of the tub for discarded numbers.

"Don't worry," he said. The microphone seemed to have developed a fault that distorted and slurred his words. "We'll just re-run the last few balls."

"Will we fuck!" exclaimed one of the old ladies.

Many people in the crowd were now on their feet. One of the lads from the back had reached the gang of old ladies surrounding the winner and was trying to snatch the card from her hand. Some of his friends were close behind him.

"Leave my granny alone, you tosser!" said a huge man who rose from the middle of the crowd like a leviathan. He was wearing a police uniform.

"You might be a copper, Ally Vickery," replied the lad, "but you're still a cunt."

"Yes, yes, that is the truth," came a voice with a strong Polish accent, "he is cunt!"

"You can fuck off back to where you came from, mate," said someone close to the last speaker, and there was a sound of a flesh colliding with flesh.

"Sit down, everyone, for goodness sake!" shrieked one of the Laura Ashley types, plucking aggressively at the sleeve of an old lady who was standing next to her. The old lady spun around, whirling an ancient, massive handbag, and hit the woman on the side of the head with it, sending her glasses flying off her nose.

"My glasses! Don't step on them, anyone! I've lost my glasses!"

"See if you can find some fucking manners while you're looking for them," growled the old lady.

Another voice, louder than all the rest, bellowed above the growing tumult: "It's all that wanker's fault! Yes, you! You fucking wanker!"

James saw Terry Pringle pointing at him from the back of the marquee. His face was contorted with rage, which he directed with such force that James felt it like a physical blow. He recoiled and took a step back. There was nothing behind him, and he fell off the platform.

As he lay gazing up at the warm glow of sunlight softened by the canvas of the marquee roof he thought, for the second time that day, of being under the sheets in his childhood bedroom on a sunny morning. He heard Mandy speaking into the microphone:

"All right, ladies and gentlemen," she said, soothingly, "nothing to worry about. We'll work it all out. If you can all just--"

She was cut off by a squawk of static and then the microphone went dead. Not a good sign, thought James. The level of noise was increasing and it sounded as if several separate large-scale fights had broken out.

A face loomed over James. After a moment he recognized it as Sylvia Silver's.

"Come along, dear," she said, and pulled him to his feet. She was surprisingly strong. "I think we'd better get you out of here, don't you? I've got the feeling you're not very popular at the moment."

"I thought it was going quite well. It was just a little problem with the balls."

"There'll be a little problem with your balls if you don't get going. Come on." Sylvia spun him around firmly and began to march him out of the back of the marquee.

"Wait," James said, "don't you think I should stay and try to sort things out?"

"Definitely not," she said, and gave him a powerful shove that sent him staggering out into the open. She kept one hand on the small of his back and trotted along beside him as she propelled him up the slope towards the house. James noticed that today she was dressed like an extra from an American high school movie, with her blouse knotted beneath her vast bosom, tight leopard-skin patterned toreador pants, and basketball sneakers. She was chewing bubblegum, which she popped occasionally.

They passed people who were converging on the marquee, attracted by the prospect of mayhem. "I thought it might all kick off down there," James heard someone say as they passed, "when I heard they had some twat from London doing the numbers. That's like a red rag to Terry Pringle's lot."

"Oh, look, there's Terry coming out now," said someone else. "I hope we haven't missed it all. Perhaps they've already killed him."

James glanced over his shoulder. The Pringle brothers and some of their friends were fighting their way out through the crowds swarming into the enclosure. Posses of old ladies were also emerging. Some of them seemed to be trying to catch up with the Pringle faction, swinging their handbags and walking sticks, limbering up for an attack, while others fanned out with the distinct look of search parties, scanning the area.

"Keep down, dear," said Sylvia, "but keep going. I don't think we'd better try and get up to the house. It's a bit exposed up on the lawn there. Let's pop in here, shall we?"

James saw that Sylvia was steering him towards the windmill. They approached it at high speed, with James now scuttling along in a low, galloping crouch. Max Fennel looked up from his table and rose from his seat with a puzzled expression.

"Hello, Sylvia, my dear, what can I--"

"Sanctuary, Max!" cried Sylvia as she pushed James past him, "we need to get this boy out of the way for bit. Be a treasure and guard the door with your life!"

James stumbled into the windmill and turned to face Sylvia as the door closed behind her. Blades of sunlight created a strobe effect on her as she walked through them to join him by the central grindstone mechanism. They stood looking at each other and breathing heavily.

"Well. You seem to have made quite an impression," she said.

"You see, the great thing about a windmill," James was saying a few minutes later, as he paced around the grindstones, "is that it's the perfect device to demonstrate the transfer of stored, or pogential tenergy. I mean, potential energy."

"Yes, dear, I'm sure," Sylvia said. She was sitting next to the door on the narrow bench that ran all the way around the inside wall, massaging her ankles.

"You could think of it as a giant spring, wound up by the wind. Except it's not really a spring, it's more of a kind of boat. A sailing vessel. And the grain is the sea. And the flour, when it's ground, that's the destination!" He chuckled happily, then saw that the analogy was seriously flawed. "No, wait, it's more like a... a..."

"A windmill."

"Exactly!" James said, slapping the upper grindstone, which was rough and cool beneath his hand, "it's completely and utterly, uniquely itself. And that applies even to this one which isn't really - no, wait, I'm not meant to say that. Oops. What I mean is that this one isn't really any different from a real windmill. Because it is a real one! Just as real as any other windmill. Authentic. It's provenance is not indeterminate at all."

"Don't be upset if I say I've no idea what you're talking about, will you?"

"Not at all. I may not be expressing myself terribly coherently. I drink I'm a bit thunker than I thought I was."

The door was flung open and someone stood silhouetted in the light. Sylvia sprang up and placed herself between James and the door. Like a tigress with a cub, James thought admiringly.

"It's all right, it's only me!" Jessica stepped inside and closed the door behind her. She turned to James. "My God, it's a total riot down there," she said happily. "How did you do it?"

"It's a gift," he said. He saw that Jessica was flushed and excited. He thought it made her look particularly beautiful.

"Quite a lot of people are looking for you, as a matter of fact," she said.

"In that case," Sylvia said, "I think we should get him out of here altogether and back to your place, to sleep it off. They're bound to find him here sooner or later."

"I know. We'll have to smuggle him out, somehow."

"I don't know about that. I was thinking we should get hold of Dave and a few other people and just escort him out. Under protection. I mean, what can they do?"

"You don't know what Terry Pringle is capable of. The more people we get involved, the more they'll just see it as us getting our own gang together and offering to fight them in a pitched battle. They'd love it. No, we'll obviously have to disguise him."

"As what?"

"Just wait. I've got a brilliant idea. I'll be back in a minute. See you later."

Five minutes later James was sitting on the grindstones having his face painted and his hair braided into tight little spikes by two giggling young women who were treating him like a life-sized doll. The one doing the braids was pressing herself against him as she pulled and twisted his hair into painfully tight strands.

"What you're doing to my hair - is that what they call corn rows?" James said.

"Well, I'm not doing them in rows, because we lie them flat to do that, and yours is too short. But it's the same difference, just these ones are sticking up, that's all."

"Stay still, will you?" said the one painting his face, laughing at him.

James looked into her eyes, which were level with his own and very close. They sparkled with pure, innocent fun. Her breath was sweet and warm. She was only about fifteen. Earlier on he'd passed the face-painting stall where she was working with another, older girl. They had a real talent for it, and the kids James had seen wandering around after being painted by them sported some wonderful designs. They were mostly of animals, but some were like carnival masks, or landscapes, or visions of the night sky, with a moon and stars, and some were completely abstract. He'd glimpsed one teenager whose face they'd somehow made to look like a Picasso portrait, with both eyes on the same side, and a crooked, pointy nose in the wrong place.

"Come on, tell me what you're doing to me," he said to her.

"Don't be so impatient, you! You'll just have to wait, innit? I got a mirror you can look in when I finished, all right?"

The girl doing his hair laid a cool hand on his bare shoulder.

"You're quite buff, aren't you?" she said. "Do you work out?"

They'd made him take his shirt off before they started. Jessica pointed out that it was far too distinctive, anyway, and she'd bought him another one from one of the second-hand clothing stalls.

"The only working out I do," James said, "is working out how to get into the gym without paying, so I can use the bar."

Both girls giggled and the one doing his face slapped his arm lightly.

"You're mad, you are!" she said.

"He's not mad," said the other one, "just paralytic on that cider punch."

"No, I'm not," James said, "I'm just in a good mood. Who wouldn't be, with two beautiful girls lavishing so much skill and devotion on them?"

Both the girls shrieked and collapsed into giggles.

"Sorry, but we really need to get on with it," said Jessica, who was regarding the operation critically from a few feet away. James hoped the sharpness he heard in her voice was caused by jealousy. He'd been far too docile with her so far. By turning on the charm with these girls, and letting her see that he was attractive to other women, it would make her want him. It would inflame her desire. Any man of the world knew that.

"Come on, James," Jessica said, "stop pissing about. When I went out for the shirt, the whole place was crawling with people looking for you. They might look in here at any moment."

"Yeah, you didn't half wind them up," said the face-painter, "and we can't let that bastard Terry Pringle and his lot get hold of you, can we?" She stroked his arm.

"Never mind them," the other girl said, "it's those stuck-up bitches you got to watch out for. They're spitting tacks out there."

"All right, I'm finished," said the face-painter, "what about you, Sapphire?"

"Last one," the other girl said, and gave the strand she was plaiting a final tweak.

James stood up. "Right, let's have a look!"

"I hope you like it," said the girl who'd painted his face, suddenly shy. "Here," she said, passing a small mirror to Jessica, "you show him."

Jessica held the mirror up and James peered into it.

For a moment he thought it was a trick, and she was holding up a picture, then he blinked and confirmed that it must be his own face he was looking at. But it wasn't his face at all. It was utterly alien, exotic and strange. He was a different being altogether.

"Fuck... me!" he whispered slowly.

"Any time," he heard one of the girls whisper behind him, followed by stifled shrieks and giggles.

He gazed at the vision in the mirror. His hair was covered in tight little spikes that radiated out from his head like blond firecrackers, or the detonators on a mine, and the effect was both bizarre and strangely beautiful. But it was his face that was truly extraordinary. She'd painted him as a tiger. But it was more than just a painted design. She'd subtly followed and altered the contours of his own face, and created such a realistic depth of texture, that every tiny change of expression caused ripples and pulses in what looked so convincingly like real fur that James tried to stroke it.

"Don't smudge it!" she cried from behind him.

"Sorry. It's just so... realistic. It's more than realistic. It's amazing."

"Glad you like it."

"And the hair," said James, aware of a silence from the other girl, "it's great." He turned his head this way and that, widening his eyes and making them glint in the mirror. It was so good that it was disturbing. He *was* a tiger. He bared his teeth and roared.

The girls laughed and clapped.

"Wow," he said, turning to them, "thank you so much. It's just fantastic. You're both really talented, you know that?"

"All right," Sylvia said, "let's get that shirt on him, Jess."

Jessica helped him slip it on. It was a nondescript faded green check.

"Perfect," Sylvia said. "Now, I think we'd better head up to the main entrance. It's shorter that way. We'll circle around and go up by the side of the lawn, then, at the top, cross to the house and slip along the side. The thing is, we can't stay too close to you, James, or it'll give the game away. Especially Jess; they'll expect you to be with her. So she'll have to walk a good way in front of you, and make it look very casual, and you'll have to follow her at a distance. You'll just have to look like you've had your face painted and you're wandering about because you're a bit pissed. Which shouldn't be too difficult. But for God's sake don't speak to anyone. Got it?"

"Right," James said. "Got it."

"Okay," said Sylvia, "I'll just have a quick check on things outside. Won't be long." She opened the door, looked around cautiously, then slipped outside, closing the door softly behind her.

The girl who'd painted James's face was examining the grindstone mechanism. "Does this lot actually work?" she said.

"Oh, yes," James said, "it's a fully functional replica. That is, a replica of itself, I mean, because it's all real. You see these gears over here? That's what transfers the power generated by the wind turning the sails to the big shaft in the middle there."

"Actually, Chantelle," Jessica said, "there's an old guy outside who can tell you all about it. Professor Max Fennel, he's a friend of mine. He's the expert."

"That's all right, thanks, Jessica, I wouldn't want to bother an important friend of yours. And James seems to know quite a bit about it, anyway. What were you saying about the gears, James?"

"Oh, just that it's all very simple: the wind turns the sails, the sails turn the shaft, and the shaft turns the grindstones. And all the power is on tap, ready to use. All you have to do is release it." He put both hands on a large lever that was attached to the main gear machinery and showed them how it could be detached from the cogs. "And then, if the wind isn't blowing in the right direction, the whole top of the windmill can revolve to find the best position. You just have to set it free, which is what this handle does, I think. Yes, that's it. Like all classic design, there's an elegance to its simplicity, and--"

"Okay, let's get going!" Sylvia called from the door "It's all clear."

"I was just explaining--"

"Never mind that, dear, we've got to move while the time is right."

"Yes, James," Jessica said, "stop waffling, and get moving."

"You first, Jess, " Sylvia said. "James, give her about thirty seconds, then you leave. Then I'll come out after you and bring up the rear. All right, Jess? Off you go."

Jessica moved to the door. "Only thirty seconds, remember, James?" She looked at him darkly, and glanced significantly at the two girls. James nodded.

"Right, try not to get killed," Jessica said, and slunk out through an impossibly narrow gap.

James turned to the girls. "Thank you so much, you've been fantastic."

"So have you," Chantelle said.

"Come on, James," Sylvia said, "wait by the door."

James smiled at the girls, then positioned himself next to the door.

"And... go!" Sylvia said, giving him a little shove.

He slipped out of the windmill and blinked in the light.

James tried to keep his eyes fixed firmly on the back of Jessica's head, about twenty yards ahead of him. But it wasn't easy. People kept looking at him.

Jessica had just begun to circle around to reach the shrubbery running up the side of the lawn when James heard a sound like the ticking of a giant clock. It was coming from behind him. Then there was an immense groan, followed by a tortured creaking noise that was drowned by shouts and screams, along with some excited cheering. Even before James turned around he knew what was happening.

The windmill's sails were beginning to turn as the cap slowly swivelled this way and that in a tight, ever-decreasing arc, hunting the wind. Several people were gathering around the base of the mill. Some of them were trying to stop the sails from moving by hanging on to them, encouraged by a large audience. Different factions of the swelling crowd provided confident but conflicting advice, leading to disagreements that showed signs of escalating.

James tried to think of an explanation for the mill's sudden activity, other than the obvious one, which was that he hadn't returned the levers he'd been fiddling with to their original position. It was his fault. He heard Max's voice, raised above the commotion.

"No, stop, for God's sake!" Max screamed, swatting ineffectually at the people attempting to restrain the sails. "You'll damage the machinery! Let me get inside!"

Suddenly the sails found the wind. Max's table was directly beneath their trajectory, and the bottom of one of the sails smashed into it, sending all the merchandise flying and scattering the contents of a cash box. Max dropped to his knees and scrabbled on the grass, pouncing on stray banknotes. As he stood up, the next sail clipped him smartly on the side of the head. He fell forward and lay on the ground.

At that moment, James caught Sylvia's eye. She shook her head despairingly and then made a shooing gesture to James, urging him to carry on. He saw that someone who looked as if he knew what he was doing was kneeling beside Max and gesturing at the crowd to give him space. Just then, the sails stopped turning. A moment later, Chantelle and Sapphire emerged from the windmill. Sapphire raised her arms above her head like a victorious boxer. There was a big cheer, tinged with a hint of disappointment.

James breathed a sigh of relief. He nodded to Sylvia, and turned to walk back up the slope, searching for a sight of Jessica ahead of him.

Jason Pringle, Terry's younger brother, was blocking his path, along with two of his friends. Jason stood directly in front of him and peered into his face intently. James's heart stopped and he held his breath. Earlier on he'd stood within inches of Jason in the queue. He was sure to recognize him. James was preparing himself to run when Jason's massive black eyebrows shot upwards, like startled, hairy caterpillars, and his round, red face was split by a huge grin.

"Nice one, mate!" he yelled into James's face. "Go, tiger, go!" He leaned back to admire James's face, then turned to his friends.

"Reckon I should have one done, then? I could be a fucking lion."

"Or a gorilla," said one of the others.

Jason scowled at him. "Fuck off." He turned back to James. "How much they charge to do them paintings, then?"

James shrugged. He swayed around and tried to make his eyes looked glazed.

Jason peered at him closely again, then laughed. "You're as pissed up as I am, aren't you, pal?"

James nodded and smiled. He kept his mouth firmly shut, worried that Jason might recognize his teeth.

Jason clapped him on the shoulder, bringing his face even closer. "Go, tiger, go!" he said again. "Nice one, our kid." He stepped out of James's path, and his posse began to shamble away.

Just as James took a tentative step forward, Jason whirled around and pointed at him. "Hey!" he cried, frowning fiercely. James froze.

"Tiger, tiger, burning bright!" Jason bellowed, "in the forest of the night!"

"The fuck are you on about, J?" said one of his friends.

"Don't you remember that supply teacher we had that time? He used to walk about reciting that, didn't he? It's a famous pome. He was mad, he was."

"Oh, yeah," said his friend, "you set fire to his car, didn't you?"

"That's right. And he killed himself soon after that. Pity, he was a good bloke."

"Yeah, he was a laugh."

"Go, tiger, go!" yelled Jason yet again, then he swung his arms around his friends' shoulders and they all lurched away.

No one else stopped James on his way to the house. As he slipped around the side, hugging the wall, he paused to look at one of the windows. If it hadn't been restored, he could get an accurate date for the house. He found that it was solidly constructed and didn't appear to have been touched. Between 1830 and 1850, he thought.

He heard a loud hissing, and turned to see Jessica, standing at the far end of the side wall. She frowned at him crossly, and gestured for him to hurry up. He gave the bevelled frame around the window a parting caress and turned away from it. As he was approaching Jessica, a door that he was walking past was flung open. He leaped away from it, his feet scrabbling on the gravel. Sylvia poked her head out.

"It's only me," she said. She turned to Jessica. "Everything all right?"

Jessica nodded.

"I would say to come in here for a bit," Sylvia continued, "but it's probably best if you get him straight home and put him to bed."

"I don't need to go to bed," James said. "I'm perfectly all right."

"I might be more inclined to believe you, dear," Sylvia said, "if you weren't sitting flat on your arse."

James discovered that he was, indeed, sitting on the ground. He didn't remember falling over. His legs must have given way when Sylvia had popped out of the door so suddenly. What did people expect if they surprised you like that? As he got to his feet he found that his legs were wobbly. Perhaps he was suffering from mild shock. That would be understandable after what he'd been through. But he was feeling better already, and the walk back to the Longbourne's would do him good, and would also give him a chance to capitalize on the advances he'd clearly made in Jessica's estimation of him during the fete. Even now she was clutching his arm and pretending he needed her help to walk. She couldn't keep her hands off him.

*

Jarvis tried to ignore the familiar, weary bitterness of disappointment. It was five, and the Post Office was closing. He watched as the fat woman waddled out and pulled down the shutters. No one had tried to collect any parcels. A geriatric old biddy had shuffled in to drop one off, and that was all. Probably sending a set of bloody tea towels to her bloody grand-daughter in New bloody Zealand. Other than that, hardly anyone had visited the Post Office at all, just a couple of people buying groceries from the shop. Everyone was at the fete at the big house along the road.

And now he was on his own. Phil Beamish had just left. Nothing that Jarvis could say would persuade him to stay for a moment longer. The only useful thing he'd done all day was to inform Jarvis that Naked Man had disappeared into the garden of a house just opposite the lane where he'd been parked. Jarvis persuaded him to make some enquiries and Phil had established that the place was owned by some posh local family called the Longbournes. Which was quite interesting, as it happened. Jarvis was convinced that Naked Man was mixed up in the coke parcel plot, and this meant there was now a further connection, involving this Longbourne family, or some member of it, in the conspiracy with Raymond Norfolk.

All's fish that come to my net, thought Jarvis.

And yet he'd been certain that there would be an attempt to collect the parcel today. He could hardly believe that it hadn't happened. But perhaps the idea that someone would just stroll in and collect it had always been too easy. Yes, there must be something else afoot, something more complex and devious. The criminal mind was pathetically predictable. These people thought they were so clever. There always had to be a plot, a scheme, a blag, a conspiracy - that's why they always tripped themselves up. Well, almost always. But whatever it was, he would get to the bottom of it. They couldn't fool him. Who did they think they were dealing with?

He began to feel better. His mind started working more clearly. Now that the Post Office was closed he would be wiser to shift his surveillance to the spot that Phil had vacated, where he could keep an eye on the approach to the rear of the place. It was likely that any attempt to retrieve the parcel from now on would be made from the back.

He started his engine and drove slowly around the village green, then up the main road that led to Nether Gurney. When he reached the entrance to the narrow lane, he saw that it was almost opposite the dilapidated gate posts of a property that must be the Longbourne place, just as Phil had said. This was looking promising. Perhaps Raymond Norfolk had a plan for the attempt on the parcel to be co-ordinated from the Longbourne house, with Naked Man playing some as yet unspecified role. Jarvis reversed into the narrow lane, parking just where it began to curve downwards to the back of the Post Office. From this position he could cover any activity in the lane itself, but he could also just see the entrance to the Longbourne House. And he was far enough along the lane for his car not to be immediately visible from the main road unless anyone took a really good look. Best of all, he could finally get out for a piss.

He had just begun to release the pent-up stream into a hedge when he heard raised voices. He forced himself to contain the flow and stuffed himself hastily back into his trousers, adding to the damp patch from earlier that still hadn't dried completely. He crouched down beside his car and edged forward.

Two people were approaching the gates to the Longbourne place along the main road. One of them was a very pretty girl. She was half-supporting the other person, who was some kind of terrifying freak with a rare, outlandish affliction.

Not long ago Jarvis had seen a documentary about a wolf-boy in South America whose face was covered in hair. But this man was far stranger: he had the face of a tiger. Also, his hair was exploding. As they got nearer, Jarvis realized the man's face was painted, and the explosive effect of his hair was created by dozens of little braids erupting from his scalp. He kept shouting something at the top of his voice. Jarvis strained his ears and caught the words, "Eye of the Tiger." He remembered a pop song of that name, but the title was the only bit Tiger-Face seemed to know, and he repeated it monotonously while punching the air, as the girl tried to shut him up and get him inside the gates.

There was something familiar about the guy. Something about his height, and his general bearing which Jarvis recognized, even though he was lurching about fairly erratically. If he hadn't been heading for the Longbourne place, Jarvis wouldn't have made the connection, but suddenly he was sure. It was Naked Man.

Naked Man, now disguised as a tiger. And the chanting. Was it a code? What did it all mean? Another attempt at distraction? No. It was something deeper and more sinister than that, Jarvis felt sure.

The couple finally disappeared through the gates.

So, there was now a definite connection between the parcel of cocaine, Raymond Norfolk, the Longbourne family, and Naked Man aka Tiger-Face. It was all very, very promising.

Jarvis waited a moment, then got up stiffly. He walked to the hedge and unzipped his fly. Tears of relief welled up in his eyes as he finally opened the floodgates.

Six

James was woken by his mobile phone. Its eerie glow, pulsing in time with the ring tone, was the only light he could see. It seemed to be floating beside his head. He reached for it and answered it.

"Hello?"

"James? Is that you?" whispered a familiar voice.

"Olly! Where are you?"

"I'm still in the nick," Oliver hissed.

"The what?"

"The police station. I've had a hard time getting them to let me make another call and I'm near the front desk, because they won't let you keep your mobile, so I'll have to be discreet. It's ridiculous, they even take your belt and shoe laces away, in case you try to kill yourself."

"But how would you kill yourself with your mobile? Unless you try to swallow it, I suppose."

"No, that's not why-- oh, never mind. Where are you?"

He was lying on a bed in a darkened room. That was all he knew. He peered around, searching for a clue, but the blackness was impenetrable. He tried to remember what he'd been doing before he went to sleep. He found himself groping blindly through an inner darkness that was indistinguishable from the inky void surrounding him, as if it had seeped in through his ears and filled up his head while he slept.

"James?" Oliver whispered, "are you still there?"

"Yes. But I don't know where 'there' is in the first place."

"Are you at home?"

"No, it's never as dark as this."

"No, I mean my place. The house. In Ullage."

"Oh, God. Yes, of course. I remember. Oh, shit."

"So, did you collect it?"

"Collect what?"

"The parcel."

"What parcel?"

"Oh, fuck. Didn't you get my text? I sent it just before they took my phone."

"No, but--"

"What about Ivan? Didn't Ivan phone you?"

"The thing is, I haven't had my phone with me."

"Why not? What have you been doing?"

"I'm not quite sure. It's only just beginning to come back to me."

"Have you been drinking?"

94

"Sort of, but mostly by accident. Who's Ivan?"

"Friend of mine. He will have left a message. Check your messages. It's too late now, but you've got to phone him back and tell him what's happening. Shit. Right, plan B. Have you met a ridiculous person called Richard yet?"

"Who calls himself Reuben?"

"You have, then, obviously. You've got to tell him something, from me, okay? Will you do that?"

"Tell him what?"

"Tell him to go for it."

"Go for what?"

"Never mind. Just say 'Olly says go for it'. He'll know what it means."

"What does it mean?"

"I'll tell you another time."

"Is it something to do with this parcel?"

"It's just a little favour. In fact, you'll still get the parcel, but Richard will give it to you. But don't open it until I get there on Monday, okay? It's a surprise."

"So you'll be here on Monday?"

"I should be. If they can't find a magistrate who's sitting on Monday morning, they'll release me anyway, on my own bail. I'm just banged up for the weekend, basically. that's the idea, anyway."

"What idea?"

"Nothing. I mean, that's the idea of keeping me in. So don't open the parcel."

"Listen, Olly, I'm not happy about this. I mean, you've got to tell me what this is all about. It sounds totally dodgy to me."

"No, no, it's all good. No problem. I would tell you, but they're saying I've got to get off the phone now." He raised his voice: "Yeah, okay, mate, just finishing!"

"No, listen," James said, "I really need to know,"

"Honestly," Oliver said, whispering again now, "they're really hassling me. I've got to go. Please don't forget to phone Ivan."

"No, wait!"

"I can't. Just one thing. Was it Jackie Leppard's cider punch?"

"Oh, God! I think I'm beginning to remember."

"Thought so. Got to go. Stay cool. See you Monday. Love ya."

The phone went dead.

Jackie Leppard's cider punch. At the fete. Everything suddenly came back to him in a cascade of pin-sharp recollections. He saw it all in sequence: arriving, Jane Cottle, the Pringle brothers, the windmill, the traction engine, bingo, cider punch, rhyming numbers, lost balls, riot, lynch mobs, windmill, mayhem. He had complete recall of the afternoon's events, and wished he didn't. He forced the memories to the back of his mind, where time might soften them before he had to confront them again.

Time. What time was it? He looked at the display on his mobile. Eight in the evening. He checked the date on the display. It was still Saturday. He'd been asleep for three hours. He remembered Jessica telling him it was five and he should sleep it off and she'd wake him up later. Sleep it off. The cider punch. At the fete. With the bingo, and the numbers, and the riot, the windmill - no, stop, this was no good. The memories were creeping out of the back of his mind, like repulsive goblins emerging from a cave.

He needed to do something. He'd better find out what this Ivan person was all about. He remembered there was a lamp on the table beside the bed. He groped for it and switched it on, squeezing his eyes shut and opening them in short blinks until he got used to the light.

He checked his phone. Apart from a text from Olly telling him to expect a call, he had four voicemail messages. He accessed the first one.

"Hi, James, right? This is Ivan, you don't know me, I'm, like, a friend of Olly's, right, and he's asked me to call you, to ask you to pop into the Post Office down there, pick up a little parcel, yeah? It's addressed to you, just a little package, no big deal, bit of a favour, actually, but make sure you do it today before five, yeah? I mean, no big deal, as I say, but just make sure you do, if you see what I mean, and be sure to phone me back, let me know, okay? Great, look forward to hearing from you mate, don't open it, that's cool, just wait for Olly, he'll fill you in, fine, great, bye!"

The other three messages were requests from Ivan for James to call him and tell him if he'd picked up the parcel. In each one he was increasingly hyper. James decided he'd better phone him back, but when he checked to get the number from his phone's caller ID memory he found that it was listed as 'withheld'. Somehow he wasn't surprised. It was typical of the logistics that characterized any scheme of Oliver's. He considered forgetting about the whole thing, but Olly had been very insistent that he should call Ivan. Maybe he could get hold of Olly. He checked his incoming calls and found that the number Olly had called from was displayed. He called it. A weary voice answered:

"You're through to the duty desk sergeant at Vine Street, how may I help you?"

"Oh, hello," James said, "can I speak to Oliver Longbourne, please?"

There was a sigh. "No, you may not speak to Oliver Longbourne. Nor may you leave a message for him, or arrange to visit him, or send him flowers, food, drink, DVDs, books, magazines or paid female companions to while away the tedium of his stay with us, for the simple reason that this is neither a hospital, nor a four star hotel, nor a brothel, but a police station, and Mr Longbourne is a prisoner in custody, and not a guest with access to twenty-four hour room service, much as he may have succeeded in persuading some of my younger and more gullible colleagues to the contrary. To which, I might add, a stop has most definitely been put. Now, is there anything else I can do for you, sir? Do you wish to report a crime? Or perhaps you'd prefer to make a confession. Have you robbed a bank recently, or murdered anyone? I assume you're familiar with our usual line of occupation, when we're not running errands for your Mr Longbourne?"

"Look, sorry, it's just that he phoned me a moment ago, and--"

"I know he did, sir, and I can assure you he won't be doing it again, Not while he's in custody at this police station. Good day, sir."

"Wait, could you just tell him--"

"No, sir, I could not. Goodbye."

James noticed that the battery on his phone had run down. Never mind, he could always charge it. If he'd brought his charger. Which he hadn't.

He looked up to see Jessica standing in the doorway, holding a plate and a mug.

"Who were you talking to?" she asked.

"A sarcastic policeman."

"Why? What's happened?"

"Actually, I was trying to speak to Olly. He phoned me from a police station."

"That's right. He said he'd probably be there for the weekend when he phoned yesterday. How was he?"

"He seemed fine, sort of. But listen, how did he know how long he'd be there? He seems to have calculated the whole thing."

"Oh, I doubt it. It's simply the type of thing that Oliver would know about. How long you get locked up for, depending on what you do. He's had a bit of experience."

"But it still seems strange, as if he organized the whole thing deliberately."

"God knows. Anyway, I've brought you some food. It's only a couple of sausage rolls and a slice of quiche, and an apple tart, and some potato salad from the fete, and a ham sandwich and cup of tea, but I thought you might be hungry."

"I'm starving. Thanks."

"I'll put it over here."

Jessica placed the plate and mug on a big mahogany dressing table. James heaved himself off the bed. He felt remarkably well, considering how drunk he'd been, and he was ravenously hungry. As he lowered himself on to the stool in front of the dressing table he caught sight of himself in the mirror on top of it. He screamed and leaped backwards, falling over the stool and landing on his back on the floor. Jessica doubled up with laughter and clamped a hand over her mouth.

"Fucking hell," James said, "I'd forgotten about that. I'm still a tiger."

Jessica helped him up, still laughing. He looked in the mirror again. It was extraordinary. Still, he'd have to get rid of it.

"Have you got some stuff I can use to wipe it all off?" he said.

"Oh, no, don't do that. It's such a shame."

"I know, but I can't stay like this for ever."

"No, I suppose so. I'll get something while you're eating. But it's such a pity to lose it. It'll be gone for ever."

"I know, it seems like a crime. But what can I do? It's getting smeared already."

"I'll bring a camera! At least we can take some pictures before it goes."

"Great. Good idea."

Jessica made for the door.

"Wait," said James, "do you know anything about a parcel?"

"A parcel of what?"

"Oh, nothing. Just part of some plan of Olly's."

"In that case," said Jessica, "include me out, as they say. See you later." She swung herself around the door and left.

James took a bite of sausage role. The pastry melted in his mouth and the meat was lightly spiced. He looked at himself in the mirror and began to chew with big, savage bites, growling and purring as he attacked the food, and slurping great gulps of tea.

From the corner of his eye he saw Spracky peering through the doorway.

"Hungry, are you?" she said. "Good for you. About time you ate something. Nice make-up, by the way." She gave him a cheery wave and disappeared.

James growled and tore at the ham sandwich with his teeth.

Jessica came back with some feminine bits and pieces to remove the face paint. Before James got to work she used a little digital camera to take a few pictures of him, then she flung herself on the bed and watched as he scrubbed off the paint, laughing as he winced and cursed at the difficulty of getting rid of it all. He was distracted by the sight of her in the mirror. She was wearing low-slung jeans and a tight T shirt, revealing a lot of her body, especially when she stretched and rolled around on the bed.

When his face was as clean as he thought he'd get it without removing a layer of skin, he began trying to undo the little braids in his hair but he found they were knotted so tightly they were like stiff spikes of rope.

"Can you give me a hand with these?"

"Oh, no - at least leave those," Jessica said, "they look great."

"Come on, I really want to get back to normal. Although from what I can remember about this afternoon, it would probably be best if I stayed in some kind of disguise for the next few years."

"Oh, don't worry about all that. Everyone had a great time."

"God, I'd forgotten to ask about Max. How is he? I mean, is he all right?"

"He's fine. Bouncing around quite happily. He might have a little bit of concussion, according to the doctor, that's all."

"Christ, I could have killed him."

"Oh, don't blame yourself."

"Why not? It was my fault."

"Well, maybe a bit. But it's probably best not to say anything about all that. Max can't really remember much about it, apparently, so there's no reason to tell him. He's a bit confused about things, they said. Anyway, it's actually his fault more than yours: he shouldn't have got in the way of the sail things when they started whizzing round."

James didn't quite see the logic of that, but decided not to object. The braids were proving extremely stubborn. So far he'd only managed to get one of them partly undone.

"Anyway," Jessica said, "a touch of concussion might do him a bit of good. At least it might shut him up for a while."

"Ouch! These things are really hard to undo! Can't you help?"

Jessica jumped off the bed and came to stand behind him. She began to attack one of the braids, twisting it quite hard as she tried to unpick it. James squirmed.

"Keep still!" she said.

James wriggled again and she giggled, grabbing him tightly for a moment to keep him still before pressing herself against him as she began to wrestle with the tight knots.

This was good. Very good. James savoured the intimacy between them. A woman needed to feel comfortable with a man, and the kind of easy, erotic playfulness they were enjoying now was a good sign. Jessica was being open and unguarded with him. Trust. That was the key. They were definitely on the threshold of the final step.

He pressed himself gently back against her, feeling her breasts against his shoulders. They had the whole evening ahead of them. There was no reason why they should even leave this room. Things would happen in their own time but James felt that any moment now, quite naturally, they'd simply embrace, and then move to the bed.

"It'll take ages if we try to do them all now," Jessica said. "Come on, you can do some more of them on the way." She patted his shoulders and turned away.

"On the way?"

"Yes, come on."

"On the way where?"

"Oh, didn't I tell you? Sorry. Yes, I thought we could go and see a friend of mine. It's only a ten minute drive and you'll really like him."

"Why?"

"He's very interesting. He used to be this rock star. He still is, actually, because he still makes records and does gigs. Raymond Norfolk. He's got this huge mansion just up the road. He used to be in a band called The Hangmen but he left about five years ago. He's quite famous. Haven't you heard of him?"

"I may have done," James said grudgingly. "It sort of rings a bell."

"It was all before my time, but the band used to make hit records, and Raymond still does, sometimes. The others have tried to carry on as well, but he wrote all their best stuff and he was the front man, so they're all a bit sad, really, still trying to be famous. I think it's pathetic, these ancient old men, bulging out of their leather trousers and trying to jump around like teenagers. Not that Ray's ancient, of course."

"But he must be pretty old. Isn't he?"

"He's forty-five, but he looks much younger. And he can still belt out his old rock hits when he wants to. I saw him play in Bath not long ago and the whole place was going mental. He wrote some brilliant songs, actually."

"Oh, yes. One of them's being used in a TV advert for acne cream or something."

"Sun lotion. The song's called 'Blister'. They just use the chorus, but he makes a fortune every time they play it, apparently. Anyway, I thought we could call in on him."

"I'm a bit tired, to tell you the truth," James said. "I thought maybe it would be good to chill out here. Have a nice quiet evening, you know?"

"That's fine. I'll just go over there by myself. You stay here and take it easy, if you want."

"No, no, I didn't mean - no, it was only a thought. In fact, come to think of it, I'd quite like to get out for a bit."

"Great. I just thought you might like to meet him, that's all."

"I'd love to." Meet him, James thought, then kill him slowly, and bury the body in a shallow grave. "But are you sure it's all right?" he said. "I mean, is he expecting me?"

"Oh, it's fine. I pop over there all the time. He's got my horse there."

"What horse? I didn't know you had a horse."

"Well, it's not completely my horse. Not yet. But we can't keep her here, and Raymond's got a whole proper stable, so she lives there with his other horses. It's huge, his place; he's converted a whole wing of it into a recording studio, and bands go and stay there. There's one there now, as it happens."

"What sort of house is it?"

"A really old one. And you're into all that, old mansions and things, and Raymond is, too, so you've got stuff you can talk about. I'll just go and get another top. It might get cold later on. Meet me outside, by the sheds, and we'll take the wagon. See you later."

James was surprised to find that it was still quite light outside. But it was only about eight-thirty, and it would be the longest day of the year soon. He looked up at the pale moon and breathed in the fresh evening air. He felt okay. Even if the effects of Jackie Leppard's cider punch were dramatic, they seemed easy to sleep off. Maybe that was why it was so popular: you could get totally legless on it for a few hours, and a few hours after that you were back to normal. The ideal alcoholic bender.

He heard the sound of an engine starting, then Jessica reversed a shiny black Range Rover out of one of the open-fronted sheds at the side of the house and swung it around in an expert, gravel-churning two-point turn so that the passenger door was next to him. He opened it and got in.

"Nice car," he said.

"Don't tell Mummy I'm driving this one, will you? I'm only meant to drive my little Polo until I... until they let me drive this one."

"Have you got a licence?"

"Nearly. I've got a provisional. I just need to be in a better mood the next time I take my test."

"How many times have you taken it so far?"

"Only one or two. Three, if you count the first time, but I don't count that because I was totally not ready and I had a filthy hangover, but I had to go ahead because the stupid man turned up. He was an idiot. It wasn't the usual one, the local one, that was the trouble. He kept trying to surprise me by suddenly banging the dashboard and expecting me to stop, or start, or turn or something, with no warning at all. He kept saying that was the whole point, as if his job was to try and trick me, instead of helping me pass, like any normal person would have done. Don't worry, though, I'm a really good driver."

She powered the Range Rover through the gateway at high speed, with an inch or so to spare on either side, then screeched to a violent halt and made a great show of peering keenly up and down the main road before swinging out and accelerating up the hill with such velocity that James was flung back in his seat.

"See?" Jessica said, "I looked really carefully before I pulled out. Both ways."

"Well done."

"Don't be like that. I suppose you'll want to drive now."

"I can't drive."

"Can't you? How brilliant!" She seemed genuinely delighted. She drove on in silence, glancing at James occasionally as he ran his fingers over his hair and started unpicking another one of the braids, having finally unknotted the first one. He was beginning to get the hang of it, but it was still going to take a long time.

"Hello," said a low voice from behind them.

"Fuck!" Jessica yelled, slamming on the brakes and nearly sending James through the windscreen.

"Sorry," said the voice.

James craned around and saw Reuben, rising up from the space between the front and back seats, where he'd been covered by an old blanket. He looked thoroughly dishevelled. He picked up his hat from the floor and clamped it on his head.

101

"Out," Jessica said.

"Please, Jess."

"No way."

"Why can't I come to Raymond's?."

"Why do you think that's where we're going?"

"There's a new band there. You always like to go and check them out."

"Bollocks! That's got nothing to do with it. I'm going to introduce James to Raymond, because I think they'd enjoy meeting each other and get on well together, and you are totally not invited. So you can get out now."

"No, I can't. We've gone too far. I'd have to walk back miles."

"Tough shit."

"Anyway, I get on well with Raymond."

"You've hardly ever spoken to him!"

"Yes, I have. That time at your place, that party, and the time I met you out riding. We had a really interesting conversation, as it happens."

"Oh, yes, I seem to remember you boring him about something. Religion, probably. I expect he was just being polite."

"No, he said he'd like to talk to me again, and to come over some time."

"And that's why you were hiding in the car, was it, because you thought we might be going there this evening?"

"Not completely," Reuben said. "I had a bit of an argument at home. I just needed somewhere to be."

"Well, you can go and be somewhere else."

"Wait a minute," James said, "why couldn't he come?" Apart from feeling sorry for Reuben, James wanted to talk to him. His suspicion that Olly was leading Reuben into trouble had been confirmed by the phone conversation. Oliver had more or less admitted to some kind of plot that involved not only Reuben, but James as well. And whatever it was, it sounded like it was going to happen soon. James felt safer with Reuben where he could keep an eye on him.

Jessica sighed. "You don't realize, James. It's not the first time he's done this kind of thing."

"I don't know about that. but I think you should let him stay. I mean, I'd actually like him to come with us, if that's all right."

"Fine!" Jessica rammed the car back into gear and floored the accelerator at the same time as she released the handbrake. The Range Rover fishtailed, with its wheels burning rubber until they took a grip on the road and the big engine thrust the car smoothly back up the hill.

"Thanks," Reuben said.

"Don't mention it," James said as he fastened his seat belt.

Rueben craned forward and peered at James. "What happened to your hair?"

*

102

Jarvis had to make a quick decision. When he saw the Range Rover pause just outside the gates to the Longbourne place there was still enough light to recognize the driver as the pretty young girl he'd seen earlier. He noticed that she hadn't turned her headlights on, which was probably just as well, because their beam might have caught the front of his car, tucked away down the lane on the other side of the road. He also saw that Naked Man was in the front passenger seat. He no longer had his face painted as a tiger, but his hair was still framing his head in a mad halo.

When the Range Rover swung out to the left and roared off up the hill towards Nether Gurney, that settled it. They were going to Raymond Norfolk's place. They must be. And while it was a risk to abandon his surveillance of the Post Office, he had a strong hunch that any action from now on would originate with the principals in the web of conspirators he'd unearthed. And squatting in the centre of that web was Raymond Norfolk, alert to every twitch and tremor in the gossamer network of deception he'd woven so cunningly and patiently. The bastard. He decided to follow them.

They'd only gone about half a mile when the silly bitch slammed the anchors on. Luckily, Jarvis was having difficulty keeping up with them anyway. His old Nissan was displaying its usual problem with hills, even though this was a relatively gentle one. But at least he had plenty of time to check the view ahead and swerve smoothly around the big black vehicle sitting in the middle of the road. Unbelievable: the little cow hadn't even bothered to pull in, as if she owned the highway. Typical. He drove on for few hundred yards and pulled into a lay-by where the road levelled off. He'd wait for them to pass him, then follow them again. But what if they didn't? What if it was another trick to draw him away from the Post Office? Jarvis was tormented by doubt. He manoeuvred his car into a position that would allow him to pull out in either direction. He'd give it five minutes, then get back to the Post Office as fast as he could if they didn't reappear. Meanwhile, he had some new information to process. While Naked Man might have dropped his Tiger Face disguise, there was now a new player in whatever twisted little game it was that they were playing. Jarvis had distinctly seen a rabbi in the back of the vehicle. Or possibly a cowboy. Interesting. Very interesting.

*

"Good to meet you, James. Like the hair."

"It's not always been like this."

"No, I didn't think you were born that way."

James couldn't think of a witty reply.

Jessica laughed and kissed Raymond on both cheeks.

James was distracted by what he could see of the house. It had been quite dark by the time they'd approached it, and James had only been able to tell that it was a vast, sprawling old building with interesting chimneys. Now they were standing around a back porch, where Jessica had parked after swinging along the side of some outbuildings, and James could see it was a classic early Tudor manor house, in what looked like an excellent state of preservation.

"And you're Reuben, aren't you?" Raymond said, looking over Jessica's shoulder. Reuben stepped around her and shook Raymond's hand.

"Oh, right," Jessica said, "he's come along, too."

"Great to see you again, Reuben. I remember we had an interesting talk when we met last time. But I didn't realize you were Orthodox."

"I'm not, really. Well, I suppose I am, now, sort of. I don't know. Sorry, I'm sort of working on it." Reuben took his hat off and wiped his lank hair away from his brow.

"Don't apologize, mate. Faith is the choice that chooses us, right? Keep the hat on, if you want. Whatever you're comfortable with. But I would ask you all to take your shoes off before we go any further, if that's cool with you."

"Oh, Ray, do we have to?" Jessica said.

"Sorry if it's a drag, folks," Raymond said, "but just humour an old hippie if you don't mind."

James thought Raymond Norfolk looked nothing like an old hippie. His thick, dark hair was neatly cut, with just a touch of grey at the temples. He looked very fit, and had the kind of discreet, healthy tan maintained by someone who can go skiing whenever they feel like it. He was as tall as James and was dressed in a loose brown velour track suit. Even though James still wanted to murder him, he also wanted Raymond to like him.

"I hope we're not disturbing you," James said.

"No way, I was just doing a bit of the old yoga, that's all. That's why you've caught me in my pyjamas."

"Oh, listen, sorry," Reuben said. He seemed genuinely embarrassed. "Do you want to carry on and we can wait until you've finished? Wait outside, or something?"

"Of course not. No problem, buddy. I might just finish off while we have a drink, if that's okay. Bevvies for you, *chakras* for me. Refreshment for mind, body and spirit."

"God, Raymond," Jessica said, "now you do sound like a hippie."

"Whatever you say, darling. Peace, love and cheap vibrations. Have you got those shoes off? Yeah? Great, then come on in."

Raymond handed Jessica a gin and tonic. "What about you, Reuben?"

"Er, nothing, thanks."

"Are you sure? I've got pretty much everything."

"Maybe I will, actually."

"Soft drink? Hard liquor? Anything in between? I've got some Belgian beer in the fridge. And some nice fresh smoothies as well, if you're feeling virtuous."

"Okay, maybe one of them, thanks."

"What flavour? I've got all the fruits."

"Actually, maybe I'll have a drink after all. I mean, an alcoholic drink."

"Sure. Whiskey, gin, rum, vodka, wine, beer, grappa, tequila? I've got the lot."

"Whiskey, please. No, vodka. Actually, no; whiskey. I think."

"For God's sake!" Jessica said.

"Tell you what," Raymond said, "why don't you come over and have a look?"

Reuben got up from his armchair, shambled over to the huge oak sideboard, and started inspecting the vast array of bottles on top of it.

"There's a couple of pretty good single malts there," Raymond said. "Branch water in the jug, and ice in the bucket if you want to ruin it, like I do, and risk outraging any passing Scotsman."

Reuben laughed knowingly, but James was pretty sure he had no idea what Raymond was talking about. However, he knew what a good single malt was. James watched him fill half a crystal tumbler with Glenfiddich Special Reserve.

"What would you like, James?" asked Raymond.

"I'd better have a soft drink, I think."

"You sound like a man with regrets."

"It's just that I got a bit legless this afternoon."

"Of course, it was the fete, wasn't it? Don't tell me: Jackie Leppard's cider punch, right?"

"I'm afraid so."

"And I bet you feel okay now, don't you? Fragile but functional. I couldn't believe it the first time I had it. But if you're still a bit spaced out, then I'll tell you exactly what you need. Cold Guinness, mate. That'll do the trick. Trust me on this."

"How do you know about that, Ray?" Jessica said. "I mean about the cider punch. I thought you hadn't had a drink for years."

"I sometimes have a drink. I don't get Taliban about these things. I do whatever's appropriate. And the year after I bought this place, it was appropriate to go to the fete and get slaughtered on the cider punch. So, what about it, James? Cold Guinness?"

"Sounds good."

Raymond flipped open a door in the ancient sideboard and a fridge light came on. James felt a twinge of disappointment. He hated it when people messed around with lovely old furniture, no matter how discreetly. It always seemed like a desecration.

"Not guilty, by the way," Raymond said as he poured Guinness slowly into a tall glass. He glanced at James. "In case you were thinking it was me that put the fridge in there. It wasn't."

James was taken aback to find that Raymond could read his mind. "No, not at all," he said, "I was just interested in it, that's all."

"I know. I can always tell by the way people look around, as soon as they walk in. I can tell who appreciates these things. Here you go." He passed the beer to James over the back of the sofa where he was sitting next to Jessica, and walked back to the sideboard. "I would never fuck around with a lovely old piece like this," he said, stroking the gnarled wood. "You might as well do the whole rock-trash ethic and turn it into a cocktail bar. Get a pool table in. No, the guy I bought the place from had the fridge put in. He didn't have a clue about any of the old stuff in here. Not that I was much better. But I'm learning. I've still got a long way to go, though. I expect you could probably give me some good advice. Jess said you're a bit of an expert."

"Oh, yes," Jessica said, "he knows all about that kind of thing. That's partly why I brought him over, actually, Ray."

"No, listen," James said, "I'm not an expert at all. Just an enthusiast."

"That's even better," Raymond said. "Go with your heart, right?"

"I haven't got much choice, really, since my head is pretty much empty when it comes to any real expertise."

"Who needs it? You can find out everything on the web these days. As it happens, I think I've tracked down where this sideboard came from. It could have been a dower chest originally, which a local girl brought with her when she married someone who lived here. What do you reckon?"

James twisted around on the sofa to look at the sideboard but was distracted by Raymond, who was slowly raising one arm perpendicularly into the air. He stretched it as far as he could, then raised the other one, clasped his fingers together and began to bend over from the waist. James remembered: yoga. He tried to concentrate on the sideboard. "It's very big for an ordinary Tudor dower chest," he said, "even early period. Actually, it could be two or three older chests that were joined together later on and converted."

"Spot on," Raymond said. His torso and extended arms were now at a perfect right angle to his legs. He swept his upper body down in a curve until his fingers touched the floor. "That's exactly what I've been told by someone who's meant to know about these things." He stretched down still father, placing his palms flat on the floor.

James was impressed. He wasn't even sure that he could touch his toes. "So, in fact," he said without thinking, "you did get an expert to have a look at it."

"That's right," said Raymond, nestling his face into his legs, but still speaking perfectly clearly, "I was lying." He chuckled from somewhere between his knees.

"Sorry," James said, "I didn't... it's just that when you said to go with your heart--"

"I was full of shit. I'm always spouting crap like that. It's amazing how few people call me on it." Raymond laughed again. He bent his legs and crouched down on the ground, then clasped his hands behind his head. He raised his legs slowly, and then straightened them out. He was now standing on his head.

106

"Listen, if you want to wander round and have a look at the place, go ahead. Feel free. There are some other pieces around that might interest you. And pictures, too."

James had the feeling he'd passed some sort of test.

"How's that Guinness going down?" Raymond's inverted face said.

James found that he'd nearly finished it. "Great. Hit the spot." He decided to ignore the fact that Raymond was upside down. "You were absolutely right; I was feeling okay, but I was still a bit shaky. What does she put in that punch? Apart from gallons of cider and vodka."

"Who knows? Absinthe, magic mushrooms, hair restorer. People keep trying to steal the recipe, but no dice. Mess with big Jackie, and you're toast. The only thing that everyone knows for sure is that it blows your fucking head off."

"God, yes," Jessica said, "you should have seen James. He was so funny!" She bounced herself around on the sofa to talk to Raymond, and gave a little squeal when she found herself looking at his legs. "For God's sake, Ray!"

Raymond brought his legs down slowly, uncurled himself, and got to his feet in one graceful movement. He raised his arms and stretched again. "I should really do a counter-pose after that one, but it can wait. Ah, that feels good." He shook himself loosely. "That one's great. You should try it. Very good for you, standing on your head."

"No thanks," James said, "it feels like someone's already stood on mine."

Raymond laughed.

"Let me tell you about this afternoon," Jessica said.

James became increasingly irritated by Jessica's version of events, which made him sound like a complete idiot by exaggerating his occasional minor mistakes and overlooking all the intelligent and resourceful things he distinctly remembered doing. He had to admit she was turning it into a very funny story but she was infantilizing the whole episode, with him in the role of chief infant. However, the advantage of this was that she kept snuggling up to him on the sofa, stroking him sympathetically as she described all the trouble he'd got into, and squeezing him impulsively at particularly exciting moments. James was pleased she wasn't hiding her affection for him from Raymond. A good sign.

Raymond listened to the story politely but James could tell he was used to Jessica's unreliable narrative style. At one point, as he was laughing indulgently at her description of the final stages of the bingo, he caught James's eye and winked at him.

James realized that his initial reaction when Jessica had told him about Raymond had been immature. Raymond was a very intelligent, interesting man. And it was ridiculous for James to have been jealous.

Reuben, who was on his second large drink, was laughing a lot at the story, which James thought was a bit impertinent. He wondered when he'd get a chance to give him Olly's message and ask him what it all meant. He'd begun to

107

raise the topic discreetly on the way over in the car, but Reuben had scowled and grimaced ferociously, making it clear that he didn't want to say anything in front of Jessica. But James was aware of the need to catch Reuben while he was still sober, and time was running out.

"It's just such a shame you didn't see James with his face painted," Jessica said, "because he looked amazing. I honestly think that girl might be genuinely talented. For someone like her, I mean. She probably won't make anything of herself. None of them ever do. Five years from now she'll be fat and married with a couple of brats." She stood up suddenly. "Come on then, Ray, let's go and see Bodie."

"Sure." Raymond stood up. "Would you two like to come?"

"No, they wouldn't," Jessica said.

"Who's Bodie?" asked James.

"My horse," Jessica said. "Bodie, short for Boudicca."

"Not exactly your horse, Jess," Raymond said. "Not yet."

"Oh, don't be such a miser. You'll get your money. Not that you need it."

"It's not about the money. Anyway, let's not talk about that now."

"No, let's not. I just want to see her. And we can ride tomorrow, can't we?"

"I'm not sure if I can. I'll have to see."

"Of course you can."

"I'd like to come to the stables," Reuben said.

"No you wouldn't," Jessica said. "You'd just be bored."

"All right, then I won't," Reuben said, throwing himself back into his chair.

James saw his chance to get Reuben on his own. "Actually, I might stay here, as well. I'd like to have a look around, if that's okay."

"Absolutely. The only thing is, you can't go into the annexe as I've got a band in there. It's through the blue door on the other side of the kitchen. Pity, really. The studio is actually the old dairy, and I've knocked through to the adjoining building and made it residential. I put in a couple of extra bedrooms, but most of it is still original. I'll show you another time. Everywhere else is fine. *Mi casa es su casa.* But I don't want to disturb them in the studio."

He turned to Jessica. "I think they're pulling an all-nighter in there. I get the impression things are a bit fraught. They're using their own engineer so I'm not getting my usual gossip from Guy, but I don't think it's a very happy ship. We'd better leave them to it." He gave her a sly smile. "Shame about that; I know you wanted to check them out."

"I most certainly did not, it hadn't crossed my mind. Who's in there, anyway?"

"Some boy band or other."

"Bazooka aren't a boy band!" Jessica said, then bit her lip and blushed. "If that's who's in there, I mean. They play their own instruments, as it happens, and write their own songs. Most of them. I mean, I think I remember hearing

108

that somewhere. But all I'm saying is you don't have to go around calling them a boy band in that patronizing way."

"Sorry, I didn't realize you were a secret fan."

"I'm not, don't be ridiculous."

"Then why did you ask me who was in the there when you knew all along?"

"Oh, stop being so stupid. I must have just happened to hear it. Someone from the village must have told me. I expect it was probably one of those silly girls who did James's face. Come on, are we going to the stables or not?"

She walked to the door and waited for him. Raymond paused on his way out. "Are you sure you don't want to come, Reuben?"

"Actually, I would like to. If that's okay."

"That's fine."

"Oh, leave it, Richard," Jessica said, "you don't know anything about horses."

"I know," he said, getting up from his chair, "and now I can find out. Raymond doesn't mind."

"Not at all, mate. Come on, then."

Reuben smirked at Jessica and followed them out of the door. Raymond turned back and called to James:

"Help yourself to drinks, or whatever you want. We'll leave you to have a good old wander around by yourself without being distracted. See you in a while. Enjoy."

*

"May I look around your house, please?" the polite little boy would ask almost as soon as he walked in.

"Oh, James!" his mother would exclaim, half-embarrassed and half-pleased. His father would shrug helplessly at the man of the house, and perhaps ruffle James's hair, also secretly proud that his child was a bit unusual. The two men might exchange a few words about curiosity being a healthy quality in a child, within reason.

"Of course you can, my love," the wife would say, "but there's nothing very special to see. Although we're quite pleased with the loft conversion. In fact, your mum and dad might like to have a look at that, as well. Shall we all go up?"

"Let the poor people have a drink first, dear," her husband would say, and turn to James's parents with a tentative smile, wondering whether it had been a good idea to invite these new acquaintances. "What can I offer you? How was the drive, by the way? Did you take that little short-cut I mentioned over the phone, to avoid the bottleneck on the main road?"

"Very grown-up," the woman might whisper as James made his way upstairs or through to the back of the house, "wanting to look around like that. Perhaps he'll be an estate agent."

Sometimes there was a child James was expected to play with, which made exploration more difficult. Often it would be a family they'd met on holiday. Which usually happened on the second or third day, once his parents' social instincts started working again in their new surroundings. If James wasn't present for the first contact he would get the news in the early evening as he was grappling with the unfamiliar food his parents encouraged him to eat, to develop the 'sophisticated palette' which they were convinced that a boy of seven should take the opportunity to acquire away from home.

"We met such a nice English couple on the beach, James, while you were off looking for shells. And guess what? They've got a little boy almost exactly your age! So that'll be fun, won't it? We've arranged to have a picnic together tomorrow."

For the rest of the holiday James would have to pretend to enjoy playing with this child, who would quite often turn out to be the little thug who'd kicked over his sandcastle on his first day.

The two families would arrange to meet up after the holiday, and once or twice a genuine friendship developed and persisted for a few years, but didn't survive the death of James's father. But usually it would fade away after a few visits. In a couple of instances it ended abruptly, when the grown-ups discovered they'd been very mistaken about each other. On one occasion, when James was nine, he'd overheard his parents talking about some kind of misunderstanding that had taken place.

"It took me a moment to realize exactly what it was they were suggesting," his father said. "I was quite shocked, I don't mind admitting it. Even though I like to think I'm as broad-minded as the next man."

"No, you're not, Jerry."

There was a short silence. His father muttered, "No, I suppose not." Then he chuckled, and James's mother joined in.

*

James heard music coming from downstairs. They must be back from the stables. He was disappointed; they'd been gone less than half an hour and he'd only just reached the top floor. Raymond Norfolk either had very good taste, or the sense to trust people who did. There was a lot of very good English furniture, and old paintings and tapestries that James suspected were good. There were also several statues of the Buddha, sitting calmly on windowsills or smiling shyly in nooks and corners. Hindu deities writhed and leered around the place, and various tribal masks hung from the walls. But all the exotica blended discreetly into the general decoration. A lot of care had been taken.

The building itself was a warren, full of unexpected turnings and floors at slightly different levels, joined by odd little sets of steps and sloping passages. As James began to make his way back down to the living room he avoided the main staircase he'd gone up, weaving his way down flights of narrow, twisting back stairs. When he reached the first floor he found that the final flight of back stairs was at the far end of a long passage. It was quite unlike the rest of the house. There was only one door in the whole corridor, and as he approached it he began to hear a faint sound above the music that drifted up from downstairs: a rhythmic cacophony of propulsive shuttling, clicking and rattling, all woven into a dense wall of sound. There was something urgent but unflustered about the noise, a businesslike quality that James found tantalizingly familiar. He reached the door and stopped. The noise was definitely coming from behind it. He opened the door.

It was amazing.

One Christmas when he was eight his father had taken him to Hamley's toyshop in Regent's Street to see the famous model railway they displayed every year. Even though such things were old fashioned by then, not as desirable as the video games and movie tie-in products that were beginning to dominate the toy market, James and the other boys (and some girls, too) stood gazing at it, fascinated by its intricacy, by the almost religious perfection of every tiny detail, and by its sheer size.

But this was bigger. Much bigger. And the whole, vast system was in motion.

The room was immense, with a high, vaulted ceiling. James's best guess was that he was looking into the upper half of a banqueting hall, or something similar, bisected horizontally when the floor was put in.

The whole space was filled with a labyrinth of purpose-built, waist-high trestle tables supporting a model railway network of astounding complexity. Dozens of trains sped busily around the tracks, clattering past each other, narrowly avoiding collisions with hair's-breadth precision at intersections, and travelling side by side for long sections where the tracks ran in parallel.

But there was far more than the railway itself. There were fields and forests full of exquisitely detailed trees and bushes that you wanted to touch, to see if they were real; hills and valleys where the railway tracks ran through tunnels and over viaducts whose stonework you would swear was genuine. In one place a bridge spanned a swiftly flowing river of real water. Everything was constructed with astonishing accuracy.

In places, the trains passed through small country stations with miniature villages around them, and at the far end of the layout there was an entire town, served by a station with several platforms and a goods yard. Some of the trains stopped there, or shunted around the web of tracks in complicated, inscrutable manoeuvres. Behind the station, in the centre of the town, an electric tram shuttled among the large municipal buildings before making a circuit of the extensive suburbs.

111

And then there were the people. The tiny figures were horribly realistic. There was something disturbing about the minute creases and wrinkles in their skin. James wouldn't have been particularly surprised if they'd started scuttling around, chattering to each other in high-pitched, squeaky little voices as they went in and out of the shops, or perhaps lurched from the pub slightly the worse for drink.

In the middle of the system there was a command centre where two tall swivel chairs stood on a raised area, surrounded by computers which were all silently displaying flickering streams of data. Over the back of each chair a neatly-pressed dark blue jacket was draped. Each jacket was decorated with insignia, one more elaborately than the other. There was a hook on the side of each chair, from which hung a cap with an embossed metal plate above a shiny black peak. James could see the word 'Driver' on one of them, and 'Station Master' on the other. The station master was also equipped with a whistle.

James was disturbed by the way the computers quietly went about their business, running the network of trains, unconcerned about whether anyone was there to see them or not. It made him feel, as he left the room, that he was closing the door on a parallel universe with an entirely independent existence.

When James reached the living room he paused in the doorway. He'd assumed the music he'd been hearing on his way downstairs was coming from a sound system, but it wasn't. There was a baby grand piano in the far corner of the big room near the sideboard, which he hadn't noticed before. Reuben was playing it, hunched over the keys, his eyes half closed. He was improvising around a simple, catchy melody, keeping the elaborations anchored to a solid rhythm. James thought the effect was both delicate and soulful, and Reuben seemed to be creating it with casual brilliance.

There was no sign of Raymond or Jessica. Perhaps Reuben had been bored at the stables, or, more likely, Jessica had bullied him into coming back. James knew this was his opportunity to ask him about Olly's plan, but he stayed in the doorway.

He heard a noise behind him and turned to see Jessica and Raymond coming along the passage. He put his finger to his lips. Jessica began to speak, but Raymond clamped his hand around her mouth from behind. He didn't do it very hard, but she acted as though he'd clutched her in a tight embrace, and wriggled and squirmed against him, giggling. James noticed there was straw on her clothes. She must have been mucking out the horses. He didn't know exactly what mucking out meant, but he was pretty sure it involved something to do with straw. Or hay, which was possibly the same thing.

Reuben looked up and saw them in the doorway, and stopped playing abruptly.

"Sorry," he said, getting up from the piano stool and closing the keyboard lid. He picked up his glass of whiskey from the top of the piano and took a swig from it. James noticed that the level in the Glenfiddich bottle had fallen considerably.

"Don't stop," Raymond said.

"No, I was just messing about, really."

"It sounded nice," Jessica said. "I didn't know you could play the piano."

They all came into the room. Reuben sat down on the piano stool again, spinning around on it slowly, not looking at them.

"That really took it somewhere else," Raymond said.

"I hope you don't mind," Reuben said. "I mean, it's your song."

"Of course not, man. I love what you were doing with it."

"What song?" Jessica said.

"Have you been trained?" asked Raymond.

"I had some lessons when I was younger, because my parents were keen. But I didn't like it. I didn't really have the concentration for it. To learn properly."

"Who told you that?"

"The teacher."

"Bullshit. You've got everything you need, mate. Otherwise you wouldn't be able to do what you were doing."

"What?" said Jessica. "What was he doing?"

"Improvising with 'White Line Fever'. One of my old songs."

"I was just noodling around, that's all. I noticed the record on the wall; that's what set me off. "

James saw there was a framed platinum disc on the wall above the piano. He'd thought there was something familiar about what Reuben had been playing.

"Oh, right," Jessica said, "your famous druggy song."

Raymond sighed. "The number of times I've sworn I'd never say this again. But for your information, 'White Line Fever' isn't about drugs."

"Everyone thinks it is, though, don't they?" Jessica said.

"I know. But it's actually about touring, in the States. The white line in the middle of the road, stretching to the horizon for days on end. Going crazy in the bus. That's what it's about. But people always love to think that everything is code for something else. It's like that song called 'Perfect Day' by Lou Reed. Remember that?"

"Who?" Jessica said.

"I remember," James said, "they released a new version of it a few years ago, with a whole lot of famous people singing it, didn't they? Bowie and people."

"Right," Raymond said, "and everyone kept saying, 'Oh, that song's all about heroin, it's all a secret message.' But years before that, when he was still in the Velvet Underground, Lou Reed wrote a song that was about heroin. Know what it was called?"

"What?" Jessica said.

"It was called 'Heroin'."

James laughed.

"But people were bound to think all your songs are about drugs," Jessica said, "what with your reputation. Everyone knows what you lot got up to."

"They may think they do," Raymond said.

"What, are you saying you didn't do drugs?"

"Of course I did drugs. There was so much coke around you could ski across London on it. But the rest of the band were more into it than I was. I mean, the way Bill, the drummer, hoovered it up was unbelievable. And our second manager, as well. Although he was certifiably insane. At least, he was by the time he spent our royalties on a racehorse. Everyone was pretty much off their heads most of the time, and I was caning it along with everyone else, but I was never a real hound for it like some people."

"But you were the one who went to prison," Jessica said.

Raymond walked over to the sideboard, giving Reuben's shoulder a squeeze as he passed him. He took a jug from the fridge and poured himself a glass of juice.

"True," he said, and took a long drink. "Maybe I was the one who deserved it."

"What do you mean?" Jessica said.

"It doesn't matter. Is everyone okay for a drink?"

"I'm fine, thanks," James said.

Reuben raised his glass and squinted at Raymond through it. "Yes, please."

Raymond took the glass and picked up the whiskey bottle from the sideboard.

"I thought you were framed on that drug thing," persisted Jessica.

Raymond frowned and turned away. James saw that he was keeping his back to Reuben as he filled his glass with a very small splash of whiskey and a lot of ice and water. He turned and handed Reuben the drink. "James and Reuben don't want to hear about all this."

"Yes, they do. Don't you, James?"

"Well," James said, "if Ray doesn't want to talk about it--"

"Oh, stop being so fucking polite," Jessica said. "It's exciting! Drugs, crime, celebs, we're all mad for it, be honest. So, Ray, were the drugs planted on you or not?"

"Yup. They were."

"Oh, wow," Jessica said. "Why? I mean, who did it?"

"It was this cop. Strange guy. For some reason he got obsessed with busting me, and he went a bit nuts. And I think he stayed nuts, actually, because he's still around and he's still got this weird thing about me. Basically, he's a very disturbed individual on a bizarre mission to fuck me over. God knows why. It's like stalkers: they delude themselves that it's all about you, but really it's just about them."

"Then why did you say you deserved it?" Jessica said.

114

Raymond leaned back against the sideboard and looked at her. "Put it this way," he said, finally, "I was playing games and I didn't think about the consequences."

"Karma," Reuben said. He took a gulp of his drink, which he'd nearly finished, and stared at the floor, swivelling slowly around on the piano stool.

"Exactly," Raymond said. "Karma."

"Oh, God, don't start with the hippie stuff," Jessica said.

Raymond laughed.

"All is vanity and vexation of spirit," Reuben intoned.

"That's Ecclesiastes!" Jessica said. "We had a teacher who used to quote that every time we turned up with a bit of make-up on, or our skirts too short. Old bitch."

"There's some good stuff in the bible," Raymond said.

"Actually," Reuben said, "I'm looking into the kabbalah."

"What do you want?" Raymond said abruptly. James wondered why he'd spoken so harshly to Reuben, then he saw that someone had appeared in the doorway.

The man was short and stocky, with a pale, fleshy face. He was about Raymond's age, James thought, but he looked tired and unhealthy, and his clothes made him appear even less fit than he would have done if he hadn't tried to dress like a teenager about to go windsurfing. He took off his baseball cap and ran his hand over his close-cropped, receding hair.

"Listen, I'm really sorry, Ray, I know this is out of order, coming in here, but I really need to talk to you."

"Why?"

"We've got a bit of a problem."

"Anything technical, phone Guy. He can be here in half an hour."

"No, it's not actually technical, mate. It's more a personal kind of thing."

"I don't want to hear about it, Bruce. No personal disputes, no business shit, no dramas, nothing. I make it all clear when you sign the contract. I don't interfere."

"I know, I know. You've been great. It's just we've got a problem with Spike."

"Who?"

"One of the kids."

"Your band, Bruce, your problem. I won't get involved."

"The thing is," Bruce said, sidling into the room, "it sort of involves you already, without me being able to help it. Fuck knows, I wouldn't dream of coming in here and disturbing you unless I had to. No way."

"How does it involve me? I don't even know this kid. What was his name again?"

"Spike. The lead singer. Singer-songwriter. Well, he thinks he writes the songs, because he pitches in with some ideas when I get the writers in, and we give him a credit. Keeps him happy. You know how it works with these kids."

"Doesn't he play guitar, as well?" Jessica said.

Bruce turned to gaze at her. He seemed to have difficulty focussing. "Yeah, that's right, guitar," he said vaguely, "singer-songwriter-guitarist."

"He's hot," Jessica said.

"Yeah. Nice kid." Bruce looked around the room, now apparently noticing James and Reuben for the first time as well. "Listen, mate," he said to Raymond, "can we have a word in private?"

"No. Just go and deal with it."

"The only way I can deal with it is if you talk to him."

"Bullshit."

"No, really, he's been asking for you. That's the whole thing, Ray. He's a big fan, you see. That's one of the reasons we booked in the studio here in the first place. I think he's a bit disappointed he hasn't met you, actually. I'm not saying he's got any right to expect it, don't get me wrong, I know the score. But we've been working hard, and he's been overdoing it a bit, and he's a bit highly-strung, that's the thing."

"Highly strung-out, more likely," Raymond said.

"Well, I don't know about that, obviously--"

"Yes you do. I expect you're the one giving them the stuff in the first place."

"Look, Ray, these kids are going to do what they want anyway, right? Whatever I try and do. Isn't it better if I at least know what they're taking, and keep an eye on it all?"

"I don't want to know, Bruce."

"Right, no, of course. Let's just say that Spike is having a bit of a breakdown, then, okay? Overwork, right? But he had a big barney with the others and stormed out. I think he's wandering around in the grounds somewhere. I'm worried about him, Ray, he's in a right state. I don't know what he might do. Might, you know, harm himself."

"What do you expect me to do?"

"Well, maybe you could help me look for him."

"No way."

"But if he hears you calling for him or something, he might come in. He's got this idea he needs to talk to you. You're his idol, mate, straight up. If you could just have a quick word with him, Ray. I'm really worried about him, honestly. Otherwise I wouldn't ask. I'm very attached to that boy. He's a lovely kid, I'm like a father to him."

Raymond looked at him with undisguised distaste. Bruce shifted his weight from foot to foot, breathing through his mouth and swaying slightly.

Raymond sighed. "You can tell him I'll talk to him tomorrow. But you'll have to go and find him yourself. I'm not coming out there now."

"Thanks, Ray, mate. I appreciate it." Bruce hesitated, revolving his baseball cap in his hands. "What about just coming out for five minutes? Give him a shout?"

"No. That's it. Now fuck off."

"Sure, yes. I'll try and find him. I'll tell him you'll see him tomorrow."

"But only if he's straight and sober. I'm not talking to him if he's off his face."

Bruce nodded and walked from the room without saying anything else.

Jessica finally broke the silence. "You don't like him very much, do you?"

"No shit, Sherlock," Raymond said.

Reuben laughed and spun himself around on the piano stool. James saw that he'd topped up his drink while Raymond had been talking to Bruce.

"I can see he's a bit of a creep," Jessica said.

"He's a reptile. He's been managing boy bands for years. Or whatever you want to call them. These kids. He signs them up to outrageous contracts, controls everything, and dumps them when it suits him. He just exploits them, basically."

"Come on, I bet they know what they're getting into, most of them. They're not all totally dumb and innocent, you know."

"They don't have to be. I'm sure a lot of them are pretty smart. They probably know a lot more about the music business than I did at their age. But when it comes to it, they'll still do anything to make it. And people like Bruce exploit that." He stretched, and rolled the tension out of his neck and shoulders. "I guess I just don't like him. I shouldn't have taken the booking, that's the truth. That's why I'm so pissed off, I think. I'm angry with myself. Do I really need to do business with a nasty little shit like him?"

"Right livelihood," Reuben said, speaking slowly and carefully.

"What?" Jessica said.

Reuben gazed at them owlishly. "Buddhist thing. Izznit, Ray?"

"Sort of. It's the idea that if you need to make a living, you do whatever's necessary to conduct your ordinary day-to-day life with integrity."

"Good old Buddha," Reuben said.

"Let me top that up," Raymond said, casually taking Reuben's glass from him. He put it on the sideboard. "Apart from anything else," he said, apparently forgetting about Reuben's drink, "if Bruce is giving drugs to those kids, and he's doing it on my property, that makes me liable. And you know what really creeps me out? He has sex with those boys as well, some of them."

"But they're not underage, are they?" said Jessica.

"He's still exploiting them. What do you think, James?"

James was startled. "I don't know. I was just thinking about this young guy who's wandering around outside. I mean, do you think he'd do anything drastic?"

117

"If he does," Raymond said, "I'd prefer him to do it off the premises."

"God, Ray," Jessica said, "you're being a bit harsh, aren't you? You might at least pop out there for a few minutes and have a quick look for him. He might be just about to jump in the fishpond or something."

"Okay, Jess," Reuben said, swivelling around slowly on the piano stool, "why don't you go and look for him, then?"

"Me? Why? It's got nothing to do with me."

"That's the spirit, Jess," Raymond said.

*

Tragic Rock Star Death, big headline. Or maybe Troubled Spike in Suicide Riddle. Yeah, that'll be cool. Do it so they can't tell if I meant to or not. Like Hendrix or one of those dudes. So they'll still be making TV programmes about it in fifty years. Did brilliant rising young talent Harvey 'Spike' Tindall take his own life? Was the tormented lead singer of boy band, no, not boy band, fuck that. Was tormented singer-songwriter Spike, no, I think I'll stop calling myself Spike, just be Harvey, that sounds more mature, it was Bruce's idea to give us all fucking nicknames. Was rock genius Harvey Tindall driven to suicide by the cruel jealousy of his less talented bandmates, or was it the callous neglect of the music industry itself, which is only now beginning to recognize the immensity of its loss as his timeless songs become the anthems for a whole generation? Not that I'm going to do it, I wouldn't give them the fucking satisfaction, although if I did it would serve them right, they'd realize what they've lost. They'd play my songs at the funeral and everyone would be crying, police trying to keep all the fans away, probably a couple of them driven mad with grief trying to throw themselves into the grave, unless I get cremated, I haven't decided, then they'd try and jump into the furnace or whatever, it'd probably be those two sisters from Bolton we all shagged in the tour bus that night, they're fucking mad they are OW! what the fuck was that? Stubbed my fucking toe. Shitfuckettybollockscunt that hurts. Fucking garden gnome. Oh, it's a whatsit, a Buddha statue. In the middle of the fucking lawn. Oh, yeah, Raymond, he's into all of that. Cool. If I could just talk to him, he'd see how much we've got in common. That whole attitude he had, he'd see that I'm like his natural successor, the heir to his legacy, the whole anarchist attitude although not in a punk way because he was never a punk, more a serious political statement, like a situationist kind if thing. I must read that book Bruce gave me, that whole thing about using art to take a stand against the establishment, that's my thing too, so why doesn't Bruce arrange for me to talk to Raymond? Fucking Bruce, he's probably jealous. God, that was pathetic when he said he loved me, standing there all short and fat with his little cock sticking out. It wasn't bad, though, I've got to admit, he knows what he's doing. Better than some of those girls, in a way. Some of them are right slags. At least

118

Bruce is gentle. I wonder what it would be like without the drugs? Maybe I should take another E. I'm a bit wired, that's the trouble. I'll go down through these trees, they look good in the moonlight, I'm into nature, it's a good influence, helps you chill. Bruce said that pill he gave me earlier was a downer but it feels more like speed. Or maybe that's just the E. Hang on, did I take a second one already? I can't remember. I'll see how many I've got left in a minute. I could always do a couple of valium. Or maybe just one. No, what I really need is some more of that opium. Our little secret, as Bruce says. That was great, that opium. And like Bruce says, you don't get addicted, it's got all the buzz you get from heroin but it doesn't fuck you up because it's organic. I mean, those Chinese dudes have been taking it for thousands of years. I could go back inside and raid his stash again. He's so funny, Bruce, he thinks I don't know where he keeps it all. Wasn't he ever a kid? Looking for things they've hidden. Christmas and birthday prezzies, your mum's little purse of emergency cash, your dad's porn stash, there's nowhere they can hide things where you won't find it. Fucking dad, he's another one who'll be sorry at the funeral. If he turns up. Yeah, he'd turn up. Beg forgiveness from mum. Maybe I should have a big reconciliation with him first. Not that I'm going to do it, but if I did. Why does she always defend him? He fucking deserted us. What a nerve, that phone call last year when we got to number one. Just to congratulate you, son, yeah, bollocks, how much money are you after, dad, crawling out of the woodwork when I haven't seen you for five years... what the fuck is that car doing there? Oh, right, I've come out next to the bottom of the drive. Geezer inside the car looks asleep. Press. Got to be the press. Found out we're recording down here and staking it out. Can't be very important, that's a rubbish motor. Or maybe that's just for cover. Yeah, low profile. Fuck, that's it! I'll go and give him an interview. Get my side of the story in. Brilliant. Give him an exclusive. I'll just have another one of those valium, chill me out a bit so I can think straight.

*

Jarvis was just dozing off when, for the second time that day, a kid banged on his car window and he jumped out of his skin. At first he thought he was having a deja vu, but as his head cleared and he rolled down his window he saw that this kid was older than the boy in the village; he looked about eighteen, with a thin, pale face and spiky hair.

"What do you want, son?"

"It's not what I want. It's what you want, isn't it?"

Jarvis tried to keep his temper. "Really? What do I want?"

"If you're just going to play games, I'm going back inside and you can forget it."

Inside. Inside where? Where was he, anyway? Then Jarvis remembered. Raymond Norfolk's place. And this kid was talking about going back inside there. He might have something to do with the whole set-up. With a bit of luck, he was on drugs. Yes, look at the state of his eyes. And chewing his lips off. All the signs. Perfect. Better go carefully, though. Get him in the car, that was the first step.

"Are you cold out there?"

"No."

"Oh. How about some coffee?" Jarvis showed him the thermos.

"I don't drink coffee, man. It's a bad drug. Fucks you up."

Not so promising. If the kid wasn't into drugs he probably wouldn't be able to tell him about Norfolk's operation. Jarvis peered at him. He certainly looked off his head.

The boy leaned in through the window. "Do you want an interview or not?"

An interview! Was he saying he wanted to turn himself in? He must have some information after all. Maybe he'd fallen out with Norfolk and wanted to cut a deal. Or maybe he was an innocent employee who'd stumbled on the drugs operation, and, like he said, he wasn't into that whole scene, and now he was going to squeal on Norfolk.

"An interview?" Jarvis said. "Of course. Great. Get in, son."

"Wait a minute. Who are you with?"

Jarvis was just about to say he was with the drugs squad, so he'd come to the right shop, when the boy saw yesterday's Daily Mail lying on the back seat.

"Daily Mail, right? Cool. Freelance or staff?"

Jarvis got it. This kid was in a band, recording at the studio. He'd mistaken Jarvis for the press and now, for some reason, wanted to do an interview. Fine. Play along with that. Pretend to interview him and probe him subtly about the drugs operation. Perfect.

"That's right," Jarvis said. "Freelance. I'm Phil Beamish. Jump in."

The boy went around to the passenger side and got in, slamming the door much harder than he needed to. He looked around the car and sniffed.

"Smells like a fucking toilet in here."

Jarvis chuckled indulgently. "Us reporters can't be too particular when we're on a big story. In case we miss something. And you're a big story, after all."

That seemed to make the boy happy. He nodded several times. He stared through the windscreen with his mouth slightly open, tapping his foot on the floor and scratching himself. Definitely on drugs, thought Jarvis, whatever he said about coffee.

"Yes," Jarvis continued, "you lead us a merry old dance, you celebrity pop stars."

"I'm not a pop star!" snapped the boy.

Shit. Had he got it wrong? Maybe the kid was wasting his time.

The boy turned to him. "And don't say I'm in a boy band, either. We've never been a boy band. They might think they are, but I'm not. Fuck that. I'm a singer-songwriter."

120

"Of course," said Jarvis, relieved that he was on the right track after all. "I know that. You're an artist. I'll tell it like it is, don't worry. Trust me, son."

"And don't call me son."

"No, right, sorry. Just a habit, son. Sorry. What shall I call you, then?"

"What the fuck do you think?"

This was dangerous. If this little turd realized Jarvis had no idea who he was it might all go pear-shaped. He might throw a wobbler and storm off.

"No, wait, actually," the boy said, "don't call me that. I'm not Spike any more. Just Harvey. In fact, you can have that as an exclusive. I'm dropping the nickname."

"Right, thanks for the scoop. Nice one." That was a stroke of luck. "So, Harvey. What's it all about?"

"What the fuck is that supposed to mean?"

Jarvis took a chance. "I mean what are the new songs all about? Are you doing some new ones, there in the studio?"

"Where's your tape? Aren't you going to tape this?"

Jarvis took out his notebook. "I'll use this. Get it all down in black and white."

"Right. Old school, yeah? All right, cool. But I still want approval."

"Oh, yes, naturally. So. What's the scoop on the new songs, Harvey?"

"The usual shit from Nick and Tony. Saying they don't think my stuff is right for the band at this stage in our career. Saying we should do more covers, just because that's how we broke through. Okay, so we got to the semi-finals on some stupid bogus TV talent show by singing covers. But that was two years ago! They don't seem to realize, I've evolved as an artist since then. And does Bruce support me? Does he fuck. Oh, sure, when we're alone he tells me how much he loves where I'm taking the whole vibe, then when we're in the studio he won't back me up when those two start dissing my creativity. As for Gavin, he doesn't give a fuck, anything for an easy life, thick as shit, dozy twat."

Jarvis shook his head and tutted. He wrote 'Bruce?' in his notebook. He had no idea what the kid was talking about. He needed to move things on but he also needed to tread carefully. "So," he said sympathetically, "Bruce doesn't back you up?"

"No. Two-faced cunt."

"What about Norfolk? Does he back you up?"

Harvey looked at him suspiciously. "What do you mean?"

"Raymond Norfolk. Does he, you know, give you... what you want?"

Harvey turned away and gazed out of the window. "What do I want? Ultimately? That's the question. I don't even know if I know what I want. I'm conflicted."

"But he could give you pretty much anything, could he?"

"Actually, he's already given me so much."

This was more like it. "Has he? What's he given you, son? I mean, Harvey?"

121

"Everything. And I'm giving it to other people. Passing it on."

"You're passing it on? What exactly are you passing on? And how much of it would you say you're passing on? And who to?"

Harvey turned on him, scowling. "You just don't get it, do you? It's like a chain. It's given to him, and he passes it on to people like me and I pass it on to other people, but only people who are open to it. It's like a sacred trust. But they won't let it happen. They're keeping us apart. It's all a big conspiracy, that's what it is. There are forces at work. Dark forces. Some people are just evil, that's what I believe."

This was definitely promising, especially the stuff about the supply chain, and the conspiracy. But dark, evil forces at work? What was all that about? A rival drugs gang? Or maybe something to do with Naked Man? The bestial make-up and weird dancing could have satanic implications. Maybe a cult. The kid was addled, that was the trouble. Best to try and pin down some basic facts. Jarvis chose his words carefully:

"So, you're saying Raymond Norfolk can supply you with anything you want, is that right?"

"What the fuck are you talking about?"

"I'm just asking what Raymond Norfolk is giving you."

"Why do you keep talking about him? I thought this was meant to be an interview with me! I don't want to talk about him any more." Harvey turned away from him and gazed out of the window.

"Fine, no problem," Jarvis said. "Let's talk about you."

Harvey didn't seem to hear him.

"In your own time," Jarvis said.

No response. Shit. Had he pushed him too hard? Best to let him settle down. Jarvis opened his thermos and poured some coffee into the plastic lid that doubled as a cup. It was almost cold. Still, better than nothing. He sipped it slowly. Experience of interrogations told him that he'd just have to wait. The boy would probably start talking again of his own accord, especially considering the state he was in. Drugs always made them talk, especially about themselves. They could talk about themselves all night, and frequently did, unless they were nodding out on smack or jellies or the like.

Jarvis revised his opinion of the coffee. Perhaps it wasn't better than nothing. And it would make him want to piss, as well. Or even worse, although he'd been pretty solidly constipated for the last three days, so he was probably safe.

"Do you want a picture?" Harvey said suddenly, twitching his head from side to side and then half turning towards Jarvis without looking at him.

Jarvis realized that the boy was gazing at his own reflection. Had been all the time. Narcissistic little sod. Completely engrossed. Still, best to humour him, and luckily he had the little digital Casio with him, that he'd brought along to get a record of everything so they couldn't accuse him of staging a moody bust.

He heaved himself around and rummaged in the pockets of his car coat on the back seat.

"Yeah, great. I've got a camera right here, as it happens." He found the camera and blew fluff off the lens.

Harvey turned to look at it. "That's a small one."

"Yeah, right. Discreet, you see."

"Not like the fucking paps. In your face all the time."

"Oh, no, not like them. They've got no class, have they? Here, I'll just turn the interior light on. Throw some illumination on the situation, yeah?" He flipped the switch above him, then he remembered about the battery, and turned on the ignition.

Harvey looked around wildly. "What the fuck are you doing? What's happening?"

"Relax, son!" Jarvis shouted over the howling grind of the ignition. The engine sparked at the last possible moment, as usual, and the car coughed into life. "The battery's a bit knackered, that's all. Doesn't hold much of a charge these days so it's best to run the engine if I want the lights or the radio or anything like that. Right, let's see."

He examined the camera. It all looked pretty simple. He raised it to his eye. Yes, it all looked fine. The kid's face more or less filled the frame and there was quite a nice effect with the darkness outside. He took the snap.

"Let's see it, then," Harvey said.

"Oh, right." Jarvis had forgotten you could look at the pictures right away on these things. He peered at the display. Not bad. He let Harvey see it.

"I look like shit."

"No, son, you look lovely."

"Lovely? Do you think so?"

Jarvis looked at the picture again. "Yeah. Very handsome. Brooding. Very nice."

"Do you want to suck my cock?'

Jarvis dropped the camera and it fell into the cup that was clamped between his thighs. Coffee splashed onto the lap of his trousers, joining the other stains that had accumulated there. At least it wasn't hot. He fished out the camera, shook it, and wiped it on his sleeve.

"I beg you pardon?"

"I just wondered if you want to suck me off. If you think I look nice."

"Er, not just now, thanks."

"Suit yourself."

"Thanks for the offer, though. Very kind."

"I'm not gay, you know."

"No, I didn't think so. Not at all."

"But I am tormented about my sexual identity."

"Are you? Oh, well, happens to the best of us."

"Write that down. It's an exclusive. 'As he opened his heart to me Spike revealed, no, Harvey revealed that he was tormented about his sexual identity.' Go on."

"Yes, right, of course." Jarvis put the camera and the coffee cup carefully on top of the dashboard, wiped his hands on the car seat and wrote 'queer' in his notebook. He smiled at Harvey. "Thanks. Nice one."

Harvey turned away. He seemed to be drifting off again. He'd be back. Jarvis groped for the box of tissues on the floor behind his seat. Only a few left. He began to dab at the damp patch on his trousers, trying to soak up the worst of it.

*

This guy is a complete twat. He just doesn't get it. Why does he keep asking about Raymond Norfolk? I'm the one who should decide if we talk about him, tell him about the, what's the word, the affinity we've got going between us, even though Raymond might not know it, although he probably does, he probably picks up on the vibe people like me put out, even without actually meeting me. Because I've got a very strong psychic aura, that woman in Blackpool said, I'm very sensitive, very in touch with my essence. And it's true, I am in touch with it, and when I feel things I just go with them, very natural, like a beautiful animal. That's why I asked this dude if he wanted to suck me off, because I suddenly got a horny rush from the E, that mellow sex vibe, wanting to be touched and come. That's what this guy here needs, a good hit of E, open his mind a bit. Then he might be able to understand me. None of them really understand me. Even Raymond Norfolk might not, if they ever let me talk to him. Because I'm a very complex person. Conflicted. That's what people like this dude just don't get. They're all too obsessed with themselves and their own identity. Seriously, maybe I should spike this guy. I'm Spike the spiker! Except I'm not Spike any more. But I could just drop a tab of E into his coffee thermos while he's busy dabbing at his bollocks like some horrible old pervert. Fuck it, I will. I'll turn him on to what's really happening, the whole space where my creativity comes from, then he'll get it. Why not? I'm doing him a favour. Two tabs, that's what he needs to really get him out of his mind. I've got plenty, and Bruce has got that whole fucking bagful stashed in the cistern. I'll do it now, while he's not looking. Just slip them out of my pocket here. Got them. Two tabs, that'll do it. Here you go, mate, try this for size. This'll spread your head. Brilliant. He'll go mental. Maybe I should stay and watch. But I get bored when other people start tripping, they just start talking bollocks, so I don't think I will. Fuck me, that last valium has just hit the spot. I feel good now. What am I doing in this loser's car anyway? I'm going to go back and tell Nick and Tony what's happening, really happening, get them to see the truth behind all the mind games. Even if it takes all night. Because I love them, really. I love everyone, That's my whole thing, actually, I've got so much love to give. Okay, I'm out of here.

*

"Wait," Jarvis said, "what are you doing?"

"Got to go, mate."

"No, no, hold on. What about the interview?"

"I'm bored with it now. I've given you some good stuff, anyway. Just make the rest of it up and then email it to Bruce for approval. No, wait, not to Bruce. I don't want him to see it. I'm the one who should have approval. Except I can't be bothered. Just write what I told you. And maybe drop some hints that I might be thinking about leaving the band. Yeah, that'd be good. That'll make them see how much they need me."

"But there's still a lot we haven't covered. Insights."

"What sort of insights?"

"Well, I was wondering about drugs, for example."

Harvey turned and looked at him suspiciously. "What about drugs?"

"Um, torment."

"What are you talking about?"

"Drugs torment. Like when you said you were tormented by sex."

"My sexual identity, I said."

"Right, exactly. I just wondered if there was another good story there. All about how you were driven to do things. Led astray, perhaps. By someone older for example. And you got mixed up in drugs, even though it's not your fault. Got tormented. You know. My Drugs Hell. That kind of thing."

Harvey started laughing and didn't stop until he had a severe coughing fit that left him heaving and wheezing.

"What's so funny?"

Harvey shook his head, hanging onto the half-open car door to stop himself from falling out. When he could finally speak, he gasped, "It's just funny, that's all."

"Why? Come on, tell me?"

"Nothing. My Drugs Hell." He burst into uncontrollable laughter again. Finally he calmed down.

"Tell me about it, Harvey," Jarvis said. "Get it off your chest. You'll feel better." Jarvis picked up the thermos mug from the top of the dashboard and took a swig of cold coffee while he waited for Harvey's response.

The boy watched him closely. For a moment it seemed as if he was about to go into hysterics again, but he controlled himself. He looked away. "You'll find out," he said.

"What do you mean? How will I find out?"

125

"Never mind. I've got to go. And don't use that picture. Get one of my latest ones from our publicity people. I mean it, if you use that other one I'll say you molested me. Slipped me drugs and took advantage." He started laughing again as he flung open the car door, tumbled out, and staggered away into the darkness. Jarvis listened to the sound of his laughter fade away into the darkness.

Shit. It had all looked so promising. But he'd got some useful information. The boy was definitely on drugs, and he was very touchy on the subject of Raymond Norfolk, so that confirmed a connection. And then there was all that stuff about a conspiracy. Meanwhile, Naked Man and Rabbi Cowboy were still inside. They had some kind of role in all this. Yes, it was all fitting into place. Jarvis sipped the cold coffee. Christ, it tasted foul. Even worse than before. Bitter. Oh, well. He finished what was in the cup anyway. He gazed out into the night. The sky was very clear and the moon was rising. He had a strong hunch that something interesting would develop tonight.

*

James, Jessica and Reuben left just before midnight.

Reuben was a bit unsteady but not as bad as he'd been earlier. He'd gone very quiet not long after Raymond's confrontation with Bruce, and not long after that he fell off the piano stool. He lay on the floor laughing, and when James tried to help him up he became belligerent and asked James if he wanted a fight. When James declined, Reuben scrambled to his feet, apologized profusely and tried to kiss him. He then delivered a few snatches of song before lying on the sofa and going to sleep. After twenty minutes he woke up suddenly and made his way rapidly from the room. A few moments later the others heard him being sick outside the window. When he returned he said he'd managed to direct most of the vomit into an empty flowerpot, announcing the achievement with the air of someone who'd pulled off a delicate feat of engineering under difficult conditions. He claimed to be completely refreshed, but when he showed signs of wanting to continue drinking the others persuaded him it was time to leave. He allowed himself to be helped from the house quite happily.

As they were getting into the Range Rover Jessica said there was something she'd forgotten to talk to Raymond about, and she ran back to speak to him in the porch, where he was waiting to see them off.

James helped Reuben do up his seat belt. Now was his chance. He only hoped Reuben was sober enough to make sense.

"Listen, I had a call from Oliver."

"Oliver? Our Oliver?"

"Yes, Oliver. Olly. He asked me to give you a message."

"Ah. Aha. I've been expecting a message. What did he say?"

"I'll only tell you if you tell me what this plan of yours is all about."

Reuben considered this for a while. "All right. I like you. Have I told you that?"

"Yes, you told me last night."

"Did I? Oh. Well, I still like you. So I'll tell you. What's the message?"

"If I tell you, promise you'll tell me what's happening?"

"Promise."

"Okay. Olly said to tell you to go for it."

"Aha! Great. It's on. Good."

"What does it mean? Go for it. Go for what? Quick, before she comes back."

"Tomorrow."

"No, tell me now!"

"No, I mean it's happening tomorrow."

"What? What's happening tomorrow?"

"That's when I'm doing it."

"Doing what?"

"The robbery."

"Oh, God. What robbery?"

"It's a secret. I can't tell anyone until afterwards. Wait, I've got to give you something, after I've done it. I can't remember all the details exactly, but I've got it all written down at home. Don't worry, it's in code. It's a brilliant code, it uses mystical number sequences from the kabbalah. It works by--"

"Just tell me about the robbery. Oh, shit, she's coming back. Quick, tell me! What are you stealing? Where? When?"

"Tomorrow."

"I know it's tomorrow, but when? Quick!"

"No, I mean I'll tell you tomorrow. When you come to lunch."

"What lunch?"

"You're all coming. Isn't that right, Jess?"

Jessica clambered into the driver's seat. "Isn't what right?"

"You're all coming to lunch tomorrow. All you lot. Isn't that right?"

"Oh, yes," Jessica said, starting the engine. She blew Raymond a kiss and reversed away from the porch. He waved and went back inside.

"After church," Jessica said.

James was going to ask Jessica more about going to church, but he was distracted by a car that was driving behind them, very erratically.

"Have you seen that guy behind us?" he asked Jessica.

"I know, he's all over the place." She put her foot down and they left the car's headlights far behind them. But the next time James looked over his shoulder, to check on Reuben, snoring in the back seat, he could still see the beams, weaving around in the far distance like unmanned searchlights.

They dropped Reuben off at the manor, where they watched him lurch in through the side door, then Jessica sped back down the drive and swung back on to the main road. There was no sign of the car that had been following them. Neither of them spoke for the few minutes it took to get back to the Longbourne's. James was wrestling with an important decision and Jessica seemed engrossed in her own thoughts.

Back inside the house James found himself facing her at the foot of the stairs, just as he had the previous night. He was determined not to go through the same uncertainty that had tormented him then.

"You know last night," he said.

"What about it?"

"Were you waiting for me?"

"To do what?"

"To come to your room. Tell me honestly."

Jessica shrugged. "I don't know. I thought I'd leave it up to you."

"I did come, you know. But I got the wrong room."

"Which room did you go to?"

"The one on the other side. Spracky was in there. And your great aunt."

"Oh. Were they being eccentric?"

"I've been trying not to think about what they were doing, to be honest. It was very embarrassing. I felt terrible about it."

"Probably best if you don't wander about in the middle of the night, then."

"All right, will you come to my room?"

Jessica smiled. She leaned close and kissed him on the cheek. "Wait and see," she whispered, then she brushed past him and began to trot upstairs.

"Wait," James said. "Tell me."

She turned and continued walking up the stairs backwards, smiling down at him. "I just told you," she said. "See you later!" She spun around again and trotted up the rest of the stairs without looking back.

James lay on his bed. It must mean she was coming. She couldn't not come, not after what she'd said. Wait and see. That must mean she was coming. He stretched and yawned. It had been a long day and he felt pleasantly tired. In a way, that would make it even better. To begin with they'd make love almost lazily, lingering deliciously over long, languid caresses, then slowly their hunger for each other would overtake them until they were transported into an uncontrollable frenzy of passion. She'd be here soon. He strained to hear a sound in the passage outside. He thought about opening the door and looking out. No, give her time, He'd only been waiting a few minutes. He closed his eyes.

*

Jarvis lay looking up at the stars. His car was parked a few yards away, at the edge of the village green, more or less in the spot where it had been that afternoon. The car door was open and the radio was on, tuned to some classical music, which was the only thing he could find at three in the morning, although he could only just hear it because he had to keep the engine running. But it didn't matter. The sound of the engine was just as beautiful as the music. It was just a different kind of music.

What an amazing thing a car was. When he'd first tried to leave Norfolk's place, to follow the Range Rover, he found that for some reason he'd forgotten how to drive. He was completely baffled. Then he understood. He realized that it was supremely arrogant to imagine that he could control the car, as if he was somehow superior to it. Once he accepted that, it was easy. The car could drive itself. All you had to do was lay your hands upon the lovely cool steering wheel, press the clutch pedal softly, caress the gear lever at just the right moment, allow your foot to rest on the accelerator in perfect sympathy with the vehicle. It was a partnership, based on trust, and understanding, and love. It was so simple. Everything was simple.

His body felt wonderful. Every fibre of his being was alive. The very air around him was stroking him like a lover. He could feel every blade of grass underneath him, every speck of earth. He understood Naked Man. The delicious feeling of having nothing between you and the world. In many ways he wished he could be completely naked, too. But somewhere in his mind was the certain knowledge that a police officer on duty could not remove all his clothes. That was why he'd kept his underpants on.

Jarvis heard a soft rustling, snuffling sound. He turned his head. It was a miracle. A living creature. A fellow organism, a partner in the great, glad dance of being. Like him, a child of the infinite cosmos. It was a hedgehog.

He lay as still as he could. Very slowly the hedgehog shuffled closer, wrinkling its delicate snout. Its bright black eyes glittered. Closer. He could see every miniscule hair on its tiny pink feet. Closer. He could smell it. Very carefully he reached out and touched its nose. The hedgehog froze, then curled itself into a ball. Amazing! He stroked the quills. He could feel it trembling beneath his hand. Tenderly he lifted it up and placed it on his chest. He rested his hand on top of it, feeling the life force within it, identical to the force within himself. He and the hedgehog were the same. What kept them apart? Only the ridiculous conventions of society. This little creature was his bride. He felt its paws scrabble against his skin. It felt exquisite. He loved the hedgehog with all his heart.

Seven

"I went to sleep last night."

"How very conventional of you."

"You know what I mean," James said. "I was waiting for you, but I must have just been exhausted after everything that happened yesterday."

"Sounds like you needed to sleep, then."

"But did you come?"

Jessica didn't say anything and kept walking towards the gates. James skipped around in front of her and turned to face her, walking backwards. She wouldn't meet his eye, and looked down with a shy smile, which made her appear even more demure than she already did in the simple little flowered summer dress she'd put on to go to church. She was also carrying a light raincoat because, incredibly, a few spots of rain had fallen earlier from an utterly cloudless blue sky. There was no sign of rain now, but the coat, folded neatly over her arm, completed the impression of a well-behaved schoolgirl dressed for a special outing. Daphne Longbourne and Auntie Pru, who were ahead of them, both wore hats, and John Longbourne was in a dark suit. James had done his best, with some slightly shiny black trousers and a shirt that had once been white before it had fallen into bad company with a mixed wash at the launderette.

"You've got to tell me," he said. "Did you come to my room?"

"You'll never know, will you?"

"That's not fair. Please tell me."

He'd woken up at about five, still fully dressed, and hadn't gone back to sleep. He lay on the bed, tormenting himself with visions of Jessica, wearing a transparent nightdress, or, in some versions, nothing at all, tapping softly at his bedroom door, and then walking away sadly when there was no response.

She still wouldn't look at him. "Some people might say that what's not fair is someone asking you to come to their room and then going to sleep."

"Oh, God. So you did come?"

"I didn't say that."

"But did you?"

"Like I said, you'll never know. Look out, you're going into the bushes."

James turned around and fell back into step beside her.

"Gangway!" cried a voice from behind them.

Spracky trotted past. She was wearing a large straw bonnet, tied under her chin with a ribbon, and she was pushing a wheelchair.

"Who's that for?" James said.

"Auntie Pru. She doesn't actually need it, she can walk for miles. Quite often does. She just likes to be wheeled to church and sit there in it. She says it's

130

because her bottom's so bony, and she's entitled to have a comfy seat at her age."

As the path curved around through the bushes James saw that ahead of them the others were waiting at the gates. Spracky was patting down some cushions in the wheelchair while Auntie Pru stood by, giving instructions.

A figure emerged from the shrubbery beside the gates. It was Bill Longbourne. He was dressed in smarter versions of the tweed and corduroy clothes that James had first seen him in, and a faded brown Trilby. His moustache looked cleaner and he'd either trimmed or brushed it for the occasion. He exchanged a few words with his wife and his brother as Spracky settled Auntie Pru into the wheelchair.

"There's your father," James said.

"I know."

"I just didn't expect to see him. Is he coming to church?"

"Yes, he and Mummy always sit together in the family pew."

"As if they were still married?"

"They are still married."

"Yes, of course. But don't people know? You know, about the arrangement."

"Oh, yes," said Jessica, "everyone knows. But you wouldn't expect Mummy and Uncle John to sit there in church together, would you?"

"Why not?"

Jessica glanced at him, frowning. "It's just not done, is it?"

They had nearly reached the gates.

"Listen," James said, "can we, you know, get together later on?"

She grabbed his arm and whispered, "I expect so, but I can't possibly discuss it now. We're on our way to church, after all. Try to have some respect for the religious feelings of others." She licked his ear, and then skipped ahead to join the family.

James squinted up at the bell tower. It appeared to be leaning slightly. The church was set back from the road at a slight angle, and the tower was taller than it looked at first glance. It loomed over the Post Office, which partly obscured its base from the road, so James only got a sense of its true height when he was standing in the churchyard, where the grass was dotted with tipsy gravestones, some of which had sunk so far into the soil that they were little more than mossy humps. An ancient yew stood on one side of the path that led to the porch, and the church windows displayed some simple tracery. Thirteenth century, thought James.

He'd been vaguely aware that someone in a dark cassock was greeting people at the church door but it was only when he and Jessica were almost under the porch, shuffling in behind John Longbourne, that he saw it was Raymond Norfolk.

"Hello, mate," Raymond said, shaking James's hand.

Jessica kissed Raymond on both cheeks.

"What are you doing here?" James asked.

"I'm a verger. I prefer it to my local in Nether Gurney, which is a bit of a Victorian monstrosity. This place has got some awesome brasses. I do a bit of rubbing every now and again."

James remembered seeing some framed brass rubbings when he was looking around Raymond's place the night before. "I thought you were a Buddhist," he said.

"I am. Among other things."

"What about the vicar? I mean, does he mind? You being other things?"

"Simon? Oh, he's happy about it. He's an old fan of the band, as it happens. And I think he'd rather have me inside the tent pissing out, if you know what I mean."

"Don't use language like that on Sunday," Jessica said.

"Sorry."

"Do vergers always wear a cassock?" asked James.

"It's optional," Raymond said, doing a little twirl so that the skirt of the cassock flared out. "But Simon runs quite a High Church operation here. You'll like it. It's worth listening up: he gives great sermon. What do you think of the place, anyway?"

"Is it thirteenth century?"

"Early fourteenth, most of it."

"It's surprisingly large."

"Ullage used to be a sizeable market town," Raymond said. "It declined along with the wool trade, and now it's three separate villages, like islands. This part is what's left of Ullage proper, then there's Ullage Bottom, down where the council houses are, then there's Ullage Parva, along the road, where the pub is. So this church was built for a large congregation. It's got some lovely features. There's a nice little Lepers' Squint around the side. I'll show it to you later."

"Poor old lepers," Jessica said. "As if they didn't have enough problems already, without squinting."

"No," James said, "a Lepers' Squint is a kind of slit in the wall so that they could stand outside and look in, and see the altar during the service, without being seen by the congregation. So they wouldn't be denied a sight of the sacrament."

"Oh, how sad," Jessica said. "I can just see the brave little lepers, huddled out here in the rain with bits dropping off them."

"Sounds like the title for a song," Raymond said. "Lepers in the Rain."

"By the way," James said, "what happened about that guy from the band last night? The singer guy."

"He wandered back in eventually. Stayed up all night talking crap, apparently. And, after all that bullshit about needing to talk to me, he couldn't even be bothered to get up in time to catch me before I left. So, fuck him. Greetings in

132

the body of Christ, Mrs Rosser!" Raymond flashed a dazzling smile over James's shoulder. "It's a glorious day!"

James turned to see a small, beaky woman, gripping a very old man firmly by the elbow. She shoved the old man through the porch ahead of her and simpered girlishly at Raymond as she slithered past him.

"God bless you, Raymond," she said, and followed the tottering old man inside, prodding him in the back to keep him going.

"That's probably the last of the punters," Raymond said, looking at his watch. "You'd better get inside. Nearly show time. Good house today. Go on, in you go. I stay out here for a while in case there's any latecomers. See you afterwards."

James considered the problem of his knees. They were wedged tightly between the back of pew in front of him, and the shelf for hymn books that jutted out from it, pressing down on them. He was sitting at the end of the pew, so he'd been able to slide in from the side aisle with his legs already bent, but now he couldn't move them. Of course, people had been smaller many years ago, but this seating seemed to have been designed for a congregation of midgets. The Little People. James had a sudden vision of ghastly, shrunken figures capering around in the woods; elderly children with wizened, simian faces, cackling with laughter. It made him shiver. He tried to shift his legs, and collected a splinter in the top of his shin.

He leaned forward and peered along the pew to see how everyone else was coping. When Jessica had spoken of 'the family pew' he'd imagined something in its own separate nook, with plush velvet upholstery, but the Longbournes were in the third row from the front, in a hard wooden pew that was no different from any of the others.

Jessica, who was next to him, saw him looking at her legs, and crossed them, exposing more flesh. He was surprised she had room for the manoeuvre, which was out of the question for him, even though he wasn't all that much taller than her. Perhaps he just had uncommonly long thighs. He saw that Daphne Longbourne, next to Jessica, appeared to have plenty of space. Her husband, on her right, didn't seem to have a problem, and neither did John Longbourne, who was more or less the same size as Bill, and sat next to him. At the far end of the pew, Spracky's stumpy little legs barely reached the floor. Auntie Pru's wheelchair was parked in the nave, next to Spracky. It took up more than half of the width of the nave, but no one seemed to mind. When a couple of latecomers had to negotiate the obstruction to get to the front pew, they simply smiled and nodded to her deferentially as they squeezed past.

James heard a heavy door close behind him. He craned around and saw Raymond Norfolk striding up the nave, his cassock swirling. He took his place at the end of the front pew, directly below the pulpit.

The church was full. James had been astonished to see so many people when he'd come in. Nearly two hundred, he estimated. The news that Anglican church attendance was in severe decline all over Britain obviously hadn't reached Ullage. As James looked around, he recognized several faces from yesterday's fete, including some of the young, unruly element, which was a surprise. He spotted Jason Pringle and one of his friends, right at the back. Jason looked clean and sleek, and when he caught James's eye, he nodded solemnly at him and then looked down.

The congregation fell silent. Someone coughed. For several moments nothing happened, then a door beside the altar opened and Simon Cottle emerged.

James hadn't been to church very much. He thought his parents probably saw religion as something exotic and slightly embarrassing that was best not done in public, like crying or homosexuality. He and his parents went to church at Christmas and sang carols, which was a purely social activity, but the topic was avoided the rest of the time. Then, just after his father died, his mother became a churchgoer for a while. James's memory of that time was patchy - blanketed in a kind of fog - but he recalled going to services with her, where he sat, and stood, and sang, and prayed, obeying the murmured instructions that drifted through the damp, almost empty church like the hopeless pleas of an exhausted ghost. He seemed to remember that she went quite frequently but she only took him with her occasionally. He had no idea if his mother found what she was looking for in the bland, apologetic Anglican services conducted in the local church but she stopped going after a few months. Not long after that James went to a new school that was nominally a church establishment, with prayers and hymns in morning assembly, but he and his mother moved to a different area within the year, and his next school was less concerned with spiritual welfare than with the prevention of truancy, arson, and gang warfare in the playground.

This sporadic acquaintance with the Church of England now enabled James to recognize most of the morning's hymns and prayers, but the service itself seemed more elaborate than those he remembered. Raymond was right about it being High Church. It seemed to James that if it got any higher it would leave the gentle Anglican foothills altogether and stray up into the incense-shrouded precipices of Rome.

The most flamboyant sign of this tendency was the vicar himself. Simon Cottle's vestments frothed with embroidery and lace, and were adorned with accessories that favoured various shades of purple. His plump, pink face was serene and serious, and he moved with ceremonial deliberation, investing each action with solemn reverence.

134

James found himself unexpectedly impressed. Simon seemed to have acquired dignity and stature here in his own church. James hadn't really considered Simon in this capacity. Until now, he'd thought of him as a good sport who'd agreed to play the role of a vicar in a kind of community amateur dramatic production. But he was the real thing.

Simon began to intone something in Latin that James vaguely recognized. It sounded stern and implacable, but strangely comforting at the same time.

Looking around, James saw some of the brasses that Raymond had mentioned. They were highly polished, and glittered in the light from the small stained-glass windows. There was also an interesting tomb in a recess in the wall, further along the aisle. The life-size marble figures of a medieval lord and lady lay side by side on top of it. A carved shield rested on the knight's breast, and a hound was curled at his feet. There was some kind of animal nestling at the lady's feet as well: a small, spiky creature. A porcupine? James strained to see it. The quills seemed too short for a porcupine. No, it looked more like a hedgehog.

James became aware of a tense silence. He looked up to see that Simon Cottle was walking slowly up the steps to the pulpit. When he reached the top, he lifted the hem of his vestments aside so they didn't get caught in the little wooden gate as he closed it behind him. He produced a sheaf of notes from somewhere within his robes, and studied them for a few moments. Finally he looked up and gazed around at the congregation.

"Today's sermon," he said, "is about ecumenical co-operation in the worldwide Christian communion."

He paused, then leaned forward.

"But let's be honest. How boring is that?"

A few people in the congregation made a polite, amused sound, that wasn't actual laughter, but indicated a willingness to produce some if required.

"So I'm not going to deliver that sermon," Simon continued. "I changed my mind. And one thing that made me change my mind, apart from deciding that no one deserved the balls-aching tedium of hearing me talk about such a dull subject - including me - was something that struck me as I wandered around the fete yesterday.

"And let me just take this opportunity to thank everyone involved in the fete. Not least, of course, Dave and Sylvia Silver. Although they don't share our faith, I don't think they'd be offended if I say that I find their generosity truly Christian. But the whole event was a magnificent effort, that raised a lot of money for a number of good causes, not least the restoration fund for our bell tower. As you know, its condition is giving increasing cause for concern, but I'm delighted to say that we're now very close to our target. Anyone who'd like to dig into their pocket or purse one more time to ensure that work can start even sooner should speak to Raymond afterwards."

Simon glanced down towards the front pew, and James saw Raymond nod.

"So, we can all give thanks for that," Simon said. "But now let me tell you what it was that struck me yesterday, as I wandered around, watching everyone enjoying themselves. What struck me was how absolutely hammered a lot of you got."

There were a few uneasy chuckles as Simon looked slowly around the church. His eyes came to rest on James. For a terrible, chilling moment he thought he was going to be singled out in front of everyone. But then Simon's gaze moved on, and when he'd taken in the whole congregation he smiled and shook his head.

"Don't get me wrong," he said, "I like a drink as much as the next person. Nothing wrong with the occasional beer, or glass of wine. What was it that St Paul said? 'Take a little wine for thy stomach's sake.' Although he might have had second thoughts about that if he'd been pole-axed by Jackie Leppard's cider punch."

That got a laugh, but it was tentative. You couldn't tell where Simon was going with this, thought James, and it was effective. He was keeping it light for the moment, but you got the sense that something was on the way. A storm brewing.

"But Jackie doesn't force you to drink the stuff," Simon continued. "You could just have a glass or two, and leave it at that. A medical friend of mine used to talk about The Plateau of Maximum Contentment. We reach it, and that's as good as we're going to feel, and we know it. And yet we persist in pushing ourselves over the edge of that plateau, and down the steep, slippery slope that ends in a drunken brawl, or a puddle of vomit, or both. Or worse. Why do we do it? Why do some of us feel that we're not enjoying ourselves unless we over-indulge? And what, exactly, is over-indulgence?

"Well, it's fine line. But it's always there. Everyone has a different capacity, of course, but each of us knows where that line lies for us. And what happens once we cross over that line? We change. We're still ourselves, but we're our worst selves. Vicious, ugly, brutes. Animals. Worse than animals. Because animals have no choice. But we can choose. And when we choose to abandon all the special, finer qualities that make us uniquely human, we choose to sin."

James felt something fluttering against his thigh. He looked down to see that Jessica's light blue raincoat, which had been draped across the back of the pew, was now on the bench between them, partly covering his leg. It must have slipped down. Unless Jessica had moved it, but why would she do that? Then he felt her hand creep under the coat and come to rest on his thigh.

For a moment James thought she didn't realize what she was doing. He glanced at her. She was gazing up at Simon, apparently engrossed. Then, quite deliberately, she moved her hand up his leg.

Even though James could hardly believe it was happening, he had a calm, elated sense of things fitting, finally, into place. He closed his eyes.

"Damnation!"

James looked up with a start to see Simon leaning forward in the pulpit, gripping its sides. The exclamation seemed to be the conclusion to something he'd been saying, and now he paused, looking around and nodding slowly.

"Yes," he continued, finally, "it's the same fine line. The line between salvation and damnation. But there's no recovery from damnation. No sleeping it off. No long walk to clear your head, no lunchtime in the pub for a hair-of-the-dog to make you feel better. No cure. It's the hangover from hell. It's the hangover *in* hell. And it goes on for ever."

Jessica moved her hand further up, burrowing in between the top of James's thigh and his groin. His cock swelled and stiffened.

"Damnation!" Simon cried again. He shook his head. "Do we really understand what that means? Do we have any sense of its reality? It's just a swear word for most of us, and a relatively mild one at that, in these days of casual obscenity and profanity, a word we might use in front of an elderly aunt, instead of stronger language. Although, believe me, if that elderly aunt had used the word when she was a girl, she might have been sent to her room, or had her mouth washed out with soap. It was a word that used to mean something. Something real."

James caught a movement out of the corner of his eye. He leaned forward slightly and looked along the pew. In the nave, Auntie Pru was shaking her head slowly, a sardonic smile twisting her handsome face. As he leaned back, Jessica turned her hand slightly and nestled it around his groin, cupping it and moving her fingers lightly. He gasped, and tried to cover the sound with a light cough.

"So, what does it mean? What happens when we are damned? When, through our own choice to sin, and sin, and sin again, we finally cross that line for ever? When, after all the warnings, and the second chances, and the promises, we suddenly find that we can't go back? What does it feel like?

"I'll tell you what it feels like. It feels like being lost. Utterly, hopelessly lost. Abandoned. You yearn for home. But you have no home. You ache for love, and kindness, and comfort. But there is no love for you; no kindness, not even a word; no comfort, not for a second. You feel cold. You turn, and try to cross back over the line. But you can't. Then you realize that you're trapped. And that's when it starts."

Jessica began to stroke the fabric of James's trousers where his cock was straining against it. He was convulsed by a sharp intake of breath, which he disguised as a hiccup. Jessica's mother leaned forward and shot him a quick, irritated glance.

"I read a fascinating article the other day," Simon said, adopting a more conversational tone. "It was about the atoms in our bodies. It said that there's so much space between them that if you took away all the space, the atoms themselves would have almost no volume at all. In fact, without the gaps

137

between them, all the atoms that make up all the people in the world would fit inside a matchbox. Amazing. That would be a very crowded matchbox. Imagine being inside it. Stuffed in there along with billions of other tiny little people. Literally billions. Billions of souls, crying out in torment."

James shot Jessica another sidelong glance. She squeezed his groin gently, still gazing serenely up at Simon, who had paused again. James tried to distract himself by thinking about what Simon had just said. There was something familiar about that last phrase. Souls crying out in torment. What was it? Star Wars, that was it. When Obi-Wan talks about a huge disturbance in the force. As if a million voices suddenly cried out in terror, and then were silenced. It was still the best film, that first one. The next two were pretty good, but those later ones - what was George Lucas thinking of?

"Help!"

Simon's voice made James jump, pressing him more tightly into Jessica's cupped hand. He felt as if his cock was about to rip through the fabric of his trousers. He tried to breathe deeply and evenly. He had a sudden vision of Raymond Norfolk doing yoga, breathing deeply as he bent over and touched his toes. James found the image erotic, which was disturbing. But then, he thought, almost anything would seem erotic in his present condition. The cold marble image of the lady on the tomb would seemed erotic. He glanced at it. It did.

"Help!" Simon shouted again. He looked around, his eyebrows raised theatrically. He cupped his hand to his ear and turned from side to side. He shook his head slowly.

"Nothing. And yet each one of those doomed souls crammed inside that tiny matchbox still believes they have a right to God's mercy. Each one is so preoccupied with their own petty, selfish concerns, they don't understand that they've been abandoned. 'Lord have mercy on me,' one of them might cry out, 'for I am sick!' Sorry, chum. He's not listening. Another might cry out, 'Oh, God, help me, my family are starving!' So what? Join the queue. Yet another might say, 'Lord, pity me in my misery, my wife and children have been raped and murdered, and I'm being tortured in a dungeon by an oppressive regime.' Tough luck, mate. Write to Amnesty International. Does that seem harsh? Maybe. But it's nothing - nothing at all - compared to the harshness of hell.

"You see, these lost, doomed souls don't realize where they are. They're in a matchbox. That's all we are to God, all of us: billions of tiny, insignificant nonentities, stuffed into the matchbox of our universe. That universe may seem big to us, but not to God. Where is our wonderful, vast universe, that's so special and unique? In a matchbox, crammed away at the back of a drawer. And that drawer is in the kitchen of a house, and that house is in a street in a small town, in an unremarkable country, on a world that is one of billions of worlds in a vast galaxy that is just one of billions of galaxies, and those billions of galaxies are all - all of them, every single one of them - all crammed into another matchbox, in another drawer, in another house on another world in another galaxy and so on, and on and on, for ever and ever and ever."

A bolt of electricity shot up James's spine as Jessica's fingers closed around his cock, which leapt and twitched under her grip. It struggled to spring upright but was painfully constrained. If only he could move, just a little. Oh, God, he thought, how much longer can I bear this?

"Why cry out to God?" Simon asked. "Do you think He hears us, as we bleat and wail about our little problems? It would be a miracle if He did. But then, of course, He's in the business of miracles. So maybe He does hear us. He hears billions of tiny, squeaking voices, wafting out of that matchbox in the drawer. But why should He do anything about it? We've rejected Him. We'd rather hide in the matchbox of our own sin. We deserve to be left in there to rot. Stewing in alcohol, groping and poking at each other in the damp, fetid darkness. Spitting and cursing, spewing vile obscenities, cowering in loathing and terror, punching and kicking each other in rage, rutting like beasts in a frenzy of lust, reproducing blindly, filling up the matchbox with more and more doomed souls, until there's no room to move at all. We're squashing each other. The life is being pressed out of us. We're suffocating! Can you feel it? The air is getting thicker. It's getting difficult to breathe. It's getting warm, isn't it? Warmer and warmer, as we fight for those last precious molecules of oxygen, but they're all being used up, hardly any left as we squirm in the teeming throng, pressed in so tight we can't even raise our arms to shove our neighbour out of the way in the sweltering mass, the sweaty, heaving bodies steaming in the heat, the itching, throbbing heat, it's unbearable, it's so hot!"

James heard someone behind him wheezing asthmatically. He felt that the temperature in the church had, in fact, risen in the last few moments.

"And we're trapped!" Simon cried. "Really and truly trapped!"

He placed hands on the edge of the pulpit and leaned forward. When he spoke, his tone was conversational again.

"You know," he said, "it's a well-attested fact that up until quite recently, people were buried alive on a regular basis. Quite a lot of people. Oh, yes. Before medical science began to understand about things like coma and unconsciousness. Especially in the days when it was important to get people buried quickly. Think about it."

Simon flung out his arm and pointed to one of the windows.

"Statistically," he said, "it's an absolute certainty that at least one person in that churchyard out there was buried alive. Possibly several. And what's more, we know, from archaeological evidence, that sometimes people regained consciousness once they had been buried. Yes. They woke up. Think about that. All of you."

Keeping his arm outstretched, he swivelled it around, pointing at every section of the church in turn. When he had swept the whole congregation he dropped his arm.

"Imagine it," he said, lowering his voice. "You open your eyes. You're drowsy. It's pitch black. Not a glimmer of light. It's stuffy. Where am I? The last thing you remember is being ill. Lying in bed. The doctor was there. He looked unhappy, poor man. Then you smell it. Damp wood. That's strange. And something else. Earth. Lots of earth. Very close. No. Surely not. It can't be! Oh, dear God, no! Panic. You shake and twitch with utter, howling panic. You scream, you beat your fists against the wood, you kick with all your might, but all the time the paralyzing horror is creeping through your veins like ice as the certainty takes possession of you: there's no way out, you're doomed, you're already dead and buried, buried alive; you gasp for air, you take great heaving, shuddering gasps - of what? Of nothing, there's no air left, only your own warm, moist breath, pumping in and out of you, getting thicker and hotter every time, it's no good, there's nothing left to breathe, strange, sickly lights flare and pop in your eyeballs, you're fainting, losing it, fading away, no, you've got to get out, you claw at the wood that's only inches from your face, ripping your fingernails out as you tear at it, you rip your nails to bloody stumps and the blood drips down into your eyes and mingles with the tears that choke you as you scream and scream and scream for help, help, HELP!"

James could hear many of the people around him taking quick, feverish gulps of air. His own breathing was far from steady, but that was at least partly because Jessica was rubbing his cock through his trousers with hard, rhythmic strokes. He couldn't take much more of this. He wanted to come, to explode, but his cock was trapped so tightly that he didn't think he could. The effect was agonizing.

"You scream, you wail, you howl," Simon said, gazing fiercely at the congregation, "but all the time you know that nobody will hear. Of course they won't. They buried you, you're dead!"

Suddenly he raised his hand, dramatically.

"But wait. What's this? A sound? Did the wood just creak? Maybe it's just settling. No, listen! A scrape of earth against the coffin lid? Can it be? Did someone hear you screaming? Someone who happened to be in the graveyard? Who could it be? Who could possibly have heard your hopeless, muffled cries through the wood, the earth, the grass? You know the answer."

Simon nodded slowly.

" 'And they heard the voice of the Lord God walking in the garden in the cool of the day.' Genesis, chapter three, verse eight. Who else could it be? God walks in his garden. All his gardens. He hears. He hears everything. Every sound, every tiny, muffled cry in every one of His infinite worlds within worlds. He's present all the time in every inch of every one of them. And His mercy is boundless. Even for the dead, abandoned wretch who rejected his maker through the foulest sin, who cast Him off, who thought that he knew better, who didn't want God's love, who crawled into a hole to rot in shame and depravity, who had another chance, and then another, and then another,

140

and lost them all; even for you, God gives you yet another chance. He hears our cry. And now it happens - the miracle! Just as you're about to give up, just as you lose all hope and faith, just as you're sinking for the last time, deeper and deeper, down to the very bottom of the pit of despair, you feel a slight movement, a trembling, then a shaking, a dislodging, a lifting, the whole coffin is being raised, you hear the soil tumbling away, you feel yourself soaring upwards, you can smell fresher air, then chinks of light appear, wood parts from wood, light pours in, fresh, blessed air and light, bright sunlight, glorious blinding light, this is salvation, an end to sin, new life begins, reborn in love and light, this is salvation, this is resurrection, this is new life in death, you're saved! You're saved!"

James felt himself about to come. He closed his eyes and groaned.

The sound that escaped him seemed to act like a general signal for several people in the congregation. Groans and inarticulate cries filled the church.

"Hallelujah!" someone called out.

"Praise be!" from someone else.

"Stop!" cried Simon.

Jessica disengaged her hand from James's groin. He felt it slither away quickly, back under the raincoat. He teetered on the edge of orgasm, tensing every muscle in his body to avert the plunge.

"Stop!" Simon said again.

James opened his eyes to see Simon gripping the edge of the pulpit with white knuckles. The veins in his neck throbbed like strings on a double bass.

"That's enough!" he shouted. "I will not have this, this... this evangelical exhibitionism in my church!"

He glared around, his eyes bulging. "I know what you're trying to do! But you're not going to turn this holy place into some kind of mad, gibbering, circus!"

James was entranced by the way the fine spray of spittle that flew from Simon's mouth created a tiny rainbow as it was caught in the light from the stained glass windows.

"What was that?" Simon shouted, looking around wildly. "Did I hear a tambourine? Come on, did one of you bring a tambourine in here?"

The church was completely silent.

Simon stood still, breathing heavily. Gradually his face flushed a deep crimson.

"I'm sorry," he said, after a few moments. "But we simply can't have that kind of thing. Groaning, and shouting out. It's just not on. This is a church service. It's not intended as some kind of feel-good therapy session. That's not what we're here for. And we're not here for vague, comforting waffle about spirituality and enlightenment. There's no place in this church for that kind of self-centred indulgence. This is not about 'personal growth.' People don't seem to realize nowadays..."

He trailed off and looked down. When he looked up, his expression was clearer.

"We're here to reflect," he said. "To think. Yes, we want to be uplifted, of course we do. But we're not here to lose ourselves in some kind of... mindless... ecstasy. Quite the opposite, in fact. We're here to find ourselves. To be mindful. To remain in ourselves, to stay in this place, in this moment, to reflect, seriously and soberly, on the words of the service, and of my sermon, and their meaning for us. And the message of my sermon, the point I was trying to make, is that God sets us free from sin. We are trapped by our sin, and God sets us free. Simple as that. God sets us free from sin." He crossed himself. "In the name of the Father, and of the Son, and of the Holy Ghost, Amen."

James didn't take much notice of the rest of the service. He wanted to attract Jessica's attention but she seemed to be ignoring him. He kept trying to catch a glimpse of her expression without turning to look at her directly, but after a while he found he was straining the muscles of his eyeballs. When it was time for the final hymn she stood up without looking at him. James found it difficult to stand up straight, and his oddly hunched posture attracted another withering glance from Daphne Longbourne. At the end of the hymn, as he toppled back into his seat, Jessica briefly flashed him a smile of pure, unsullied innocence.

When the service ended James shuffled out along the pew behind Jessica. His thwarted erection had just about subsided and his posture was nearly normal. He could have left by the aisle next to him, but he wanted to stay close to Jessica, so that he could talk to her quietly if there was a chance. Her mother was directly in front of her, so it might be tricky. The procession came to halt as it disgorged into the nave, which was jammed with people milling around, chatting to each other on the way out, and gradually coalescing into factions, families and parties for their next activity. The pub, then lunch, probably. James took a deep breath and reached for Jessica's elbow.

"Lunch," said a voice behind him, and a hand clapped him on the shoulder. He turned to see John Longbourne exposing his teeth at him. He'd been ahead of James a moment ago, but perhaps he'd stopped to talk to someone in the nave. Probably the extremely fat man with a shaved head James could now see, standing behind him.

"I assume you're joining all of us for lunch?" John said.

"Yes, I assume so. I mean, I'd love to, thank you."

"Don't thank me, thank the Silvers."

"The Silvers?"

"Yes. We're all lunching there. Didn't anyone tell you?"

"Oh. I'm not sure. Oh, yes, I think..."

142

"It's usually terrific. They've got a chef. A real maestro. And none of that kosher nonsense, either. Or is it halal? I can never remember with these buggers and their funny diets. Although why God should give a toss if you eat a prawn cocktail or not has always eluded me. Or is it something to do with cheese? Anyway, there's none of that with Dave and Sylvia. It'll probably be something traditional, like roast beef or lamb, but you wait and see what Antonio does with it. God, he's good."

John Longbourne licked his moustache.

"I look forward to it," James said.

"Good." John squeezed his arm. "By the way, do you need a car by any chance?"

"No, I can walk back, thanks."

"No, I mean to buy. A good, reliable, motor. My friend Perry, here, has got one for sale." He jerked a thumb over his shoulder at the fat man, who hoisted his eyebrows at James. "Bloody shame," John continued, "because he doesn't want to part with it, but he's just lost his licence. Haven't you, Perry?"

The man nodded ruefully, exercising a few of his chins.

"Mondeo," John said. "Beautiful condition. It's a real bargain because he needs the cash. Now he's got no licence he's lost his delivery job, and his mother needs specialist care in a home, and the fees are something shocking if you want anything over the bare minimum. Fuck-all help from the state, of course. Positively cruel, this government, don't you agree?"

"Yes, but--"

"Very economical, the Mondeo. And this one's a lovely runner. I'd buy it myself if I could."

"Actually," James said, "I can't drive."

"Oh. How about some driving lessons, then? Perry happens to be a qualified driving instructor as well, don't you, Perry?"

Perry smiled modestly.

"But if he's just lost his driving licence..." James began.

"Not yet. Nearly. Soon. The court case is soon. But not yet. Still plenty of time. And this would be the place to learn. Much better than London. We're on quite good terms with the local test examiner, you see, so I'm sure you wouldn't have too much trouble passing, if you know what I mean. In fact, we can guarantee it."

Behind him, Perry laughed, bringing all his chins into play.

John leaned in close to James. "A couple of lessons would do it. One this afternoon, one first thing tomorrow, get the test done by lunchtime. We can always get hold of the examiner, arrange for the fast-track option. Of course, the fees would have to reflect that. Basic economics. Time is money."

"That's very kind of you, but I don't think I can, really. Thank you, though."

"Oh, well. Let me know if you change your mind. Or if you want to take a bit of game back to town. Perry's got some lovely fresh venison, haven't you, Perry?"

Perry pursed his moist, pink lips and winked at James.

"I'll certainly think about it," James said.

"Good, good. Right, better have a word with old Simon. What did you think of the sermon? Not bad, was it?"

"It was quite unusual, I thought. Distinctive."

"Distinctive. Very good word for it. Yes, he puts on a good show. Gives me quite an appetite. Good, good. See you at the trough, then!"

John Longbourne squeezed around James and began to shove his way vigorously through the press of people in front of him. Nobody seemed to mind. Most of them were only hanging around and gossiping, and weren't in any hurry to get out. Auntie Pru's wheelchair appeared to be causing a fairly severe obstruction up ahead, although Spracky was using her elbows quite effectively.

James thought that perhaps he should do the same, as Jessica was now well ahead of him, nearly at the door. Maybe he could catch up with her in the porch, where there seemed to be another major bottleneck.

When he finally got there he found that the delay was caused by people stopping to talk to Simon. They were congratulating him on his sermon, and he was being modest, and apologizing for getting angry, and they were apologizing, in turn, for anything anyone in the congregation might have done to cause offence, and he was assuring them that they mustn't blame themselves, and they were insisting that he mustn't, on any account, blame himself, either. James felt a deep ancestral urge to join in with this quintessentially English pastime, and go and apologize for something, but resisted it.

He pushed his way out through the crowd, and found an even bigger throng of people in the churchyard. He peered around, standing on tiptoe, looking for Jessica.

"I think she's gone, mate."

Raymond Norfolk was beside him.

"Oh. Why do you think that?"

"Because she told me she was going."

"When was that?"

"Just a minute ago. She had to wheel the old lady home. Mother Sprackling wanted to do a bit of business with Perry Mason." He nodded towards the gate at the end of the path, where Spracky was talking to the fat man, who must have overtaken James on the way out, somehow.

"Is that really his name? Like on the TV?" James said.

144

"Yes. Quite funny, isn't it? He actually looks a bit like that actor, in a way. He was a big lad, too, Raymond Burr."

"But he wasn't actually fat," James said, "just bulky."

"That's true. And he had all his hair, as well. Unless it was a rug. You never know with these film stars. And Perry's fair complexioned. No, you're right, he doesn't look anything like him. Just wishful thinking, really. It would be fun if he did, but he doesn't. Things are as they are. Om Shanti. All is as it is. Holy shit, he's fat, though, isn't he?"

They watched as Perry threw back his head and laughed, sending ripples down the full set of chins, through his shoulders, and into his stomach, which undulated with its own internal tides, like a waterbed. Spracky laughed, too, and slapped him playfully on his bicep, which was so thick that his arms wouldn't hang straight down, and stuck out at an angle.

"She's probably negotiating to buy some of his venison," Raymond said. "She'll be able to feed the whole family for a week with a nice haunch of that."

"He tried to sell me some venison, actually," James said. "And a car."

"Was it the Mondeo? I hope you didn't buy it."

"God, no. Why, is there something wrong with it?"

"He's probably had it patched up by now, but the whole front end got smashed up when he hit the deer. Which is where the venison came from."

"John Longbourne told me he was selling it because he's lost his licence and he needs to pay for his mother's medical treatment."

"Bollocks," Raymond said, fondly. "I doubt if he's ever had a licence. Or a mother, come to that." He looked around at the crowd, which was thinning now. "Right. It looks like nobody wants to slip me any more dosh for the bell tower fund. I think I'll go and get changed, before someone decides to come and talk to me about God."

James felt a bit lost. "I'd better get back, I suppose."

"Hang on. Jessica asked me to tell you something."

"What was that?"

"She said, why don't you go straight on to the Silver's, and she'll see you there?"

James checked his watch. "Won't I be a bit early? It's only eleven-thirty."

"No, we'll be eating at one. And they like to get a few drinks in first."

"Are you coming, too?"

"Yup. In fact, if you wait a couple of minutes while I nip into the vestry, I'll walk over there with you. I wanted to talk to you anyway, as it happens. About Jessica."

Most people had gone by the time Raymond came back out, including Spracky. James hadn't seen her conclude her business with fat Perry, but he'd been looking at the church most of the time. Some of the masonry around the top of the bell tower had fallen off, and a couple of sizeable chunks were lying in the grass among the graves. The tower was definitely leaning. James took a few steps back along the path.

When he turned to get another look at the tower he saw Raymond emerging from the church. Simon was still chatting with a few parishioners in the porch. Raymond paused to shake hands with him. James noticed that he was wearing leather trousers.

"I came on the bike," Raymond said as he approached, "but I'll leave it here and walk over with you. It's around the back. Do you know anything about motorbikes?"

"Nothing at all. I've only been on the back of one a few times."

"Never driven one?"

"Well, I had a go once, but it tried to throw me."

Raymond laughed. "Sure that wasn't a horse?"

"Pretty sure, but I was a bit drunk. I was all right until I tried to change gear. Luckily I was on the grass. Well, I ended up on the grass, anyway. Mind you, if it was a horse, that might explain why I had problems trying to change gear."

Raymond laughed again, politely, then stopped. "Anyway, about my bike. It's an old Norton, and I'm trying to convert it."

"To Buddhism?"

"That would be interesting, but no, in fact I want to convert the engine to run on methane. You can do it with cars quite easily, but it's a lot harder with a bike. But I've got a very good mechanic working on it. There's a big TV celebrity living not far from me, I won't mention his name, but he's got a high profile as a tree-hugger, supports every ecological cause that's going. Anyway, he hired this same mechanic to get his Bentley and his SUV running on methane from chicken shit. The only trouble is they use an awful lot of it. So the guy's had to get a lot more chickens. Thousands of them. And he has to keep them all in a big shed, in cages, otherwise it's too difficult to collect all the shit. So, to get the chicken shit he needs to save the environment by running his cars ecologically he's ended up owning an ecologically disgusting industrial battery farm. And he throws all the eggs away. Amazing."

They walked through the gate and out into the road at the top of the village green. Raymond paused. He narrowed his eyes and looked around, scanning the green.

"What are you looking for?" James said.

"Here's a weird thing. You remember me telling you last night about that policeman who's obsessed with busting me?"

"Yes. You said he was a bit mad."

"Definitely. But I haven't heard anything about him for ages. At least a year. And then, when I was on my way into the church this morning, I could swear I saw him."

"Where?"

"In a tree."

146

"Really? Which one?"

"That big one at the far side of the green. He was right at the top. And he looked awful. Looked like he'd been sleeping rough for a while. But I'm sure it was him. I waved to him, but he ignored me. Or maybe he didn't see me. He was talking to himself. He was in a bad way, I thought. No one else was about yet, so I thought I'd just check in with Simon, then come out and see if he was all right. But when I got back out here, people were beginning to arrive, and there was no sign of him."

"Is he dangerous, do you think?" James said.

"He's never actually tried anything violent, all these years he's been harassing me. I think I might come back a bit later and have a look for him. I wouldn't like anything to happen to him."

"That's a very charitable attitude, considering what he's done to you."

"Not really. I'd like to talk to him. I might finally find out what his problem is with me. I'm intrigued. Yes, I might do that." He took another look around, peering up and down the street, and squinting in the sun as he scanned the village green again. "Nope. Can't spot him. Okay, let's go to the Silver's. We can go along the main road, or take the scenic route, around the back, which is a bit longer but it's nice country. Do you fancy a bit of a walk?"

"Sure," James said. "Let's go the long way."

*

Jarvis watched them from his nest inside the hedge on the village green. Raymond Norfolk and Naked Tiger Man, blatantly consorting in public. They were getting cocky. But they didn't know who they were dealing with. No sign of Rabbi Cowboy today, but he'd seen the young girl, pushing an old woman in a wheelchair. That was a classic ploy: using an invalid as a decoy. But a decoy for what? And there was something fishy about the handshake that Norfolk had given the vicar. Was there a Masonic connection? He hated freemasons. The force was full of them, and he was sure that his career had been held back because he wasn't one. Their tentacles spread everywhere. But if the vicar was involved, maybe that confirmed the information he'd received about a possible satanic connection. Where had that information come from, now he came to think of it? He couldn't remember, but it was firmly lodged in his mind. He tried to piece it all together: Norfolk, Naked Man and Rabbi Cowboy, the invalid decoy, the vicar, Satanism, the drugs operation... it was all getting confusing. He was finding it very hard to think clearly.

And he was extremely uncomfortable. But at least he couldn't be seen, inside the hedge. Not like the tree. He wasn't quite sure why - or how - he'd climbed a tree. But when Norfolk had arrived, he'd spotted him easily. Then, other people had started to appear in the distance, and he began to realize that his presence in the top of the tree might draw unwelcome attention. He'd climbed down as quickly as he could. Fallen, really, more than climbed, but he was pretty sure he'd managed to complete the descent before anyone had noticed him.

Luckily, he didn't think anyone had seen him burrowing into the hedge, either. He'd collected a lot of scratches in the process, to add to the ones he'd picked up on his way down from the tree. But neither the tree nor the hedge could explain the strange marks on his chest. Those were more than scratches, they were wounds. He undid the top of his shirt and looked at them. There were two kinds of marks: deep punctures, as though someone had been poking needles into him, and sets of gouges, like furrows. Almost like claw marks. Where had they come from? They were fantastically painful, and very itchy. But he tried not to scratch them because he could now see that some of the deeper wounds were going septic, with pus oozing out of them. The flesh around them was swollen and tender, displaying unhealthy shades of purple and yellow. He shivered. About a minute later he had another spasm of shivering, even though it was sweltering inside the hedge.

If Jarvis's mind had been working clearly, and if the relevant medical knowledge could have been found in it, he might have recognized the first stages of septicaemia, as the poison in his wounds began to enter his bloodstream. He would have known that the blood poisoning would get worse, and he would develop a fever, with the strong likelihood of delirium, which would combine with the ecstasy in his system to interesting effect. But the information wasn't there, and he simply wondered why he was feeling so cold, even though he also seemed to be sweating.

*

"What did you think of the sermon?" Raymond said. They'd just climbed over a stile and were walking across a wide field that sloped up to some trees. James had lost his bearings after Raymond led him through a series of lanes on the far side of the green, and he couldn't tell where they'd emerged in relation to the village.

"It was pretty scary," James said. "Does he always get like that?"

"Oh, Simon likes to give it a bit of fire and brimstone. The punters love it. They like to feel they're getting their money's worth. That stuff about being buried alive, that was classic. That really got them going."

"Exactly, yes, he got them going, but then he got angry when they started getting into it. What's all that about?"

"He's paranoid. He thinks New Age evangelical Christians are trying to infiltrate the place. Like I said, he's very High Church. They hate all that happy-clappy stuff. They still think that Methodists are the spawn of the devil."

"But if he doesn't want people to get - I don't know - elevated, or carried away, then why does he wind them up like that?"

"He gets carried away himself. I know the feeling, actually. It's like being on stage. You get taken over, in a way. A bit like being possessed, in fact." Raymond gazed into the distance, smiling.

"But it doesn't make sense," James said.

"It's not about making sense. That's not always what people want, is it?"

"I suppose not."

"Watch out for this next bit. It's a bit boggy down in the dip here. It never dries out, there must be a spring under there somewhere. Just follow me."

James was slightly out of breath when they got up to the trees, where the ground levelled out. He was glad of their cool shade as he and Raymond walked into the woods.

Neither of them had spoken as they'd negotiated the swampy dip in the middle of the field, or climbed up the slope, which was steeper than it looked. Now, as they walked through patches of dappled sunlight between the tall trees, James was anxious to find out what Raymond wanted to say about Jessica.

"How long have you known Jessica?" he said, by way of a hint.

"About four years. I met the Longbournes through the Silvers, actually. I used to know Dave Silver in London, when he was making money in the music business."

"Jessica didn't say he'd been in the music business."

"He's done all sorts. He's always been a wheeler-dealer. But he's cool. People like doing business with him, he's got this warm, friendly vibe. Good heart. But he's no fool. Sylvia gets all the attention, of course, and people think Dave's just this nice rich guy who drifts around in the background and pays for everything. But he's a very astute man."

"I thought he made all his money in computers. That's what Jessica said."

"Funnily enough, the computer business is about the only one he didn't make money from. I think he got a bit bored with it. So now he just concentrates on his environmental projects."

"Right, like this film about elephants. Jessica told me about that."

"Yeah. He's asked me to do the music for it. He's got some interesting ideas."

"But how did the Silvers get to know Jessica's family?"

James felt that if he kept mentioning Jessica's name, he might be able to focus Raymond's mind on what he was going to tell him about her.

"It was when they bought the house," Raymond said. "Which I turned Dave on to, as it happens. He said he wanted to buy a place in the country, and I knew Ullage Manor was up for sale. He and Sylvia came down, took one look, and bought it on the spot. Then Dave wanted to find out all about its history, so he got in touch with the Longbournes, because it used to belong to them years ago. Did you know that?"

"Yes. Jessica told me," James lied. "So, how did you meet her? Jessica."

"Dave found out she wanted to do some riding but she had nowhere to keep a horse. Bill's taken over all the spare outbuildings down there for workshops, and Dave has converted all the stables up at the manor. So she started riding one of my horses. We've been talking about her buying it, but nothing's settled. Do you ride?"

"Nothing with legs or an engine. I find that even bicycles can get a bit frisky."

"You should learn. It's fun. Especially riding to hounds."

"You mean hunting?"

"Yes. It's a blast."

"But you can't actually hunt foxes any more, can you? They changed the law."

"No one takes any notice of that. It's a joke. We had a big meet almost every week last winter. A lot of good kills, as well. Simon's hounds are awesome."

"You mean you kill the foxes?" James was shocked.

"Are you shocked?"

"No, not at all. Just a bit surprised. I just thought that with your beliefs..."

"I believe in the balance of nature. Why, do you think it's immoral?"

"No. Well, I don't know, really. What does Jessica think?"

"Jessica? Oh, she hates the idea of the little foxy-woxy being hurt."

"Right. And did you teach Jessica to ride?"

"No, she learned at one of those schools she went to. She's probably a better rider than me. Although she's completely reckless. She's a bit of a menace, actually. And not just on a horse. That's what I was going to mention to you."

They emerged from the trees. James saw that the side of the manor house was a few hundred yards ahead of them. On their right the lawn swept down to the ornamental lake, beyond which the ground rose in a patchwork of bright green and yellow fields, dotted with hedgerows and woods, stretching away to the hazy hills on the horizon.

"Nice view, isn't it?" Raymond said. "Apart from the windmill. Rather fucks the picture up, if you ask me."

They began to walk along the top of the lawn to the house.

"You were just telling me that Jessica was a menace," James said.

"Yes. The thing is, I can see you're a bit smitten. If you don't mind me saying so."

"No, of course not," James said, minding a lot, "but I don't know about being smitten. I mean, she's very attractive, but I hardly know her. And she's only seventeen."

"Nearly."

"Nearly what?"

"Nearly seventeen. She's still only sixteen at the moment."

"Oh. I see."

"Look, I'm sure you can take care of yourself. But I've watched her putting the moves on men since she was thirteen. And she was probably at it long before that. She's always been a heartbreaker and she knows it. And she loves it. She likes to get men excited about her. And she's very good at getting her own way. So, just take care, okay?"

"Well, thank you for the warning."

"Look, don't be pissed off. It's a bit like I'm her uncle or something. So I feel I can say these things."

"I'm not pissed off."

"Yes you are."

"Okay. I am. A bit."

"That's cool. I just wanted to let you know."

They walked on in silence.

"And then there's Oliver," Raymond said after a few moments. "Can I just ask how well you know him?"

"We work together. Not exactly together, but for the same company. And we hang out a bit. But you know what he's like. Do you? I mean, do you know him quite well?

"Does anyone?"

"I don't know. He tends to have a life of his own. I've no idea what he's up to, a lot of the time."

"That's probably quite a good thing."

"Yes, I expect so." James paused. Perhaps Raymond knew something about this scheme of Oliver's. Maybe he was even involved. "But why do you say that?" he asked cautiously. "Is there anything particular I should know?"

They were very nearly at the house. Raymond stopped and turned to him. As he opened his mouth to speak, a shrill whistle split the air.

They saw Max Fennel trotting towards them. A referee's whistle was clamped between his teeth. A bandage covered the whole of the top of his head so that his hair frothed out on either side of it, making him look like an elderly, absent-minded pirate. He was wearing a striped rugby shirt, baggy khaki shorts and dirty tennis shoes. His legs were spindly and leprously pale beneath a sparse, fuzzy coating of ginger hair.

He gave another blast on the whistle, and jogged up to James and Raymond. He was holding a stopwatch that was attached to a lanyard around his neck, and a clip-board was tucked under his arm. He removed the whistle from his mouth.

"Hello, you chaps," he panted, "have you seen the boys?"

"Which boys are you talking about, professor?" Raymond asked politely.

"The upper fifth. Always a bit of a troublesome lot. I sent them on a run to let off some steam. I'm giving them a pretty stiff history test later, based on the Balliol entrance exam. It'll be a tough challenge for them, but I think they're up to it. They're decent lads, really, even though they do get a bit boisterous. I thought they should blow the cobwebs away before they get down to it."

He stopped suddenly and peered at James.

"Ah, you're the new man, aren't you? Pleased to meet you." He thrust his hand out, then checked himself. He frowned. "No, hang on, sorry, we've already met, haven't we? Yes, of course, it must have been at the headmaster's cocktail party. Sorry, my mistake!" He beamed at both of them, then stuck his little finger in his right ear and began to excavate it enthusiastically while jogging on the spot. James got the impression he wasn't really seeing them.

Sylvia Silver walked up behind Max. She shrugged at James and Raymond, and spread her hands in a gesture of amused helplessness. She coughed, and laid a hand gently on Max's shoulder.

"It won't be long until lunch, Dr Fennel," she said, "why don't you come inside?"

"Oh, thank you, Matron. I'd completely forgotten about lunch."

He turned to James and Raymond again. "I'll forget my own head next!" He slapped himself on the head. He seemed perplexed to find the bandage there. He fingered it for a moment, then gave them a vacant smile. "I'll see you chaps in the dining hall."

He turned and began to walk back to the house. Sylvia went with him, hovering at his side, her hand discreetly poised to grasp his elbow, although Max seemed perfectly steady, and even began to jog again, consulting his clip-board.

Sylvia glanced back over her shoulder and smiled at James and Raymond, raising her eyes heavenwards.

Max stopped just before he reached the house, and turned to call back to them.

"I say," he shouted, "if you do see those boys before I do, remind them to clean up properly before lunch, will you? And that includes their kit, the grubby little beggars! But tell them to make it sharpish - no horseplay in the showers! All right?"

James and Raymond watched him turn and trot towards the house.

"Lunch could be interesting," Raymond said.

Eight.

"Don't worry," Dave Silver said, "he'll be all right. Eventually."

"What did the doctor say, exactly?"

James glanced over his shoulder at Max Fennel, on the far side of the room. He was explaining something to Auntie Pru, who was regarding him with distaste. She was installed in an old, high-backed armchair and Max was squatting beside her. He was still wearing his baggy khaki shorts, and as he bounced lightly on his heels with his legs apart, as if preparing for some gymnastic feat, James suspected that he was inadvertently exposing himself to her. Spracky was watching him closely from her position beside Auntie Pru's chair, on the look-out for any unpleasant developments.

"It's quite common, apparently," Dave Silver said. "But it's usually only temporary."

"Usually?"

"Well, almost always. The memory gets a bit scrambled, but when the concussion wears off, everything goes back to normal. It seems to be coming over him in waves. He's perfectly all right some of the time, then suddenly he's off with the fairies."

"But it's so weird," James said, "he actually seems to be reliving an earlier period of his life. It's more like regression."

Dave chuckled. "Not just one period. We've been getting a whole selection. You should have seen him with the doctor, he started acting like he was about ten. I think he must have had some kind of trouble with a doctor when he was a kid. As soon as poor old Martin Bulmer walked in the room Max started stamping his foot and screaming that he didn't like him because his hands were always cold."

"When we arrived he seemed to think he was back at some public school he used to teach at, organizing games and things for the boys."

"Yes, it's strange," Dave said, "because he never taught at a public school."

"What, he wasn't a teacher at all?"

"Oh, yes, he was a teacher. He taught at a grammar school near Croydon. But all this Tom Brown's Schooldays performance is a fantasy. He's been doing that a lot, mixing up things he really did with things he didn't. Enhancing things, you might say."

Dave turned to gaze out of the French windows. "It's wishful thinking, I suppose. I was out having a walk this morning and he popped out of the shrubbery and chatted away to me for a good ten minutes as if we were both a pair of Cambridge professors strolling around the quad, asking me what I thought about the restoration plans for some library or other." He turned back to James with a smile. "But he didn't go to Cambridge, he was at Manchester. Nothing wrong with that, very good university, so I hear. But it's interesting, isn't it?" .

They were in the room at the back of the house that James had seen from the grounds. It ran across the whole width of the building and was an extension to the rooms behind it, which could be made into a ballroom by opening a set of doors between them. People could drift out of the ballroom - James visualized Georgian couples, flirting mercilessly - and either dally in this extension or, weather permitting, continue out through the French windows onto the gravel walk running across the top of the lawn.

Big, dark paintings lined the wall opposite the windows, many of them featuring unattractive horses and dogs. Auntie Pru's chair was beneath one of them, on one side of a fireplace; on the other was a sofa where Raymond sat talking to Jessica. Simon Cottle and Daphne Longbourne were standing nearby, chatting politely. Next to them John Longbourne was talking earnestly to Jane Cottle and staring at her cleavage, while most of her attention was devoted to her usual close surveillance of her husband. She'd been conducting a discreet but furious argument with him when they'd walked in, and seemed impatient to continue it. There was no sign of Bill Longbourne or Reuben.

Sylvia Silver moved graciously among her guests. Today she was dressed in a cream silk blouse and a light tweed skirt, with a rope of pearls and flat, chunky shoes. She'd also done something severe to her hair to complete the impersonation of an English country house chatelaine in her element. As she moved around the room she fingered her pearls and trilled with refined laughter, heroically subduing her natural ear-splitting honk.

James looked anxiously at Jessica, who had now moved closer to Raymond on the sofa and was talking to him earnestly. He still hadn't been able to speak to her since what had happened in church. Strangely, even though what she'd done should have encouraged him - it was only a step away from actual sex, for God's sake - there was something about it that made him uneasy. He desperately wanted to talk to her, but as soon as he'd entered the house he'd been claimed by Sylvia, who steered him around the place in a brisk tour, then handed him over to Dave, whose voice now claimed his attention again:

"It's a bit like this business with the windmill."

James turned and followed Dave Silver's gaze out of the window. If he was going to talk about the windmill, James would have to be careful.

"What do you think of it?" Dave said.

"Interesting." James nodded vigorously. "Very interesting."

Dave turned to look at him. He wasn't smiling but the skin around his eyes crinkled a little. "Really?" He pursed his lips for a moment, then nodded. "You've sussed it, haven't you?"

"Sussed what?"

154

Dave gave a snort of laughter. "You're not a very good liar, are you? Never mind, your mother would be pleased." He turned back to look at the windmill and gestured to it with his drink. "Our authentic olde worlde windmill, as used by genuine peasants in the good old days of Merrie England. Which you don't believe for a moment, do you?"

"Well, there's always a certain doubt about authenticating historical artefacts."

"Not if someone tells you they've found a long-lost Shakespeare play, and it's written in biro. Not that Max is trying to sell a forgery, exactly. But he is taking the piss. That place isn't what he says it is. I know that, and so do you, don't you?"

James didn't look at him. "Well, yes, I think it's quite possible it's a Georgian replica, built at the same time as the house. Perhaps it's a kind of folly."

"Of course it is. And you know what?"

James turned to face him.

Dave raised his eyebrows and beamed at him. "I don't give a toss. As long as she's happy." He nodded in the direction of his wife, who was gliding away from Daphne Longbourne with the satisfied smile of a woman who's clocked up some worthwhile condescension before lunch.

"That's all I care about," Dave said. "And I'll tell you something." He put his hand on James's shoulder. "You seem like a nice bloke, and I won't try to bullshit you. Max is running a bit of racket, but I've come across a lot worse. He's not doing much harm, and he's keeping her happy. You've probably figured it all out for yourself. Fine." He leaned in closer to James. "But if you breathe a word to Sylvia, I'll have you boiled alive in dirty motor oil. I mean it. You can understand that, can't you?"

He gave James's shoulder a squeeze. He had a surprisingly powerful grip for a small man.

"Absolutely. I wouldn't dream of it."

Dave patted his shoulder and dropped his hand. "The thing is, I love my wife." He chuckled, seeming to find the proposition pleasantly surprising. "Yes, she's a good woman," he said, stroking his hard, round little belly, as if he was perhaps thinking of eating her, "a very good woman. That's why I bought her this place. I mean, I'm very fond of it, and I love all the history, but I don't really mind where I live. I've always been a bit of a gypsy. But Sylvia's thrilled to bits with the whole set-up. Especially the windmill, what with the ecological angle we've got now, as well. And if she's happy, I'm happy."

He finished his drink and looked at the glass in James's hand. "You'll want some more of that, I expect." He looked around the room. Just then a door at the far end of it opened.

"Ah, just the man!" Dave said. "He must have read my mind. Uncanny. He's a marvel, is George. What I call a proper fucking butler."

155

The figure who had just entered the room with a tray of champagne glasses was tall and thin, with sleek black hair brushed back from a long, narrow face. His tailcoat, pinstriped trousers and gleaming black shoes were immaculate, and he wore his eyelids at half-mast in the traditional expression of supercilious imperturbability. The only thing that spoiled the complete fulfilment of a Hollywood producer's fantasy of what a perfect English butler should look like was a broken nose.

"I'll introduce you when he gets to us," Dave said, "he's very good value, is George." He watched admiringly as George made his way around the room, supplying everyone with champagne. As he lowered the tray to serve Max Fennel, who was still squatting beside Auntie Pru, he deftly swivelled it around so that Max took a particular glass which, James suspected, contained something innocuous. When he reached Jane Cottle she indicated that her glass was still half full, and declined another one. As George turned away from her, John Longbourne took an extra glass from the tray.

"I'll have hers," James heard him say. "No point in wasting the stuff. It goes flat if you don't drink it." He grinned at Jane, but she was peering over his shoulder at her husband, presumably checking that he wasn't standing too close to Daphne Longbourne, or any other woman, preparing to drag her from the room and ravish her.

"Here he comes," Dave said, "you'll love this."

George approached them and inclined his head slightly. They put their empty glasses on the proffered tray and took the two remaining full ones.

"Are we all right for supplies, George?" Dave asked. "No danger of running out of the good stuff, is there?"

"Indeed not, sir," George replied in voice that made James think of treacle being poured into a bowl of cream. "There is an ample sufficiency of the superior vintage."

"An ample sufficiency, is there?" Dave said, glancing meaningfully at James. "That sounds like quite a lot."

"Yes, sir; one might say that we are plentitudinously supplied."

Dave made a small noise like a stifled sneeze. He took a sip of his drink. "That's good," he said, "I like to be plentitudinously supplied with this stuff."

"A noble beverage, sir, that when consumed in moderation, and with the precaution of selecting only the finest vintages, enables one to enjoy the more agreeable aspects of intoxication while avoiding the unpleasant concomitant sensations that sometimes result from over-indulgence."

Dave turned away quickly to the window. James saw his cheek muscles twitching. When he turned back his face was serious. "George, have you ever had the unpleasant concomitant sensations that sometimes result from over-indulgence?"

George took a moment to reply, during which Dave stared hard at him.

"Alas, sir," George said, lowering his voice and his eyes, "in my younger days, which were, I regret to say, to a certain extent misspent, an excessive predilection for stimulants occasionally led to my debilitation by their after-effects."

Dave clenched his jaw and breathed heavily through his nose. "Debilitation," he repeated finally. "It sounds as if you were a bit of a rogue, George."

"My conduct, sir, to put it bluntly, was reprehensible."

"Reprehensible, was it?" Dave's shoulders began to shake. He pressed his lips together and his face turned red. Finally he burst out laughing. "Reprehensible!" he gasped, "you bastard, that's got me!" He wiped his eyes. "Come on," he said, looking closely at George, "you're going to crack. I know you are."

For an instant James thought he saw George's lips quiver fractionally.

"There!" Dave said, "I saw it, you definitely smiled! Go on, laugh, you bugger!"

"I beg your pardon, sir, but I would never presume to succumb to risibility while performing my duties."

Dave snorted. "All right, but I'll get you. One day, I'll do it, I swear."

"A challenging assertion, sir."

"Fuck off. But before you do, I want to introduce you to my friend James Burridge. George this is James; James, George."

"Highly gratified to make your acquaintance, sir."

"Yes, me too."

"Will there be anything else, sir?"

"No, you're all right," Dave said. "Are you taking the evening off, by the way?"

"If that is agreeable to you, sir."

"Of course it is. It's your choice, you know that. Either tonight or tomorrow, whatever you've arranged with Sylvia."

"Thank you, sir."

"Are you going out somewhere?"

"No, sir. I believe I shall refresh my acquaintance with the work of Mr Updike, and perhaps carry out some further small improvements to my quarters."

"You should see what he's done to his flat," Dave said to James, "he's a genius at the DIY. He's got his own apartment over in the old stable block, above my edit suite, and he's transformed the place, haven't you, George?"

"You were generous enough to provide me with exceptionally commodious and well-appointed accommodation, sir. I have merely added some minor personal touches."

"Bollocks, it's like a palace. Or a harem, eh, George?" Dave winked at him and said to James, "He's a bit of a ladies' man, is George. He's got the gift in

157

that department. He has to beat them off with a stick. I don't know how he does it."

George tilted his head to one side and nodded gravely, as if conceding a good point, well made.

"All right," Dave said, "we won't keep you. I'll catch you some time later, I expect."

George gave a little bow, swivelled around and walked away. James noticed that the pale leather undersides of his shoes were spotlessly clean.

Dave shook his head and chuckled as he watched George walk away. "Bloody marvellous, isn't he?"

"He's quite a character."

"You'll never guess how I found him."

"How?"

"He was trying to rob me."

"Really? Was he a burglar?"

"No. Well, yes and no, you might say. He was actually a con artist by profession. A very good one in his earlier days, too, by all accounts. One of the best in the business. But he was losing the plot by the time I met him. He was an alcoholic, and the drink had started affecting his judgment. He used to specialize in what they call the long con, and that's all about selecting the right mark, and cultivating them. But the point is, for a con to really work properly, especially the long game, the mark has got to be a bit greedy. And I'm not. I've got plenty of other faults, and I always liked making money, but I'm not greedy. Never have been."

Dave glanced at James as if he wasn't sure if he believed him.

"Right," James said, "so he picked the wrong man."

"He did. But like I say, George was a bit addled by the time he tried to set me up. I was in the music publishing game at that time, and there was a lot of money in it if you knew what you were doing and you were lucky. George tried to sell me a lovely little swindle involving two or three bogus companies, non-existent overseas partners, VAT fiddles, all very complex. But I wasn't falling for it. He played it well, mind you, made all the right moves, took me to lunch at The Ivy and insisted on paying the bill, that type of thing - you've got to lay out a bit of money to make the long con work - but none of it's any use unless you've got the right mark, and he hadn't. By the time he realized that, he was well out of pocket. And he got desperate. So he tried to burgle my office. Pokey little place up the top of a building in Dean Street. And I walked in on him, didn't I? I'd gone back to pick up some contracts I'd forgotten, and there he was, with a bloody mask on and everything, tearing the place apart with a fucking great crowbar."

"That must have been quite frightening. Walking in to find that going on."

"Just a bit, yes. But he'd had a few drinks and he wasn't really on top of things. And I can look after myself. I did a bit of Judo when I was younger, as it happens."

James didn't find it hard to imagine Dave flipping someone over his shoulder.

Dave gave a brisk little sniff. "No big deal, but if you grow up Jewish where I did, you sometimes want to be able make your point. But George was harmless, anyway. I took the crowbar off him, and we had a little chat, and I took him out for meal. I tried to stop him drinking too much but he wasn't having it and I had to practically carry him out of the restaurant. When we were outside and I was trying to flag down a cab for him, he started chatting up two women who were passing, trotting along beside them, giving them the gab, and he walked straight into a lamp-post. That's how he broke his nose.

"So, I had to take him to hospital. Of course, it took hours for him to get it seen to, but the broken nose had sobered him up, and we ended up talking for most of the night. He's a very interesting man. Very cultured. I'd always liked him, even when I could see he was trying to con me. And in a funny way, I liked the fact that he tried to burgle me, as well. He wouldn't give up, you see. I admire that. I admire tenacity."

He chuckled and turned to look out of the window again. "Don't get me wrong, I'm not saying I approve of criminal behaviour. But somehow I never really thought of him as a criminal, know what I mean?"

"He seems more like an actor than anything else," James said.

"Exactly. Very true. All con men are actors, the good ones. And now he's playing a butler, and doing a lovely job of it. I made a deal with him, you see, because it turned out he was in quite a bad way and he owed money to some very nasty people. I was in the middle of buying this place at the time, and I said that I'd take care of the money problem and give him a job if he cleaned up his act, and promised to stick with it. He gave me his word, and that was good enough for me, because I knew he was an honest man in his own way, so I put him through rehab and when he came out we turned him into a butler. Four years he's been sober now. And although we have a good laugh, he works hard, too, and takes the job very seriously. Like I say, he's a proper butler."

Dave drained his glass and laughed. "Of course, I might wake up tomorrow and find he's robbed me blind and run off. You never know with people, do you?"

The sound of a gong shimmered through the room.

"Luncheon is served," George declared.

James was acutely aware of Jessica's thigh, inches from his own. He'd been pleased to find himself sitting next to her at first, but it wasn't doing him much good. She was being perfectly nice to him, and she wasn't actively ignoring him, but she seemed more interested in continuing her discussion with

159

Raymond, who was sitting next to her on the other side. As far as James could tell they were arguing about horses.

Unnervingly, James was sitting opposite Auntie Pru again. And, once again, every time he glanced at her, he found himself the object of her inscrutable inspection. When they'd sat down he'd remarked laughingly that they couldn't go on meeting like this, and he'd received the wintry ghost of a smile, but otherwise she remained expressionless. She didn't seem to expect him to talk to her, which gave him plenty of time to consider how inane his remark had been and then to wonder, with a sudden chill, if it might have prompted her to recall their other encounter, after dinner on Friday night. The image of what he'd witnessed sprang into his mind. He shuddered, grabbed his glass, and drained it of red wine. It was warm and full-bodied, and tasted expensive. He replaced the empty glass on the table and looked up to see Auntie Pru staring at him.

He felt a tug on his sleeve. Max Fennel was sitting on his left but until now he hadn't said anything. James took a deep breath and turned to face him.

Max glanced around disapprovingly, then leaned towards him, frowning.

"What do you think of this new notion of admitting ladies to High Table?" he said in a low voice. He'd now assumed the port-sodden rumble of an elderly Oxbridge don.

"I expect there's no harm in it," James said, trying to sound neutral.

"But what is one to say to the creatures? I'm at a complete loss with my neighbour here." Max jerked his thumb over his shoulder at Daphne Longbourne, sitting next to him. She was talking to Dave Silver, at the head of the table. John Longbourne, opposite her, was leaning back in his chair and drumming his fingers on the table. James saw him catch Daphne's eye and frown, nodding towards Dave.

"I mean, what can I talk to her about?" Max continued. "I heard some gossip about a member of the royal family recently. Isn't that the sort of thing they're interested in? Or popular music, do you think? Unfortunately I know very little about that."

"You could always talk about the weather."

"Do you think so? It seems rather a dull topic."

"Ah," James said, "but you can lead on to all kinds of things. Farming, perhaps. Or the battle of Waterloo. Don't they say the weather was crucial to the outcome?"

"That's true," Max said. "Very true. Thanks for the tip."

Max nodded happily and turned towards Daphne. When there was a lull in her conversation with Dave Silver, he coughed loudly. Daphne turned towards him with a tense smile.

"Are you interested in rainfall?" Max said to her.

In the pause that followed, James heard John Longbourne addressing Dave.

"It's just struck me, David," he said, "we haven't had a chance to discuss that little business opportunity I was telling you about the other day. My colleagues tell me it's all looking very promising, and I wouldn't want to you to miss out."

Dave smiled down at the table for a moment, and turned to him.

Before James could hear what he said, Jessica tapped him on the arm. He turned to find her passing him a plate with thin slices of goose in some kind of sauce on it.

"Pass it on," she said. Beyond her, at the end of the table, Sylvia was serving the meat from a large platter and passing the plates to her left and right.

"I do hope you don't mind helping yourselves to everything else," Sylvia called out, "it's all on the table."

Whatever other duties George performed, serving at the table clearly wasn't one of them. A few moments ago Sylvia had gone to collect the main course herself from the kitchen, where the legendary Antonio was presumably lurking, the task of serving his own food far beneath him. If the Silvers had any other staff, there was no sign of them.

When Sylvia had returned with the food, Reuben was with her. It was the first time he'd appeared that day and it looked as if he'd only recently got out of bed, or been dragged out of it by his mother. At her prompting, he shuffled around the table, moodily collecting the plates from the first course. It had been a fish terrine with an exquisitely delicate flavour, and little triangles of toast with something dark and gamey on them, which James thought was probably an outcome of Fat Perry's encounter with the deer.

When Reuben reached James and leaned down for his plate, James caught a blast of fresh alcohol on his breath, overlaying the stale intake from last night. He was obviously dealing with his hangover by preparing the foundations of another one.

Reuben shuffled from the room with the plates and when he came back a moment later he flung himself into an empty chair at the end of the table, between Simon Cottle and his mother. Sylvia passed him a plate with meat on it and whispered to him. He rolled his eyes and heaved a huge sigh, then hauled himself up and stumped around the table, spooning up a selection vegetables from the various side dishes. Then he glared at his mother and lumbered from the room again. Sylvia smiled around brightly.

"Does everyone have enough goose?" she asked.

There was a muffled chorus of assent. Most people were already eating.

James wondered if Reuben had been banished to eat alone, but he reappeared almost instantly without the plate. It occurred to James that he'd taken it to George, who must be eating somewhere nearby. Reuben wouldn't have had time to get to the stable block and back. Perhaps he was in a Butler's Pantry. Wasn't that a kind of little den they had? James envied him; he imagined him enjoying a leisurely lunch in a comfortable chair, reading the Sunday papers in his shirtsleeves, perhaps even wearing slippers.

161

James tried some of the food on his plate. The meat was succulent; rich but not heavy. Its sauce was light and creamy with a slight tang of citrus, and something that hinted at sweetness without actually being sweet. Delicate little sausages clustered around the slices of goose. And while the vegetables were familiar - broccoli, carrots, parsnips, spinach and sweet corn, with the only remotely unusual addition being a concoction involving chestnuts - James felt that he was tasting them for the first time. There were also three kinds of potato.

After the pudding, which was a simple but spectacular conspiracy between some raspberries and a chocolate sauce, with a sorbet collaborating from the sidelines, people began to talk to each other again. There had been some fitful murmurs of conversation after the main course, but everyone seemed unwilling to emerge from a private sensory trance while there was still a prospect of more food. Once the spell was broken they leaned back and sighed, already nostalgic for the tastes that still lingered on their palettes.

James thought he might now have a chance to speak to Jessica. It had been so quiet when everyone was eating that any conversational approach would have attracted attention, particularly on the topic of masturbation in church, which is what he wanted to talk to her about.

But when he turned to Jessica he found that she and Raymond had already resumed their discussion about riding, gradually becoming more animated as they shook off the gastronomic stupor. James thought it was unfair that she wasn't talking to him. He just wanted to confirm that what she'd done in church was a prelude to proper sex, and to arrange for it to take place as soon as possible. But perhaps her reluctance to speak to him was a good sign. They'd gone beyond small talk. All they had to do was fix the time and place to take things further. She was probably waiting for them to be alone.

James looked around the table. John Longbourne was slumped in his chair with his arms crossed, not listening to something Jane Cottle was telling him. He stared at the tablecloth, darting occasional dark glances from under his brow at Dave Silver, who was talking to Daphne again. Jane said something to him, laughed at her own remark, and leaned towards him, perhaps missing his usual close attention to her cleavage. With Auntie Pru and Spracky between her and her husband, she'd abandoned a policy of constant scrutiny, just checking occasionally that Simon wasn't trying to talk to Jessica, who was opposite him. But Jessica was occupied with Raymond, and Simon was reduced to talking to Reuben, who turned around in his chair to face him so that his back was to his mother. Nodding solemnly at what Simon was saying, his hand crept towards a bottle of wine in the middle of the table. He managed to pour himself a large glass, and drink most of it in one go, before Sylvia noticed and took the bottle away.

James felt himself being prodded on the shoulder.

162

"Yes, yes, yes," he heard Max say, "now I remember: you were in the windmill, weren't you? It's all coming back to me."

James took a moment to compose his features into the bland expression of someone who hasn't inflicted brain damage on the person sitting next to him at lunch.

He turned to Max.

A change had come over him. His expression was clear, and his voice had returned to normal. James's heart sank.

"That's right," James said, "you very kindly showed me how it all worked."

"No, after that," Max said. "Didn't you go in there again?"

James was aware that everyone else had stopped talking. He took a deep breath. Before he could say anything, Max continued:

"And you were the one who managed to stop it! The hero of the hour! I owe you a real debt of gratitude, dear boy. If it weren't for you, there's no telling what damage might have been done, in addition to my little knock on the noggin!"

Max beamed at him and patted his shoulder.

There was a palpable sense of relief around the table.

Max's face darkened. "And there were a couple of girls in there, too, I seem to remember. Isn't that right? They were obviously the ones who caused the problem. Mucking about with the machinery, no doubt. Girls from the village." He shook his head. "I'm sorry to have to say it, but I'm afraid that type of person can't really be trusted."

James couldn't let that pass. It was one thing to take credit for something he hadn't done, but another to blame someone else for a disaster that was his fault. And he didn't like the way Max was talking about Chantelle and Saphire.

"Actually," he said, "that's not quite what happened."

Jessica kicked him under the table, hard.

James ignored her and continued, "It was the girls who managed to stop it. Chantelle and Saphire. They were the ones who stopped the machinery."

Max looked confused. "In that case, how did it get released in the first place?"

"I'm afraid it was my fault," James said.

Sylvia's voice cut across the table. "What he means," she said, "is that he feels responsible for making you show him how it all worked. Because that's when it must have happened."

"Really?" Max said. "But that was earlier on."

"Yes," Sylvia said, "but the wind didn't pick up until later."

"That's quite possible," Max said. He turned to James. "There was no wind at all for most of the afternoon. Good God, do you think I left the machinery disengaged after I demonstrated it to you, and it was just waiting for a bit of a gust to swing into action?"

James looked down at the table. He thought about his father, and the way he always became very serious whenever he'd spoken about honesty. James heard his gentle voice telling him that a lie could only ever be excused if it prevented some great harm.

Jessica kicked him again.

He knew that if he told the complete truth she'd think he was a fool.

Before he'd decided what to say Max gave a yelp of laughter. "Fancy that," he cried, "it was all my own silly fault!" He shook his head with a rueful chuckle. "Well, how very embarrassing. So, I have only myself to blame for this little mishap." He pointed to the bandages on his head then picked up his wine glass. "Here's to the very model of an absent-minded professor!" He paused with the glass half way to his lips and frowned. "No, wait a moment." He put the glass down and turned to James again. "That still doesn't explain what you were doing in there later on. Didn't you go in there a second time, without me?"

"No," Sylvia said, firmly. "I think you're getting mixed up again, Max."

"Am I?" Max frowned down at the table. "Yes, that's possible. I am having some difficulty remembering things. It's quite a strain, trying to sort things out in my mind." He raised his hand to his head and gently felt his bandages.

"Don't tax yourself, my dear," Sylvia said. "It'll all come back to you, I'm sure."

"Yes, I expect you're right." Max said, vaguely. He seemed to be losing interest.

"Let's all take a little break," Sylvia said, "and then have coffee in the big room."

Sylvia started to clear the table.

"Help Sylvia, Jess," Daphne said.

Jessica began to get up reluctantly.

"No, no, sit down," Sylvia said. "I won't hear of it. It's only a few plates and things. Richard will help me take them into the kitchen, won't you, darling?"

Reuben looked at her as if she'd asked him to carry several back-breaking loads of radioactive waste for many miles over difficult terrain.

He pushed himself away from the table slowly, deliberately making his chair squeal unpleasantly on the parquet floor. "Yes," he sighed mournfully, "I'll do it."

James stood up. "Let me help. Reuben did it earlier."

Sylvia smiled at him. "That's very kind of you, dear."

Five minutes later James was surprised to find himself doing the washing up. After he and Sylvia had finished taking everything into the kitchen, and he asked if there was anything else he could do, he hadn't expected her to say yes.

164

She'd loaded most of the crockery and cutlery into a cavernous dishwasher, and now they were tackling the things that couldn't go in there, including a jumble of pans abandoned on the ten-ring gas range and cooker that hulked in the middle of the room like an altar. Antonio, its high priest, had vanished after presiding over the miracles performed upon it, leaving behind the stained sacrificial vessels.

"I hope you didn't mind me interrupting your little confession to Max," Sylvia said as she handed James a crystal glass to dry. "It's just that he's confused enough already, and I didn't want him getting into a state about it. But it was good of you to try and stop him blaming those girls."

"It was the least I could do, really. And I still feel guilty."

"Well, don't. He'll be fine. And even if he's not," Sylvia said, laughing, "how could you tell the difference? He talks a lot of nonsense most of the time even when he's meant to be normal. Not what you'd call completely reliable." She handed him another glass. "Like with the windmill, for example."

James held the glass carefully and began to dry it without saying anything.

"What do you think of it, by the way?" Sylvia said.

"Interesting,"

"Yes, it is, isn't it?"

She swirled the water around in the sink, then gazed out of the window above it.

"Of course," she said, "it might not be quite what it seems. A bit like Max. Do you know what I mean, dear?"

"I think so," James said. He sensed a need for caution.

"You seemed to be quite knowledgeable about it. Do you think it was really ever used as the village mill? Is it that old?"

"Umm, it's quite difficult to tell with these things. There's always some doubt."

Sylvia laughed. "Right. Let's cut to the chase. You obviously know it's a load of bollocks. No, don't worry, I know the score. Max is telling us what he thinks we want to hear. And why not? He's doing well out of it, and he thinks he's keeping us happy."

She turned to hand him another glass and when he reached for it she grasped his wrist so he was forced to meet her eye.

"The thing is," she said, "I don't want Dave to be disappointed. He keeps telling me it's the real thing. He's obviously got his heart set on believing it, bless him."

"I see. Yes, right."

"He loves this place. So do I, but he's a real nut for all the historical side. He's thrilled to think they really used the windmill in the olden days. I'm not really bothered about all that, I just like a nice place to live, and having all the lovely things we've got, and all the fun I can have. I expect you think I'm just a silly, vain, vulgar old woman--"

165

"No, of course I don't," James said, truthfully. He knew that when he first met her he had thought exactly that about her, and now he felt ashamed.

"Thank you. But I wouldn't care if you did, quite frankly. No offence. I love Dave and what matters most to me is making him happy. So, please don't tell him."

"I won't. I promise."

"Good. You're a nice boy."

She released his wrist and turned back to the sink.

"How are you getting on at the Longbourne's, by the way? It must be a bit strange for you, without Oliver being there. They can be a bit daunting, can't they?"

"They can, a bit. Meeting them for the first time."

"Especially Daphne, I expect."

"Mmm. She can be a bit... formidable."

"Don't you be frightened of Daphne Longbourne. She has to wash her knickers, just like the rest of us. I'm fond of her in a way, but let me tell you something about her. Daphne married well above herself when she got her hands on poor old Bill Longbourne. She came out of a different drawer altogether." She turned to James and raised her nose in the air. "Frightfully common," she said, putting on a refined drawl. "Comes from trade, don't you know. My deah! Can you imagine?"

James laughed.

"Daphne Snape, she used to be. Her father had a pork butcher's shop in Shepton Mallet and she grew up above the shop. He was a smart bloke, the old man, and in the sixties, just when the supermarkets were starting up, he saw they'd need big suppliers. So he started buying up local pig farms, bringing in intensive production methods. Made a fortune. Daphne likes to say she comes from a farming background, as if the old man was some kind of sturdy yeoman from the landed gentry. But he never did any farming. Just took the money. So, the next time Daphne looks at you as if you were something she just stepped in, think of her behind the counter, wrapping the sausages."

"I will," James said. "That'll help a lot."

"Daphne always knew exactly what she wanted." Sylvia said, handing him a big saucepan. "Oh, yes, she probably looked around at all the genuine old upper-crust families in the vicinity, chose the Longbournes, and set about catching Bill. You might think I'm being cynical, but she's not the only one who's done that, let me tell you."

"No, I can believe it. Quite easily."

"Bill didn't stand a chance. She was quite a beauty, by all accounts, and she was only young when they married, and he was a good twenty years older. The Longbournes were in a bad way financially, and poor old Bill was nailing down the coffin lid, trying to raise money on the property. He was hopeless with money. And he was letting John drain the coffers, as well. Well, she soon put a

166

stop to that. The way she saw it, it was a perfect match. Old blood, new money. She had a good head for business, too. Bill was happy to let her take over. Now, of course, he's just faded into the background, pottering about with his steamrollers. No one takes much notice of him, but I think that suits him."

"Jessica seems fond of him."

"Oh, they dote on each other. Late child, you see. Bill was about sixty when she was born. Frankly, I don't think Daphne planned on any children at all. She was past thirty when she had Oliver. And when Jessica came along - well, some people say Daphne had already started carrying on with John by then. So there's always been a bit of talk about that."

James took a moment to understand what she meant. "Oh. Right."

"I don't believe it, myself. But people are bound to talk." Daphne handed him a another pan. "You're pretty keen on her, aren't you?"

"Is it that obvious?"

"Oh, yes. She has that effect on men. You're like dogs with your tongues out. Poor Richard is hopelessly in love with her. At least, he thinks he is, which amounts to the same thing. I'm hoping he'll get over it. Like this religious thing he's going through. What do you think? Do you think it's just a phase? Has he talked to you about it?"

"Not really. He seems to be a bit confused, to be honest."

"Well, he's still only a teenager, after all. At least he's not into drugs, as far as I know. He's never even smoked, I don't think. Of course, hardly anybody smokes anymore, so that helps He does tend to drink a bit too much, though. But that's a typical teenage thing, isn't it?"

James knew that when he was Reuben's age, getting drunk had been a major preoccupation for him and his friends. But he didn't think he'd shown quite the same impressive commitment as Reuben. "It would probably be a good idea if he cut down a bit," he said.

"Yes, I expect so," Sylvia said, although her mind seemed to be on something else. She took the plug out of the sink and peeled off her yellow rubber gloves. She turned to him. "I think the real problem is that he's very easily influenced. Like with Oliver. He looks up to Oliver a tremendous amount, you know."

"Does he?"

"Yes. Thinks he's the cat's pyjamas." She turned away and began to take coffee cups from a cabinet next to the sink. "How long have you known him, by the way?"

"Only a couple of years, I suppose. Two or three years."

"He's a very charming young man. I expect you're great friends."

"I don't see all that much of him, actually."

"Really?" Sylvia nodded thoughtfully as she laid the cups out on a tray. "I wonder if I could ask you a favour?"

"Of course. Go ahead."

167

"I like Oliver, but I'm not sure he's a suitable friend for Richard at the moment. Oh, I know better than to try and tell Richard that. He'd just get even more infatuated. But I can't help feeling that Oliver is bit irresponsible. Do you mind me saying that?"

"Not at all. You're right. He's not the world's most reliable person."

"No. And Richard will be leaving home soon, and he'll probably be in London for a while, and if he's going to see Oliver there I just... I wondered if I could ask you to keep an eye on him. Try to stop him getting into trouble."

James didn't know what to say. Almost ever since he'd met Rueben he'd been trying to stop him getting into trouble, so far without much success.

"I'm not asking you to be his best friend," Sylvia said. "You've got plenty of friends of your own, and I know a boy that age can be a real nuisance." She looked down at the water gurgling out of the sink. "Although he does need a real friend," she said.

"I'll be happy to keep in touch with him in London," James said. "I know what it's like. When I first arrived there, I was very lonely."

This wasn't entirely true, as he'd moved in with a girl he'd been seeing as soon as he got to London. But he'd known loneliness as a child, and he felt qualified to import that emotional experience into an imaginary situation, and fantasise about what it would be like to be young and friendless in London. As he did so he began to be quite moved by bogus memories of himself, wandering the streets, gazing sadly at scenes of conviviality inaccessible to him behind the steamy windows of expensive restaurants. He added some rain to the Dickensian picture, modified it to freezing sleet, gave himself an unspecified but tragic illness, and his eyes pricked with tears.

"That's so kind of you, dear." Sylvia patted his arm. "Thank you."

"No problem. Really."

"Right. Let's get this coffee organized."

When James and Sylvia arrived with the coffee in the room they'd been in before lunch, the first thing he noticed was that Jessica wasn't there. The second thing he noticed was that Raymond wasn't there either. The sofa they'd been sitting on earlier was now occupied by Reuben, who was asleep. A thin rope of drool dangled just above his chest.

James took a cup of coffee and stood next to the sofa. He wanted to know where Jessica and Raymond were. Reuben might know, and James also needed to have a serious talk with him about his plan to commit a robbery, especially as it appeared to involve him, and was due to be put into action tonight. He decided it would be a good idea to wake Reuben up.

He slowly lowered his cup and saucer and rattled them in Reuben's ear, coughing to cover the noise. Reuben continued to snore peacefully. James glanced around the room. Daphne Longbourne, standing by the French windows with Dave Silver, was staring at him. He smiled at her. She turned away from him slowly and shook her head. James rattled the cup and saucer again as violently as he dared, covering the noise with a series of even louder coughs. Reuben slept on.

"Would you like a lozenge, dear?"

He turned to find Spracky hovering beside him.

"I'm sorry?"

"A lozenge. A pastille. A throat sweet."

"Oh, no, I'm fine, thanks."

"Just a frog in your throat, is it?"

"Yes, that was it. Gone now. Hopped off." James cleared his throat and giggled.

Spracky looked at Reuben. "They need a lot of sleep at that age, don't they?"

"Yes. All part of growing up." He gave Reuben a hearty pat on the shoulder.

"Of course, the boy's completely shitfaced most of the time, as well."

"Ah, yes. There is that."

"What did you think of the lunch?" Spracky said.

"Wonderful. He's a brilliant cook."

"Yes, he is, isn't he?"

James thought he detected a note of sadness in her voice.

"I loved the dinner on Friday, too," he said loyally. "That was delicious."

"Very kind of you, but I know my limitations. I'm a good cook, but I'm not a chef. That's the difference. I just haven't got the gene. Antonio is out of my league."

"But you might get tired of all that gourmet stuff if you had it all the time. Sometimes it's nice just to have some good, well prepared, simple, honest food. Like that fantastic breakfast you made me."

Spracky laughed. "Oh, stop it."

"No, I bet Antonio doesn't know how to make a really perfect bacon sandwich."

"I bet he does. I suspect he has supernatural powers."

"What's he like?"

"No one knows."

"Really? What do you mean?"

"No one's ever seen him. Apart from Sylvia."

"Seriously?"

"Well, did you see him?"

"No, he'd already gone."

"Exactly. There's a rumour that he's hideously deformed."

"In what way?"

"I don't know. I didn't specify. I'll have to think about that."

James was puzzled. "What difference will that make?"

"Well, I started the rumour, you see. Not bad, is it?"

They heard a loud hammering noise coming from the garden.

"Oh, Christ," Spracky said, "what's the mad bugger up to now?"

He followed her gaze to see Max, battering a croquet hoop into the lawn.

"I don't think he'll get many takers for that," Spracky muttered.

Max finished with the hoop, and peered at the house. He gestured to Dave Silver, who opened the French windows and walked out to talk to him. They exchanged a few words, then Dave returned. He smiled around the room. "Anyone fancy a game of croquet? No, I didn't think so." He turned and called back to Max, "I think everyone's too full of lunch, Max. I'll come out a bit later and knock a few around with you, if you like."

Max nodded and paced out the distance to the next hoop, which he began hammering into the grass. Dave closed the windows.

"I find Max greatly improved since that knock on the head," Spracky said. "I always used to find him a bit of a bore, but now he's great fun. You never know what he's going to say next. It'll be a shame if he recovers. I might have to administer another wallop on a regular basis myself, just to keep him topped up. What do you think?"

"Hard to say. It's not an exact science, bashing people over the head."

"You're right; he's a bit fragile to be knocked around too much. Not like you young people. You can take it."

"Talking of young people, James said, "I wonder where Jessica is? Do you happen to know, by any chance? I haven't seen her for a while."

"No idea."

"But she hasn't gone or anything, has she?"

"Search me. Although, come to think of it, she did mention something when you were in the kitchen. What was it?"

"Sprack!" Auntie Pru's voice cut across the room. They turned to see her, now back in her chair on the other side of the fireplace, holding up her coffee cup and beckoning to Spracky.

"Sorry, duty calls," Spracky said, and went to attend to her.

James looked down at Reuben. He seemed to be sleeping even more deeply. One of his feet was propped up on the sofa and the other was resting on the floor. Very carefully, James trod on it. Reuben's snore was enriched by a soft, wheezing moan, but after a moment his snoring returned to normal. James glanced around to make sure nobody was looking and kicked his ankle sharply. Reuben paused mid-snore, and then exhaled in a series of stuttering gasps. That was more promising. James kicked him again. This time Reuben grunted and his eyelids fluttered. One more good kick should do it. James drew back his foot and took careful aim.

"What are you doing?"

James whirled around, spilling coffee on his shirt. Simon Cottle was standing next to him. "What's he done to you?" Simon asked. "Can't you find it in your heart to forgive him? Unless he really deserves a kicking. Does he?"

"Oh, no, not at all. No, I was just trying to wake him up."

"Why?"

"I was worried about him. In case he choked. You know, choked on his own vomit. He's quite drunk."

"He's always drunk. Let him sleep it off. He'll be fine." Simon patted James on the shoulder. "Thank you for coming to church, by the way. I like to see newcomers there."

"It was a pleasure," James said, then felt odd about using the word pleasure under the circumstances. "I mean, I enjoyed it. Well, not 'enjoyed' in the sense of having fun. Although it was fun, of course. In the religious sense. If you see what I mean."

"You're not drunk as well, are you?"

"No, no. I'm fine."

"Good. Yes, as I say, I like to see newcomers in the church. As long as their intentions are good, of course."

"Oh, yes, of course."

"It's a pity the sermon was rather spoiled."

"Oh, I thought it was very effective."

"At the end, I meant. All that groaning and moaning, then people trying to join in. I can't stand for that. You didn't see who started it all off, did you?"

"No, I couldn't tell."

"It seemed to be coming from somewhere near where you were sitting."

"Did it? I didn't notice."

"I'm very touchy about troublemakers. Especially outsiders, if they come in and try to promote some kind of evangelical agenda. I deal with them very strictly."

"Yes, that's probably the best way," James said.

Simon moved closer to him. "I may look like a bit of a pudding," he said quietly, "but I still play quite a lot of rugby, you know."

"Do you? Excellent. Good way to stay fit, I expect."

"I find it keeps the aggressive instincts tuned up. Nothing like a bit of rough contact sport to put you in shape for a fight. If necessary. In case I have to give someone a bloody good thrashing."

"Is that what they call Muscular Christianity?"

Simon moved even closer to James. "Don't take the piss," he said. "I'm telling you that I don't like people interfering in my church, and I'm prepared to stop them." He studied James closely with narrowed eyes. "Got it?"

"Yes," James said, "I've got that."

"Good. Just as long as that's clear."

James nodded.

Simon took a step back and smiled at him. "Coming to evensong?"

"Possibly not."

"Never mind. You'll be in my prayers. Cheerio!" He turned and walked away.

James felt that he'd been holding his breath for the last few minutes. He watched Simon stroll over to join Daphne and Dave at the window. Simon's wife made a move to intercept him, darting away from her conversation with Sylvia in the middle of the room, but Simon evaded her deftly in a move that reminded James, appropriately, of a rugby player avoiding a tackle.

James turned his attention back to Reuben. He wondered how to wake him up without attracting more attention. As he looked at him, Reuben's snoring subsided into a diminishing series of whiffles and grunts. His eyes opened slowly. From fathoms deep he gazed up at James with blind serenity. Gradually he began to focus his eyes and James saw him begin the long, slow swim up to consciousness. His eyes swivelled around as he took in as much of his surroundings as he could without moving his head. James wondered how many times in a day Reuben underwent this procedure, as he woke up somewhere and tried to process the basic information necessary to function.

"Move up," James said.

Reuben blinked. James shoved Reuben's leg off the sofa and his foot flopped onto the floor with a thud. His leg must have gone to sleep, and as he struggled to sit upright he nearly fell over. James steadied him as he sat down beside him.

"Reuben," he whispered, "listen to me. This is important. We may not have much time. You've got to tell me what's going on."

Reuben looked around. "I don't know. What is going on?"

"I mean about your plan. With Oliver. Whatever it is you're going to do tonight."

"Oh, right. Yes. That's tonight."

"I know. But what are you going to do?"

"Why are we whispering?"

"Because we don't want anyone else to know."

"Good point." Reuben nodded sagaciously. "Good thinking." he looked around again. "I think I might have just had a little nap. But I'm okay now. It's all good. All good to go for tonight."

"What? What's good to go for tonight?"

Reuben looked at him suspiciously. "Don't you know?"

James saw he might be losing him. "Yes. Of course I do," he said. "But I want you to talk me through it. As part of the drill. That's the professional way: keep going over the plan. Co-ordinate everything. Check, then check again. So it all goes like clockwork."

"Reuben's eyes lit up. "Yeah, cool. Professionals, right?"

"Right, professionals."

"Okay. Shall I go first, or will you?"

"You do it."

"Okay." Reuben took a deep breath. "Step one: as soon as it's completely dark, I get there."

"Where? Where do you get?"

172

Reuben frowned at him. "You already know that."

"Yes, yes, but you need to say it. As part of the drill. Professionals, remember?"

"Oh, God, yes, sorry. Sorry. Right, as soon as it's really dark, I get to--"

"James! Come along!"

James swivelled around to see Daphne Longbourne beckoning him from near the door. John, Spracky and Auntie Pru were standing beside her. He turned back to Reuben. "Where?" he hissed. "Where do you get to?"

"Hurry up, please, dear," Daphne called. "We have to get back. Prudence needs her tablets."

"My fault," Spracky added, "I forgot to bring them."

James looked at Reuben in desperation. Reuben smiled, and tapped his nose. "Don't worry," he whispered, "I know the drill. You get going. See you later." He leaned back complacently and nodded at James.

There was nothing for it. James got up and joined the party at the door.

Dave Silver turned away from the French windows, where he was watching Max out on the lawn, and called to his departing guests. "Thanks for coming, everyone. James, good to see you. Sylvia will see you out, if that's okay. I just want to keep an eye on Max. He's getting a bit frisky with that mallet."

Sylvia Silver appeared, holding Jessica's light raincoat. "Jess left this behind."

Daphne took the coat "I'll give it to her," she said.

James steeled himself. "Do you happen to know where Jessica is?" he said.

"She went off with Raymond," Daphne said. "I expect they've gone for a ride."

"A ride?" James said. "What do you mean?"

"Horses, dear," Daphne said. "You sit on them. It's quite a common activity in the countryside."

James remembered Jessica's conversation with Raymond the previous evening. And they'd been talking about horses earlier. It all made terrible, numbing sense. As he shuffled towards the door behind the others, who were saying goodbye to Sylvia, he glanced back at Reuben. He was on his feet, sidling towards a small table where all the glasses they'd been drinking from before lunch had been collected. Many of them still had some champagne in them.

At the door, Sylvia seized James's hands in hers and pressed then warmly. "Thank you," she said. "I really appreciate the help."

"My pleasure. It was only a bit of washing up."

"No, I mean about Richard. I feel so much better, knowing you're going to be looking out for him. As I said, he really needs someone to help keep him out of trouble. And you're such a nice, sensible boy. I hope we'll see you again soon, dear. Take care." She kissed him on the cheek.

James trooped out behind the Longbourne contingent.

When they were outside he thought about what Jessica had done. It wasn't necessarily as bad as it seemed. She'd probably wanted to say goodbye, and explain everything, but she hadn't been able to because he'd been in the kitchen with Sylvia. And for all he knew, she may not have wanted to go riding at all, and that's what her extended argument with Raymond had been about. That was the most likely explanation for it, on consideration. In fact, it was quite possible that she was missing him just as much as he was missing her, and planning to get back as soon as she could. Quite possible.

James took a deep breath and began to walk

.

Nine.

John Longbourne glanced over his shoulder and said something to Daphne. She nodded and walked on. John hung back for a moment and fell into step beside James. Auntie Pru and Spracky were about a quarter of a mile ahead, setting a brisk pace. They were all walking back the short way, along the main road. It wasn't as interesting as the route James had taken with Raymond, but he wasn't in the mood to notice much about the scenery except that there was less of it.

"Not a bad lunch," John said. "I told you it would be good, didn't I?"

"You were absolutely right."

"Of course, you can lay on that kind of spread all the time if you've got the money. Roasted swan for breakfast every day if you fancy it, and never feel the pinch."

"Still, it was good of them to invite us."

"Oh, yes. Very decent. And it keeps them happy. Got to do something with all that loot, after all. And they've got a fair bit, let me tell you. He's worth a few quid, Dave Silver. He's accumulated a nice little pile. He's got that knack for making a profit." John twitched his nose and gazed around, perhaps scanning the area for traces of spare money. "Yes," he said, "they're a canny tribe."

"Who, the Silvers?"

"No, I mean our Semitic friends in general. It's in the blood, isn't it?"

James paused before he replied. "Well, some people think so."

"Historical fact. You've only got to look at them. He's typical, Dave Silver. He's sitting on a fortune. God knows how much he's worth."

They were silent for a moment. James could see the village green in the distance.

"The only problem," John said, "is that he's not putting his money to work."

"But he's got these various environmental projects, hasn't he? He's producing a film about saving elephants, for one thing."

"Ridiculous. You can't interfere with nature. Red in tooth and claw. No, it's the survival of the fittest out there, and if the elephants aren't fit they've only got themselves to blame. It's no good mollycoddling these wild animals. If you start protecting them artificially, they over-breed and become a pest. In fact, there's a very real danger that elephants will become vermin, like squirrels. A friend of mine who knows about these things, runs safaris, used to be in the South African army, he tells me there's already a lot of concern over there about the exploding gorilla population."

James considered the problem of exploding gorillas.

"It's all a waste of money," John continued, "like this bloody nonsense with the windmill. No, Dave Silver needs to do something useful with all those shekels, that's the truth of the matter." He shook his head sadly.

They walked on in silence for a moment.

"The problem is," John burst out, "and I have to say it, no offence to them at all, but these people can't see a good business opportunity when it's staring them in the face. You've only got to look at the way they've always operated. Traditionally, and I mean it in the nicest possible way, your Jew is basically a loan shark, isn't he?"

"Well, some of the banks were founded by Jewish families," James said. "I think it was often a case of not having many choices of career. You've got to remember--"

"Exactly," John said, "banking, money-lending, usury, whatever you want to call it. You lend money out at high interest, then sit back and watch the profit roll in. To you and me it may seem greedy, but that's just their way, isn't it? And we have to respect it, of course. Different cultures, and all that. We mustn't be prejudiced. God forbid. Have to watch what we say. Otherwise we'll have the Political Correctness Gestapo on to us."

John chuckled and shot a sideways glance at James.

James took a close interest in some small white and yellow flowers growing in the hedge they were walking beside.

"Get on with them all right, do you?" John said.

"Who, the Silvers?"

"No, I mean the Jews. I imagine you come across a fair number of them in London. In the line of business, and such like."

"Well, I suppose I know quite a few Jewish people. I don't really think about it very much, to tell you the truth. I tend not to notice if they are or not."

"Yes, they're clever that way, aren't they? The way they blend in. The business types, anyway. Not the weirdoes with the whiskers and funny haircuts, of course. And those women in the God-awful wigs. But the normal ones, like Dave Silver. Now, he's a nice enough bloke, but the whole concept of the true business venture is alien to these people. The idea of a partnership, for example. Oh, no, too risky. They're quite happy to lend you money for a business deal, as long as they get a guaranteed security and a thumping great rate of interest. They want the old pound of flesh.

"For example, I've been trying to interest Dave in a nice little investment opportunity, but he's got to move fast. These people I work with don't hang about. Opportunity knocks, and you'd better pull your knickers on and open the bloody door. That's the way it works. But every time I mention it, Dave starts gassing on about lawyers, and contracts, and signing papers. A lot of useless red tape. Know what I always say? Red tape strangles enterprise at birth. What Dave can't grasp is that people like me do business on the strength of a handshake and my good name. A gentleman's agreement. And if you want something in writing, well, two gentlemen can draw up a perfectly sound business contract on the back of a napkin over lunch, and trust each other to honour it. But these people don't understand ideas like honour. Integrity. The good, old fashioned traditional values. You see, in my book, an Englishman's word is his bond."

James remembered his father using that expression. But he'd been reminiscing about a vanished world of pink-faced sales reps like his uncle, the armpits of their linen suits stained with the sweat of empire, swapping yarns over G&Ts in expats' clubs from Montevideo to Daar-es-Salaam. It was a world that was as a remote from James's father as it was from James, but the idea had seemed important to him.

John sighed. "The Jews just don't understand that kind of thing, though. Not their style." He shook his head. "Too cautious, that's their trouble. Don't want to spread it about. I expect the son's the same. Is he? have you spoken to him much?"

"Who, Reuben?"

"Reuben, or Richard, or Rabbi Goldberg, or whatever he wants to call himself. Has he mentioned anything about money to you?"

"Money? No, I don't think so. I mean, I haven't really spent that much time with him." James felt they were moving onto shaky ground.

"I heard he was coming into some money, that's all," John said. "A bit of a windfall. I overheard him talking to Jess, as a matter of fact. He was telling her he'd buy her a horse."

"A horse? What, a real one?"

John glanced at him suspiciously. "Yes, a real one. He's got the hots for her, of course, the poor little sod. But if he's going to get hold of some funds of his own, I thought he might be interested in this little investment I was talking about. Okay, the old man might be too tight to go for it, but the younger generation tend to be a bit more adventurous. People like you. You can recognize an opportunity when you see it, can't you? In fact, you might be interested yourself, if you can get hold of a bit of capital. We've set a bottom limit of twenty thousand per investor, but I could put in a word for you, if you can't raise that much. No point making rules if you can't break them, is there?"

He clapped James on the shoulder and winked at him.

"I'm afraid I haven't got any money," James said. "In fact, I've got an overdraft."

"Oh, we've all got an overdraft. It's the only way to get any respect from the bank. If you're fifty quid in credit, they treat you like dirt, but if you owe them a few million, you can't get their tongues out of your arse. No, it's not about what you've got, it's about what you can raise."

"I don't think I could raise any, to be honest."

"Pity. And what about young Richard? No idea what's going to make him rich all of a sudden?"

177

"No. He hasn't mentioned it."

"It's just that this little business deal is such a good opportunity. Sweet as a nut."

They'd reached the gates of the house. Daphne was waiting for them.

"Think about it," John said to James, "and we can talk about it again later." He walked up to Daphne and linked his arm through hers. As they walked towards the house James heard him say, "I think I'm about ready for a nap after that lunch."

*

Jarvis had glimpsed Naked Man and some members of the Longbourne family through the dense web of foliage that cocooned him. He wondered where they'd been and what they'd been doing. What did people do? They went to church. They had lunch. They went for a walk. Church. Lunch. Walk. Chunk. Lurch. Lunk, wurch, wunk. The words loomed out of the dense fog that filled his head, and then receded before he could examine them and understand what they meant.

He couldn't stay in the hedge. He was shivering and sweating and he was in agony. He didn't want to examine the wounds on his chest but they throbbed with searing pain. Yellow pus was seeping through his crusted shirt continuously now. His throat was aching with thirst. What could he drink? He remembered the vacuum flask in his car. Maybe there was still some coffee in it. He crawled out of the hedge, ignoring the fresh cuts and scratches he collected. He headed towards his car, at the bottom of the green.

He seemed to be moving without walking. Floating. It was quite pleasant in a way, even though he was in pain. Because the pain wasn't actually his. It was happening to someone else, someone very similar to him, but not quite the same. A kind of ghostly identical twin, who was suffering on his behalf. Perhaps he'd been replaced by a replica of himself. In which case, where was the real him? An interesting question. Very interesting.

He looked around. Something was wrong with the colours. Everything was shimmering slightly. If he turned his head quickly, it left an after-image. He was immensely tall. If he looked down, his feet seemed tiny. But it wasn't a good idea to look down, he discovered: his feet became shy and wouldn't work properly. Best not to embarrass them. Look straight ahead.

He reached the car and wrenched the door open. The vacuum flask was on the passenger seat. He got in, picked it up, and unscrewed the lid. There was about a cupful of coffee in the bottom. He drank straight from the flask. It was foul. Stale and bitter, with a repulsive, sour aftertaste that furred up his tongue and teeth. And something else, that he couldn't identify. A dense, chalky texture. But whatever it was, he needed liquid. He drained the flask and slumped down in his seat. It was stifling in the car, and the decaying upholstery was almost too hot to touch. He opened the windows and then leaned back again. He closed his eyes. Perhaps he should try to get some rest.

*

James didn't follow the others into the house. He didn't know what he would do in there and he didn't want to talk to any of them. His conversation with John Longbourne had distracted him from thoughts of Jessica for a while, but it had also depressed him, and left him feeling that he needed a shower.

And now he was tormented by indecision. He began to walk slowly down the sloping lawn as he tried to think things through. Should he go back to the manor under some pretext and try to get more information out of Reuben? But he didn't want to miss Jessica when she got back from riding. When would that be? In an hour? Two? Three? She'd have to go back to Raymond's first, because the horse lived there. Maybe he should go and meet them. But how long would it take him to walk there, assuming he could find his way? And he might miss her coming back a different way.

He found that he'd reached the trees and shrubbery at the bottom of the lawn. He turned to his right and scuffed along the edge of the grass. It was oppressively hot. Although the sky was still clear and blue, the air seemed to have thickened. He came to a trail leading through the trees, and walked into the shade.

He emerged from the trees into a different part of the property. A paved pathway led him between some greenhouses on one side, and lots of things growing in neat rows on the other, some of them entwined around complex bamboo frames.

A rattling, chugging noise was coming from somewhere. He turned a corner and walked into a large cobbled yard, lined with sheds and other buildings. In the middle of the yard stood Bill Longbourne's traction engine. As he watched, its drive belt rattled and whirred to a stop. A couple of puffs of cloudy grey smoke seeped gently from its chimney stack and then it stood creaking and hissing gently in the afternoon sun, at rest.

James couldn't see anyone around. He walked towards the traction engine. At close range it was even more impressive than it had looked yesterday. There was something stately and magnificent about it.

He stood beside it and touched the slender brass pipes that ran all around the great cylindrical body of the machine. They were warm but not hot. He ran his fingers around the junctions where the brass work intersected with another system of slightly larger copper tubes. The joints felt solid and reliable, tooled with care and precision. He traced the pipes along the side of the engine and walked around to the front of the machine, where he stopped abruptly. He was face-to-face with Bill Longbourne.

179

Bill was holding a grease gun with a long spout in one hand, and some rags in the other. He'd changed back into the clothes that James had first seen him in. He appeared to possess two versions of the same basic outfit: one for special occasions, in which he looked reasonably respectable from a distance, and a decayed replica of the same clothes, in which he looked like someone who lived in a cardboard box on the street.

They looked at each other in silence for a moment.

"What do you think of her?" Bill said.

James realized he still had his hand on the metalwork. He removed it hastily. "It's lovely," he said. "She. She's lovely."

Bill nodded slowly. He walked past James, around to the side of the machine. He inserted the nozzle of the grease gun into an aperture next to one of the drive-belt spindles, latched it onto a recessed nipple and squeezed the handle of the gun gently. He removed the nozzle and carefully wiped away the excess grease with one of the rags, then polished the surrounding metal with another, cleaner one.

He turned to face James. "You like old things, do you?"

"Yes. Well, what I actually like is the way they used to make things."

"Craftsmanship."

"Exactly. It's all to do with care and attention."

"I hear you like old houses, too."

James looked at him in surprise.

"Oh, I hear things," Bill said. "Spracky keeps me up to date. She said you were keen on architecture."

"I suppose I'm interested in anything that's well made, really. Craftsmanship, as you say. And there seems to be more of that in old things than in new ones."

"And the manor house? What do you think of that?"

"I love it. I love the simplicity of that period. The clean lines. And it's great the way the Silvers haven't cluttered it up. I know some people say these buildings shouldn't be in private hands, but Dave and Sylvia obviously take such good care of the place I can't help thinking they deserve to live there. I mean, when you look at--" He stopped. He was aware of sweat breaking out on his upper lip. "God, I'm sorry, I forgot. It used to be in your family. Sorry."

"Don't apologize. That was years ago. To tell you the truth I don't really care who owns the place, as long as they look after it. And I'd be no good at it, I can tell you that. I'm pretty hopeless with money, even if I had any. And Dave Silver is doing an excellent job up there. He's a good man. I like the wife, too. Great fun." He paused. "I'd like to see more of them, actually, but I don't socialize much these days."

Bill turned back to the traction engine and inserted the nozzle of the grease gun into another crevice. "I dare say my brother would like to get his hands on the place, if the family could get it back." He squeezed the handle of the gun.

"But there's not much chance of that." The ends of his moustache twitched. "Not much chance at all."

He withdrew the gun and wiped the metalwork. "You can't take it with you, can you? You can only hope someone else will look after it. Like this beauty. She was made by craftsmen, all right." He waved the nozzle of the grease gun at a brass plaque mounted on the side of the boiler. James stepped up to look at it. The embossed inscription declared that the traction engine was manufactured by Arbuthnot and Sons of Taunton in nineteen hundred and ten.

"It's in amazing condition," James said.

"She was in poor shape when I found her, though. Hadn't been properly looked after for years. I had to do a lot of work to restore her. Luckily there are a few of us in the area who are interested in these things. We've got a sort of club. So I had some help." The ends of his moustache twitched again. "I'm not the only crackpot around here, you see."

He turned away, and steadying himself with one hand on the huge, ribbed back wheel, he used two footplates set into the bodywork to climb up into the cab, where he sat down. His battered shoes were level with the top of James's head.

"Come on up," he said.

James clambered up and hoisted himself into the cab. There was another seat beside Bill, like an oversized, perforated metal bicycle saddle, mounted on an armature. James sat in it. It was surprisingly comfortable. He gazed around at the instruments and controls. The various valves, taps, levers, wheels, handles and pedals were worn and polished with years of use. The calibrations on the dials evoked arcane systems of measurement. Everything looked both outdated and quaintly futuristic, like the poignant technology in an old sci-fi film.

"I often sit up here," Bill said. "I find it's a good place to think. Or not think, if you know what I mean. I find I can drift off. I don't know where. Nowhere in particular. I can just... be here. I expect I'm talking rubbish. But I do find it very restful. Tranquil."

"No, I understand completely."

"Like being in church, perhaps," Bill said.

"Yes." James looked around at the gleaming metal and the polished wood, and the deep shadows cast by the canopy that covered the cab. "Like a sort of chapel."

"That's an idea," Bill said. "We could start our own little religion up here, couldn't we? It couldn't do much more harm than the real ones." He chuckled. "They'll burn us at the stake if we're not careful. Talking blasphemy. Or is it heresy?"

"I don't think they care any more. Well, not the C of E, anyway. Although the vicar got quite worked up today, didn't he?"

"Did he?" Bill said. "I was asleep. I'm very lucky. I've developed the knack of going to sleep with my eyes open. It's a great comfort."

"God, yes. Very handy."

"Always been a bit of a sore point for me, actually, religion. My mother was half French, you see. Did you know that?"

"No, I didn't. French. Was that a problem?"

"Catholic."

"Oh, right. Of course."

"She only agreed to marry my father if he promised that any children they had would be brought up as Catholics. He would have promised anything, he was mad about her. There's a picture of her in the house. Wearing a purple dress, you may have seen it."

"The big one, in the living room?"

"That's it. Anyway, when it came to it, Father went back on his promise. So there was always a tremendous amount of trouble about religion in the house. I think it broke her heart, in a way. He was a good man, don't get me wrong. He loved her desperately. He had a great struggle with his conscience. But he had his own family to think about, you see? My grandfather was terribly cut up about it. There were awful rows."

Bill paused and examined the grease gun that was still in his hand.

"Then she died," he said. "I was still quite young, and John was just an infant. I never really knew her that well. Or Father, for that matter. But things were different in those days, you see. Men didn't make a great fuss over their children. It simply wasn't done. You spent most of your time with Nanny, if you were of a certain sort. And she'd bring you in to see him at tea-time every so often, and he'd try to remember who the hell you were and think of something to say. And you stood there, trying not to stammer when he asked you about your lessons, or games, or hobbies, until he sent you away again. But everyone was like that. Apart from anything else, they never knew how long the children were going to last. Because of what happened to their own generation, of course. He was one of five children, and only two survived. Him and Prudence. His older brother, Arthur, was lost in the Great War. Although they don't call it that any more."

"The First World War," James said.

"Well, fair play, there was nothing great about it, as it turned out. Or any of them. They're all a bloody waste. I was a bit too young to fight in the next one. I was terribly disappointed at the time, of course. I wanted to go off and kill the Huns, like all the older boys. I thank my lucky stars now, though. All those men who didn't come back. Or got smashed up. What a bloody waste."

Bill fell silent. James didn't feel the need to say anything.

"Yes," Bill said suddenly, "poor old uncle Arthur copped it in the trenches. Then the other two were taken by the flu just after the war. That was cruel, that epidemic. All those millions dead in the war, and then even more of them snuffed out by a bloody germ. Alice and Bertie went within a week of each other. Only Father and Prudence were left. We were a bit luckier, my generation. Two out of three. John and I had a sister who died, you see. Did they tell you?"

"No. No one's mentioned it."

"No, well, they wouldn't, probably. Not done. She was a sweet little thing, but there was something wrong with her. Not right in the head. I can't remember what they call it now, something different. Poor little Julia. She was always so jolly. Always smiling and laughing. Wanted to hug you all the time. No trouble, really, but you could tell she wasn't right. And when Mother died, Father rather went to pieces, and Auntie Pru moved in. She was much younger than him, but she more or less took charge of things, and brought us up, really. And she couldn't stand little Julia. Couldn't bear to be touched by her. Said it made her sick. So they put her away. In a home. That's what they called it, anyway, but I don't think it was much of a home. We weren't allowed to visit her. Pru said it was unhealthy to brood on these things and it would be better if we were encouraged to forget about her."

Bill sighed. James tried to imagine him and John as children, but all he could visualise were smaller versions of them as they were now, complete with little moustaches.

"Poor little thing," Bill continued, "all by herself in that ghastly place. She died after a year or two. John was terribly upset. She was nearer his age, you see. He went off the rails for a while, got chucked out of various schools, and so forth. God, it's all so bloody sad. Poor little Julia. To think of her all alone there, wondering why we'd locked her up, what she'd done wrong. And we never saw her again. I still think about her. Every day. Poor little thing."

Bill sniffed loudly. James glanced at him and saw that tears were rolling down his cheeks. He made no attempt to hide them. He gazed vacantly into space for a moment, then wiped his eyes with the filthy sleeve of his jacket.

"Sorry," he said. "I seem to get more sentimental as I get older. You wouldn't think that would happen, would you? You'd think it would be the other way. That you'd get used to all these damned things. But you don't. I don't, anyway." He examined the rags in his hand and blew his nose on the cleaner one. "Sorry," he muttered again.

James felt he should say something. "That's all right. I understand. Well, in a way. My father died when I was quite young. I seem to be thinking about him more and more as I get older."

"Older." Bill laughed. "You have no idea."

"Obviously, I'm not old, as such."

"No, I'm sorry, I shouldn't laugh. It doesn't make any difference. It's damn well miserable and that's all there is too it, no matter how old you are. I'm sure you've suffered dreadfully from your loss. But don't you start blubbing, too, or we'll be here all day."

"I'd better be going," James said. "I expect you've got things to do."

Bill nodded. "I expect so."

"Thanks for letting me see her."

"You're welcome. Nice to meet someone who appreciates her."

James slid off the seat and climbed down from the cab.

"Oh, by the way," Bill said.

James looked up at him. "Yes?"

"I hear you caused quite a stir at the fete yesterday."

"I think I drank a bit too much, actually."

"Good for you." A wistful look came over Bill's face. "Jackie Leppard's scrumpy punch. She's a got a real talent, that woman." He peered down at James again. "And I understand you had a bit of trouble with the windmill."

"There was rather an unfortunate accident."

"Well, anyone who manages to give a good whack on the head to that bumptious little fraud who pretends to be a professor stands high in my estimation."

"I didn't do it on purpose."

"No, of course not. How is he, by the way?"

"I'm told he'll recover."

"Not too soon, I hope. It'd be nice to think you've shut him up for a while. I had him over here when he first arrived, you know. Tried to teach me about traction engines. He'd obviously just read some book or other. Ridiculous man. Well, goodbye."

"Goodbye." James turned away.

"One more thing," Bill called to him.

"Yes?"

"You know my brother, John?"

"Yes, of course."

"Don't lend him any money."

"Right. I haven't got any, actually."

"That's what you think. Everyone's worth something. You could probably get a loan, or a mortgage, or something. And he'll get it out of you, if you give him half a chance." He shook his head. "It's all too much trouble, in the end. Money."

"I expect you're right. Although I wouldn't mind the chance to find out."

"Of course, you might turn out to be very good with it. Who knows. Some people are. But much as I dearly love my little brother, just be careful of him."

"I will."

"And don't let any of them bother you, for that matter. Up at the house."

"Thanks. I'll try not to."

"Good man."

James ambled up the lawn towards the house. He thought about the way the tears had trickled down the furrows in Bill Longbourne's leathery cheeks as he talked about a little girl who died seventy years ago.

As he reached the gravel driveway he allowed himself to consider an idea that he'd been carefully avoiding.

Perhaps Jessica was back.

He'd been aware of the thought, lurking hopefully at the edge of his attention, but he'd been denying it access, like a club doorman turning away a customer wearing the wrong shoes. Now he allowed it into his mind, where it immediately ran riot:

Jessica had returned without going riding. It was all a mistake. Or she'd gone riding, then realized she wanted to see him. She'd rushed back. She was waiting for him. She would take him by the hand and lead him upstairs. They'd close the curtains and make love in the cool, dim light. It would be wonderful, magical, transcendent.

He opened the door and stepped into the shadowed hallway.

He pitched his voice to reach the rooms on either side of the hall. "Jessica?"

The house was silent.

He walked towards the stairs. "Hello? Jessica?"

Spracky's voice drifted from the kitchen. "She's not here! Riding!"

"Sorry! Thanks!"

He turned and went back outside.

James stood at the top of the lawn. There was a very faint impression of cloud beginning to form in the sky, or behind it, like a light charcoal sketch of clouds beyond a deep blue veil.

He heard the noise of a car engine, approaching from the gateway. There was a sound of stone scraping against metal, then a furious grinding of gears followed by a whine of acceleration. After a couple of seconds a large grey car shot around the curve of the drive, destroying some of the flower beds as it swerved wildly from side to side. James thought it might hit the house, until it skidded to a halt a few yards away from him, churning up the gravel. The engine revved, then stalled. Nothing happened for a moment, then the driver's door swung open. A powerful arc of projectile vomit shot out, flying horizontally for several feet over the gravel before it splashed down onto the grass.

James walked towards the car. "Reuben?"

It was a BMW saloon and it looked a few years old. Reuben was behind the wheel. No one else was in the car. He looked up at James, trying to focus.

"She here?"

"No. What are you doing, Reuben? Come inside."

Reuben shook his head. "Got to find her." He turned the ignition key. The car bucked and leapt forward, then stalled, making James jump out of the way as the open door swung to and fro. Reuben grabbed the gear stick, wrenched it into neutral, and turned the key again. The engine fired and he waggled the stick around violently, mashing the gears as he tried to find reverse.

"Reuben, stop! I might be wrong. Maybe she's inside! Let's go and see!"

Reuben gazed up at him. He narrowed his eyes. "Lying."

"No, really, she might be!"

Reuben pushed and pulled the gear stick angrily, slapping it around as he pumped the clutch. "Get in gear, you fucking fucker!"

"No, wait! I can't let you drive like this."

Reuben stared up at him through bloodshot eyes. "You can't stop me."

He was probably right, James thought. He was quite big and he was very drunk. James calculated his chances if he tried to reach past him, turn the ignition off, remove the key, and get out of the way before Reuben could do him some damage. Not good.

"I'm not going to try and stop you. I promise. Just wait a moment. Please. I just want to talk to you. Just for two seconds."

"Can't. Got to go. Got to find her." He hauled at the gear stick again.

"Wait! It's about Jessica. I've got something to tell you."

Reuben wavered.

"Turn the engine off," James said. "Just for a moment."

"No."

The engine stalled.

"Fuck." Reuben fumbled for the ignition key.

"No, hold on. Wait."

Reuben slumped back in his seat. "What? What is it?"

"Whose car is this?"

"Parents. Their old one. They got a green one. Eco-thing green. You know."

"Do they know you've got it?'

Reuben shrugged. "Dunno."

"Have you got a licence?"

"No."

"Why don't you just come inside for a minute?"

"No! Fuck off!" Reuben reached for the key again.

"Stop! Don't you want to hear about Jessica?"

"What about her?"

James thought furiously. "Well, she said she liked you. She told me."

"When?"

"Last night. No, this morning. At church. On the way to church."

"She likes me?"

"Yes, she really likes you. Except for one thing."

"What?"

"She doesn't like you getting drunk. She said she hates seeing you drunk. She'd rather not see you at all than see you drunk, even though she really likes you."

Reuben squinted at him for a long time. "Really?"

"Yes. So, you see, it would be much better if you didn't try and find her now, wouldn't it? So she doesn't see you drunk. Better to come inside and have a rest."

Reuben's face hardened. James knew he'd overplayed it. He should have left out the last bit, about having a rest. Reuben tried to close the car door. James hung on to it.

"Fuck off!" Reuben said.

"Wait," James said in desperation, "I'll come with you!"

Reuben considered this. "Actually," he said, "you could help me drive."

*

"Down!" Reuben shouted, gripping the steering wheel.

"What?"

"Down! Change down! Quick!"

They were at the foot of the hill on the route they'd taken last night, and the car was losing power. James manoeuvred the gear stick down into third.

"And again! Down!" Reuben pumped the clutch.

James found second gear. "And again?"

"No, it's okay."

The car gained power and began to climb the hill steadily.

Reuben leaned back in the driver's seat. They'd agreed that he should steer and operate the pedals, and James would take over the duty of shifting the gear stick. They'd managed to make it out of the driveway using this system, with only some minor damage to the lawn and the loss of a wing mirror as they went through the gateposts.

"This is the road to Raymond's," James said.

"I know."

"Is that where we're going?"

"Got to find them."

"But they've gone riding. Haven't they?"

"Might be a bluff. But we can pick up their trail."

"But why is it so important to find them right now? Why can't it wait?"

"Got to stop them."

"Doing what?"

"Shagging."

"What?"

"Shagging, Having sex."

"That's ridiculous! What makes you think they're going to have sex?"

"I just know."

"How? How do you know?"

"I just do. Up! Change up!"

They'd reached the top of the hill. Reuben depressed the clutch and James slipped the gear stick up into third. The car shot over the crest of the hill.

"And again!" Reuben said. "I'm doing the clutch again now!"

James changed to fourth. They accelerated along the flat, straight road.

"Slow down," James said.

"It's all right. I'm fine. Oops."

James grabbed the wheel. Between them they wrestled the car back on to the road after a brief interlude on the grass verge.

"I don't believe it," James said, "about them having sex. Raymond's far too old for her. He wouldn't do that."

Reuben glanced at him. "Why not? Wouldn't you?"

"Me? No. I mean, I don't know. But that's not the point. Anyway, I'm only a few years older than her. Not that I would do it. But he's - he's much older."

"Doesn't matter. He's a man."

"Watch the road!"

"Oops."

"Slow down, please!"

"No."

"All right. But how do you know they're going to have sex?"

"Last night. When I went to the stables with them? And then I left? I didn't really leave. Not completely. Not straight away. I heard them talk about it. Arranging it."

"You definitely heard them?"

"Sort of. It was a bit muffled. Then I had to go because the hay made me sneeze."

"So you can't be sure."

"It's true! She's going to let him take her virginity."

"What!"

"Her virginity."

"What makes you think she's a virgin?"

"I know she is. She told me."

"But why's she going to let Raymond do it?"

"Because then he'll give her the horse."

"If she has sex with him?"

"Yes."

"You heard him say he'd give her the horse if she let him take her virginity."

"Not exactly. But I definitely heard them talking about having sex. Today. And she wants the horse. So it stands to reason; that's why she's going to let him do it."

"But that's awful," James said. "He's just exploiting her. It's blackmail. It's abusive. It's almost rape. I can't believe Raymond would do something like that."

"He's probably shagged millions of women. You know what these rock stars are like. That's why he wants a virgin. They get jaded. Everything's like a hobby for them."

James thought about the model railway. What did he really know about Raymond? He was like an assemblage of ingredients, as if he'd constructed himself from a catalogue. Even his weird mixture of beliefs were like clothes selected from a dressing-up box. He was utterly unfathomable. Oh, God. What if Reuben was right? They had to stop Jessica from making a terrible mistake.

A horn blared. A car coming the other way passed within a inch of them, "Wanker," Reuben muttered.

"Look," James said, "we'd better think this through before we try to find them. Pull over, and we can work out what to do."

"No."

Reuben swerved violently to avoid another oncoming car.

"Christ," James said, "pull over. Really, I mean it. We can work out a plan, and you can take a bit of a break. You're going to kill us in a minute."

"No!" Reuben said fiercely. "I'm fine. It's a straight road from here."

James seemed to remember that he was right, although he was pretty sure there was a major crossroads somewhere. As he began to look out for it, he realized they weren't very far from Raymond's place. There was no telling what Reuben would do when they got there.

Suddenly he remembered that the robbery plan was still lurking in the background like some nightmarish surgical appointment. Much as he wanted to focus on what to do about Jessica, he had to try and get some more information from Reuben urgently.

"Reuben, listen. You know this plan of yours?"

"What plan?"

"This plan you and Olly have cooked up. The one that's happening tonight."

"I thought we were talking about Jessica."

"We are. But we need to talk about the other plan as well. I need you to tell me what you're going to do. Quickly, before we get there."

Reuben scowled. "I already told you. Why do you keep asking me?"

"Yes, we ran through it all after lunch. Very professional. Good briefing. But we didn't cover all the details before I had to leave, did we? Remember? For example, where exactly is the robbery happening?"

"Where do you think? The Post Office."

James was astonished. "You're going to break in? To the Post Office?"

"How else am I going to get inside in the middle of the fucking night?"

"But--" James sat back in his seat. "Why?"

"For the fucking money!"

"Look out!"

"Why? What?"

"Oh, shit!"

189

They sped past a stop sign and shot across the major intersection that James remembered. From the corner of his eye he saw a car that was approaching from their left swerve wildly, and glimpsed the driver's ashen face as he hit his brakes.

"What?" Reuben said.

"Nothing." James unbraced himself from the dashboard. His legs were rigid with the effort of trying to press himself back into his seat. He unbent them slowly. "Listen, Reuben," he said, "it's a tiny village Post Office. Think about it. How much money can there be in there?"

Reuben snickered. "Maybe thousands. Thousand and thousands."

"What has Oliver told you?"

Reuben glanced at him suspiciously. "It's inside information. If he hasn't told you, I can't tell you."

"I'm just checking to see if he's told you the full story. The one that he's told me."

"Oh, right."

"So, what has he told you?"

"It's old money. Old notes, so they can't be traced. On its way to be destroyed. Burned. It's just there for this weekend. Being stored. In transit."

"Why would they do that? Why would they store large sums of money in a tiny village Post Office over a weekend? It's not very likely."

"Exactly! That's what they want you to think. No one suspects it's there. It's the last place they'd look. It's brilliant."

James focused on his breathing for a moment. It was important to be calm. He tried to keep his tone casual. "Actually, why does the money have to be stored at all? That's the interesting question, isn't it? Why can't it just go straight to the incinerator, or whatever it is? Under guard. That would make more sense."

Reuben frowned. "Something about chemicals. I can't remember exactly. Olly told me. He knows all about it. He knows a man who works for the Royal Mint. They do it all the time. It's top secret. Right?"

"Right. And what about the parcel?"

"Ah, we're here!" Reuben hauled at the wheel, scissoring his arms. The car spun across the road and slewed into Raymond's driveway which, luckily, was wide enough to admit it sideways. Reuben had to slow down to get them pointed in the right direction, and by the time he took the final corner of the drive on the approach to the house they were doing no more than fifty.

"The parcel," James said. "What about the parcel?"

"Oh, yes. Very important. Even more important than the money, Olly said. He said I had to find it and give it to you, no matter what. No matter how much money I found there. He said you'd know what was in it. You do know, don't you?"

James sighed. "Yes," he said, "I do."

Reuben slammed the brakes on. The car skidded to a halt in the yard where Jessica had parked last night. Reuben flung open his door and tumbled out. "Stay there!" he shouted.

"No, wait!" James said, struggling with his seat belt, "I'll come too!"

Reuben lurched back to the car and leaned on the open door. "No, no, stay here. In case they're out riding, and they come back while I'm inside. I won't be long." He staggered to the porch and disappeared inside the house.

After five minutes James began to worry. He got out of the car. He wondered if he should follow Reuben inside. On the one hand, if Jessica and Raymond were out riding, and they returned now, it would be much better if he encountered them before Reuben did. But if they were inside, and Reuben had found them, he felt he should be there. He strained to hear the sound of raised voices or breaking glass. Everything was silent. He scanned the windows, opaque as they reflected the afternoon sun, and pictured a body suddenly crashing out through one of them.

James thought about the robbery plan. The story about the money was clearly preposterous. It was amazing what people would believe when they wanted to. Reuben was being shamelessly manipulated by Oliver, who'd obviously been nurturing his delusions about Jessica in order to persuade him to break into the Post Office.

And why? James finally admitted to himself what he'd known ever since he first heard about the parcel. It was a drug deal, and, like all Oliver's deals, it was needlessly complex, astoundingly ill-conceived, and potentially dangerous to everyone except Oliver. As far as James could tell, the original plan was to get him to collect the parcel, so that Oliver wouldn't be exposed to the risk. Oliver had got himself arrested in London in order to give himself an alibi for the whole weekend. And in the event that the police had somehow found out about the parcel, and were waiting to pounce on whoever collected it, Oliver probably expected James to claim ignorance, and insist it was all a mistake, or that he was an innocent dupe of some unknown criminal. He knew James wouldn't shop him.

The whole insane enterprise with Reuben and the burglary was the back-up plan, to be used in case James failed to collect the parcel during opening hours. Which is what had happened, naturally, given Oliver's administrative skills. And now Reuben was going to execute Plan B. No matter how little money he found in the Post Office, he would dutifully extract the parcel and hand it over to James. Oliver would spin Reuben some ridiculous explanation about why the money wasn't there, and Reuben would swallow it.

And if he was caught, or James was caught, or they were both caught, and they were in real, serious trouble, what would Oliver do? James pictured his handsome, laughing face, as he greeted you and made you feel you were the one person he most wanted to see in the whole world, and you sat in a bar or a restaurant with him, and he took you into his confidence, and made you feel special, so you were quite happy to pay the bill when he had to leave suddenly. What would Oliver do?

Fuck all.

He'd simply abandon them. That was the truth.

James heard the sudden clatter of hooves on cobbles. He turned towards the drive. But the sound was coming from behind him. He turned back. A horse was galloping towards him from the stables.

Reuben was on its back, clinging on for dear life.

James flattened himself against the car. He caught a scent of the horse as it rushed past him, huge and very close. Stale sweat, dust, damp carpets, leather.

He glimpsed Reuben's white, pinched face. "Wait there!" Reuben shouted in a strangled croak, his voice drifting back to James as the horse thundered out of the yard.

For a while James considered the question of how Reuben's hat stayed on. Was there some very thin cord, or filament of elastic, that James hadn't noticed, buried in his wispy beard as it ran under his chin? Or perhaps it was something religious, a mystery of the faith. Or even faith itself.

After a few moments, he began to try and understand what he'd just seen. There were several reasons why it was impossible, but unless he was hallucinating, he had to accept that Reuben had ridden past him on a horse.

He became aware that a short, chubby man was inspecting him from the far side of the yard. James had seen him before. Last night. It was Bruce, the manager of the band who were recording in the studio. He sported the same inappropriately youthful clothes that he wore last night, but with a different baseball cap. He raised his arm in greeting and walked towards James.

"Are you sure he can ride, your friend?"

James paused before answering. "Why do you ask?"

"Well, he looked a bit shaky when he got going just then. He told me he was an experienced rider. Otherwise I wouldn't have saddled up the mare for him. He told me that Ray had said to let him ride one of the nags so he can catch up with him and the girl. What's her name again?"

"Jessica. Sorry, did you say you'd saddled the horse up for him?"

"Yeah, why not?" There was a note of defiance in Bruce's voice. "Seems like a nice boy. He said he was a bit rusty, and he asked me do it for him. I can give him a hand if I want, can't I? Nothing wrong with that, is there?"

"No, no, fine. But you know how to do all that, do you? That's all I was asking."

"Oh, I see what you mean. Sorry. Yeah, I know how to do all that." He gave James a shy smile. "I grew up near Newbury. I was a stable lad for years. I know all about horses, mate. Horrible fucking animals."

"But does Raymond know?"

192

"Know what?"

"About you using one of his horses."

"Of course he does. We've got an arrangement. I paid a bit extra, well, a lot extra, actually, to be able to use a couple of them. Ray knows I can handle them." He shook his head sadly. "I was hoping to teach a couple of the guys to ride. I've always thought Spike would have a good seat. Thought he might be a natural. But he wasn't interested. I was very disappointed. Gavin, the drummer, he had a crack, but he was hopeless. He was treating her like a computer game. She threw him, eventually. That nice big mare I put your friend on, as it happens. She's as good as gold normally."

"Oh, God. But you think Reuben will be all right?"

"As long as he treats her properly. I told him she's got a bit of a soft mouth on her, that one."

"Did he say he knew which way to go?"

"Yeah. Said he did. And even if he doesn't, Polly does. She'll find her own way. Ray takes them all on the same ride, you see, so they're all used to it. They all know the route. Up the first meadow, nice little run over the heath at the top, past the golf course, and down around the back of that village where he goes to church. What's it called?"

"Ullage."

"That's it. Round through the fields behind there, then back up through the village, then there's a bridle path through the woods next to the main road, nice gentle canter all the way home."

"But will the horse be going fast?"

Bruce looked worried. "It sounds like you're saying your mate doesn't know what he's doing. Why did he tell me he could ride? Can he? Can he ride?"

"No."

"Oh, fuck. Ray's going to kill me."

"We've got to stop him."

"It's all right. He'll just be a bit angry. I'll pay for the horse if she's hurt."

"No, I mean stop Reuben."

"Oh. I see."

James looked dubiously at the car. "Can you drive?"

"Me? Of course I can."

"Can you drive me? To catch up with Reuben."

"That won't do much good. They'll be cross-country most of the way. Apart from going back up through that village. I suppose you could try to catch him there, but that's more than half way, and it's just as likely you'll miss him."

James came to a decision. "What about the other horse?"

"What other horse?"

"The other horse Raymond's letting you use."

"Damien? What about him?"

"Can you saddle it up for me? Him? So I can ride him?"

"You want to ride Damien?"

"Yes. Raymond said I could. Last night. He said it was fine."

Bruce took off his baseball cap and scratched his head. "Are you sure?"

"Positive. But we need to hurry. I've got to find Reuben. He might get hurt."

"And you can ride, can you?"

"Oh, yes."

"How much riding have you done?"

"Oh, I was practically born on a horse."

Bruce raised his eyebrows. "Then you can saddle him up yourself, can't you?"

"No. No, I've got a bad arm. Shoulder. Bad shoulder. Can't lift things."

"Perhaps you'd better not ride, then."

"Oh, no, riding's good for it. It's what's called a neurological referred spasmodic reaction of the sciatic system, which derives a therapeutic stimulation of the nerve endings from agitation of the *gluteus maximus*. As I'm sure you know. So, if you can just do all the saddling part, I'll be fine."

"Oh. All right. Come on."

"What are you doing?"

James took his foot out of the stirrup. He was obviously about to do something wrong, but couldn't see what. How difficult could it be? You just put your foot in the stirrup and jumped on the horse. Perhaps he'd overlooked some minor point of equestrian etiquette. He laughed. "Oh, nothing, I always do that." He shook his leg, then raised the other one and shook it. "Silly, really. Just a little ritual I have. For luck."

"Well, you won't have much luck if you walk up from behind him like that. He's liable to give you a nasty kick."

James stepped away from the horse quickly. "Why, what's the matter with him?"

"Nothing. They just don't like it, do they? When you get behind them. And he's just a bit nervous, this one. But he's a sweetheart, really. He's lovely and friendly." Bruce tightened his grip on the bridle and rubbed the horse behind its ear. "Aren't you mate? Yes, that's right, you're a sweetheart."

James stood beside the animal's head. Its eye bulged at him. James smiled encouragingly. He reached out and touched its nose. It snorted and shook its head. James withdrew his hand hastily. "Good boy," he said. "Good boy."

"You need to be a bit firm with him," Bruce said. He patted the horse's long, tapering skull just above its nostrils.

James patted the horse in the same place. It gave a little snuffle, but didn't seem to mind. James got more confident. He patted the animal's neck, with no ill effects. Yes, you needed to show it who was boss. The worst thing you could do was let it see you were nervous. He gave the horse a friendly whack on its flank. It bucked violently and pawed at the ground. James leapt back, nearly losing his footing in the straw.

"Steady," Bruce said. "He'll think you want him to go."

"Oh, I do. When I'm on, of course." He turned to Bruce and laughed.

Bruce nodded. "You're ready, then, are you?"

"Yes, sure."

James saw a sudden image of someone getting on a horse in a film he'd watched recently. Of course: you faced the rear of the animal and swung around as you got up, so you ended up facing the front. It was completely logical, when you thought about it. He casually turned towards the horse's backside, lifted his left leg, and put it in the stirrup. He reached up and grasped the pommel of the saddle. As he put his weight on it the horse shuffled sideways away from him. James hopped along with it, trying to stay upright.

"Whoa there, Damien, steady boy, steady," Bruce said, pulling the horse back into position. He peered around the horse's head at James. "You'll have to hop on a bit quick, mate, once he knows what you're up to. Go on, jump up quick."

James pushed himself up off his right leg and tried to swing it over the horse's back, hoisting himself up by the pommel at the same time. But he failed to achieve sufficient elevation, and flopped down again, staggering slightly.

"I'll help you," Bruce said, walking around to James's side of the horse.

As James flexed his leg, ready to spring, he felt Bruce's hand slide under his bottom. He leapt in the air like a trout, slung himself onto the horse's back in a low crouch, and nearly slipped off the other side. He righted himself, and sat up in the saddle.

God, he was high up off the ground. He clung on to the pommel, trying to get his right foot into the other stirrup.

"He's tall, isn't he?" James said.

Bruce grunted as he walked around the horse and grabbed James's foot, which he guided roughly into the stirrup. He held on to James's ankle for a moment, then moved his hand slowly up his leg, looking up at him. James coughed loudly and looked away.

Bruce let his hand rest on James's thigh for a moment. James froze. Bruce squeezed his leg, then took his hand away. He handed the reins up to him and stepped back. He eyed James critically.

"If you're going to sit that far back, I'd better adjust those stirrups."

"No, it's all right, just getting used to this saddle." James shuffled his bottom along the saddle, using the reins to pull himself forward. This had the effect of hauling the horse's head violently up and back, which it objected to. It snorted, and dipped its head down suddenly so that James was jerked forward and his arms were nearly yanked out of their sockets.

"Go easy, mate!" Bruce said. "He won't like that."

"No," James said, "I thought not. Good. Fine." He let the reins go loose for a moment, then took a tight grip on them when the horse had stopped jerking its head around and seemed to have settled down. He saw Bruce looking closely at his hands.

"Are you sure you know what you're doing?" Bruce said.

"Yes, no problem. Right. Let's go." James clicked his tongue and flicked the reins.

Nothing happened. Bruce shook his head.

"You'll have to use your heels."

James slapped his heels against the horse's flanks. It sprang forward, throwing him back in the saddle so that he nearly lost his balance. He hauled desperately on the reins and the horse skidded to a sudden stop, sending James sprawling forward. He sat up straight again, breathing heavily. The horse was half in and half out of the stable. Bruce appeared at his side, and took hold of the bridle.

"Right, I think you'd better get off, mate."

"No, I'm just getting used to him. We're fine," James leaned forward and patted the horse's neck. "Aren't we, boy?"

"No, come on. I can't risk it. You can't ride at all, can you? Off you get."

Bruce let go of the bridle and tried to take the reins. James yanked them away from him, leaned forward, and dug his heels into the horse several times in quick succession. He felt a surge of power beneath him, and they shot out of the stable.

"Stop! For fuck's sake!" Bruce staggered along beside them as they crossed the yard, but James lowered his head, and slapped his heels against the horse's flanks again. The horse broke into a gallop, and James buried his face in the coarse, dusty hair on the back of its neck.

He could hear Bruce's voice getting fainter behind him. He felt bad about the way he'd treated him, but he had to find Reuben. And Jessica. In fact, it would be best if he found Jessica first. The truth was that he wanted to be the one to save her. Save her from herself, if necessary. She would thank him for it later. He was riding to Jessica's rescue.

He raised his head fractionally. They were flying along the driveway at incredible speed. He was clutching the horse's mane just behind its ears, with the reins bunched up in his hands, which were sweating profusely, like the rest of him. He was being bounced around so much he thought he was sure to fall off at any moment. He was just about to try using the reins to slow them down when the horse decided to slacken its pace anyway.

James risked sitting up a little. He was still being bounced around, but felt in less danger of falling off. He saw that the horse had slowed down because they were turning off the drive towards a path through the trees on their right. James hung on tightly as the horse took the curve and began to trot up the path.

The path emerged from the trees into a broad meadow that sloped gently up to the horizon. The horse followed a track worn into the grass. They weren't going nearly so fast now. In fact, the horse was more or less walking. James began to relax a little. He sat up straight, and found himself swaying gently as he picked up the horse's rhythm. It felt quite good, although his whole body ached. Perhaps he had a knack for riding. What had Bruce said? A good seat. Yes, maybe he had a good seat. He clicked his tongue at the horse. Its ears twitched. Good. They were bonding now, definitely.

They got to the top of the meadow and emerged onto a wide, flat expanse of gorse bushes and scrubby vegetation. The horse began to quicken its pace. James remembered what Bruce had said about 'a nice little run over the heath'. Oh, shit. He pulled tentatively on the reins. The horse slowed down a little. He did it again, with the same result. It wasn't so difficult after all. He gave the reins a series of little tweaks, trying to bring the horse back down to a slow walking pace. Suddenly the animal dipped its head, just as it had done in the stables. James was jerked forward, and the reins slipped through his fingers. As he scrabbled around trying to pick them up, the horse broke into a fast trot. James found himself being bounced around again, which made it even harder to pick up the reins. When he finally got them back in his hands, there was something wrong with them. Both strands now seemed to be on the same side of the horse's head. When he pulled on them, the horse veered sharply to the left. He could see that if he kept pulling, the horse would simply go around in circles. He now had no means of slowing it down. Also, it didn't seem to like the new arrangement with the reins at all. James decided he'd better let them go slack.

Immediately the horse changed its rhythm and went faster. Cantering, James thought, that was the word. It wasn't trotting any more, it was cantering. He was now being bounced around so much that he hardly touched the saddle. Feeling that he was about to fall off again, he leaned right forward, with his head beside the horse's neck. The horse began to gallop. Its hooves thudded against the hardened mud of the narrow track, sending gobbets of turf flying up into the air.

From the corner of his eye James noticed that they were passing the golf course. Someone waved at him. He closed his eyes.

A moment later he became aware that they were going downhill. He raised his head a little and peered around. They were pelting down a sloping field, towards a dry stone wall at the bottom of it. James looked for a gate or some kind of opening. He spotted a gap in the wall over to their left - mercifully, the direction he could steer in.

He risked a light tweak on the reins. The horse snorted angrily, shook its head, and seemed to increase its speed.

They were approaching the wall, but the horse didn't seem to care. A terrible suspicion began to form in James's mind. The animal began twitching and bucking underneath him as it galloped towards the wall, as if preparing itself for something. James was now sure he knew what that was.

He let go of the reins altogether and clasped his arms around the horse's neck. The beast seemed to take this as a final confirmation to proceed with what it had in mind, and put on an extra burst of speed. James closed his eyes and hung on with all his strength.

He felt himself soaring upwards. He experienced a moment of complete weightlessness, then a sickening lurch in his stomach as he began his descent. He thumped back down on the saddle, and his whole body was shaken by a tremendous, juddering impact. Immediately, he was flung into the air again. He found that he was no longer holding on to the horse, or anything at all.

He felt himself turn completely over in a full somersault. Suddenly all the air was sucked violently out if his body. It took him a moment to realize that he'd landed, and was lying on his back. There was a hard lump under his head. He heard the horse snorting briefly - and, he thought, derisively - then the sound of its departing hooves.

He gazed up at the sky. It was darker than it had been earlier, and was full of murky grey clouds. It looked as though it might rain heavily quite soon. Maybe a storm was on the way. As he watched, the sky got darker very quickly. And not just the sky: the air around him was glooming, too. It was like the sudden onset of night. That was what happened in the tropics, apparently. Night fell very suddenly. But he wasn't in the tropics. He was lying in a field in England. He knew that much. With this thought in his mind, he allowed the encroaching blackness to envelop him.

*

Jarvis stood beside his car. He'd begun to feel trapped in there, even with all the windows open. But it wasn't any better outside. The sky was low and dark, pressing down on him. Someone, somewhere, was interfering with the force of gravity. He could hardly move. His limbs were heavy and sluggish.

His mind, however, was racing. It scampered away from him, constantly changing direction, scattering a trail of random, inconsequential thoughts. When he caught up with one and tried to pin it down, it evaporated.

His head felt very large but very light, as if it was made of sponge, or possibly pumice stone. Every few minutes a wave of dizziness swept over him and he closed his eyes, which produced an interesting display of swirling coloured lights.

He was aware that the wounds on his chest were getting worse and should be causing him pain, but he didn't feel any.

He wondered where his notebook was. Probably somewhere in the filthy mess inside the car, which reminded Jarvis of the squalid disorder he associated with a domestic crime scene. Or pictures he'd seen of so-called art installations, where someone lived in bed for a month, then put the results in an art gallery.

And then some pretentious wanker bought it for thousands of quid. Maybe he could sell his car to an art gallery.

He wanted his notebook so he could write down the important things he'd seen. First, there had been Norfolk, and the girl, on horseback. They'd ambled up the far side of the green, and disappeared along the road leading to the Longbourne place. About twenty minutes later Rabbi Cowboy had appeared, also on a horse. That wasn't so surprising. You expected to see a cowboy on a horse. But this one seemed to be having trouble. When the horse appeared, it was going very fast, with the Cowboy hanging on precariously. Then it stopped abruptly to eat some grass, and he was thrown forward, nearly sliding over its head. When it set off again, just as suddenly, he lurched back and very nearly fell off its rear end. He was still struggling to claw his way back into the saddle as Jarvis watched him disappear from view, following the others at high speed.

But where? They might all be heading for the Longbourne's. Alternatively, they might be continuing along the main road all the way back to Norfolk's place. Or maybe they'd turned off the main road just out of sight, and gone along the little lane that ran behind the Post Office. Where they might be planning to do that thing which cowboys did in the films, when they tied a rope to the bars of the window in the back of the jail, and tied the other end to the knobby bit on top of the horse's saddle, then dug their spurs into the horse and shouted "Yeehah!" and ripped the bars out of the wall.

They might be breaking in at this moment. Or they might be hiding, waiting for Jarvis to follow them, and when he was safely at the other end of the lane, they'd sneak back, and make a lightning attempt on the front of the building.

What could he do? He needed to be able to watch the front and the back of the Post Office at the same time. It was impossible. He needed to be able to hover above the scene, getting a birds-eye view.

The church clock began to strike. Jarvis looked up at the bell tower. It made him dizzy, and it seemed as if the tower was constantly in the process of toppling down on him. He lowered his head. He was looking straight at the Post Office. The tower was directly behind it. As the sixth stroke died away, throbbing in the thickening evening air, the solution suddenly came to him.

Ten

"What were you thinking?"

James heard Jessica's voice and opened his eyes. Confusingly, it was Raymond, not Jessica, he found himself looking at. Raymond's face was close to his, and oddly distorted. James realized he was lying on his back. Raymond was looming over him, looking down at him with narrowed eyes. The flesh around his jaw sagged slightly, and James was comforted to know that Raymond would probably develop jowls quite soon.

"All right, champ?" Raymond said.

James heard Jessica's voice again: "I mean, really, what the fuck?"

He turned his head and saw that Jessica was standing a few feet away, facing Reuben, who was scowling at a spot between her feet.

"Whoa, steady there," Raymond said to James, "don't move your head sharply, mate. No sudden movements. Just turn your head back slowly. Nice and easy."

James turned his head back to gaze up at Raymond again.

"Good," Raymond said. "Now, can you move your fingers?"

James fluttered his hands about.

"Great. What about your feet?"

"He's fine," Jessica said. "There's no need for all that."

"You never know," Raymond said, without taking his eyes from James's face, "you can't be too careful with a fall. Especially when someone's been sparked out."

"How long was I unconscious?" James said. He felt a bit sick.

"Only a minute or so. We just caught your act from the top of the field. You should join the circus. It was pretty spectacular."

"Pretty fucking stupid," Jessica said.

"I think I'm okay," James said. He propped himself up on his elbows.

"Want to get up?" Raymond said.

"Yes, I think so."

"Okay. Nice and slow."

Raymond held out his hands. James gripped them and hauled himself up. As he stood upright an intense flash of white light seared his eyeballs. Almost certainly brain damage, he thought. That would be a nice irony, after what he'd done to Max Fennel. A good example of karma for Raymond to ponder.

James became aware of Reuben's voice: "Three elephant, four elephant, five-
-"

There was a deep rumble of thunder.

"Oh," James said, "it was lightning."

Raymond gave him a sharp look then squinted at the sky. "With a bit of luck we'll get back ahead of the storm. Bruce'll be here with the horse box in a minute."

James peered around. They didn't seem to be close to any paths or tracks.

"The main road's only just behind there," Raymond said, nodding towards a line of trees about two hundred yards away. "We'll walk the horses down to the box, and put Damien and Polly in, then you and Reuben can go back in the Land Rover with Bruce."

"I can ride," Reuben said.

"No, you bloody well can't," Raymond said. "And then Jess can drive you lot back in your car."

"His parents' car," Jessica muttered.

"Why?" Reuben said. "She hasn't got a licence, either."

"I can drive a fuck of a sight better than you."

"Well, maybe it's not such a good idea," Raymond said. "I can drive you all back later and we'll arrange to have the car picked up some other time."

"No," Jessica said fiercely, "I'll drive!"

Raymond looked at her for a moment. "Okay," he said.

James heard a whinnying noise behind him. He turned to see that four horses were loosely tethered to a pair of stunted trees a few yards away. He recognized his horse, and glared at it. It blinked at him, insolently.

A mobile phone rang.

"Bruce?" Raymond said. "That was quick, mate. Thanks. Okay, won't be long. Couple of minutes. See you." Raymond frowned at the phone. "Now he's going to think I owe him a favour," he said. "Actually, I do owe him a favour." He sighed, and dropped the phone into the pocket of his tweed hacking jacket. "I lose face, he gains face. Oh, well, that's what I get for despising him. The fat turd."

Raymond went up to James's horse and did something deft with the straps around its nose. "I'll just make it easier for you two to walk them," he said, and did the same thing to Reuben's horse. "Okay, let's get going."

Jessica unhitched her horse and got on it in one easy movement.

"Hey, Jess," Raymond said, "we're all going to walk them down there."

Jessica looked away from him. "I'm on now. Do you want me to get off?"

"No," Raymond said, "it's okay." He handed Reuben a set of reins. "Just keep slightly in front of her nose," he said, "and grip the reins as high up as you can."

Reuben bunched the reins under the big mare's jaw and took a few steps. The horse ambled forward. Raymond handed James the reins for his horse.

"All right, James?"

James nodded and took the reins. He felt the horse stiffen.

Raymond unhitched his own horse and began to walk it towards the trees, falling in beside Reuben. Jessica's horse trotted ahead of them. She didn't look back.

James tugged at his horse's reins. Nothing happened. He heard the sound of running water. The horse was releasing a powerful stream of steaming piss onto the dusty grass, staring calmly at James as it did so. James waited until it had finished, then pulled at the reins again. The horse moved forward obligingly, having made its point.

Bruce eased the Land Rover into the yard and stopped. James felt a soft jolt through the back of his seat as the horse box they were hauling thudded against the tow bar. He could see that Jessica was already sitting in the driver's seat of the old BMW, a few yards away. She was staring straight ahead and didn't turn to look at them. There was no sign of Raymond. Bruce honked the horn. Raymond immediately emerged from the stables and went straight to the back of the horse box.

James and Reuben got out of the back of the Land Rover. Reuben walked to the car and wrenched open the back door. He slid inside and slammed the door. James joined Bruce at the back of the box and stood there awkwardly as Raymond lowered the ramp.

"I can manage now, thanks," Raymond said. He nodded to James. "You get going, mate. Go on. Look after yourself."

"Are you sure?"

"Yes, go on. I'll see you another time."

"Thanks for... everything. And I'm really sorry about... everything."

"No worries, James. Take it easy."

James hesitated.

"Excuse me." Bruce stepped past him and began to waddle up the ramp into the box. Raymond blocked his way.

"You're all right now, thanks, Bruce," Raymond said. "I'll get them in."

"It's all right, I'll give you a hand."

"No, really, I'd rather do it myself. Give them a bit of quality time."

Bruce nodded gravely and shuffled back down the ramp. He held out his hand to James, and when James took it he held it in a moist grip. "Nice to meet you," he said. "Don't give up on the riding." He smiled broadly. James noticed that some of his teeth were missing. "You've got good, strong legs." He released James's hand, and walked towards the house, waving at Jessica and Reuben in the car as he passed it.

James peered into the gloom inside the horse box and raised his hand, but he couldn't tell whether Raymond saw him.

He turned away and nearly bumped into a short youth with spiky hair the colour and texture of dirty straw. James wondered where he'd suddenly appeared from. He was very pale. He didn't look well.

202

"Where's Ray?" he said.

"In there." As James nodded at the box the rear end of a horse emerged from it. The rest of the horse followed, shuffling backwards. James recognized the animal as the one he'd ridden. Raymond appeared, holding the bridle as he coaxed the animal down the ramp. He stopped when he saw the straw-haired youth, and frowned.

"Ray," the boy said.

"What do you want?"

"I've got to talk to you, dude."

"You had your chance this morning, mate. You blew it, Spike."

"I know, I'm really sorry. But I'm totally straight now. I'm a bit, like, frazzled, but it's cool. I'm sorted. Honestly. Can I talk to you? Please?"

Raymond began to lead the horse to the stable. "Maybe later."

"Wait!"

Raymond stopped and turned to him. "What?"

"Here's the thing. I think I might have done something a bit... uncool."

"What kind of thing?"

"With this journalist dude. You haven't seen him, have you?"

Raymond narrowed his eyes. He shook his head slowly.

The boy turned to James. "Old guy? Shabby looking?"

"I don't think so," James said.

"You'd know if you had, I think. He'd probably be acting a bit strange."

"Spike," Raymond said quietly, "does this involve drugs?"

Spike gazed around the yard. "Er, yeah, sort of. Probably."

"Fuck," Raymond said. "And this guy's a journalist, is he?"

"Yeah. I think he's with The Mail."

"How do you know?"

"He had a copy with him. In his car."

"And what else? Did he have a tape?"

"No, he was old-school. Wrote shit down in a notebook."

Raymond expelled a deep breath. "Give me twenty minutes," he said. "I'll meet you in the studio." He led the horse away without looking back.

Spike turned and walked to the house, placing his feet with care, as if he suspected the ground might be unstable.

James got into the front of the car beside Jessica. The engine was already running. Jessica swung the car in a wide arc all the way around the Land Rover and horse box, and drove out of the yard with her eyes fixed straight ahead all the time.

James suddenly felt immensely tired. His body ached and his head throbbed. He needed to sort things out. He needed to prevent Reuben from going ahead with the robbery plan. But if he did, what about the large parcel of drugs with his name on it sitting in the Post Office? They couldn't talk about it now, in front of Jessica. What could he do? He leaned back and tried to think.

James awoke to the sound of heavy rain drumming on the car roof and the angry slap of the windscreen wipers. He was aware that the car had just stopped. He peered out of the window. They were beside the manor house, close to the side door. Sylvia Silver was standing in the doorway, holding an umbrella. Jessica got out of the car and ran to the doorway, huddling under Sylvia's umbrella as she spoke to her.

Reuben opened the back door of the car.

"Wait!" James said.

"What?"

"Tonight. What time? What time are you going to do it?"

Jessica was coming back to the car, holding the umbrella.

"When it gets dark," Reuben hissed. "About ten. Whatever."

"Come on," Jessica said through the open back door, "it's wet out here."

Reuben got out and Jessica held the umbrella over both of them. In the doorway Reuben allowed his mother to hug him briefly, then pushed past her into the house.

Jessica said something to Sylvia and held out the car keys. Sylvia shook her head and bobbed down, peering at James through the rain-streaked window. He smiled feebly and raised his hand. He felt like a disappointing specimen in a fish tank. Sylvia turned back to Jessica, handed her the umbrella, and went into the house.

Jessica ran back to the car, closing the umbrella as she slid into the driver's seat, and thrusting it at James. He took it from her awkwardly and tried to manoeuvre it into a position where it wouldn't drip on his trousers.

As a concession to the torrential rain that reduced visibility to a few yards Jessica kept her eyes on the road and stayed on her half of it most of the time, driving at a speed that was only moderately dangerous. Neither of them spoke.

As they pulled up outside the Longbourne house the rain stopped suddenly. Jessica turned the engine off but made no attempt to move, and continued to gaze through the windscreen.

"It's stopped," James said.

Jessica said nothing.

James craned forward and looked up at the sky. "But it looks like there's more to come. Still a lot of dark clouds. I think it's just a lull. A lull in the storm." James was making a huge effort not to ask the question that was tormenting him. But he felt that he was trying to hold a door closed while an exceptionally strong man pushed against it from the other side. He took a deep breath.

"Look--"

"What?" Jessica snapped.

"I just wanted to say. To ask. Please don't be upset. But I really need to know."

"What?"

"Did you have sex with Raymond?"

"None of your business."

"So you did."

"I said it's none of your business."

"Well, it is a bit. Isn't it?"

"Why?"

"After what happened this morning, for one thing. In church."

Jessica sighed. "Oh, that."

"Yes, that."

"I thought you might like it. It was meant to be fun."

"Oh. I suppose you do that to all of Oliver's friends."

"No. Not all of them."

James felt something sag inside him. He turned to look out of his side window.

"Look," Jessica said quietly, "I'm sorry, all right?"

He turned back to look at her. She was still staring straight ahead. He saw that her eyes were swimming and her face was red and puffy. She bit her lower lip.

James sensed that he should on no account say anything else.

"So," he said, "did you have sex with him?"

Jessica burst into tears and buried her face in her hands.

James suddenly felt better. It had been awful for her. A terrible mistake. She was bitterly disillusioned. It had been loveless and impersonal. She felt violated and betrayed. But he would be patient. He would heal her. Slowly and tenderly he would re-awaken her feelings, as only a truly considerate lover could, until she gave herself to him, not just willingly, but gratefully, joyfully, ecstatically.

"I'm so sorry," he said quietly. "Was it terrible for you?"

Jessica lifted her head from her hands. Her face was red and swollen. She wiped her eyes and gazed through the windscreen. "Nothing happened," she said.

James saw that her tears had splashed down and made two dark patches on her jeans, where the material was stretched across her thighs. He tried to decide whether he was relieved that Jessica hadn't had sex with Raymond or whether he'd have preferred it if she'd had sex with him and not liked it. Meanwhile she was clearly upset, which at least gave him the chance to comfort her. He put his hand tentatively on her shoulder. She didn't react. After a few seconds he took it away again.

"Are you all right?" he said.

She shook her head.

"But what... what's the matter? You can tell me."

"I've been such an idiot."

"What do you mean?"

She turned a tear-streaked face to James. She looked utterly miserable. She really was very young, he thought. She was like a little girl.

"I've fucked everything up," she said. Her nose was running and she wiped it with the back of her hand. She turned to look through the windscreen again. "We were going to do it. In this little secret place we know, completely hidden, off the track where we go riding. But when we started it felt all wrong. I was doing it for all the wrong reasons."

She shot him a very quick glance. Before he could say anything she continued:

"So I wanted to stop, but it was a bit... difficult. And then we heard Richard, crashing through the undergrowth, off the track. So we had to go and help him. And then we saw you, and you know the rest. And ever since then, Ray's been all... all..."

"Distant?" James offered.

"No. No, he was all... kindly, and grown-up. It was awful."

"A bit patronizing, right?" James said hopefully.

"No, he was just trying to be nice. But now it's all ruined." She slumped forward, and rested her head on the steering wheel. "My life is horrible," she muttered.

"But perhaps it was good thing," James said..

"What?"

"That Reuben came along."

Jessica laughed bitterly. "What a dickhead. And you." She raised her head from the steering wheel and glanced at him. "I mean, totally stupid, with those horses. Like, duh. Neither of you can ride! What was all that about?"

"We were trying to stop you."

"Stop me doing what?"

"Stop you from... you know. What you were going to do. Reuben knew all about it. I think he'd been spying on you. Anyway, he knew."

"Oh, God." Jessica screwed up her face. "It's none of his business, the little prick."

"He's in love with you."

Jessica pressed her lips together. After a while she said, "I know."

James looked away from her. "And so am I," he said. "I think."

Jessica didn't say anything. James glanced at her. Tears were welling up in her eyes, but she continued to sit very still, staring straight ahead.

Finally she spoke. "I know," she said quietly, "and I'm not sorry. But I'm sorry you got so serious about me before I realized."

James worked up a wry, worldly smile. As he waited for her to look at him and see it, she continued, "People are always doing that."

James turned away quickly and disposed of the smile.

"All kinds of people," Jessica said. "I don't know why. I mean, I don't do anything to encourage them, particularly. Much. But I've certainly never done anything to give that idiot down the road any ideas. But he won't leave me alone. What am I supposed to do?"

"Well, he's planning to do something really stupid."

"What a surprise."

"No, I mean something really, really stupid. Genuinely deranged."

"Like what?"

"He's going to rob the Post Office."

Jessica screwed up her nose. "What on earth for?"

"He's convinced there's a huge amount of money in there. Actually, it was Olly who convinced him."

"Typical."

"Yes, very Olly."

"No, I mean typical of those people."

"What people?"

"Jews. That's all they think about, isn't it? Money."

"Jessica," James said gently, "you just can't say things like that."

"Why not?"

"Well, it's not true for one thing. And it's anti-Semitic, for another."

"Oh, God, don't start with that stuff. Anyway, what's turned you into such a saint all of a sudden? You think exactly the same thing."

"No, I don't. Why do you say that?"

"Yes you do. You said so."

"When?"

"The other night. In the bathroom. When I told you about Dave Silver and all the money he made. You said you thought they were, like, a whole different species."

"No, I was talking about people who understand computers! I said people like that must have completely different brains to people like me, or something like that. It was nothing to do with him being Jewish."

"Oh." She looked down and rubbed at the damp patches on her thighs. "Now I suppose you're going to tell me I'm a racist, or something."

"No, I was just--"

"Because I'm not! I listen to loads of rap music. And there's some black guys I really fancy. And that footballer. The one who's a sort of mixture of black and Chinese or something. Anyway, him. And that Paki doctor who used to shag Princess Di. I'd go out with him any day. So I can't be a racist, can I?"

"That's not quite the same thing."

"I bet you won't like it so much when there's more of them in England than us and they take over your job."

"Who do you mean by 'them' and 'us', exactly?"

"Oh, come on. You know what I mean." Jessica sighed and assumed the patient voice of a teacher explaining something to a child. "James, it's just common sense. Everyone's different. And all these different people are the same. I mean, the same as each other. All these different nationalities. They've all got their own national characters. Like when you go to France and everyone's rude if you can't speak French. And the Muslims, they've got completely different beliefs to us, like terrorism and veils and things. And the same with all these asylum seekers."

"Asylum seekers aren't all the same nationality. Neither are Muslims."

"Aren't they? Oh. No, right. Of course not." She frowned.

"And many of them have a legitimate--"

"But they're all foreigners!" she broke in triumphantly. "You can't deny that."

"Actually, they're not all foreigners. There are lots of British Muslims."

"Exactly. Like I said, they're taking over. There's millions of immigrants now."

"Look, we were all immigrants if you go back far enough."

Jessica ran her fingers through her hair. "Whatever."

She reached up and flipped the driver's sun visor down, then bounced forward in her seat and examined her face in the little mirror that was set into it. "God," she said, turning her head from side to side, "I look like shit." She snapped the visor shut. "So, why does Richard want to get hold of all this money? His parents are loaded."

"He's doing it to impress you."

Jessica snorted. "Well, it's not going to. You can tell him that if you want."

"He wants to buy you a horse."

"Oh, fuck." Jessica turned to face him. She looked pale.

"What?" James said. "What is it?"

"Is that really why he's doing it?"

"That's what he said."

"Oh, fuck. That sort of makes me involved, doesn't it?"

"Not really. Why should it?"

"If he got caught. And people thought I'd... encouraged him."

"Did you encourage him?"

Jessica turned away, bit her lip, then buried her face in her hands again. "Oh, God," she muttered, "you are *so* going to hate me."

"No, I'm not. Why? Why would I hate you?"

She raised her head but didn't look at him. She seemed scared.

"I'm such a fool. Oh, shit, what have I done?"

"I don't know. What have you done?"

"You've got to understand. I really, really want a horse. And I thought that if things didn't work out with Raymond, then I should have a kind of back-up plan."

"Reuben."

Jessica nodded. "I think I might have made him a kind of promise."

James tried to make his voice cold and impassive. "Sex."

She turned to him. "But I didn't think-- I mean, I had no idea he'd..."

"So you promised you'd have sex with him if he'd get you a horse."

"I didn't think he'd do something like this! Oh, God, what if he gets caught and everyone finds out? They'll think I'm some kind of horrible slut. Not that I'm only thinking of that, obviously. But I might even get into trouble with the police! Oh, fuck, James, you've got to stop him! Please!" She looked down. "Because I'm not a horrible slut. I'm not. In fact, you may not believe this, but... I'm a virgin."

James arranged his face into an expression of surprise. "Wow," he said.

"So when I do it, it should be with someone... someone I care about, shouldn't it?"

She turned and looked at him shyly from beneath her tear-sparkled lashes.

James nodded.

She took his hand.

James wondered what he should say. The answer came to him in a blinding flash of unassailable wisdom. Nothing. Say nothing. Keep your mouth shut.

"That's partly what I meant earlier," Jessica said. "About it not feeling right when I was going to... you know. And doing it for the wrong reasons. And not just the wrong reasons. With the wrong person. That's what I meant, as well."

James frowned, and nodded again slowly, aiming for a grave, judicious look.

She squeezed his hand. "So, please! For me. You've got to stop him."

"Why? Because it might get you into trouble?"

"No! Not just that. Because of us!" She looked down again. "You see," she said quietly, "I don't want it to ruin everything. Because I know what I really want now. I've found the right person. And I'm ready, James."

James made a great effort, and took his hand away. "So now you're making me a promise, aren't you?" he said sternly. "Just like the others."

"No! It's not like that at all!"

"Why is it different?"

Jessica's eyes began to fill with tears. "Please don't be like that! All cold and angry. It's completely different. Because it's with you! Don't you see?"

The tears overflowed and she began to sob uncontrollably.

James reached across to her and took her in his arms. The handbrake got in the way, but he tried to ignore it. "It's all right," he whispered, "don't worry. Everything's going to be all right. I'll take care of it."

She clung on to him and pulled him close. "Oh, James," she breathed, "will you?"

"Yes."

She gave him a long, passionate kiss. Finally she pulled away and looked deep into his eyes. "You really are special, you know," she said in a husky voice.

"Mind you," James said, "I'm not quite sure exactly how I'm--

She stopped him by laying a finger on his lips. "You'd probably better not tell me how you're going to do it. The less I know the better, really, isn't that right? I mean legally, and all that kind of thing."

"Absolutely right." He frowned. "We'd better proceed on a strictly need-to-know basis." He was pleased. He'd always wanted a good reason to use that phrase.

Jessica stroked his cheek and gave him a wistful smile. "I'd better get inside. It's nearly eight. They'll be wondering what's happened. I expect Sylvia's already phoned them up with the whole story. She's probably told them we all got trampled to death in a stampede or something" She opened her door. "I might have a bath, actually. Oh, listen, we won't be having dinner, because of going out to lunch. But Spracky puts things out on the kitchen table, for sandwiches and things, so just help yourself whenever you want." She began to get out of the car then saw James hadn't moved. "Aren't you coming?"

"I'll stay out here, if that's okay. I need to make a plan. I thought--"

"Don't say a word. I trust you. Need-to-know basis, remember? And when you've got it all sorted we can finally be together properly." She kissed her fingertips and brushed them lingeringly against his lips. "See you later." She slammed the door.

James could still feel the pressure of Jessica's lips, and the luscious sensation of her tongue. She'd wanted to show him that she thought he was special. Different.

Did she mean it? He thought about how she'd clutched him so desperately when he'd taken her in his arms. Yes. She meant it. And she wanted him as much as he wanted her, he was sure of it. And it was no fickle teenage whim, it went deeper than that.

But he had to remember that she was, in fact, still very young. That was why she sometimes seemed a bit thoughtless and self-centred. Like the things she was saying about Jews and Muslims and immigrants. She'd obviously just picked all that up from her uncle John, and was repeating it without thinking. But that's what teenagers were like: thoughtless. It was the same when he'd told her about the robbery plan. The only person she'd been worried about was herself. But in a way it showed how innocent she was: she didn't even have the guile to pretend to be concerned about anyone else. She just came out with exactly what she thought and felt about things. She was totally sincere. That's why he knew she meant what she said about having been a fool, and only wanting him.

And he would protect her, and make sure that she didn't get into trouble. Which meant, in effect, keeping Reuben out of trouble. Of course, there were other reasons why he needed to intervene in Reuben's attempt on the Post Office. Like a parcel of cocaine with his name on it that was sitting in there.

Which was a big problem. On the one hand, he didn't want to let Reuben undertake the kind of foolhardy assault that might go horribly wrong. On the other hand he didn't want to leave the parcel in the Post Office. He couldn't just wait until Tuesday, march in there and collect it. Olly had concocted the whole teetering edifice of plans and backup plans in the first place because he'd been sufficiently concerned about the possibility of detection and surveillance, and the risk of arrest, to try and ensure that if it happened, it didn't happen to him. James was going to make bloody sure it didn't happen to him, either.

He realized that what he needed to do was not so much thwart the robbery as supervise it. Which made it even more important to contact Reuben. Collaborating with him was going to be more difficult than stopping him, especially taking into account the impossibility of knowing what his condition might be, or his ability to process incoming information of any kind.

James checked his watch again. Just after eight. Reuben had said he was going to make his attempt on the Post Office at about ten. But he'd also said he was going to do it when it got dark. James peered up at the sky. It was pretty dark already, but that was mainly because of the storm clouds. Maybe he should go directly to the Post Office and wait. But that still wouldn't guarantee that he could intercept Rueben. For one thing, he had no idea how Reuben was planning to get into the place. Through a window? He tried to visualize the Post Office. All he could see was the fat woman standing in the doorway and then closing the door. So there was definitely a door. But Reuben might be planning to break in from the back. Or through the roof. Or he might have dug a tunnel. He might have been working on it for months, disposing of the soil by using special bags sewn into his trousers, like the British POWs in that film. He could be underneath the Post Office at this very moment, about to break through. No. Pull yourself together.

It was more likely that Reuben was still at home. James decided he should go there immediately and try to head him off. True, it would take him a good twenty minutes to walk to the manor house, and it might start pouring with rain again at any moment, but he had to get to him. It was a race against the clock.

As he got out of the car he noticed that directly ahead of him was the open-fronted shed he'd seen when he first arrived, with the ancient, rusting sports car in it. He now saw that leaning against the wall beside it was an old-fashioned bicycle.

James had nearly reached the manor house when the rain began again. It had been falling in isolated bursts ever since the first downpour, but each deluge seemed like a rehearsal for a storm that was still gathering. Lightning crackled on the horizon against a layer of deep, bruised purple, while tall, dark clouds towered overhead.

211

James pedalled up the rest of the driveway as fast as he could. The bike worked fairly well, although the tyres were a bit flat. He steered it towards the side wall of the house, then discovered that the brakes had almost no effect. He scraped along the wall, taking the skin off his knuckles. When he came to a halt he leaned the bike against the wall near the side door. The rain wasn't stopping, but it hadn't got any worse, either.

Now he'd arrived he had to think of what to do. So far he'd been relying on a vague idea that he'd find Reuben alone and sober, without having to look for him. That now seemed a bit optimistic. He considered his options. If he knocked at the door, one of the parents might answer, and he couldn't imagine how he'd explain himself to them, especially if it was Sylvia. He needed a better plan.

After soaking up some more of the rain, he decided to have a look around. It wasn't exactly a plan, but it was better than simply standing in one place and getting wet.

He edged his way around to the back of the house. Light was spilling from the windows in the big room on the ground floor where they'd congregated before and after lunch. The curtains were open but it was dark enough now for him not to be seen from inside if he was careful. He crept up to the nearest window and risked a quick look. He couldn't see anyone in there.

He took a few steps back. Lights were showing in some of the first floor windows, and in one or two of the smaller ones above them. Those would be the old servants' quarters. But where was Reuben's room? If he knew that, he could at least throw some gravel at a window. Did Reuben have one of the big bedrooms, or did he have his own lair on the top floor, as far away from his parents as possible?

As James squinted at the windows, searching for clues, there was a bright flash of lightning, followed immediately by a clap of thunder. The rain began to hammer down on him as if he was standing under a tap. In a few seconds he was soaked. Water cascaded down every inch of his exposed skin and although his clothes were utterly sodden and couldn't possibly absorb any more moisture he seemed to be getting wetter all the time.

He had to get under cover. He looked around desperately. The windmill was only about a hundred yards away. It might be locked, of course. But it was his best hope.

James huddled in the   mill doorway, groping for the door handle. There was another intense flash of lighting, even closer than the last one. He saw the handle, pressed down on it and pushed at the door. It refused to budge. Maybe it was locked. After a while he wondered if perhaps it opened outwards. It did. He opened it and stepped inside.

It was pitch black. Gradually he began to make out the dim shape of the huge stone in the middle of the floor. Then the wind slammed the door shut and he was plunged into total darkness again. He stood completely still. The whole mill creaked and groaned as if it was in pain. The wind was creating an odd effect in the interior that sounded almost like breathing.

James remembered he had some matches on him. He was wearing the same trousers he'd had on the other night when he went to the club with Olly, and he'd slipped a book of their complimentary matches into his pocket. He fished them out and found they were in a laminated cover, which seemed to have kept them relatively dry. Carefully he broke off a match and tried to light it. There was a brief sputter of flame and then it went out. He tried again. After three more matches he got one to stay alight. He held it up and turned around slowly.

He found himself staring at Max Fennel.

Max Fennel stared back at him. The match burnt his fingers and went out. A second later the inside of the mill was flooded with light. Max stood at the door with his hand on a light switch.

"Ha," he cried, "got you, professor Quinn!"

"What?" James said.

"You unspeakable shit, Quinn. It wasn't enough to try and destroy my reputation with that vicious review. Now you try to burn down my windmill!"

"I'm not trying to burn it down. I was just trying to see."

"Pathetic! I caught you red-handed! You've got the matches in your hand! Do you take me for a complete fool, Quinn?"

"My name's not Quinn," James said. "It's me, James, don't you remember?"

"Oh, so that's your game, is it? False identity."

"Look, I'm not this person you think I am."

"Oh, no? And who else but a jealous, spiteful, so-called expert on early Tudor naval history like you would come here and try to ruin my life's work?"

James was distracted by a sound that he tried to identify. It was an absence of sound, he realized. The mill's timbers were still creaking in the wind but the rain, which had provided a constant background, was no longer drumming against the outside.

"It's stopped raining," he said.

"Oh, yes!" Max cried, "and that suits your plans very nicely, doesn't it? No rain to douse the conflagration you intend to cause. But we'll have no arson today, thank you very much! Hand over those matches."

"Okay." James walked up to him and gave him the matches. "Look, I need to go," he said, and stepped around Max to get to the door.

Max sprang back and planted himself in front of the door. "Oh, no, you don't! You think you can just walk out of here like that?"

"Well, I'd like to. I've got something rather urgent to do." James was aware that Reuben might be setting off from the house at this very moment.

"You're not leaving here until you and I have settled one or two things!"

"Look," James said, "I think you're mixing me up with someone else."

"Oh, drop it, Quinn! I've seen through the disguise and there's no point in trying to pretend any more. No, my friend, you're not getting out of here until I get what I want."

"All right, what do you want?"

"A full, written confession of your felonious intentions here, a copy of which I will lodge with a trusted legal advisor in case you get any funny ideas, and which I will publish if you ever attack me, or my achievements, again. That includes any more vile, untruthful and unwarranted criticisms of any written work that I may publish in the future. Meanwhile, I want a full retraction of the stream of bile that you spewed over my last book in the pages of the Historical Review."

Max reached into his pocket and took out a wallet, from which he unfolded a creased and yellowing press clipping. He began to read from it:

"'On the rare occasions that Dr Fennel blunders against a verifiable fact or a plausible hypothesis, its origin as the work of other, more diligent historians, is transparently obvious. In most instances he doesn't even offer his victims the fundamental courtesy of attempting to conceal his wholesale plagiarism, and when he does, his attempts are as crude as the shame-faced efforts of a guilty schoolboy.'"

Max was shaking with rage. He shoved his glasses back up his nose and continued: "'This laughable travesty displays all the worst failings of *soi-disant* populism, with none of the simple but honest entertainment which the form can provide in the hands of writers who possess some vestige of academic rigour, not to mention basic literacy.'"

Max waved the piece of paper under James's nose. "Take it back! All of it! Admit you're wrong! It's time for you to tell the truth for once, Quinn, you vindictive swine!"

James recoiled from the insults, even though he wasn't the person for whom the insults were intended. He felt that having been put in the position of representing the absent professor Quinn the least he could do was offer some defence on his behalf.

"You can't stop people expressing their opinions, you know," he said, "Otherwise you open the door to censorship and the suppression of free and frank debate."

"How dare you!" Max screamed. "How dare you stand there and lecture me about freedom of expression when it's sneaking, snivelling, self-righteous bastards like you who try to stifle the work of anyone who's not as supercilious and spiteful as you!"

James suddenly got angry. The abuse may have been intended for someone else but it still hurt. "I'm sorry," he said coldly, "but I've really got to go."

He tried to push his way past Max, who responded by shoving him violently backwards. James recovered himself and sprang at him, seizing him by the shoulders and trying to move him aside from the door. Max was quite short but he was surprisingly strong, and his rage made him formidable. James couldn't move him, and Max began to swing wildly at him. James spun him around and let go. Max staggered back, trying to keep his footing on the loose straw, then he lost his balance and fell backwards. His head struck the millstone with a sickening thud, ricocheted forward, then bounced back and hit the stone again. His eyes widened in a look of blank astonishment, then closed like a pair of shutters. He slumped down, sprawling against the side of the millstone like a drunk.

But he's not drunk, James thought. He's dead. I've killed him.

James went to the door and switched the light off. If he couldn't see the body, perhaps it wasn't there. He knew this was absurd, but it still felt better to be standing in the dark than to be staring at the body of a man he'd just killed.

He heard a groan, followed by the unmistakeable sound of someone vomiting. His first impulse was to run away, but then a mixture of relief, guilt and curiosity got the better of him. He switched on the light.

Max Fennel was struggling into a sitting position. He looked up at James without seeming to see him. He peered down at his clothes, spattered with vomit, then looked back up at James.

"What time is it?" he said.

James checked his watch. "Just after nine."

"I feel a bit strange," Max said. "What's going on? Do you know?"

"You fell down and hit your head."

"Did I?" Max ran his hand over the back of his head. "Oh, yes, my goodness, quite lump there. Two, in fact. No, three. That's odd."

James noticed for the first time that Max was no longer wearing his piratical bandage, and he'd changed back into his tweed suit.

"I seem to have been sick," Max said. "That's quite common when you've been unconscious. I must have been knocked out. How long was I out? Any idea?"

"Only a couple of seconds."

"It's all a bit fuzzy. I remember turning the light off when I heard someone rattling the door, because I thought it might be an intruder." He frowned. "For some reason I thought it might be an old colleague of mine. I wonder where that idea came from."

"It was me," James said, "and you mistook me for someone else."

"Did I? How silly. Because I know you, don't I? Jeremy, is it?"

"James."

"James, that's it. Friend of young Jess. And I met you at the fete." He frowned again. "When was that, actually? The fete?"

"Yesterday afternoon."

"Really? Good Lord, it seems much longer ago than that."

James had to agree. It seemed a very long time since yesterday afternoon.

"I can't seem to remember anything much since then," Max said. He touched the back of his head again. "You know, I think this little bump on the noggin has given me a touch of temporary amnesia. Nothing to worry about, it'll probably clear up. I can remember everything before the fete perfectly well. And I feel fine now."

He struggled to his feet. James stepped forward and reached out to support him, but Max brushed him away and steadied himself against the millstone. "No, no, I'm fine," he said, "I just need a moment to get my bearings. That's better."

There was a loud bang and the lights went out.

"Oh, damn," Max said in the darkness, "It's that bloody fuse again. Have you got any matches?"

"I gave you some earlier on."

"Did you? Oh yes, I'm holding them. How odd."

After a moment Max got a match lit. He held it up and looked around. "Ah yes," he said, "there are some oil lamps in that chest over there."

He shuffled around the millstone to a large cabinet by the far wall. The match went out. He lit another one and opened the cabinet. After a bit of scrabbling about he pulled out an old-fashioned hurricane lamp and flipped open the cover. The second match went out. He lit another one and touched it to the wick of the lamp, which flared into life immediately. The lamp cast a surprising amount of light. Max shook it around and James heard a sloshing noise. "Yes, plenty of juice in there," Max said.

"Be careful with that," James said.

"It's all right, these old things are very safe."

"Look," James said, "if you think you're going to be okay--"

"You're not leaving, are you?"

"Sorry, but I've really got to go. I've got a very urgent appointment."

"And just remind me: why did you come here in the first place?"

"I'll have to explain later. But I really must go now."

"What a pity. Here, I'll see you out."

Max made his way towards him erratically, waving the lamp around.

"Are you sure you're all right?" James said.

"Yes, I'm fine. Tickety-boo." Suddenly he stopped, raised the lamp, and peered at him. "Do you happen to know professor Quinn?" he said.

"No. I've never heard of him," James said, edging towards the door.

"He's a swine. He's trying to discredit me. He wants to destroy me, and given half the chance he'd probably try to destroy this place as well. The bastard."

"I'm sorry to hear that," James said as he got the door open. "Well, if you're sure you're okay, I'll say goodbye."

"But I'll tell you this, " Max said, ignoring him. "This is my windmill, and I'm the only one who decides what'll happen to it!"

"Of course. Take care now."

James stepped out of the door and closed it behind him. He didn't give much thought to Max's last remark, but he had cause to remember it later.

He set off for the house at a run.

Had he missed Rueben? He'd only been in the windmill about twenty minutes but Reuben might have left the house when the rain stopped. James decided he'd better make straight for the Post Office.

He reached the bicycle, and paused to catch his breath.

The side door of the house opened and Dave Silver stepped out. He regarded James with mild curiosity. "Hello," he said.

"Hello," James gasped.

"What are you up to?"

James couldn't think of a viable alternative to telling the truth. He probably needed the practice, anyway. "I'm looking for Reuben," he said.

"Are you? So am I."

"Oh, right. He's not inside, then?"

Dave shook his head. "Not unless he's hiding somewhere. And wherever he's gone, he's taken one of my bottles of good whiskey with him. Which is a bit ironic, really, given that the reason I wanted to find him was to have a serious talk about his drinking." Dave looked around doubtfully. "He must be pissed already if he's left the house in this weather."

James stood the bike upright and tried to brush water off the saddle. "If I see him," he said, "I'll tell him you want to talk to him."

Dave looked him up and down. "Do you want to come in for a bit? You look like you could use a drink yourself. Or a cup of tea, or something. Dry yourself off."

"No, that's all right. I'd better be going."

Dave looked at him thoughtfully. "So, you've got no idea where he might be?"

"No, sorry."

So much for the idea of telling the truth, James thought. He hoped it had done him some good while it had lasted.

Dave nodded. "All right. Take care, then."

"Thanks. You too."

James scooted the bike forward and jumped on.

He soon discovered that the tyres were now completely flat, which meant he couldn't go very fast. But as the brakes didn't work, perhaps that wasn't such a bad thing. He grunted with the effort of pedalling along the gravel drive at slightly less than walking pace. When he reached the road, with its smoother surface, the going got a little easier, but not much.

He kept on the lookout for Reuben. With a bit of luck he might not be far ahead, unless he'd taken the cross-country route. No one in their right mind would go that way in these conditions, of course, but Reuben couldn't safely be included in that category. James would just have to hope that he was having a rare attack of common sense.

He was about half way back to Ullage when the storm erupted again. He hunched over the handlebars and tried to pull his head into his shoulders like a tortoise. In a barrage of lightning he saw something glinting momentarily at the side of the road. He pedalled towards the spot where he'd seen it. The next burst of lightning showed him that it was a bottle of single malt whiskey. The good news was that it meant Reuben had definitely come this way. The bad news was that the bottle was empty.

James reached the village square about ten minutes later. He hadn't encountered Reuben, and he half expected to see him now, attacking the door of the Post Office with an axe. But there was no sign of him, and when he reached the building it seemed intact. He hunched in the doorway, and checked his watch. Just after ten. He put his ear to the door. He couldn't hear anything, although Reuben would need to be using a pneumatic drill in there to be heard above the rain. Which was quite possible, of course. James pressed himself into the doorway and waited.

*

From his kingdom in the sky Jarvis looked down and beheld a mortal approaching the Post Office. It was Naked Man, also known as Tiger Face. Jarvis was vexed, and waxed wrathful. He was not awaiting Naked Man. He was awaiting the arrival of The Dark One. What if Naked Man tried to get into the Post Office? He could not permit such a thing. He uttered a stern command, forbidding it. Naked Man heeded the command, and didn't try to enter the building, but merely lurked in the doorway.

Jarvis chuckled, and withdrew his head back inside the belfry. He liked it up here, although there wasn't much room to move as most of the space was taken up by the bells. There were four of them, but only the smallest one, for the clock, was working. It had struck the hour three times since he'd been here. The first time it had happened Jarvis had been taken by surprise, and was nearly deafened. But the next time, he heard the whirring and grinding of gears just before it struck, and was able to huddle in the far corner and cover his ears. The other bells were hung on separate beams - huge lengths of timber, spanning the belfry - with frayed ropes dangling down from them. They looked as though they hadn't been rung for a long time.

It had been easy to break into the church, and just as easy to get up to the top of the bell tower, although some of the steps were broken. There had been a sign on the door to the tower that said, 'Danger. Please Keep Out. The Tower is Unsafe'. But the words had no power over him. They were puny, spindly things. He'd decided to eat them. He tore the flimsy cardboard sign

218

into pieces and stuffed them into his mouth. It was hard work, but he chewed remorselessly, and eventually he disposed of them. That was the way to deal with enemies. By eating them, you ingested their power, and grew stronger. In fact, that was what he should do with The Dark One. His old enemy. He would eat Raymond Norfolk, and take away his power for ever. But should he be raw, or cooked? On the one hand, some of the goodness was lost in cooking. But on the other, his mouth was very dry and he wasn't sure he could manage to eat someone raw, even if he just ate the important sources of power - the heart, brain, liver, and genitals.

He leaned against the largest bell, and considered the question.

*

James checked his watch again, and established that it was ten-fifteen: exactly a minute later than when he'd last checked his watch. He pressed himself further back into the doorway, and squinted into the rain-lashed darkness in front of him. He could barely make out the bus shelter on the green, fifteen yards away.

He became aware of a rumbling sound. At first he thought it was thunder, but the sound was continuous and seemed to be getting louder. He peered into the dense curtain of glittering rain. Slowly something emerged from within it. James watched in horror as a huge, panting beast lumbered towards him up the green. As it got closer he saw that it was Bill Longbourne's traction engine. It was heading straight for him, and a familiar figure was in the cab, hunched over the steering wheel. James had finally discovered how Reuben intended to break into the Post Office.

He stepped out of the doorway. "Reuben!" he shouted, "stop!"

Reuben couldn't hear him. James ran forward, waving his arms.

Reuben saw him, and stood up in the cab, swaying precariously as he leaned out of the side, yelling something which James couldn't hear. Whatever it was he clearly had no intention of aborting the slow-motion ram-raid.

James stood his ground. The machine chugged implacably towards him. The front wheels were now only a few yards away. He cupped his hands to his mouth and shouted, "Reuben, this is crazy!"

Reuben hung on to the wheel and waved his free arm frantically out of the side of the cab at James, gesturing for him to get out of the way.

James shook his head. He could feel the heat coming off the traction engine's boiler, and see the steam as the rain sizzled on it. Just as one of the huge front wheels was about to hit him Reuben wrenched the steering wheel to one side and the machine swerved. Reuben lost his balance and toppled out of the cab. He landed at James's feet and lay on his back, gasping as the rain drummed down on his face.

The traction engine had changed course. James watched, spellbound, as it bypassed the Post Office and rumbled up to the churchyard wall. It smashed neatly through the gateway, then trundled along the winding path towards the church porch, as if guided by a phantom hand. In fact, James realized after a moment, the path was lined with large, whitewashed stones, and every time the machine veered off course, a wheel glanced against one of the stones, and it was nudged back onto the path.

The progress of the huge machine was inexorable. James briefly considered trying to catch up with it, climb up into the cab while it was still moving, find the brakes, and stop it. He decided against it, strongly influenced by the likelihood of being killed.

He felt something tugging at his trousers. Reuben was using James's leg to haul himself up off the ground. He achieved a kneeling position, then let go and staggered to his feet. He swayed around, gazing at James vacantly, then peering out into the rain, looking puzzled. Finally he turned around and caught sight of the traction engine.

"Oh, God," he said.

The traction engine ploughed into the church just to one side of the doorway. For a moment it paused, its wheels grinding angrily, then something seemed to give way and it lurched forward. The porch collapsed around it. Chunks of masonry began to tumble down from the tower. There was a blinding flash of lightning and an explosion of thunder. The whole tower trembled, then began to topple forward with a booming clang of cracked, ancient bells that drowned the noise of the storm.

As the tower fell, it disintegrated like a jigsaw. James could see that it was going to crash down onto the Post Office. He grabbed Reuben's arm and dragged him away from the building just as lumps of brickwork began to thud down beside them. As they scrambled onto the green they bounced into each other and fell to the ground. James struggled to his feet and hauled Reuben up. They slithered a few more yards on the wet grass and slipped over again. James curled himself up and pulled Reuben towards him, trying to cover his head.

A series of thundering crashes shook the ground beneath them and compressed James's eardrums. When the noise stopped he raised his head carefully and looked back. All he could see was a huge, roiling cloud of rubble slowly collapsing in on itself. A secondary cloud of fine dust surrounded the central core, settling quickly as it was stifled by the rain.

The church tower had vanished. In the rubble-filled gap where the Post Office had been, an isolated slab of its back wall remained, like a single tooth, with a calendar advertising farm machinery still hanging on it. In the debris James saw a set of scales that were completely intact, and some tins of baked beans still stacked in a neat pyramid. Several melons were scattered around, like cannonballs. Everything was garnished with a fine layer of soggy, shredded paper. Here and there great chunks of jagged metal protruded from the rubble: fragments of the church bells.

The rain stopped abruptly. The storm seemed to have exhausted itself. James stood up. Next to him, Reuben struggled to his feet. They gazed at the devastation without speaking. Suddenly Reuben grabbed his arm. James turned to look at him. His mouth was hanging open and he was making a croaking noise as he stared at something with an expression of terror. James followed his gaze. At first he couldn't tell what Reuben was looking at, then he saw that directly ahead of them a figure was standing in the ruins. It seemed to be an integral part of the debris, and James was staring at it for a long time before he realized it was there at all, a separate entity from its background, and that he was looking at a living person, although it was barely recognizable as a human being. Its clothes were in shreds and its eyes burned with an unearthly glow.

The figure began to walk forward very slowly, holding itself rigidly upright as it picked its way through the chaos. James saw that it was a man, and he appeared to be several hundred years old. After a few steps he stopped and looked down. There, at his feet, was a neatly wrapped brown paper parcel, about the size of a portable television. James felt a sudden lurch in the pit of his stomach. Very slowly the man sank to his knees like a worshipper in a trance. Trembling, he reached out to the parcel, as if it was a holy relic with the power to transfigure him. As he leaned forward to touch it he lost his balance and toppled over. He landed face-first in the parcel, which disintegrated in an explosion of white dust. For several moments he lay still, then his body began to twitch. He raised his face, and a cloud of the white powder bloomed around his head. His bloodshot eyes blazed through a mask of greyish paste, as if he was participating in some crazed tribal ritual. Slowly he stood upright, appearing to unfold himself from the ground and rise up smoothly to his full height by a process of levitation. He took a deep breath, then threw back his head and unleashed a piercing, inhuman howl that seemed to erupt from some ancient core of his being. Still howling, he raised his arms; his whole body shivered in a single, heaving spasm, then he toppled over backwards and lay still.

James prised Reuben's fingers from his arm. He took few steps forward, then stopped. What if the man was dead? Or worse, not dead?

Someone put a hand on James's shoulder. He turned to find Raymond Norfolk standing beside him.

"It's all right," Raymond said, "I'll take a look at him."

James stared at him. "How did you get here?"

"On the bike." Raymond nodded at a motorbike parked at the side of the green.

"Did you see... what happened?"

"Oh, yes. And I think you two should get out of here."

"No, we can't do that. I mean, we can't just leave." James paused. "Can we?"

"Yeah, get going. I'll take care of that guy. See he gets to hospital. It's the guy I told you about."

As they looked at the man on the ground he moved a little, and began to make a strange noise. After a moment James realized he was laughing.

"There you go," Raymond said, "he's okay. Go on, you need to leave. Now."

"But what about... all this?"

"It's done now, isn't it? The question is, can you do any good by staying?"

"I suppose not."

"Well, fuck off, then. And don't say anything. Either of you. It'll be all right."

"Are you sure?"

Raymond sighed. "Of course I'm not sure," he said. He patted James on the shoulder, then turned away and walked towards the man lying on the ground.

James noticed that Reuben had his eyes closed and was swaying around.

James prodded him. "Come on," he said, "wake up."

Reuben turned to him sharply. "I was just thinking."

"Well, don't," James said.

*

Jarvis gazed up at the sky. The sky was dark but there was light everywhere. He was surrounded by a thick dome of roaring silence. He was made of earth, but a few moments ago he'd been flying. Even now, a gigantic bird beat its wings in his chest. In the silence he heard everything.

He considered these mysteries. His mind was a diamond, expanding all the time, its infinite facets glittering with light.

He laughed.

And then the miracle happened. He saw the face of the Dark One, radiant with light. The Dark One spoke, his lips moved, but he spoke in words of deep silence and Jarvis heard nothing. The Dark One smiled down at him. Jarvis smiled back.

He'd been right. All along, despite them all. He'd found the package, and now Raymond Norfolk had arrived to collect it, just as he'd predicted. Yes, he'd been right.

He smiled again, and allowed the light to enfold him in its darkness.

*

James parted company with Reuben at the entrance to the Longbourne's drive. Reuben solemnly assured him that he understood the need to keep quiet about everything.

"And you can get home okay, right?" James said. The only thing he cared about now was getting back to Jessica.

"I'll be fine," Reuben said, showing no signs of leaving.

"Good. Well. It's been quite a night. I expect you should go home and try to get some sleep, then."

"I don't have to try," Reuben said. "I can always get some. I know where to find it." He tapped the side of his head. "I keep it in here." He released a cackle of laughter.

James smiled politely. Reuben opened his arms slowly and lumbered towards him. James realized that Reuben wanted to hug him. They grappled in a clumsy embrace and walloped each other manfully on the back. Reuben finally let go of him and backed away. He raised his hand, palm outwards, nodded slowly, and turned away.

As James watched him stagger along the road he noticed a faint, reddish glow in the sky beyond him. Perhaps the clouds were finally clearing over there and the moon was breaking through. The tinge of red probably meant it was a harvest moon, James thought, or a hunter's moon, or one of those other special moons they get in the country.

James picked his way along the drive and worked on a version of recent events to tell Jessica. There was no need to describe the full extent of the mayhem. She would find out about all that tomorrow in any case. For now he could simply emphasize that he'd kept her out of serious trouble by ensuring that Reuben hadn't been caught - entirely thanks to him, in the narrative he was now developing. As he refined his coverage of the story he decided he could reasonably claim to have saved Reuben's life, as well.

He could also imply that he himself was still in considerable danger, underplaying Raymond's assessment that they might get away with it if everyone kept quiet. In fact there was probably no need to mention Raymond's involvement in the story at all at this stage. It might be too much for Jessica to take in.

The house looked completely dark. When he got inside there didn't seem to be any lights on anywhere. It was just after eleven. Perhaps everyone else had gone to bed and Jessica was waiting for him upstairs. He groped for the light switches but couldn't find them so he shuffled forward, feeling his way along the wall. He stumbled against something and remembered a small table with various things on it, among them an old telephone, a vase of dried flowers, and a bowl full of rusting keys, old batteries, useless pens, and a range of nails, bolts and screws. All of these now crashed to the floor.

"Shit!" James hopped around on one leg, clutching his shin.

Someone turned the lights on.

Spracky stood beside the foot of the stairs. She must have emerged from the passage leading to the kitchen. She was wearing what appeared to be a lightweight tent that covered her from her chin to the floor, and a long, pointed nightcap. Even though the cap concealed the top of her scalp it still left a disturbing amount of smooth, pink skin visible where hair should have been, and which James tried no to stare at.

"Oh, it's you," Spracky said. "We shan't be needing this, then." She propped the cricket bat she was carrying against the side of the stairs.

James wondered for a moment why Spracky imagined someone would turn up at this time of night wanting to play cricket. Then he realised the bat was intended as a weapon. "Oh, I see," he said, "did you think I was burglar or something?"

"I doubt if a burglar would make as much ness as you have."

"Sorry about that, I'll clear it up." James crouched down and scrabbled around ineffectually. He put the receiver back on the big, old-fashioned phone, lifted it again, and listened. "Still working!" he said.

"Leave it, leave it. Get up. I'll do it later."

James got to his feet.

"Want anything?" Spracky said. "Sandwich? Egg and bacon? Kippers? Tea?"

James hadn't eaten since lunch but he didn't feel hungry. "No, thanks."

"In that case you should probably take yourself off to bed. That's where everyone else is. I'm just feeding the cat."

"Is everyone in bed? Jessica as well?"

"Jess? No, she's not."

"Oh, good. Where is she?"

"She's out."

James tried to think of reasons why Jessica could be out of the house. Perhaps she'd gone to find him and he'd missed her. "Where is she," he said, "do you know?"

"She's gone to Serena's," Spracky said. "What's the time?"

"Not long after eleven."

"Yes, that's where she'll be now."

"Do you know when she's likely to get back?"

"She won't come back tonight, now it's this late."

"What do you mean?"

"She'll stay over there. Serena phoned earlier to say that Charlie was down from Cambridge with a friend, and they were all going to the pub. So Jess drove over to join them. Daphne's very strict about Jess driving by herself when it gets late, especially if she's had a drink. They'll probably have a few, as Charlie's a great chum of hers. A great chum. So she'll stay over at Serena's. It's practically next door to the pub."

"Who's Charlie?"

"Serena's brother. Nice chap. Great fun." Spracky turned away and began to stump back towards the kitchen.

"So she won't be back at all," James said. "I mean, tonight."

Spracky turned and glanced at him sharply. "That's what I just said."

James stared at her. Not only had Jessica not waited for him, but at the slightest inducement she'd raced off to the pub to go and get drunk with the ominously fun-filled Charlie. The Great Chum. It could be the name of a foul medieval pestilence.

Spracky's expression softened. "I know," she said. "It's not easy." She turned away again. "Sleep well," she called over her shoulder.

When James switched on the light in his own room he saw a piece of paper on his bed. He picked it up. It was a note from Jessica:

Darling James, had to rush out - bit of an emergency, friend in need, got to go and be social with boring people to make up the numbers yawn yawn but duty calls, you know how it is?!! Hope you managed to sort everything. I'm sure you did, clever you. I'll see you in the morning. Can't wait!! Sleep well. Big hugs, kisses, licks and other things!!! lots and lots and lots of love, Jess.

James sat on his bed with the note in his hand for a long time.

Eleven

"This is all a bit Agatha Christie, isn't it?" the sergeant said.

"Who?" Auntie Pru said in a stage whisper from the other side of the Longbourne's sitting room. Spracky leaned down and spoke to her quietly. Pru muttered a reply in which James caught the word 'vulgar'.

"If only you had a library for us to assemble in," the sergeant continued, "we'd be in business." He chuckled. "After all, we've even got a visiting butler."

He turned to George, who nodded politely. James had been mildly shocked to see him in casual clothes, although the cream linen jacket, crisply pressed grey flannel trousers, open-necked shirt and paisley cravat looked just as formal as the butler's outfit.

"However, I'd like to make it clear," the sergeant said to George, "that as far as I'm concerned, you're here this morning purely because you've kindly agreed to come and represent your employers down the road. I'm sure they'd like to be here themselves if they could, especially as they put a lot of money into restoring that church tower. They'd like to find out what happened just like the rest of us. And we will, don't you worry." The sergeant narrowed his eyes and looked around the room, nodding slowly. "Oh, yes, we'll find out. Definitely. However, we all know why the Silvers can't be here and I'm sure we all sympathize with their loss down at the manor there."

No one had seemed particularly shocked by the news that the windmill had burned down in the night. Raised eyebrows, quiet smiles, and knowing looks were the general reaction. The information that there was no sign of Max or any trace of his body was met by a similar lack of surprise and a few more knowing looks. The official view was that the mill had been struck by lightning and that Max, already traumatized, had fled in panic and was now wandering the countryside. Several far more elaborate theories were in circulation in the village, some of them involving aliens or the Mafia. But James remembered the last thing Max had said to him, about being the one to decide the fate of the windmill, and was pretty sure that Max had simply set fire to it and run away.

"So, George," the sergeant continued, "I'd like to thank you for coming and to emphasize that there's no implication you're under any kind of suspicion, I can assure you. None at all."

He turned away from George and picked up a china shepherdess from the small table beside him. "Although as it happens," he continued, examining the ornament closely, "you haven't actually got an alibi, have you?" He spun around and pointed the shepherdess at George, who gazed at him impassively. The sergeant smiled at him and tapped the shepherdess in the palm of his hand. "Which may not be significant in itself, but there are other factors to consider, aren't there?"

"Sergeant," Daphne Longbourne said, "do you mind? That's Dresden china."

"Strictly speaking," the sergeant said, glancing at the base of the ornament, "it's Meissen, as it was made after seventeen-ten. And a very fine piece it is, too. Although this bucolic stuff is a little kitsch for my tastes." He replaced the shepherdess on the table and turned back to George. "As I say, there are other factors. Because while you may not be the only person here without an alibi, you are the only one with a criminal record. Isn't that true? Nothing personal, by the way, George. Just doing my job."

Before George could reply, Daphne Longbourne said, "What I fail to understand, sergeant, is which part of your job requires you to stage this absurd melodrama. Perhaps you've been watching too much television."

"I tend to favour the radio, as it happens," the sergeant said, "but I take your point. The fact is, I thought it might help us to get to the bottom of all this more quickly. I agree, it's not entirely orthodox. But today's a bank holiday: it gives us a chance to clear this up locally before the police from Bath get involved. Because none of us want that, do we?"

There was a general murmur of assent. Daphne pursed her lips but didn't disagree. The sergeant looked around the room with a broad smile. He seemed to be enjoying himself. As soon as he'd arrived, James recognized him as the same huge policeman who'd got involved in the fight at the bingo. He had a black eye, and his upper lip was swollen, which thickened his natural Somerset accent.

"Right," he continued, consulting a notebook, "The matter of a criminal record. As I say, George, you're the only person in the room with a bit of form."

John Longbourne gave a discreet cough from the sofa where he was sitting next to Daphne. She shifted in her seat, and James saw her kick him surreptitiously.

John winced. "It's all right," he said, "there's no point in denying it. It'll be easy enough for him to find out." He turned to the sergeant. "As a matter of fact," he said, "I was involved in a little business misunderstanding that ended up in court, and I received a conviction. The truth is, I was rather badly let down by some people I trusted, and I took the blame for some funds that went missing. It was the only decent thing to do."

Jessica sniggered. Daphne turned to glare at her. She was sprawled across a small armchair in a corner of the room, with her legs dangling over one side. James was sitting almost opposite her on a sofa that matched the one Daphne and John occupied, on the other side of the room. Reuben was slumped beside him. He'd been reading a glossy magazine when James came in, and had been quite alert, but he was fading fast. The hangover was winning. Jessica had been the last to arrive, and when she rushed in James had shoved Rueben along to make room for her between them, but she hadn't noticed.

"Oh," the sergeant said, "I see. Well, thank you for being so frank, Mr Longbourne. But I assume you can account for your whereabouts last night, can you?"

"I can vouch for him," Daphne said.

Jessica snorted quietly. James smiled at her.

He hadn't managed to speak to her this morning, apart from a hurried exchange on the stairs. He asked if she'd enjoyed herself the night before. She rolled her eyes and said she'd been totally bored but she was sure he understood, she'd had to go and rescue Serena from this friend of her brother's who was being a pest, and she'd waited quite a long time for James and was really, really sorry to have missed him and they'd catch up later. She grabbed his face and gave him a quick, wet kiss, then bounded away.

The sergeant tapped his pencil against his notebook and nodded to John and Daphne. "Good. Well, I don't think we need to go into that any further. Thank you."

"Actually," said Spracky, "I've got a criminal record, too."

"Oh, shut up, Sprack," Auntie Pru said.

"No," Spracky said, "it's only fair. It was a long time ago, but I believe certain offences remain on one's record. Isn't that so, sergeant?"

"It depends on the offence. What was the charge?"

"I was in a public house, and a drunken oaf made certain vile and filthy insinuations about me. I was obliged to give him a good hiding."

"A good hiding?" the sergeant said with a chuckle. "That one's not on the statute books, I don't think."

"I believe the actual charge was Grievous Bodily Harm. The man had to spend some time in hospital, you see, but I'm told that reconstructive surgery eventually made most of his wounds almost imperceptible. Apart from the ears, unfortunately. They couldn't rebuild them very well in those days."

"Christ," the sergeant muttered.

Jessica whistled. "Good for you, Sprack."

"In case you want to know, officer," Auntie Pru said, "I can provide Miss Sprackling with an alibi for last night."

"Thank you, miss, most helpful," the sergeant said. He was beginning to look a bit flustered. "However, I believe we'll leave this particular line of enquiry for now."

"You're the one who brought it up," Jane Cottle said. She was perched on the arm of a chair that her husband was sitting in, effectively trapping him in it.

James gazed through the open window behind her. Birds were singing in the morning sunshine. It was only half past ten but it was beginning to feel much later. Next to him Reuben released a soft belch of withering toxicity. Raymond

Norfolk, leaning against the wall beside Reuben, grimaced and fanned himself with his panama hat.

"Yes, I know I was the one who brought it up," the sergeant said testily. "The point I was trying to make was that George here not only has a criminal record, but also has no alibi. Do you see?"

"However, sergeant" George murmured, "and with respect, I must point out that the offence of which I was convicted, like Mr Longbourne's, fell into the category of what is commonly referred to as white collar crime. It hardly proves a predilection on my part for stealing vehicles - let alone a vehicle of the extraordinary type that featured in this unfortunate incident - and using them as instruments of wanton destruction. And, even more to the point, what possible motive could I have for such a deed?"

The sergeant sighed and folded his arms. "Look," he said, "I wasn't suggesting--"

"He's right, you know, sergeant," Simon Cottle broke in. He wriggled in his chair, trying to work his way free from the impediment of his wife's sizeable rump. She shifted a little on her perch and he lurched forward, nearly falling off the chair.

"It's all a question of motive, isn't it?" he said, as he and his wife rearranged themselves. "I mean, if it comes down to it, there are plenty of people with a far better motive than George for destroying the bell tower."

The sergeant frowned. "Really, sir? And who might they be? Is there a gang of militant atheists at work in the district, that I know nothing about? Or a guerrilla unit of disaffected campanologists, perhaps?"

Raymond laughed. Everyone turned to look at him.

"What are you laughing at?" Simon said.

"The sergeant," Raymond said. "He was being funny."

"But you can't deny it's true about the number of people with a motive."

"Oh, yes. And that's funny as well. When you think about it."

"What the fuck are you two talking about?" Jessica said.

"Jess," Daphne said, "please don't swear like that."

"We might as well tell them," Simon said.

Raymond shrugged. "Go ahead."

"Well, the thing is," Simon said, "as you may know, we've now collected a considerable sum for the bell tower restoration fund. But it wasn't quite enough yet to cover all the work involved. However, we've always been aware that it would actually cost more to restore the tower than it would to pull the whole lot down and start again."

"What do you mean, start again?" Auntie Pru said.

"He means build a replica," Raymond said.

"Bloody hell," the sergeant said, "I can't see certain people agreeing to that in a hurry."

"Yes, it's been the subject of some controversy," Simon said. "Although a surprising number of the church commissioners have been in favour, haven't they, Ray?"

"Absolutely. Why not have a nice new bell tower that duplicates all the architectural features of the old one, if you like that kind of thing, but one that's structurally sound and will last far longer?"

"I find the idea utterly repugnant," Auntie Pru said.

"So do quite a lot of people," Raymond said. "But quite a lot don't, either. There are two schools of thought. There are those who think that sacred buildings have a spiritual value by virtue of their antiquity, and those who believe that any building can become sacred through the spiritual value invested in it by the worshippers who use it."

"They should be shot," Auntie Pru said.

"Yes, that's the view of the archbishop," Simon said. "More or less."

"Of course it is," Pru said, "he's very sound."

"But he's up against Bath and Wells, who's surprisingly progressive on the question," Raymond said. "It's all become pretty acrimonious. And of course, now the tower's been destroyed it looks like the replica plan will be going ahead."

"Hang on," the sergeant said, "are you saying you had something to do with it?"

"No, I'm simply telling you how things stand. Or stood." Raymond laughed.

Auntie Pru made a noise of disgust.

The sergeant turned to Simon. "Vicar?"

"I certainly had nothing to do with what happened last night. That would be absurd. I was simply pointing out that lots of people might have had a motive. However, I don't mind telling you that I'm with the progressives on this one. I don't hold with the cult of preservation for its own sake. I don't think it's healthy." He looked around the room defiantly, then glanced up at his wife.

She was leaning back and gazing at him in amazement. "You never told me any of this," she said. "Why haven't I heard about it?"

"You never asked."

"What kind of attitude is that? Don't I have a right to know these things?"

"Do you? Why?"

"Because I'm your wife, in case you'd forgotten."

"Not much chance of that."

Jane smoothed down her dress, then adopted a tone of polite enquiry. "Does the sergeant know that you were lurking about the church last night?"

"I wasn't lurking about. And, yes, I've already told him that I was in the vestry at the time of the incident. It happens to be the only place where I can get a bit of peace and quiet to work on my sermons."

Jane snorted. "To look at filth on the internet, you mean."

"Well, thank you very much," the sergeant said loudly, "that's very interesting. About the motive, I mean." He frowned. "Although it doesn't make things any simpler, unfortunately, knowing that half the diocese had a good reason to want the bloody thing torn down. Oops, pardon my language, vicar. And ladies. And..." he glanced at Spracky. She stared at him with a heavy-lidded, dangerous look. "Yes, er, ladies," he repeated.

There was an awkward silence.

"Aren't we all overlooking something?" George said.

"What's that, then, George?" the sergeant said.

"We're assuming that the bell tower was the object of this extraordinary rampage. But remember, the Post Office was also destroyed. To say nothing of the buildings on either side of it, which were severely damaged as well."

"Christ," said the sergeant. "You mean the Post Office may have been the target?"

James shifted uneasily in his seat.

"I'm only speculating, sergeant," George said. "We should consider every possibility, don't you think?"

"Of course we should. I was just coming to the Post Office. I think I speak for all of us when I say its destruction is an absolute tragedy. An awful thing to happen. I dread to think how Mrs Ogden is taking it."

"Aren't they all being closed down anyway?" Jessica said.

"Disgraceful," Auntie Pru said.

"I agree," the sergeant said. "I mean, apart from anything else, there's the disruption to the postal service to consider."

"I heard it's all going to be taken over by private companies," Jessica said.

The sergeant looked at her disapprovingly. "The fact is, young lady, the loss of the Post Office is a terrible blow to this community. People are going to be devastated."

John Longbourne cleared his throat.

Daphne shot him a warning glance.

"Don't worry," he murmured to her, "it's got to come out soon enough."

She turned away from him and drummed her fingers on the arm of the sofa.

"As it happens," John said, "Jess is right. The dear old Post Office was earmarked for closure. Pal of mine in their legal department told me. In strict confidence, of course."

"Naturally," Auntie Pru said.

"And it's the most extraordinary co-incidence," John continued, "but there happens to be a scheme to develop the site. Some colleagues of mine are involved, actually. Very shrewd business types. Entrepreneurs."

"That's one word for them," Daphne muttered.

"The Post Office is going to be redeveloped?" Jane Cottle said.

"The whole row of buildings, actually. Once the Post Office had been closed down, there was going to be a compulsory purchase order served on the places on either side. So the whole site would become vacant for this scheme."

"And what, exactly, is the scheme?" Jane said.

John cleared his throat again. He attempted to straighten his tie and shoot his cuffs, but discovered he was wearing an open-necked, short-sleeved polo shirt. He settled for crossing his legs and making a steeple of his fingers. "As it happens," he said judiciously, "I believe the scheme represents a terrific opportunity to regenerate the whole area."

"Do we need regenerating?" the sergeant said.

"We've got to move with the times."

"Why?" said Auntie Pru.

John smiled at her patronizingly. "The sad truth is, Pru, that rural areas all over the country are in decline. The only solution is to stimulate a service economy. You've only got to look at what they've done in Bath."

"Bath isn't a rural area. It's a town. In fact, it's a city, as it's got a cathedral."

"Technically, yes. But it's a good example, all the same. They've spent millions on totally refurbishing the Roman remains, including the baths, and built a state-of-the-art Visitor Centre."

"But we don't want a Visitor Centre," Pru said. "We haven't got any visitors."

"Not at the moment, no," John said. "But when we have, the site of the old Post Office is the ideal place to build it."

'Why are all these visitors going to come here, then?" the sergeant said. "There's nothing here."

"That's where you're wrong, actually. This is a very interesting part of the country. People are getting very keen on all the history around places like this. Particularly all the mystical stuff. Druids and so forth. I mean, look at Glastonbury. Those shops selling crystals and tarot cards and pyramids and whatnot, they make a bloody fortune. And people will travel for miles to gawp at a prehistoric stone circle."

The sergeant laughed. "I know, they're mad if you ask me. But there isn't a prehistoric stone circle anywhere around here, as far as I know."

"No," John said, "not yet."

For a while the only sound was the singing of the birds outside.

Finally Jane Cottle spoke in a slightly strangled voice." Are you serious?"

"Look, people get far too precious about the English countryside," John said. "They seem to imagine it's this ancient, natural landscape, when in fact it's the product of constant human intervention. People have always messed around with it. I mean, thousands of years ago it was all forests full of bears and eagles and things, then people chopped down most of the trees, slaughtered all the wildlife, and made fields and hedges and so on. And now we've got huge industrial farms all over the place. We change it all the time. It's always been artificial, you see."

"But you're talking about deliberately deceiving people," Jane said.

"Oh, nonsense. It's been going on for years. Gormless tourists tiptoeing around every pile of earth in England that's more than three feet high in the firm belief it's King Arthur's tomb, or Merlin's spare bedroom. And who's to say they're wrong? It keeps them happy, doesn't it? And this part of the country's full of all these burial mounds, or long barrows, or earthworks, or whatever you want to call them. I'm sure we'll find a few around here if we look hard enough."

Jane shook her head in disbelief. She turned to her husband. "Did you know about all this? This scheme he's talking about?"

"Er, yes, I knew a bit about it. The general idea. Yes."

Jane stared at him. He frowned, and looked around the room as if he was searching for something he'd mislaid.

"You're involved in it, aren't you?" she said quietly.

"What? No. I mean, not really. Just a bit. John was kind enough to give me a chance to make a small investment, that's all. I was going to tell you."

"When?"

"When it all paid off. It was going to be a surprise."

Jane stood up abruptly from her perch on the arm of the chair, and turned to face him. He looked up at her with a sickly smile. She shook her head, then spun around and walked away from him. She paused in the middle of the room, looking for somewhere else to sit, then strode towards James's sofa. He shifted along, away from Reuben, and Jane dropped down between them, making them both bounce up in the air slightly. She gave James a bright smile then began to cry quietly.

"This is all rather surprising," the sergeant said. He flipped open his notebook and frowned at whatever he'd written in it.

Jessica laughed. "Well, you got all that wrong, didn't you? It looks like poor old George is about the only person who *didn't* have a reason to knock down the bell tower and demolish the Post Office. Who's next on the list?"

The sergeant snapped his notebook shut and scowled at Jessica. "I never suggested George actually did it," he said. "I was simply proceeding in a logical fashion, assessing the probabilities based on the facts available to me at the time. I'm not making any accusations against George, so don't tell me I am, if you don't mind!"

"Thank you, sergeant," George murmured, and inclined his head a fraction.

"That doesn't mean you're off the hook, pal," the sergeant said, turning to him angrily, "so you can wipe that smug little smile off your face for a start. I don't know why everyone here thinks they can make a bloody fool of me!"

James thought the sergeant probably resented the way recent dramatic revelations were upstaging him. And Jessica's remark about him getting it all wrong had probably not been the best thing to say. Now the sergeant was taking his injured feelings out on George. He took a step towards him, and wagged a sausage-sized finger in his face.

"I haven't finished with you yet, not by a long chalk," he said. "You still haven't come up with an alibi, and you refuse to account for your movements, and that doesn't look very good, as far as I'm concerned."

"He was with me," Jane Cottle said.

There was a long silence. It was broken by an unfamiliar voice.

"Fuck me, darling," George said cheerfully, "you didn't have to go that far, you silly mare. You've done it now, haven't you?" He sounded unmistakeably Cockney. The butler had vanished. He smiled at Jane and his face was split by a huge, toothy grin. "But never mind," he continued, "you're a star and I love you. Come here, doll."

Jane got up and went to stand beside him. He took her hand and looked at her proudly. She was two or three inches taller than him, and a couple of stone heavier, but she seemed suddenly girlish beside him.

Simon Cottle stood up. He pointed at George. "Did you call my wife darling?"

Jane turned on him. "Yes, he did," she said, "and it's more than you ever do."

"You bastard," Simon said, ignoring her, "how long has this been going on?"

"Now, now," the sergeant said. "Let's keep it civil, if you please." He turned to Simon. "Would you mind sitting down, vicar?"

"Oh. All right." Simon sat down. He seemed to think honour had been satisfied.

"You and your wife obviously have some things to discuss," the sergeant said, "but let's not get distracted from the matter in hand. We still have to deal with a very serious criminal offence. Very serious."

"And now that your chief suspect appears to have an alibi," Daphne Longbourne said, "are you any nearer to bringing this whole charade to a close?"

The sergeant puffed out his cheeks and expelled a long, exasperated breath. "I keep trying to tell you," he said, "that I wasn't accusing George of anything."

"Well, if he didn't do it," Daphne said, "who did?"

"Surely," Spracky broke in, "there's one very obvious candidate, isn't there? What about the poor man who was found in the ruins by Mr Norfolk?"

"Ah, yes," the sergeant said. He glanced uneasily at Raymond. "Detective Sergeant Jarvis."

"Good God," Daphne said, "are you telling us the man's a police officer?"

"Unfortunately, yes. It seems he was suffering from some kind of breakdown."

"There you are, then," Daphne said. "The man's a loony. He must have done it."

"Yes, one would think so," the sergeant said, "especially as Mr Norfolk tells us there was no one else at the scene when he arrived." He glanced at Raymond again.

"That's right," Raymond said. "I got there just after it happened. Very lucky, really. I just happened to be out for a ride on the chopper. And there was definitely no one else around. So, naturally, I assumed he must have done it, too. Seemed logical."

"Which is what you told me," the sergeant said, checking his notebook, "in your statement."

"That's right."

"But now we know he couldn't have done it."

"Seems that way," Raymond said.

Daphne tapped her foot impatiently. "Why? Why couldn't he have done it?"

"I've been on the phone to the hospital," the sergeant said, "and they say that all his injuries are consistent with a fall, so he must have been in the bell tower when it came down. Apart from some strange wounds on his chest, apparently. They can't explain those at all. But the poor man's gone completely deaf, and they say that must have been caused by the bells, when he came down with them."

"What the hell was he doing up there?" John Longbourne said.

"That," said the sergeant, "is a mystery we may never solve. It seems the man is severely disturbed, and the doctors can't get any sense out of him. It appears he's got considerable quantities of drugs in his system. Apparently, he keeps asking to 'talk to the hedgehog'. I assume that's some kind of drugs jargon. 'Talking to the hedgehog.' Similar to 'chasing the dragon', I imagine. In any event, he's pretty much off his head."

"Poor chap," Spracky said.

"I don't know about that," said Auntie Pru. "In the old days, he would have been hanged. None of this nonsense about pleading insanity."

"You can't hang a man just for being on drugs in a belfry," Spracky said.

"I don't see why not."

"I'm sorry," Daphne said, "but I've got things to do. Sergeant, can you tell us what action you now intend to take? I must go and look at my wisteria. I'm very concerned that the storm might have damaged it."

"Right," the sergeant said. He stepped into the middle of the room and looked around. He seemed to be making an effort to regain control of the situation. He held up his notebook, like a warrant of his authority, and waggled it about. "I'll tell you what I think. Which is what I've thought all along, as it happens, if only you'd give me half a chance to get to it. If you ask me, we're dealing with a case of misdirected horseplay."

"What on earth do you mean?" Daphne said.

"I mean," the sergeant said, "that this incident bears all the hallmarks of youthful high spirits that got out of hand."

James found that his mouth was dry.

"Or," the sergeant said, flipping open his notebook and consulting it, "failing that, and I admit this is a long shot, it could be the unfortunate result of an elderly person getting confused." He looked up and glanced at Auntie Pru.

"Sergeant," she said in a voice of ice, "I hope you're not suggesting that I had anything to do with this matter?"

"Nothing to be ashamed of, miss. Old people do get a bit mixed up. My own grandfather, God rest his soul, used to steal ice cream vans towards the end of his life. He used to love the chimes, he always said."

"Withdraw your allegation," Auntie Pru said.

"Oh, my gramps wouldn't mind. He used to laugh about it."

"The allegation against me, you fool!"

"Now, there's no need for personal remarks, miss."

Auntie Pru raised her arm and pointed at him with a steady hand. "If you don't withdraw that allegation and apologize to me," she said, "I shall have you horsewhipped."

The sergeant glanced around the room and began a tentative laugh, but it trickled away as he found himself pinned down by Pru's unblinking gaze.

His Adam's apple bobbed up and down. He cleared his throat. "No offence, miss," he said, "as I say, it was a long shot. I was just speculating. I'm sure you had nothing to do with it."

"Apologize!"

"Oh, right. Of course. Very sorry, I'm sure."

"Thank you."

"You're welcome."

The sergeant wiped his brow, and buried himself in his notebook for a moment. When he looked up he seemed to have regained his composure.

"So," he said, "I'm basically interested in the young people."

"Don't look at me," Jessica said, "you need to talk to those two." She kicked one of her legs up, pointing it in the general direction of James and Reuben.

"Oh, really, miss? And why do you say that?"

"Because I've got an alibi. I was here, in and out of the kitchen all evening until about ten. Ask Spracky. Then I went to the pub. Loads of people saw me there."

"Actually, that's correct, sergeant," Spracky said.

"I see, thank you very much." The sergeant wrote something in his notebook. He turned to James and Reuben. "What have you got to say for yourselves?"

"I was at home," Reuben said.

"All evening?"

"Yes."

"Can anyone corroborate that?"

"Yes."

"Who might that be? Your parents, perhaps?"

"Yes. No. Wait." Reuben frowned and stared at the carpet, biting his lip. It was obvious he was trying to think through the implications of the various lies he was considering. The strain began to tell on him, and his breathing became laboured. He wiped his nose with the back of his hand, then pulled an asthma inhaler from his pocket and shoved it in his mouth. He sucked on it deeply a few times, and absent-mindedly offered it to James.

James shook his head.

"George!" Reuben cried, triumphantly.

"What?" George said, startled. He had his arm around Jane Cottle's waist.

Reuben turned to the sergeant. "George can tell you. I was at home all evening, and he saw me. In fact, he made me a sandwich." A crafty glint appeared in Reuben's eye. "Actually, lots of sandwiches. One every half an hour or so. Didn't you, George?"

The sergeant sighed. "You haven't really been paying attention, have you, sir?"

"Yes I have. Haven't I?"

"No. We've already established that George was... otherwise engaged."

George laughed and patted Jane's rump. She giggled.

Simon Cottle glared at them. George gave him a friendly wink. Simon turned away and shook his head sadly, assuming a pious expression.

The sergeant had been composing a lengthy entry in his notebook. He regarded what he'd written with satisfaction, and turned to James.

"What about you, sir?"

"Me?"

"Yes, you."

"I was here. In the house."

"Anyone see you?"

"I'm not sure. Actually, I went to bed very early. I was quite tired."

"What time?"

"Oh, about ten. A bit earlier."

"And did you leave your room at all? Apart from the necessary?"

"Er, no, I don't think I did."

"So, no one can confirm your story."

"Er... Let me see... I'm not sure... perhaps not... er... no, I don't think so."

The sergeant wrote something in his notebook and snapped it shut. He walked up to the sofa, planted himself in front of it, and stood looking down at James and Reuben.

"I'll tell you what I think," he said. "I think that one or both of you two young gentlemen stole that machine last night and drove it up to the village green."

He looked from to the other. Neither of them spoke.

The sergeant put away his notebook and squatted down in front of them so that his eyes were level with theirs. James could smell coffee on his breath.

"I expect you were just having a lark, and you lost control of it. If that's what you want to tell me, that makes it less serious, doesn't it? So, is that what happened? It was a bit of fun that went wrong? You can tell me. It'll all be okay in the end."

He gave them an encouraging smile. "Is that what happened, then? You were having a bit of a laugh? Christ, you must have shit a brick when you lost control of that thing." He chuckled and shook his head. "What a nightmare! Still, these things happen, don't they? It can't be helped now. So, is that what happened? You can tell me."

James glanced at Reuben and caught his eye. Reuben pressed his lips together and tilted his chin defiantly.

The sergeant held up a finger. "I'd just like to say, there's nothing wrong with one of you telling me the other one was responsible. You won't hear any nonsense about being a grass. It takes a lot of courage to tell the truth and I, for one, will have nothing but respect for you. Perhaps one of you talked the other one into it. That wouldn't surprise me at all. Of course, the really brave thing to do would be if one of you owned up, and took responsibility. That would show real maturity. That really would get respect."

James found the sergeant's technique - honed, no doubt, on generations of local hooligans - quite persuasive. He wondered what the next stage might be if he and Reuben refused to confess. Would the sergeant use violence? Nothing too extreme would probably happen here in the sitting room. But what if the sergeant arrested them, and took them away? It was an isolated community. He could do anything he liked to them. James wouldn't be surprised if he was an enthusiastic practitioner of waterboarding.

"Come on," the sergeant said, "I know you want to tell me. You'll feel a lot better when you do." He seemed to be getting uncomfortable and he shifted on his haunches.

James said nothing. He tried to make his mind a blank.

The sergeant shook his head sadly. "I'm disappointed. I hoped that at least one of you would have the decency to do the right thing. You're letting me down, you know. In fact, you're letting everyone down. But most of all you're letting yourselves down."

James pictured Sylvia Silver, peering at him through the rain-streaked car window. She'd asked him to look after Reuben. Now he came to a decision. He would take the blame. He began to compose what he was going to say.

"Look," the sergeant said, getting to his feet, "someone stole that machine, and I'm pretty sure it was one or both of you. The bloody thing didn't drive up there by itself."

James took a deep breath.

"Actually," a voice said from the French windows, "it might have done."

Bill Longbourne was lounging in the open doorway. He'd been there all the time, but everyone had forgotten about him.

"What did you say, sir?" the sergeant said.

Bill removed his hands from his pockets and folded his arms. "I said it might have done. There are circumstances under which it could have driven itself, you see, extraordinary as it may sound."

"Yes, sir, it does sound rather extraordinary," the sergeant said. He glanced around the room. Everyone looked as surprised as he was. He turned back to Bill. "Would you be able to explain how that might happen?"

Bill took a step forward, then caught Daphne's eye. He looked down at his feet, and made a point of aligning them so he was still just outside the room.

"Sir?" the sergeant said. "How could it have driven itself?"

"Probably a glitch in the timing advance mechanism."

The sergeant nodded. "Ah, yes. And would you mind telling us what that might be?" His tone implied that while he knew the answer perfectly well, it would only be fair to the others to explain it.

"It's a regulator that responds to the boiler temperature and adjusts the throttle clearance. I've been having a bit of trouble with it. As you may have noticed, it's been very hot for the last couple of days. The weather, I mean."

"Yes, I think we've all been aware of that."

"And then, yesterday evening, when the storm broke, the temperature dropped very rapidly."

"Yes, I think we noticed that, too."

"Several degrees in the space of well under an hour, I would say."

"Oh, for God's sake, Bill," Daphne said, "do get on with it."

"Oh, I'm sorry," Bill said. "I thought you'd be interested. But I forgot that you've got things to do. Very well, I'll try to explain it simply."

"That would probably be best, sir," the sergeant said.

"Well, this regulator I mentioned: I was fiddling around with the damn thing all afternoon, trying to equalize the temperature response so I could retard the automatic immobilizer on the choke. And I must have over-compensated. That's the only possible explanation." Bill looked around, satisfied that he'd explained the whole mystery.

"I think some people may still be in the dark, sir," the sergeant said. "Could you just explain how the machine actually came to drive itself?"

"Ah, well, the whole system is very delicate, you see. And when the temperature dropped suddenly, the linkage must have contracted, which had the effect of pulling the starter. Normally, that wouldn't matter, but I'd left so much clearance that it actually fired up, and off she went. She was already facing the lower gate out of the yard, which happened to be open - not that that would have presented an obstacle - and so it was a straight line all the way to the bottom of the common. There was a car parked along the road there, and she must have struck it in such a way that it nudged the steering, and she

239

changed course to go all the way up the middle of the green. The steering mechanism is surprisingly sensitive, you see. Very responsive. And up at the top of the green, it was probably just the camber of the road that sent her in the direction of the church. I can't be certain on every detail, but I think that's more or less what happened."

The sergeant looked at him in silence for a long time.

"Do you mean to say," he said finally, "that no one is to blame?"

"No one except me," Bill said.

The sergeant indicated James and Reuben. "So these two weren't involved at all?"

"It's most unlikely. We're talking about a very complex machine. I doubt very much if either of them would have been able to drive her all the way up there. No, I think they're in the clear."

Bill looked slowly around the room until his bland, impassive gaze came to rest on James. They looked at each other in silence. Just for an instant, James was sure he saw the ends of Bill's moustache twitch fractionally.

"So, this whole charade has been a complete waste of time?" Daphne said.

"Good Lord," Bill said, "speaking of the time..." He fished out a pocket-watch on a chain. "I've got some friends turning up at any moment to help me tow the old girl back to the yard. Well, this has all been fascinating, but I must be off. Cheerio, everyone."

"Wait," James said.

Bill raised his eyebrows. "Yes?"

"Is she badly damaged?"

"As it happens, she's not. But thank you for asking. Very thoughtful. Yes, she's a sturdy old thing. There's a lot of craftsmanship there." He paused, and gazed at him again for a moment. This time James definitely saw the ends of his moustache twitch.

"So, it's nothing that I shan't be able to repair," Bill continued. "It'll take a bit of time, but it'll keep me out of trouble. She might even end up in better condition than ever. Well, Goodbye." He turned and walked away.

The sergeant slowly unbuttoned the top pocket of his tunic. He slid his notebook into it and buttoned it up again with great deliberation. He smoothed down his hair, looked around the room, and then walked slowly out of the French windows without a word. He paused just outside, took a deep breath, squared his shoulders, and walked off in the direction of the gates.

No one spoke or moved for a moment then Simon Cottle stood up and walked over to his wife and George, who still had his arm around Jane's waist. Simon started talking to them quietly. He seemed surprisingly friendly. James tried to imagine what was passing between them. He looked around. John Longbourne was patting Daphne's knee and whispering to her. She brushed his hand away and shook her head irritably. Spracky and Pru seemed to have resumed an argument they'd been having earlier. Reuben was asleep. James gazed across the room at Jessica, who yawned and stretched. He was about to get up and go to her when he felt a hand on his shoulder.

"I need to get back to the studio," Raymond Norfolk said, "so I'll say goodbye."

James got up and faced him. He hadn't expected him to leave so abruptly. He felt there was a lot he wanted to talk to him about but now there didn't seem to be a chance.

"Good to meet you, James. Take care."

"Yes, you too. And, listen, we must keep in touch. Or something."

"Or something." Raymond placed his palms together and inclined his head briefly. "Peace, brother. Keep up the good work." He turned and walked across the room to the French windows. He paused for a moment to say something to Simon, George and Jane, who all laughed, then Raymond stepped out into the garden.

Jessica sprang up and followed him. James saw her catch up with him on the lawn. They exchanged a few words then Raymond turned away. Jessica grabbed his arm. Raymond listened to her, nodding occasionally. He said something, put a hand on her shoulder, kissed her cheek, and walked away. Jessica stood watching him for a moment then ran back to the house. James heard the door slamming and then the sound of Jessica running up the stairs. He looked around. No one was taking any notice of him. He slipped out of the room.

Jessica's door was slightly open. As James approached it he heard her voice:

"Please! Don't hang up, Ray, please! I've really got to talk to you. I couldn't just let you walk away like that, it just didn't feel right, and it's made me so miserable!"

James flattened himself against the wall next to the door and edged closer.

"All right," Jessica was saying, "about yesterday. I'm sorry. Okay? I've already said that. It was my fault. I admit it. I should have told you before anything happened."

James risked a quick look through the crack. Jessica was sitting on her bed, hunched over her phone, half-turned away from him. With her free hand she was compulsively bunching up the bedspread, pulling and tweaking it fiercely.

"Oh, really?" Her voice rose. "Trying to seduce you? Well, I didn't have to try very hard, that's all I can say! You were all over me like--"

She listened for a moment, breathing heavily.

"I did not!" she hissed. "No way!" She paused. "Well, maybe just a bit. But you didn't try very hard to stop me, did you? Not until that stupid thing with the virginity. I mean, what's the big deal? I bet I wouldn't have been the first virgin you've had! Oh, God, why did you have to stop?" Her voice became husky: "I want you so much, Ray."

James heard the bedsprings creak. When she spoke again her voice was muffled:

"Why? Why is it about trust? Why can't it just be about sex?"

There was a pause then the bedsprings creaked again as she jumped up. "Wait a minute," she shouted, "that's not fair!"

James heard her pacing around the room and inched away from the door.

"No, really, just wait a minute," Jessica continued, making an effort to keep her voice under control. "What's he got to do with it? This is about us. Why are we suddenly talking about him? Listen Ray, I promise. I don't want to fuck James. Okay?"

James felt something like an electric shock and the sensation of falling.

"Yes, okay," Jessica said patiently, "Olly asked me to be nice to him. So what? But when he turned out to be okay, and quite good looking - well, why shouldn't I have a bit of fun?"

Pause.

"Oh, come on, Ray, what does that even mean? Prick teaser? That's probably just something you say to your groupies. And that's another thing, why is it okay for you--"

She broke off and listened.

"Him!?" Jessica shrieked. "How can you even think that? How can you say I encouraged him? I mean, you've seen what he's like. He's totally drunk all the time and he's, like, a complete nutter."

James glimpsed a flurry of movement through the crack. Jessica threw herself down on the bed again.

"Oh, don't start with all that hippie shit. Compassion. What does that even mean, either? That I can only fuck losers or something?"

There was a very brief pause. Jessica sprang up again.

"No, don't! Please, Ray. I'm sorry. Really sorry. You see, this is the trouble, this is why we need to see each other, like, face-to-face, because if we just talk on the phone we end up having these stupid arguments."

Pause.

"What do you mean?" Jessica said. She sounded frightened. "What do you mean, cooling off? How long?"

Pause.

"No! I couldn't bear it. Not seeing you for all that time, and knowing you were just up the road. I'd have to see you. You can't stop me!"

When she spoke again there was an unpleasant edge to her voice: "Oh, really? Think about this, Raymond: I could get you into a lot of trouble, you know."

Pause.

"Because some people might think you were trying to take advantage of me. Depending on how I described it. An innocent young virgin, and a much older man. And you tried to bribe me with a horse. That's what some people might think."

There was another pause then Jessica broke in, panic-stricken: "No, don't Ray! Don't hang up! It's not a threat, I didn't mean it, I take it all back, I was just being stupid, and that's right, it was despicable, that's completely true, but it's all because I want you so much! Can't you see? I love you! Ray? Ray? Hello? Ray? Hello? Fuck!"

James heard the sound of a mobile phone hitting a wall.

"Fuck," Jessica muttered. "Fuck, fuck, fuck."

James zipped his bag and took a last look around the bedroom. He hadn't brought much with him apart from all the clothes. His wallet was in his pocket and his mobile phone was on the bed beside his bag, its battery completely dead. He'd used the phone on the table in the hall to call a taxi, which he'd asked to meet him at the gates. It wasn't due for another half an hour.

He decided to go down and wait for the taxi outside. He put his mobile into his pocket and picked up his bag. Once again, he was struck by how ridiculously heavy it was. Nearly all of the vast array of clothes it contained had remained untouched. He should just dump them here. But he couldn't. What would they think of him when they found them?

He lifted up the bag, and tipped out the contents. He selected the few items he might ever be likely to wear, and put them back in. He left the rest on the bed, and walked out of the room.

James dropped his bag in the hallway and went into the living room. Simon, Jane and George had gone. There was no sign of Reuben either. Spracky and Auntie Pru were still arguing. Daphne and John Longbourne were at the French windows, looking out at the garden. Daphne was complaining about something. When she heard James come in she turned and inspected him as if she couldn't quite place him.

James walked up to them and held out his hand. "I'll say goodbye. I'm going back to London."

Daphne allowed her hand to rest in his for a moment, then withdrew it before she asked, "Are you sure you can't stay?"

"Yes, I'm sure. Thank you for having me."

"You're most welcome. What a pity Oliver didn't turn up. He will be disappointed to have missed everything. Have a good journey. Do come again. Some time." Her polite smile made it clear she never wanted to see him again.

James turned to John Longbourne and shook hands with him.

John began to mutter, "Now, are you sure you can get to the station, because I might be able give you a lift if I can get things organized..."

"It's all right, I've got a taxi coming in a--"

"Yes, yes, probably better, all things considered. Well, I won't keep you."
John released his hand and glanced at Daphne. She raised her eyebrows at him.

"The wisteria," she said. "Are you coming?"

"Right, yes, of course."

Daphne turned and stepped out into the garden. John darted in close to
James and gripped his forearm. "Don't forget about that little business
opportunity," he whispered. He winked at James, showed him his teeth, and
trotted after Daphne.

As James turned away from the windows Auntie Pru said something to
Spracky and looked away from her with a sour expression. Her eyes met
James's. She regarded him with her usual blank, icy stare.

"Well," James said, "I'm off."

"About time," Pru said.

"She's joking," Spracky said. "That's just her way." She leaned down and
spoke to Pru as if she was a sulky child. "Aren't you going to say goodbye to
James nicely?"

"Oh, all right," Pru said. "Goodbye, James. Sorry, I don't mean to be rude.
It's just that this bitch won't let me have any more coffee."

"Hardly surprising," Spracky said, "when you consider how it affects you.
Look at how you're snapping at everyone. Poor James."

"I said I was sorry, didn't I? What more does he want?"

"You could find something pleasant to say."

"Don't worry," James said, "that's fine."

"It's been very nice to meet you, James," Pru said.

"Yes," James said, "it's been very nice to meet both of you, too."

"Although, quite frankly," Pru continued, "I don't know why Oliver doesn't
invite some of his old friends from Harrow down here. I'm sure you're a
perfectly nice young man, James, but if boys are going to come here sniffing
around Jessica, we'd prefer that they had some family we knew of. Nothing
personal."

James was taken aback. He knew for a fact that Oliver hadn't gone to
Harrow. He'd attended a succession of minor public schools, and was expelled
from all of them.

Spracky turned on Pru angrily. "You really are the limit sometimes!"

Pru shrugged.

"It's all right," James said. "I understand. I'll say goodbye, then."

He left the room.

As he walked across the hall he heard a noise behind him. He turned to see
Spracky gesturing to him from the sitting room doorway.

"Psst!" she hissed, "stop a minute!"

She glanced behind her, closed the door, and stumped up to him. James
could see she was unusually pale.

"I just wanted to mention something," she said. She hesitated, then lowered her voice. "I could see you were a bit confused when Pru mentioned Harrow."

"I was a bit, yes. I mean, Oliver didn't actually go there, did he?"

"No. But Pru thinks he did."

"Wow. I see. What about everyone else?"

"Oh, everyone else knows, of course. But we don't tell Pru. We let her think that Oliver went to Harrow." She tilted her chin up at him. "That's what makes her happy."

James thought about the old lady's cold, penetrating gaze. "God, it must have been difficult to keep it up. I mean, to..."

"To maintain the deception. Yes, it was. It was very difficult."

"But... I mean, how did you manage it all?"

"Oh, Christ, it was a nightmare." Spracky looked down and shook her head. "We had to intercept all the letters, and make up stories all the time, and God knows what. And we had to make Oliver learn all about Harrow so he could tell her about it when he came home for holidays. He got pretty fed up sometimes, and kept threatening to give up on the whole thing. We had to bribe him fairly constantly. Little blighter. And a few times, Pru got it into her head that she wanted to visit him there. Go to sports day, for instance. We had to invent sudden attacks of chicken pox, and mumps, and every other ailment under the sun. If you believed what we told her, that boy had so many illnesses it's a miracle he survived at all."

"And do you think she did?"

"Did what?"

"Did she believe it all?"

Spracky turned away and squinted into the sunlight shining through the glass in the door. "She wanted to believe it," she said, "and I have to believe that she did."

"And it was all just to keep her happy?"

"No. Not entirely." She turned back to James. "I might as well tell you. You'd probably find out anyway. And I doubt if it's going to make your opinion of us any worse. Not that it could get much worse, I expect."

"No, no, not at all."

"So it couldn't get worse?"

"No, that's not what I meant. What I meant--"

"It's all right, just teasing." Spracky gave him a friendly punch on the shoulder that made James hope she never gave him one that wasn't friendly. "You're a good lad," she said, "and I know I can trust you. Strict confidence, and all that."

"Of course."

"Well, it was also about money, I'm afraid. The fact is, it was Pru's money that paid for Oliver to go to Harrow. Or not go, in fact. What I mean is, Pru thought she was paying his school fees. Which are pretty steep at Harrow, as you may know."

"Astronomical."

"Exactly. But Pru had set her heart on him going there. And he didn't get in, of course. They can be pretty flexible, and they'll take pretty much anyone with enough money and a good family but they like you to at least look as if you're making an effort. But he couldn't be bothered. Not with the exam, or the interview, or anything. None of us wanted to tell Pru. She's got a real soft spot for Oliver, you see. Dotes on him. We didn't want to disappoint her. And then John suggested we should all pretend Oliver had got in. And he came up with the idea about the money, too." She looked at him searchingly. "That doesn't surprise you, does it? That it was John's idea about the money?"

"Not really, no."

"No. Well, we all knew that Pru had set aside the money for the fees, and John persuaded her to hand it over to him, and told her he was putting it in a trust. But all the time he was sending Oliver to far less expensive schools, and pocketing the difference. For the family, he said. Quite a lot of money over the years."

"How many years? I mean, how long did all this go on for?"

Spracky looked embarrassed. "Six years," she said. "Seven."

"God. Amazing."

"Yes, I suppose it is, when you think about it."

"And what did John do with the all the money?"

"Oh, it all vanished into his various business schemes. Never to be seen again."

James thought about John Longbourne's tireless quest for money, and the transparent cunning of his efforts to extract it from everyone he met, or to use them to extract it from someone else. There was something almost heroic about it. The only conversation that James could remember having with him that wasn't about money was in the garden on Saturday morning, when John had surprised him with his nudity and offered him the papers.

"Perhaps it's all finally going to work out for him," James said. "This scheme to develop the site of the Post Office. He's been putting the whole deal together, by the sound of it. He should make some money from that, don't you think?"

"Not a bloody chance. All he's done is persuade a gang of sharks from London to get involved, and hope they'll throw him some scraps. Which they won't. They never do. The thing is, John's as innocent as a baby, basically. You should have seen some of the schemes he tried to set up with Pru's money. One of them involved getting people with various illnesses to go swimming with dolphins. He bought a bloody great boat, and a mansion on the coast of Ireland. But he could never get the money off the punters in advance. He can't even run a decent confidence trick properly. We should never have let him handle Pru's money, that's for sure. Trouble is, Daphne always lets him have his own way, and she runs the whole show, pretty much."

James was suddenly struck by a thought. "But this whole thing about Olly going to Harrow, and John taking Pru's money..."

"What about it?"

"What did Bill think about it? I mean, he's Olly's father, after all, isn't he?"

Spracky looked at him expressionlessly. After a while she gave an almost imperceptible shrug and looked away.

"Oh, God," James said, "no."

"They're the only family I've got," Spracky said quietly.

The phone on the hall table rang.

Spracky picked up the chunky, old-fashioned receiver.

"Yes?" There was a pause, and then she smiled. "Yes, and the same to you." She turned away from James. "What?" She listened to the voice on the other end. "Yes, that can be arranged." She sighed theatrically. "All right, all right. I know you don't want to talk to old Spracky." Another pause. She laughed. "Save it for the girls. Hang on."

She turned back to James and put her hand over the mouthpiece. "It's for you," she said. "So I'll say goodbye now." She seemed suddenly agitated. "But I just want to say. About what Pru said in there. I don't always... I mean..." She blushed furiously, then blurted out, "I think you're a fine young man!"

She thrust the receiver at him and turned away quickly. James watched her thump along the passage towards the kitchen, doubtless to make Pru more coffee, then raised the phone to his ear.

"Hello?"

"James, you old bastard," Oliver said, "how the hell are you?"

James had known it was Oliver on the phone but it was still somehow a shock to hear his voice. "I'm okay," he said, "under the circumstances."

"Ah, yes, the circumstances. The circumstances sound pretty lively."

"You know what happened, then, do you?"

"Oh, yes, mate. Sounds insane."

"Who told you about it?"

"Aha, I have my spies. But I've only had a rough outline so far. I'm waiting for you to give me the whole story."

James wondered if Oliver had spoken to Jessica.

"Hello? James? You still there?"

"Yes. I'm here."

"You okay? You sound a bit pissed off."

"More than a bit, actually."

"But nothing happened, did it? I mean, you're not in any trouble, are you?"

"That's not the point."

"Okay. Listen, I can understand you being a bit pissed off."

"I said more than a bit."

"Right, right. The thing is, I had this plan, and you were meant to be in the loop, but then the wheels fell off the whole thing when I got busted and I couldn't get hold of you. That was the real problem. Why didn't you answer your mobile? That's what really fucked things up, actually. There was a communication breakdown, wasn't there?"

"Unbelievable," James said.

"What is?"

"Trying to put the blame on me. Fucking unbelievable."

"James, what's the matter with you? This isn't like you at all. And if you want someone to blame, dude, then blame that twat Richard. I mean, what was he thinking, for fuck's sake?" Oliver began to laugh. "Jesus, it sounds like he demolished half the fucking village! Come on, let's be honest, that boy needs serious professional help."

"Well, he certainly didn't get any help from you, did he? You just exploited him. He's totally clueless and you exploited the shit out of him."

"James, give me a fucking break! I've just been locked up for nearly three days. Those bastards strip searched me when I arrived. And having some pervy robocop stick his hand up my arse isn't my idea of how I like to start the weekend. Seriously, the whole thing has been a pretty traumatic experience, actually. It's all right for you, getting trollied all weekend. I was in a bloody cell that whole time. Not even one drink."

"You were in a cell because you arranged to be. Don't bullshit me, Oliver. You got yourself arrested so you'd have an alibi while you left me and Reuben to do your dirty work for you. I still can't believe you did it to me, actually."

"Look, it was all perfectly simple, there was no risk at all; it was just a matter of strolling in and picking up a parcel. And that's another thing: that parcel represented a considerable investment, and now it's all gone. And I've got some pretty ugly people trying to get their money back off me. Major players. They're giving me a seriously hard time. But you don't hear me complaining, do you? No, I suck it up, get over it, and move on. That's what we've all got to do, dude. Draw a line under it."

James shifted the receiver to his other hand and shook the cramp out of the one that had been gripping it.

"Don't try to tell me there was no risk involved," he said. "For one thing, the police were lurking about, so they must have suspected something. I probably would have been arrested if I'd tried to get that parcel."

"But it was just the one cop, right?"

"I think so, yes."

"And he's no threat now, right? The cop?"

"I've no idea."

"But he's out of the picture, isn't he? I heard he'd flipped out. Gone completely off his rocker. Isn't that right? I mean, he hasn't said anything, has he?"

"About what?"

"Well, about me. Does anyone know if he's said anything?"

"God," James said, "you're a selfish bastard."

"No, look, I'm just checking, okay? Because I heard that this guy had his own agenda. Something to do with Raymond. He was off on some weird trip of his own, some weird obsessive shit, and he was basically a raving nut job. I mean, he was up in the fucking bell tower, for fuck's sake, doing a fucking Quasimodo routine, right?"

"He's lucky to be alive, Oliver. So are we for that matter. In fact it's a miracle no one was killed. Simon Cottle had only just left the vestry."

"I know. Richard missed a trick there. Extra points for squashing a vicar."

James didn't say anything.

"Hey, I'm joking!" Oliver said. "Come on, lighten up, James."

"No."

There was a long pause.

"Listen," Oliver said, "I can understand why you're a bit freaked right now, okay? I mean, more than a bit. So let's not do this on the phone. I can leave now and I should be there by six at the latest. You're the man, James. Really. I'll see you later, okay?"

"No, I'm going back to London now."

"What? No. Why? No, come on, stay there. I really want to see you, James."

"No. I'm leaving."

"Why? You're not worried about work tomorrow, are you? Fuck 'em. I'm taking the whole week off, mate. Stay there, dude, and we can do all kinds of country shit. All that country bumpkin pig-fucking shit. We can just chill together. It'll be great."

"No thanks."

Another pause.

"Maybe you're right," Oliver said. "Maybe it's best to let things settle for a bit. I probably won't stay down there very long, actually. To tell you the truth I always get bored shitless down there after a couple of days. I just need to check a few things out then I'll get back to town. So I'll see you back up here later in the week, right? We'll get together and get wasted and you can tell me all about it. Okay? How about Friday?"

"I don't think so."

James hung up.

He closed the house door behind him and put his sunglasses on.

"Hello," Jessica said. She was leaning against the wall with her thumbs in the waistband of her cut-off jeans. "I've been waiting for you. I hope you don't mind."

"No, that's fine."

"Can I walk you to the gates?"

"Sure, if you like."

She pushed away from the wall and fell in beside him.

"Do you really have to go now?" she said.

"I do. Really."

She linked her arm through his. "Why can't you stay a bit longer, though?

He glanced at her. "I think it's probably best if I go now."

She pouted, and pressed herself against him so that he could feel her breast against his arm. "But I really want you to stay."

"Why?"

"Because if you stay we can, you know, get to know each other a bit better."

"What more is there to know?'

"Don't be like that!" She squeezed his arm playfully. "That's not a very nice thing to say, is it? Now you've made me all upset."

"No, I haven't."

"You have! James, listen, I really like you. I think we've got a lot in common." She suddenly sounded shy and awkward. "And I meant what I said in the car."

"Said about what?"

"About it being right for, you know, you and me to... be together. In that way."

James stopped and turned to her. "Jessica, why are you doing this?"

"What? Doing what?" She looked at him with wide eyes.

"This whole act."

"What act? It's not an act."

"Okay. But I'm still leaving." He turned away.

"No, wait!"

He turned back to her. She scowled at him petulantly. "Why can't you just stay for a bit longer? Just stay until--"

She stopped abruptly and looked at the ground.

"Until what?"

"Nothing. Oh, go on, then, abandon me! Now you hate me like everyone else. I'll just go and be a nun or something!" She burst into tears.

James turned away and walked towards the gates. He'd only taken a few steps when a sharp, imperious command rang out behind him:

"James! Stop!"

For an instant James thought that Daphne Longbourne had called to him. He stopped and glanced back. Jessica was standing alone in the middle of the driveway, red in the face, her fists clenched at her sides.

He shook his head, waved at her, and continued on his way without looking back.

James waited at the gates for the taxi. He was a few minutes early.

He heard a noise behind him and turned to see Reuben emerging from the shrubbery. James wondered if he'd been spying on him and Jessica. If he had, it wasn't any worse than James listening to Jessica's private phone conversation, which he was glad he'd done. And maybe Reuben was glad he'd just been spying, too, if that's what he'd been doing. Maybe he'd heard something that would help him finally see the truth. Or part of it. Maybe you never saw the whole truth.

Reuben was smiling broadly. "Hello there," he said.

There was something different about him. It took James a moment to realize what it was. "Where's your hat?" he said.

Reuben lifted his shirt, and like a gangster displaying a gun, he showed James the hat, which he'd squashed, folded, and tucked into his waistband.

"Why aren't you wearing it?"

"I'm finished with all that." Reuben prised the hat out of his trousers and pummelled it back into something like its original shape. He held it out to James. "Here. Why don't you have it? As a souvenir."

"No thanks," James said hastily.

Reuben laughed. "Look at you! Backing away as if it was contaminated. Or some kind of dangerous voodoo. I thought you weren't religious."

"I'm not. Not really. I'm just..."

"Superstitious!"

"No, I'm not," James said. "Not particularly." But it was true that he'd recoiled when Reuben had thrust the hat at him, as if it was a powerful fetish object. "The thing is," he said, "I'm aware that the hat has got a religious significance for you--"

"Not any more."

"Okay, but for other people who have these... these beliefs."

"Jews."

"Yes. Some Jews."

"I'll tell you a secret," Reuben said. "It's the special hat we wear when we eat the Christian babies."

"Okay, okay. But it does represent something to some people. And I don't want to, you know, disrespect that."

"Superstition," Reuben said scornfully. "It's all superstition. It's just ignorant, primitive, magical thinking. The magic hat! Look, it can even fly!" He spun the hat away from him like a Frisbee. It skimmed across the path in lazy arc and came to rest in the shrubbery, where it snagged on a low branch and hung there.

"Superstition," Reuben repeated. "I renounce superstition and all its hats."

"What's brought this on?"

"Well, I've been thinking about things for some time. Wondering about my beliefs. And then I read this." Reuben extracted something from his shirt pocket. "It really made me see the light and realize I have no faith. Here, take a

251

look." He unfolded some torn sheets of glossy paper and held them out. James recognized them as the magazine article Reuben had been reading earlier, in the sitting room.

"It's an extraordinary piece of writing, actually," Reuben said. "Very moving."

James took the article. It was about some English doctors working for *Medecins sans Frontieres* in Africa. It also looked suspiciously like an undeclared promotion for expensive four-wheel-drive vehicles and safari clothing.

"That's what I want to be," Reuben said.

"A writer?"

"No, a doctor!"

"A doctor?"

"I want to do something useful. Something real. Something that helps people, in the real world. That's where life happens. I don't want to drift around in my head any more, with a load of ideas about God, and endless questions about what it all means. That's just self-indulgence. It's up to me to decide what life means. And life is about being with real people, in the real world, making a difference. Doing good."

"I'm amazed," James said. "But, you know, in a good way. That's great. Really wonderful. But it's not easy to be a doctor, you know."

"I know, I've got a cousin who's just about to qualify. And then you've got to do a whole lot more special training to be one of these guys. But I'm going to do it. Honestly. I'm completely determined. It'll take years, I know, but I'm going to prove I've got it in me. I'm going to dedicate myself to helping people!"

Reuben's face was glowing with pride and also a touch of sunburn. James could see that the heat had started to affect him quickly now he'd stopped wearing his hat.

"What do you think?" Reuben said.

"What can I say? Go for it. When are you going to start all this?"

"As soon as possible. Tomorrow. Today!"

"You'll have to think about the drinking, you know, if you want to be a doctor."

"I drink enough to be a doctor, don't worry." Reuben laughed. "No, seriously, I've given up."

"Since when?"

"Today."

"You were pretty drunk last night."

"I know. But I haven't had a drink at all today. And it's well after twelve."

"Well... that's good, I suppose. Yes, great. Keep it up."

"That's why I want to start as soon as I can. It'll make it easier to stay off the drink if I've got something to get totally involved in. Especially if I can get away from here. Do my medical training in Edinburgh, maybe. Take my mind off it."

"That makes sense. And it'll help you to forget about Jessica, too."

Reuben frowned. "What do you mean?"

"Well, to... you know, get over her."

"But I don't want to get over her."

"Don't you?"

"No, of course not. She's the reason I'm doing all this."

"What?"

"So I can show her I'm a mature, serious person. I should have realized she was never going to be impressed by money or anything like that. In fact, the more I was trying to impress her, the less impressed she was. No wonder she thought I was just some silly kid. But when she finds out what I'm doing, and how I'm saving people's lives and everything, she'll see what I'm really like. And when I come back, all sort of experienced, and wise, she'll want to be with me. What do you think? Good plan?"

Rueben was gazing at him earnestly. His eyes were shining.

"Yes," James said, "it's a good plan, Reuben."

"I think I'll go back to being Richard."

"Oh. I quite like Reuben."

"Really? Maybe you're right. Yes, it is a bit different, isn't it? Okay, I'll stick with Reuben. But look, I've got to go now. Start getting things organized."

"Where are you going?"

"Back home."

James looked at Reuben's peeling forehead. "I've got a taxi coming in a minute. I can drop you off on the way to the station if you like."

"No, it's okay, I fancy the walk. I'll go across the fields. I've got to make plans."

"You're getting sunburned. Why not wear the hat?"

Reuben shook his head. "I told you. It doesn't mean anything to me anymore."

"Exactly. So it's just a way to keep the sun off. Just practical."

Reuben wiped his brow and examined some curled flakes of skin that came off.

"Okay," he said. He collected the hat from the bushes, rammed it on his head and walked back. James braced himself for a hug, but Reuben only wanted to shake hands. "Great to meet you," he said. "And thanks. Thanks for everything."

"It was great to meet you, too. Good luck. I'll be thinking about you."

Reuben grinned at him, and strode away.

James watched him go. What could you do? Maybe it would all work out.

He heard the distinctive metallic gurgle of a clapped-out diesel engine and caught a whiff of burning motor oil. The minicab coasted to stop beside him.

It was the same driver who'd delivered him on Friday. "All right, chief?" he said through the open window. "Off to the station, is it?"

"Yes please." James rested an arm on the roof and leaned into the car. "How much is that going to be, by the way?"

"I can't say for definite, can I? We'll have to see what the meter says. And there's the supplement for bank holiday, of course. Somewhere between ten and twenty, I would think. All right?"

"Not really. I'd prefer you to give me a price now, if you don't mind." James gave him a friendly smile. "Just so I know what to expect."

The driver stared at him. James maintained his smile.

"Right," the driver said, "it'll be twelve pounds fifty."

"Great. Make it thirteen, and I'd like a receipt, please." James opened the back door, threw his bag onto the seat, got in behind it, and closed the door.

"Right you are, chief," the driver said, and did smooth U-turn. "Going back to London, are you?"

"That's right."

"Had a good weekend?"

"Yes."

There was a silence.

James looked out of the window. The trees and hedges were dense with greenness. Everything was lush and exuberant. He gazed at the gently sloping meadows and the undulating hills beyond them. It was lovely countryside.

"How about some music?" the driver said. Without waiting for a reply he turned up the volume on his car radio. It was an American country song about being true to various things, but most of all, buddy, to yourself.

"Actually," James said, "I'd rather not have any music."

"Oh," the driver said. He glanced at James in his rear-view mirror, then turned the radio down again. "Please yourself."

"Thanks," James said, "I will."

*

Jarvis finished his meal. A man came and picked up the plastic knife and fork. He smiled at Jarvis.

Jarvis smiled.

The man pointed at Jarvis's plate. He raised his eyebrows and rubbed his stomach.

Jarvis smiled.

The man grinned, and gave him a thumbs-up sign.

It was easy to keep them happy.

A woman came and touched his arm.

Jarvis nodded. He got up and allowed the woman to take his elbow and lead him out to the garden. He didn't need any help to get out to the garden, like some of the others, but he liked to be touched sometimes.

The woman sat him down on one of the benches. The sun was out and the garden looked nice. The woman looked around. She took a deep breath and smiled at Jarvis.

Jarvis smiled.

The woman nodded happily. She was a fat woman. She moved her mouth and began to speak words of silence. She stopped suddenly and clapped a hand over her mouth. She made a pantomime of slapping herself on the forehead.

"Silly me," she mouthed.

She swept her arm in wide arc to indicate the garden and pointed up at the sun. She turned to Jarvis and smiled at him.

Jarvis smiled.

She gave an exaggerated sigh, tapped herself on the chest, pointed back at the house, mimed the action of typing, and shrugged to say "what can you do?"

Jarvis smiled.

She smiled, and went back to the house.

He could have spoken to them if he chose to, although he no longer knew what his words sounded like.

He didn't care about that.

But he was saving his words for the Dark One. He thought about him all the time. He'd seen him in his radiance, and knew that he was known by him. One day he would meet him again. The hated enemy. How he loved him.

Jarvis smiled.

The End.

3177075R00130

Printed in Great Britain
by Amazon.co.uk, Ltd.,
Marston Gate.